Warrior's Heart

This Large Print Book carries the
Seal of Approval of N.A.V.H.

Warrior's Heart

Georgina Gentry

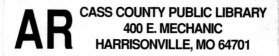
Thorndike Press • Waterville, Maine

Published in 2002 by arrangement with Zebra Books, an imprint of Kensington Publishing Corp.

Thorndike Press Large Print Basic Series.

The tree indicium is a trademark of Thorndike Press.

The text of this Large Print edition is unabridged.
Other aspects of the book may vary from the original edition.

Set in 16 pt. Plantin.

Printed in the United States on permanent paper.

Library of Congress Cataloging-in-Publication Data

Gentry, Georgina.
    Warrior's heart / Georgina Gentry.
       p. cm.
    ISBN 0-7862-4053-9 (lg. print : hc : alk. paper)
    1. Shoshoni Indians — Fiction.   2. Racially mixed
people — Fiction.   3. Women pioneers — Fiction.
    4. Large type books.   I. Title.
PS3557.E4616 W36 2002
813'.54—dc21   2002019939

This story is dedicated to the pioneers who braved the wilderness in search of new lives and to the Native Americans who became the victims of this westward expansion. Both groups have my admiration and my sympathy.

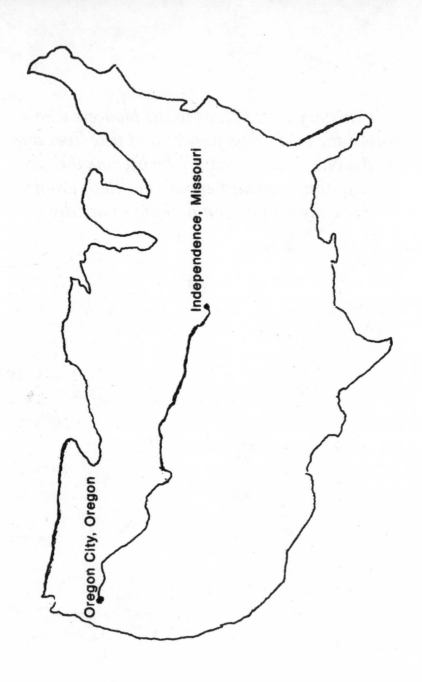

The Oregon Trail, 1862

Prologue

The Oregon Trail. Over more than thirty years, perhaps half a million hardy pioneers started the two-thousand-mile journey that began in Missouri and ended in the lush valleys of Oregon . . . if they were lucky. Probably at least ten percent died along the way of disease, accidents, and Indian attacks. These ill-fated thousands are buried in mostly unmarked graves along that terrible road.

So considering the danger, why would anyone begin this trip? Many were looking for new opportunities out West, some were on the run from the law or their own troubled past.

Emma Trent, a beautiful blond widow with a mysterious past, is traveling alone with her half-breed child, hoping to make a fresh start. The train she joins up with is unlucky and poorly equipped. Most of its travelers have already been turned down by better trains. Desperate for a wagon master to lead them, these pioneers are ready to agree to any terms for a hard man with nothing to lose who knows the trail.

Rider, a half-breed gunfighter, is on the run from the law. Unknown to the pioneers, five years ago he was a Shoshoni warrior named Rides the Thunder. At home in both the white and red world, he is welcome in neither and under a death sentence in both. *Will he risk his life to lead this wagon train through the terrible Shoshoni country?*

He will . . . for a price. The eager leaders of the train are willing to give Rider anything he wants. Anything. All he has to do is name it. Is it gold he desires? No, he wants the yellow-haired beauty to warm his blankets for the length of the trip. Some argue it isn't moral, but without Rider, the train will be stranded on the hostile plains and at the mercy of the elements and war-painted braves. The leaders agree to Rider's demands. Yes, he can have the girl.

But Emma has good reason to hate and fear most men and all Indians. Someone forgot to tell her about the gunfighter's unholy deal!

Chapter One

Late June, 1862. The frontier settlement of Independence, Missouri.

Rider wanted the girl from the first moment he saw her standing by a covered wagon on the morning he rode into town.

The yellow-haired girl did not look back at him as if she desired him, too. What intrigued him as he rode past was the glare of utter hatred and revulsion with which she returned his hot glance.

Intrigued, he reined in his Appaloosa stallion and studied the blonde. If he were still among the Shoshoni, he would consider stealing the woman and using her to warm his blankets until he tired of her, then swap her for a rifle or a good horse. Clad in faded blue gingham, she clenched her small fists and glared back at him with eyes as pale as her dress, the gold band on her left hand reflecting the hot sun. It was almost a comic gesture, he thought, seeing that though she was tall and sun-browned, she would be no match against his strength.

However, since the white man who owned this beauty would surely fight to the death to keep her, Rider would forgo the temptation of her warm, ripe body. He didn't need the kind of trouble the white girl would bring him — not with all the other problems he had right now.

Reluctantly, Rider nudged Storm into a walk and rode on past the motley cluster of covered wagons, touching the tips of his fingers to his black Stetson as he passed her. She didn't return his nod, only frowned more deeply, pressing against the big wheel of her wagon, her body tense as if ready to fight should he dismount and approach her.

Rider didn't look back as he rode down the dusty street. He had lived in two worlds, Indian and white, and was under a death sentence in both. At the moment, with those bounty hunters on his trail, what Rider needed most was a drink, some food, and a little rest for him and his horse before they moved on. Later, there would always be plenty of pretty women for his amusement and they wouldn't glare at him with revulsion and hatred as the girl with sky-blue eyes had done. He could still feel those pale eyes burning holes in his back as he threaded his way through the bustling crowds of people, buggies, and wagons heading for the small saloon sign down the street.

Emma Trent glared at the grim gunfighter's muscular back as he rode away. When he reined in to look her over, she had recognized the hunger — that man-need in his dark eyes — and it made her shudder with terrible memories that she had thought buried almost four long years. She must not allow herself to remember, but it was impossible when this half-breed gunfighter appraised her with cold, dark eyes as if he'd like to throw her down right there in the dust of the street and mount her.

Emma clenched her fists, her stomach churning, knowing instinctively that this big, silent man was someone who took what he wanted and dared anyone to stop him. The way he had stared at her made it very clear how much he desired her body, and she had no one to protect her should he decide to take her. The early morning sun reflected off the silver conchos on that hat and the fancy beadwork on the bridle as he rode away. *Indians.* She had plenty of reason to hate and fear them. Yet Emma could not stop herself from staring after the rider until his broad-shouldered back in its black shirt faded into the crowd in the street.

No ordinary cowboy, that one. The silver on his hat and gun belt, the good leather of his boots, the fine horse, but especially the pistol he wore low on his hip, told her this was a hired gun — a cold killer with a mouth like a slash across his weathered dark face, his ebony hair long, too long for a white man. She watched him as he disappeared into the bustle of the road, breathing a sigh of relief that he was gone and wondering if he'd been hired to gun down someone in the dust of this rough town's streets? *What difference did that make to her as long as he didn't return to put those dark, capable hands on her.*

A whimpering cry from inside her wagon made her turn, forgetting the gunfighter completely in her concern for her child. Hoisting her faded skirts, she climbed up on the wagon seat behind the patient oxen and reached down to pat the sleeping toddler. "Shh, Josh, it's all right. Go back to sleep now."

Her son quieted under the soothing touch of her hand as she patted his black hair and smiled down at him. Three-year-old Josh was a half-breed, too, just like the tough gunfighter who had just ridden past, but that was not the toddler's fault. Even as

Emma stroked Josh's black hair, she couldn't help but think that if this had been Ethan's son, the boy would have been as fair and blond as her dead husband.

The child dropped off to sleep again and Emma took a deep breath and squared her shoulders as she climbed down from the wagon. The fat banker, Mr. Pettigrew, in his derby hat, and several men were walking toward her. She knew by the grim set of their mouths and the way they avoided her eyes that the news would not be good.

"Miz Trent," Pettigrew wheezed as he took off his derby and fiddled with it, avoiding her eyes, "we men have talked it over, as well as our womenfolk, and well, as elected leader of this train, it's my duty to tell you we don't think you belong with us —"

"Belong? Tell me, Mr. Pettigrew, just where *do* I belong?" Her temper flared because she knew the answer: nowhere, not in any respectable white community.

The men shuffled their feet in the dust, ashamed to look at her.

The tall, elegant Southerner, Weatherford B. Carrolton, cleared his throat. "Now, see here," he drawled in a deep Mississippi accent, "there's no need for such resentment, young lady."

"Don't use that arrogant tone to me,"

Emma shot back. "I realize none of you think a respectable woman would keep a child like mine —"

"It ain't just the half-breed kid, Miz Trent —" the banker began apologetically.

"Josh," she snapped. "His name is Josh."

"Be that as it may," Mr. Weeks said, "it's a long way to Oregon — lots of problems ahead of us."

"If you're worried that I can't pull my weight, that I'll be too much trouble," she said, facing them as adversaries, "I'm a frontier girl. I can tan hides, handle a rifle, milk cows, hitch up my own team, and —"

"It ain't just that, Miz Trent," Pettigrew said and wiped the sweat from the inside of his derby before putting it back on his thinning hair. "My Francesca, well, all the womenfolk are afraid men will get to fightin' over you, seein's as how you're purty, real purty, and you got no man."

The others nodded in silent agreement.

She had been right; the women had been gossiping about her. Francesca Pettigrew, Millicent Carrolton, and the others had appeared to be whispering about Emma since she'd pulled in here yesterday with her covered wagon. Emma had noted the cold looks from the other women. She knew the gossip would center on the parentage of her half-breed son.

She didn't know whether to laugh or cry or start shrieking. Most of these men were looking at her as if they'd like to tear her clothes off. "Your women think I'm a slut? That I'll fall into the grass with any man who looks at me?"

The men's faces turned an angry, ruddy color and they glanced at each other, obviously not used to hearing women talk with such spirited defiance.

Weatherford B. Carrolton cleared his throat and adjusted the blossom in his boutonniere. "Now, ma'am. There's no need for such unladylike talk," he drawled. "It is a long trip, Miz Trent, and seein' as how you don't belong to a man —"

"I belong to me!" she flared back. "Don't you people understand? I've sold what little I had to outfit this wagon and buy these oxen," she gestured behind her. "I thought I'd get a fresh start in the Oregon country, but I can't get there alone."

A fat old farmer from Ohio sniffed disdainfully. "Most of us think we don't need women like you in the Oregon country alongside honest, respectable folk. After all, there's that half-breed kid —"

"And that's the most of it, isn't it, Mr. Adams?" Emma fired back. "You've heard the gossip and keep thinking, 'if she was a respectable woman, why didn't she kill herself and spare society the disgrace?' Well, I got news for you folks. That's the coward's way out and I'm not takin' it!"

"Nonetheless," the banker said, "the train hopes to be pulling out this afternoon, soon's our wagon master returns, and we done decided you can't join up with us —"

"Just give me a chance." She was down to pleading now, and it rankled her proud spirit. "I've already talked to Mr. McKade last night and he's willing. I promise I'll pull my own weight and won't be a hindrance. I got all I own tied up in this wagon and if I can't join the train, I don't know what I'll do."

The men shook their heads slowly and avoided her eyes. "That ain't our problem," Pettigrew said. "I have promised my Francesca that she won't have to mix with women like you, so now we're done talkin' about it. Soon's Mr. McKade gets back, we're pullin' out and you ain't goin' with us."

She had to get to Oregon, not for herself — she had long since grown immune to what people whispered about her — but for Josh. Her half-Cheyenne son was not welcome in frontier communities. Maybe things would be different out West where there was still plenty of room and the wind blew free. "But Mr. McKade said —"

"Don't care what he says," Adams, the old Ohio farmer, yelled back over his shoulder as the men walked away. "The wagon master is on our payroll and he'll see the wisdom of our vote. Good luck to you, Miz Trent."

Emma watched the men retreat and gritted her teeth so she would not cry, trying to decide what to do next. Sure, a single woman alone on a wagon train might cause some hardship if the men had to look after her, hitch up her wagon, and repair wheels and harness. But her ancestors had been tough pioneers coming through the Cumberland Gap generations ago; and she could do anything a man could do from plowing to hunting.

What was she going to do? Gossip said this was the very last train that would be leaving the "jumping off" places in Missouri and Iowa this year. All the others had left weeks ago. If this one wouldn't take her, Emma wasn't certain what to do. The Civil War was spreading all along the frontier, so she couldn't return to her old farm, and besides, she'd sold the land and house to buy this big wagon and supplies. She didn't have more than five dollars tucked away and now she was about to be stranded in this rough, wide-open town.

Mr. McKade. The train had just hired the reluctant old wagon master last night. He should be back in a few minutes and she'd talk to him again, implore him to convince the hostile pioneers to include her. No, she couldn't give up. She might have to defend her honor against some of the men late at night after the camp was asleep, but she'd take that chance — she had to. There was nothing behind her but terrifying memories and humiliation. Hope and a new life for her and her son lay ahead in the wild freedom of the Oregon country. She was in a desperate situation and she'd do whatever it took to get to Oregon!

Rider swung down off his horse and tied it to the hitching rail next to the water trough in front of a saloon. Storm bent his head and drank gratefully. "Good boy," Rider said and patted him as the horse nickered low in its throat. "I'll get me a drink, too, and maybe we'll find a place this afternoon where we can hide out and rest awhile."

The horse was the only real friend Rider had in this world. Gunfighters didn't make many attachments and they moved too often to grow any affection for a particular woman. Now, women in general, that was something different. Rider paused in front of the saloon and assessed it. This wasn't one of those fancy places that had girls up-stairs, the friendly kind who made no de-mands and asked for no commitments. Oh, yes, those were his kind of women — the ones who knew how to smile and warm a man with their soft white skin and big breasts. Never mind that in a few hours, they'd be spread beneath some other sweating, gasp-ing cowboy.

The tanned, sturdy girl back at the wagon train crossed his mind in contrast. "Forget that," he warned himself as he pushed through the creaky swinging doors. "You'd have to take it from her by force and that's not your style."

Still the woman both intrigued and mysti-fied him. Why such hatred in those pale blue eyes? Women had always been eager to plea-sure him and make him forget that he had no real home to hang his hat and that he would always have to sit with his back against the wall when he ate or gambled so that no one could come up behind him sud-den-like.

Rider stood in the doorway, letting his eyes adjust to the darkness, studying everything and everybody a long moment before he moved inside. It was a small, miserable place, reeking of dust, stale beer, and cigars. A half-dozen men leaned against the mahogany bar, their weather-beaten boots on the brass rail. Over in the corner, a drunk pecked his way across the keys of an out-of-tune piano: "Oh, Susanna, oh, don't you cry for me, I come from Alabama . . ."

Satisfied that the place contained no enemies that he recognized, Rider strode over to the bar, moving to the far side so he could watch the swinging doors. He took off his black hat and slapped it against his leg before putting it on again. "Gimme a whiskey," he said to the mustachioed man who wiped at the dust of the scarred mahogany.

The bearded old man next to him laughed and sipped his beer. "A bit early in the morning for whiskey, ain't it?"

Rider frowned at him, decided he meant no harm. The old-timer wasn't even wearing a gun. "Who thinks so?"

"McKade," the other man said and held out his hand. When Rider didn't take it, he combed through his white beard instead. "I meant no offense, stranger."

"Then none taken." Rider was bone tired and in no mood to fuss with anyone. Rider accepted the drink, threw a silver dollar on the bar so that it rang as it spun. "What goes on in this town anyway?"

The older man shrugged. "Not much this late in the season. A month ago, there was wagon trains pulling out by the dozens."

Rider sipped his whiskey, savoring the way it cleared the dust from his throat, thinking about the yellow-haired girl. "I passed a train gettin' ready as I came in."

"Oh, yeah, that one." McKade nodded and sighed. "Last night, they offered me plenty to guide them, but I'm gonna go back in a minute and tell them I've changed my mind."

"Oh?"

"I just got a bad feelin' about it, that's all. In the first place, it's too late to be takin' the trail. The trip takes four months at best, six or seven at the worst, so they'll never get to Oregon without gettin' caught in the autumn snows up in the mountains."

"That's Shoshoni country." *Oyer'ungun. Land of Peace and Plenty*, his people had named it. Rider sipped his whiskey and remembered the crisp snow and the clean, cold air of the mountains that he knew so well. It had been hotter than hell with the lid off down in Texas.

"Shoshoni, yes," McKade nodded in

agreement. "And other hostiles along the way — good place to lose your scalp. I been thinkin' about that all night. Gold don't do you no good if you ain't alive to spend it. You know that land?"

Rider didn't answer as he rolled a smoke. Yes, he knew those rugged peaks and high plains as well as he knew the back of his own hand. Long ago, he had hunted buffalo and enemy Cheyenne, Blackfoot, and Lakota there, but of course, Rider couldn't return to the land he loved. He was under a death sentence from his mother's people, the Shoshoni. "I know the country," he said finally. "A man would be risking his hair traveling through there unless he had lots of rifles and men with plenty of guts who knew how to use them."

"Well, that shore ain't this train of whiners and losers," McKade said. "Don't seem to have much grit or gumption to the lot of them."

Rider didn't answer, thinking about the yellow-haired girl. She had looked feisty and stubborn as hell. *Just what was she doing in a train like this?* Maybe her man was lazy and no-account.

"Yes, sir," McKade raked his fingers through his beard thoughtfully. "That's why after thinkin' it over, I'm goin' back and tell them I've changed my mind, even though they offered five hundred in gold."

Rider whistled low and long. "That's *mucho dinero*."

"More than most wagon masters get," the other agreed and sipped his beer. "The goin' rate is about five dollars a wagon. But I got me a bad feelin' about this bunch. First of all, there's only half a dozen wagons."

"Not enough to stand off an Injun attack," Rider said and struck a match across the bar, lighting his cigarette.

"You got that!" McKade scowled and shifted his weight. "But I doubt many of this bunch would fight — I think they'd run first."

Rider laughed. "What happened to that brave pioneer spirit?"

McKade shook his head. "These people is all rejects from other trains for one reason or another — that's why they're still stranded here tryin' to take the trail."

He didn't want to ask, but he couldn't help himself. "What about the girl, the one with yellow hair?"

"Ah, yes, that one." McKade sighed and a look of wistfulness crossed his weathered face. "Now there's a woman. Spunky little thing, but I can tell you right now this bunch ain't gonna take her along."

"Why not?" Rider blew smoke into the dim light and watched it hang on the air, remembering the beauty of her, like sunlight and blue skies.

"Well, she's too purty, to begin with — that's bound to cause some trouble on a long trip like that."

"Can't her man protect her?" Rider said. "If not, he ain't much of a man. If I had a woman like that one —"

"Oh, there's something you don't know about her," McKade said. "You see, she —"

"Who owns that Appaloosa tied out front?" a voice shouted from the doors.

Rider looked up. A man had just entered the saloon — no, more of a boy, Rider decided. "Who wants to know?"

The boy sauntered over to the middle of the worn floor and paused, his thumbs stuck in his gun belt.

Rider felt a prickle of warning go up his back. He always listened to his inner feelings; they had saved his life more than once. He tossed away the smoke and heard it sizzle as it hit the brass spittoon, then turned slightly so that his lean, experienced hand hovered just above his gun belt.

"I'm the Missouri Kid," the stranger said, and paused for effect. "I reckon you heard of me?"

"Can't say that I have," Rider answered softly. "But then, I haven't been in these parts much." He didn't want any trouble with some young stud who was looking to build his reputation. There had been too many like this one in the past five years — way too many.

The kid ran his hand through dirty brown hair and swaggered toward the bar, his hand on his gun belt. "Well, I know who you are. I heard about that stallion — finest on the frontier, they say."

The Shoshoni were famous for their fast horses. Old Chief *Washakie* himself had given Storm to the warrior Rides the Thunder. That had been in his other life, more than five years ago, when Rider was still an honored dog soldier.

"He's a good horse," Rider conceded and watched the kid's hands. Those hands were shaking slightly.

"I wanna buy him off you." The young cowboy bellied up to the bar and banged loudly for service. The bartender rushed to fill his glass, glancing nervously at Rider, sweat gathering on his lip above his mustache.

Rider shook his head. "Storm's not for sale. He's saved my life too many times."

The boy half-turned to face Rider and his hand shook a bit more as he raised his drink to his lips. "I heard of you, Rider — down in Tascosa and San Antone, over in St. Joe and the Territory. Folks say the lowdown gunfighter that rides that horse would kill anyone for a price."

A deep, shocked gasp ran through the other men at the brass railing and they began to edge away from the bar.

Rider took a deep breath. "Don't push me, kid, I've had a bad week." *It'd be even worse if those bounty hunters were as close behind him as he figured.*

The kid turned, his hands shaking even more as he slammed his empty glass down on the bar. "Maybe you didn't hear me. I hear the lowdown polecat who rides that horse would gun down anyone for a price."

"Oh, I don't know," Rider said. Even in his own ears, his voice sounded cold and hard as the Colt hanging low on his lean hip. "Sometimes I kill a man for free."

The tension hung on the air like the dust that danced in the sunlight flowing across the weatherbeaten planks from the swinging doors. Men hesitated, looking at each other uncertainly. Rider could read their faces. They knew they should run, but they were afraid they would miss the action. After a moment, they began to clear away from the pair.

McKade was the only one besides Rider and the boy who didn't retreat. He moved between them, making a soothing gesture toward the newcomer. "Now, son, back off a little. There ain't no need to throw your weight around. You can see this other gent don't want no trouble. We're just havin' us a friendly drink and I'll buy you one —"

The kid snorted. "I ain't drinkin' with him." He nodded toward Rider. "They all say you're the fastest gun on the frontier, but you seem yellow to me."

"Kid," Rider said, his voice so soft it seemed like the warning of a coiled rattler, "back off now and we'll let it go at that."

The boy looked incredulous. "You'd let a man call you yellow and take it?"

"You ain't a man," Rider said. "Come back in a couple of years when you're grown. Now get out of here. It's too nice a morning to die."

"You threatenin' me?" The boy backed away from the bar, his hands hovering just above his pistol.

So there was going to be no way around it. In the five years since he'd joined the white man's civilization, his reputation had built until there was no town he could ride into peacefully without some young buck calling him out. Rider was not yet thirty winters

27

old, but this morning he felt ancient and tired. In his mind's eye, he was Rides the Thunder again, galloping along the ridges, thrilled with the beauty of the morning, wild and free, no posse on his tail and no smart aleck kid begging for a chance to die in a dirty little saloon. "Look, there's no sense in shootin' up this place. Just move on and we'll forget it."

"No, I ain't gonna let you order me around. Let's take this out in the street!" The kid had moved to the middle of the floor, backing toward the doors, the other men watching silently as if holding their breath.

"I just came in from the street," Rider said softly, "and I ain't interested in going back out there just yet."

McKade made a placating gesture toward the boy. "Look, son, can't you see he's tryin' to avoid a fight?"

"Stay out of this!" The kid's hand hovered near his pistol — too near. "You gonna come out?" he shouted at Rider.

Rider sighed. "You really want to die in front of all those people out there?"

The boy threw back his head and laughed. "We'll see who's gonna die, you son of a bitch!"

"All right then, we'll do it your way," Rider said and finished his whiskey. He gestured to the old man to move to one side as he started for the swinging doors.

Even as he did so, the kid drew. It was a slow, clumsy draw, a dead man's draw. Rider reacted instinctively. His hand slapped leather and came up spitting fire as the Colt flashed in the dim light. His bullet caught the Missouri Kid in the heart a split second before the kid's Colt cleared its holster. The boy was dead but still firing wildly as he fell.

The mirror behind the bar shattered in a tinkling shower of glass and McKade cried out, clutching his chest as he went down. Rider took a deep breath of air that suddenly reeked of gunpowder, fear, and blood, all scents that wiped out the faint smell of stale cigars and beer. His ears still ringing from the gunfire, Rider holstered his pistol and knelt beside the old man. Cursing softly, he lifted McKade's head. "Somebody get a doc!"

Around them, men were shouting and people crowded into the saloon, asking what happened.

McKade shook his head, choking on his own blood. "Stray bullet . . . helluva way to go."

"I'm sorry as hell, oldtimer," Rider said and meant it.

"Not your fault," the old man whispered. "Your reputation . . . Someday, there'll be somebody faster —"

"And it'll be me lyin' here," Rider agreed. In his mind, he saw himself older, slower. Like McKade, he'd be lying in a pool of blood in some dirty saloon. It wasn't much of a future, but he'd play the hand he'd been dealt. "Can I do anything for you?"

". . . worried about that girl." McKade's voice was a whisper from deep inside. "She . . ." Then he smiled and died quietly, crimson staining the white beard.

Very gently, Rider laid the old man down. "I'm sorry as hell, oldtimer," he whispered again and patted the thin shoulder.

Ignoring the gawking men crowding into the saloon, Rider stood up and walked over to the Missouri Kid. The boy lay with his hazel eyes wide open in surprise as if he had known he was a dead man as he fell and could not quite believe it. Rider kicked the gun away from the still hand and cursed softly. "You all saw it," he said to the silent crowd.

They nodded and a farmer pushed back his straw hat and shook his head. "We saw it, we sure did. The kid drew first. Never in my born days seen such fancy shootin'."

"Why, don't you know who that is?" another murmured. "That half-breed is the gunfighter. . . ."

Rider was suddenly sick of being who he was. He pushed through the swinging doors and out into the bright light of the morning. Sweat plastered his shirt to his muscular body and he thought how hot the day was in the white man's dirty, crowded little town. The air in the far mountains would be cool and fresh and as Rides the Thunder, he would wear little more than a breechcloth and moccasins, his long hair trailing coup feathers to show his brave deeds as a warrior. For a long moment, he ached for the life he had known among the Shoshoni, the life that was dead to him now.

Then he caught the hushed, excited conversation around him as he stood in the middle of the dusty street and realized people were staring at him and whispering. "Somebody better get the sheriff," he said. "It was a fair fight — anyone in the saloon will tell him that."

But it hadn't been a fair fight and Rider knew it. No one could handle a gun like the legendary Rider. He'd been taught by the best, Trace Durango, down in the Texas hill country. Still, the Missouri Kid had pushed him into the duel. Life was hard and the weak couldn't survive.

Rider gritted his teeth and mounted up,

31

turning his horse to ride through the gathering crowd back down the street. He saw people running to spread the gossip about the action at the saloon. Rider wasn't quite sure where he was going, but of course he had to move on now that people had recognized him. Besides, those bounty hunters would probably be here by tomorrow.

Ignoring the curious stares, Rider stared straight ahead as he rode out. However, as he passed the stranded wagon train, he looked with curiosity toward the girl's wagon, wondering what it was the old man had been trying to tell him.

The blond girl stood there, arms folded, chin sticking out defiantly, but there were tears on those long lashes. He wondered for a split second what had happened to make her cry. She looked too stubborn to let life defeat her. Again he nodded and touched the brim of his hat as he passed.

A fat man in a derby hat hurried from behind a wagon and hailed him. "Hey, stranger, is it true?" he puffed. "Did McKade just get hisself shot?"

Rider reined in. "Yeah. He got in the way of some young kid tryin' to build a reputation."

"Damn it all to hell! Did you see it?"

Rider nodded. "I was there."

A shadow crossed the blond girl's expression. Now the hardness left her small face and for just a moment the blue eyes widened and he saw vulnerability and pain. "Mr. — Mr. McKade is dead?"

Rider nodded, looking into those eyes, thinking how they could be frozen ice one minute, and deep, warm pools the next. No, endless skies. *Sky Eyes.* "I'm afraid so."

For a moment, she sagged against the side of her wagon, her shoulders drooping as if she had no hope left and no friend in the whole world.

"Was he kin?" Rider asked, curious to know more about her and then annoyed with himself that he cared. A gunfighter didn't dare care about anything or anybody.

She swallowed hard and shook her head. "No, but he seemed like a nice old man and it's just that I was countin' on him . . ." Her voice trailed off.

The wagon train people gathered around Rider's horse. None of them seemed concerned for the old man at all. They were all grumbling and talking among themselves.

"Damn it!" said the fat one in the derby hat. "Now we ain't got a wagon master."

The girl's nostrils flared. "Is that all you can think of when a man's dead?"

The men ignored her, looking up at Rider.

"Don't pay no attention to that slut; she ain't nobody."

Rider stiffened. "You better not let her man hear you. If he's worth his salt, he'd kill you for it."

The men snickered.

"She ain't got no man," the fat old farmer in the faded overalls volunteered.

Rider blinked. "You're takin' a lone woman on a tough trip like this?"

A tall, elegant gentleman shook his head. "We've already turned her down," he drawled in a deep Southern accent. "Now it looks like we're not going ourselves."

Rider eyed the girl and she glared back at him. Why did she hate him so when she didn't even know him? She was sun-browned, her yellow hair streaked and faded even lighter, her hands rough from working in the hot sun. Sky Eyes deserved better than that faded gingham she wore. If she was his, he'd dress her fine. It wouldn't be much of a life for a woman — mostly on the run or living in cheap hotels while he gambled, but it was probably more than she had right now. It was on the tip of his tongue to invite her to ride out with him.

As if she had guessed his thoughts, she glared at him even harder. Well, there were plenty of eager women around. Rider consoled himself with that thought and started to nudge his horse forward. There was always another town over the next hill and money to be made with his gun.

"Mister," the fat man caught his fancy beaded bridle. "I've been elected captain of this here train. You wouldn't happen to know another wagon master, would you? We'd be willin' to pay plenty. We're desperate."

Rider started to shake his head, watching the girl. He disliked most white people with their pale faces. *Sooyawpi,* his people called them. *Ghost People.*

Then he reconsidered. He'd never led a wagon train before, but he knew the country they wanted to cross — knew it too well. All thoughts of danger disappeared from his mind as he looked her over and thought about how pale her skin must be under that faded blue gingham and how full and soft her breasts would be to his mouth. "I might do it," he said, surprising even himself, "but the price would be high."

"How high?" The men asked in chorus, gathering around.

Rider smiled ever so slowly and didn't answer, feeling desire building in him like a hot flame. He knew what he wanted and it wasn't gold. He wanted the girl.

Chapter Two

"Get down, stranger, and let's talk." The men gathered eagerly around his horse.

Rider tore his gaze away from the girl. Was he loco? No sane man would ride into Shoshoni country, much less try to take a small wagon train through there. For the warrior called Rides the Thunder, a very special, slow death would be waiting if the tribe captured him. He thought about death and torture. Then he looked at the girl again, at her hair like strands of ripe wheat.

"Sure." Rider dismounted, studying these settlers with a practiced eye. His ability to judge people and their reactions had kept him alive and won many a poker game for him. The plump man in the derby and the tall, elegant Southerner appeared to have wealth, judging from the fine cut of their clothes. The others were a motley-looking crew of defeated farmers, a bankrupt businessman or two, maybe some army deserters or men on the run from the law.

He glanced at the yellow-haired girl again. *Suppose he offered to lead this train, got them out on the trail, stole their gold and deserted them, taking Sky Eyes with him?* He was skilled with women; after a few nights in his blankets, she'd be glad she'd come along. Of course, after a few weeks, he'd tire of her as he always did and leave her, but in a wide-open boomtown like Virginia City or San Francisco, a beauty like Sky Eyes would have no trouble finding another man to look after her.

"Mister," one of the men asked, "couldn't you lead us if you know the country?"

Rider chewed his lip a long moment before he answered. "I have to tell you, a man would be a fool right now to take the trail with all the Indian troubles."

The aristocratic Southerner approached him, offering his hand. "I am Weatherford B. Carrolton," he said in an arrogant drawl, "of the Vicksburg Carroltons. I presume you've heard the name?"

Rider shook his hand; it was soft as a woman's. "Sorry, can't say that I have. Why aren't you in the Confederate army?"

The man drew himself up proudly. "Surely you know, sir, that as the owner of twenty slaves, I'm not required to go. Besides, those damned Yankees have utterly destroyed our lovely plantation."

A pretty, dark-haired woman had just come to his side, her nose in the air, one nervous hand lifting the hoops of her fine green dress, the other carrying a dainty lace parasol. "What my husband says is true." She dabbed at her hazel eyes with a lace kerchief. "Oh, those damned Yankees! Why, when I think of my pretty dresses that got burned up and how most of our slaves utterly deserted us —"

"Who you callin' 'damned Yankees'?" A runty, dirty-looking young man pushed through the crowd, doubling his fists. "I am proud to have served my country!"

"Now, son," the fat farmer said, holding up his hand, "don't be gettin' riled. I'm sure the lady meant no offense."

The lady only sniffed disdainfully and turned away.

Rider watched the short, younger man grit his teeth with rage. *A hothead,* Rider decided, *always looking for a fight.* The more Rider saw of this bunch, the more he knew what a disaster this wagon train would be.

A frail, sour man cleared his throat and began to cough uncontrollably. "Let's not get into all that," he suggested in a quavering voice. "Let's talk about whether this

38

gentleman might decide to lead us."

"I don't think so." Rider shook his head. "I got business elsewhere." He glanced around and saw a big, heavyset, bearded man in a nondescript cap. The man was watching the women, Mrs. Carrolton, and the blonde. The expression on his ugly face made Rider uneasy. "Who are you?"

The ugly man tore his gaze away from the blonde. "Stott. Erik Stott. I'm a black-smith."

That explained the bulging muscles, Rider thought. "At least you'd be a plus along the trail." He turned to the elegant Southerner. "Carrolton, after looking around, I'm not sure this bunch is outfitted well enough to cross this rough country."

"Well," Weatherford B. Carrolton said, "maybe not some of these others, but we have a fine buggy and good Kentucky thor-oughbreds, and a well-equipped wagon driven by our slave, Liberty."

Rider noticed the giant, silent black man who had come out from behind a wagon and stood nearby. "Isn't it sort of ironic to name a slave 'Liberty'?"

The arrogant Mrs. Carrolton sniffed. "He's just a black animal. It doesn't make no never mind what you name a slave — he doesn't know the difference."

39

Rider glanced at Liberty. The man's sullen features betrayed that he did know. Rider said, "I don't know about taking a slave clear to Oregon — I'm not sure it's legal there."

The Southern gentleman drew himself up proudly. "We must have him. Surely you don't think a gentleman should do sweaty labor like drive a team?"

"I'm not sure I ever gave gentlemen a second thought," Rider said sarcastically. "What about some of you others? Are you sure you want to try for Oregon?"

Fat Mr. Pettigrew pushed his derby back. "Some of us don't have much choice. Half my town in eastern Missouri has been wiped out, first by one side, then the other. I've got to make a fresh start for my lovely new wife, Francesca. She's used to the best — back-East aristocracy," he boasted.

Pettigrew was hiding something, Rider thought, watching the man's shifty eyes.

A thin, tired-looking little man pulled out his handkerchief and wiped his pale face. "My brother-in-law and I have lost our farms — hard times, you know. Les and I don't know what else to do but head for Oregon."

Mrs. Carrolton's refined face took on a sneer. "Poor white trash. Mr. Weeks, you and the Grays really can't make it all that way with those wagonloads of urchins."

The banker nodded agreement. "And Mrs. Weeks is in the family way, too. I say we leave those two families behind."

Immediately, there was a mutter of protest around them, although Rider, sizing up Weeks and Gray, didn't think the two weaklings had the backbone to finish this trip. He shook his head. "Hate to have a woman along who's going to give birth on the trail." He looked at the pregnant, weary little woman who had just walked up.

She in turn looked alarmed. "The baby's due in early October. We'd hoped to get there before it was borned."

October. The Hunting Moon, his people called it. Rider shook his head. "I don't know what the guidebooks promised, but we won't be in Oregon by October."

Mrs. Weeks looked up at her husband in silent appeal, but he shook his head. "Now, Aggie, you know we done sold the place in Indiana to finance this trip. We got nothin' to go back to."

Rider looked around at the crowd and sighed. The sour man was coughing again while his wife scolded him. Yes, they were a desperate bunch of losers. No wonder other wagon trains had rejected them and

McKade had decided not to lead them. Some of these people would die on the trail, some of them would turn back. Well, that wasn't his problem; he didn't intend to stay with this sorry crew but a few days. He looked toward the silent girl. "What about you?"

"Oh, she ain't goin'." Mrs. Weeks glared at the blond girl. "Emma Trent'd just cause a lotta trouble — her with her past and no husband."

Emma didn't argue, she just looked at Rider, both with appeal and loathing. "I — I've got everything I own tied up in my wagon and supplies," she said. "I even sold my grandmama's cameo brooch to get enough."

"Well," drawled Mrs. Carrolton, her nose in the air, "I reckon we all know what else you could sell to go back."

The women all laughed delightedly and Rider suddenly hated them for it.

The girl's face flamed, but she only raised her chin higher. "You ought to be ashamed to talk that way; you don't know anything about me. Besides, I got nothin' to go back to," she said. "I sold the land and I got no folks. I aim to go along, even if I have to follow after this train."

Another woman glared at the girl. "As if

we'd allow that!"

Rider gestured for silence. "Let's stop all this bickering and sit down and talk, or maybe I should just ride on."

"No, no!" The people crowded around him. "Don't be in a big hurry, now."

A fat old woman gestured. "I got a pot of coffee on. Come sit by the fire a minute."

Against his better judgment, Rider, leading his horse, followed the group as they headed into the circle of wagons. He noticed the girl hung back, listening.

They all gathered around the fire in the center of the wagons and Rider tied his horse to a wheel as the old woman put a cup of coffee in his hand. He tasted it, looking around at the expectant faces. McKade had been right; for the most part, they looked like cowards and whiners. His common sense overcame his need for the girl. "Look," he said, "now that I think about it, this is a rotten idea."

"How so?" asked the Southern gentleman. "We've all heard how Oregon is the land of milk and honey. My sister out there wrote me about how rich the land is."

"Yeah," nodded the fat farmer, "I got a brother out there already with a lot of land. He's gettin' rich."

Rider rolled a cigarette. "You got to get

there first to get rich."

The hot-tempered, short boy who favored the fat farmer snickered. "We know that, and we aim to."

Rider looked around at the wagons and livestock, not liking what he saw. He didn't have to be an experienced wagon master to realize this train was too small to protect itself against Indians. Besides, the equipment looked worn out, the oxen and horses thin. "It's more than two thousand miles through some of the roughest country you can imagine — mountains, and swift rivers, weather you can't depend on. It would be tough even for a big, well-equipped train."

"We ain't afraid," said one of the ladies.

Rider didn't answer. He was watching the men looking at each other uncertainly. "And you're starting too late. You should have left in April or early May."

A tired, gray-faced woman bouncing a fretful baby on her hip asked, "Why is that so important?"

Rider snorted and licked the paper, then stuck the cigarette in his mouth. "You've got to go in early spring when the new grass is at least four inches high so your oxen and livestock can eat. Once the frost and the blizzards come, they'll starve if they don't freeze to death along with all you people."

A murmur ran through the crowd.

"And if that don't scare you, the Indians might." Rider lit the smoke and watched the girl, who had crept into the edge of the circle.

"Injuns?" the fat banker snorted. "Why, if we come up against savages, we'll show them a thing or two."

"Yeah!" the slack-mouthed boy of the double fists snarled. "We'll whip them and send them runnin'."

"Not likely. We're talking about the Shoshoni," Rider said and took a deep drag off his cigarette, remembering.

"Is that the ones folks calls the 'Snakes'?" a man asked.

Rider nodded and without thinking, made the sign language for his tribe, a fluid motion of the arm like the fast, deadly movement of that reptile. "They're the lords of the high plains and the mountains, and nothing hardly moves through there without them noticing." Which was the best reason he could think of for him to mount up right now and ride on up toward Kansas City, Rider thought ruefully. "When I think about dealing with those warriors, I've decided maybe I don't want to do this after all."

He started to get up, but the runty, angry

boy touched his arm. "What would it take to get you to lead us?"

"Now, Willie, son," the fat farmer gave the boy a warning look, "we ain't got around to talkin' money yet, but maybe we could offer the man, oh, say, three hundred —"

"You offered McKade five hundred," Rider said. "I want two things — complete authority and a thousand dollars."

All the people gasped. "A thousand? Did that gunfighter say a thousand dollars?"

Banker Pettigrew blinked in anger. "I've been elected captain, and I don't intend to give up my authority —"

"Then don't," Rider shrugged. "I'll be movin' on now."

Carrolton drew himself up proudly. "See here, your demands are outrageous!"

"Get yourself another wagon master," Rider answered and started to untie his horse.

"There ain't none," whined the defeated little man named Weeks. "Everybody's already out on the trail."

"Which is the best reason in the world to cancel this trip," Rider shrugged. "I told you you were starting late and the group's too small, which put two strikes against you. Well, *adios*, folks. I've wasted enough time already."

He untied his horse, ignoring the buzz behind him as the people conferred. Rider took the reins and strode out of the circle, tossing his cigarette away. He passed the girl as he walked and looked over at her.

"You're a rotten bastard," she seethed, "puttin' money ahead of everything."

There was one thing he'd like more. Rider hesitated. With her looking at him like that, he didn't think she'd be agreeable to riding away with him. "What's your name again?"

"Not that it's any of your business, but Emma, Emma Trent."

Rider pushed his hat back. "What does it mean, this 'Emma'?"

The girl shrugged. "I don't know."

"Among my people, a name means something." He'd been named for the stormy night on which he'd been born.

"Injuns!" Her eyes went cold again, cold as the depths of frozen lakes.

There was something deep there, a hatred and a fear buried in her soul, Rider thought; something more terrible than just the average white's prejudice. Well, there were plenty of other women who'd be happy to warm Rider's blankets. This one would have just brought him trouble anyway. Reluctantly, Rider swung up on his horse and nudged Storm to ride out of the camp.

Behind him, the men were running, shouting, "Hey, we decided! We got the money!"

Rider drew in, half-turned in his saddle. His good sense told him to shrug and ride on, but then he looked at the girl again and wanted her more than before. So instead, he smiled and nodded to the eager crowd. "And the authority?"

They hesitated, then nodded.

Pettigrew said, "Anything you say goes."

Rider smiled. "Good, then we'll leave within the hour. Get those wagons ready and lined up."

He saw the hope in her eyes then, watched it flicker and die there. "Oh, by the way," he said to the gathering men, "there's one more thing."

"You got it!" Adams said.

"We're taking Mrs. Trent along."

"What?" half a dozen voices chorused.

"You heard me." He saw the surprise, the sudden hope on her small, sun-browned face and he was pleased, somehow, to have put it there.

"Excuse me," sniffed the elegant Mrs. Carrolton, "but the men have already held a vote and decided a single woman along on this train won't do —"

"Then hold another vote," Rider said and

48

he didn't smile, still watching the girl.

Some of the other women approached, their shoulders square and defiant as they strode toward him. "See here, Mr. Rider, we don't cotton to loose women like her comin' along among respectable people —"

"You heard her. She's got no place else to go," Rider said, wondering what had happened to her husband.

"That ain't our problem!" The fat farmer's wife crossed her chubby arms.

"Yes, it is," Rider said and kept his voice soft, "unless you want to end up without a wagon master."

"Wait! Wait!" The men set up a shout and gathered, exchanging angry words with their women.

Rider waited and as he waited, he didn't take his eyes off the girl. Her blue eyes stared back at him, the relief now replaced by suspicion. "Why are you doin' this?"

"It's just the decent thing to do." Rider tipped his hat back and smiled at her. "They got no call to treat you so bad."

"I don't think you got a decent bone in your body," the girl said, and she didn't smile back.

He'd never felt guilt in his whole life, but he was feeling it now. After all, he was doing the girl a favor, wasn't he? All she'd have to do was sleep with him a few times. Wouldn't she be as well off abandoned in some place like Santa Fe or Denver as stranded on the streets of this sleepy town?

She crossed her arms across her breasts as if to shield them from his bold stare. "Why does a gunfighter agree to lead a wagon train across dangerous country? It doesn't make any sense."

"I got nothin' else to do right now."

"The law after you?"

"In the West, it ain't considered polite to ask about a man's past. A woman's either, I reckon."

Her face flamed and she ducked her head. "I guess I brought that on myself. It's just that I'm not used to people helpin' me without wantin' something."

He wanted something, all right. He looked at where the swell of her breasts turned creamy white along the edge of the faded dress and the tangle of yellow hair that a man could bury his face in. Those curls would smell like soap and sunlight, Rider knew. His groin swelled, just imagining it.

The crowd behind them had held their hasty confab and now they hurried over, led by Mr. Carrolton. "We've talked it over," he drawled, "and she can go."

The fat farmer's wife stood with arms akimbo. "Long as that hussy doesn't try to take anyone's man!"

"There's not a man on this train I'd have!" Emma snapped back.

There's one you're gonna have, Rider decided. *Maybe not tonight,* he thought as he watched the girl's lovely face light up with hope. *Maybe not tonight, Sky Eyes, but when the time is right, you are going to be the rest of my pay. I want you under me, pleasing me and maybe if you're pleasing enough, I'll take you with me when I desert this bunch of losers.*

He must not think about that right now, he decided reluctantly. "All right, get those wagons ready to roll! We leave in less than one hour."

It took some doing to get the train moving; the more Rider surveyed the assembly, the more he regretted his agreement. The Adamses' rig looked like it needed repairs; their short, sulking son was already picking an argument with another man; the Weeks and Gray wagons were pulled by sorry-looking horses; and the strange blacksmith, Stott, seemed to be always staring at the women from under his shapeless hat as he tied down his stuff and checked his wheels. The elegant Carroltons sat in their fine buggy as if they were about to take a Sunday drive while their black slave labored and sweated to ready their big wagon ahead of them.

Rider rode up and down the line, offering suggestions, stopping now and then to check an oxen's yoke. The girl didn't seem to need any help from anyone. She had her rig ready and was already seated on the wagon box, waiting for the order to roll. He noted there was a little Jersey cow tied on behind and a brown-and-white mongrel puppy with four white feet gamboling about under her wagon. "We get in Sioux country, you better watch that dog," Rider said as he rode past her, heading up to the front of the train. "Sioux, Cheyenne, and Arapaho eat dogs."

"How would you know that?"

He curled his lip in disdain. "I've fought them and burned their villages."

"I'm not afraid. I've got a rifle and I can use it," she snapped back.

Rider made a mental note of that. He might have to disarm her before he could bed her. The challenge only made her more interesting.

He made a point to check the inventory of some of the wagons. Many of them didn't have near enough food or supplies to last five or six months and some of the wagons were rolling wrecks. No wonder all these people had been rejected by other wagon trains.

When he inspected the contents of the Carroltons' wagon, he shook his head.

Behind him, in the fancy buggy, Weatherford B. Carrolton asked, "What's the matter?"

"Your wagon is overloaded and not with necessities," Rider said. "You ought to leave half of it behind."

"Impossible!" Mrs. Carrolton snapped her lace parasol shut. "I simply can't leave my grandmother's walnut chest and my silver punch bowl. I've lost so much already."

She began to weep and her husband patted her shoulder, consoling her. "Now see what you've done?" he shouted at Rider. "My wife is a lady and she must have her things."

"That's right," she wept and dabbed at her eyes with nervous hands, "someone's got to bring civilization to Oregon, start a ladies' club, entertain the best families. I can't do that without my silver."

Rider leaned on his saddle horn and frowned. "There'll come a time you'll wish you had a lighter load," he predicted, "and Mrs. Carrolton, that fine silk dress will be

53

ruined by dust. I suggest you find a simple cotton dress."

She snapped her parasol open to protect her delicate skin and glared at Rider. "Only white trash own simple cotton dresses."

"Suit yourself." Rider shrugged and rode on. He hadn't had time to meet everyone on the train, and from what he'd seen so far, he didn't care to.

It was almost noon when Rider reined in at the front of the train and raised his hat, turning to wave it at the string of wagons. "Wagons ho!" he yelled. "Move 'em out!"

He nudged Storm forward, starting out on the dusty road leading away from town. He must be the biggest kind of fool, he thought with resignation as he rode along, glancing back to make sure the wagons were spaced far enough apart. Dogs barked and the Weeks and Gray children ran alongside the wagons, yelling with excitement. Somewhere in the line, a baby cried.

He rode up on a little rise, watching the half-dozen wagons string out along the trail. The Carroltons passed in their elegant carriage, their slave driving the covered wagon ahead of them. A group of single men sang and sipped out of their whiskey bottle as they rode along. "Put that away!" Rider yelled. "Whiskey and work don't mix!"

"Who's gonna make me?" the runty, angry Adams boy challenged.

Rider sighed. Before this trip was over, the sour young man was going to be trouble. "Let me put it this way," he said as he rode alongside, "there's plenty of rattlesnakes out there on those prairies and you'll need that liquor if you get snake bit."

"He's right," Stott grumbled. "Save it."

The boy looked as if he might argue, then tucked the bottle in his saddlebag.

Rider turned his attention to the blonde as she drove past, the clumsy puppy running along under her wagon, barking. Emma Trent drove her team of oxen with strong, capable hands, Rider thought with approval. The pioneer girl wore a sunbonnet now, but the wind had blown it back so that the sun caught the color of her yellow hair. She was probably the bravest and the smartest in the bunch, Rider thought, and wondered again why she was so desperate to go West. As pretty as she was, she could have her choice of men there in Missouri, so why was she set on going all the way to Oregon?

Rider rode down off the little rise as the train passed and headed up the line again. He glanced up at the sun. Maybe they could make ten miles today, but he doubted it. He'd heard a well-organized train sometimes got as many as twenty miles a day, but this wasn't a well-organized or well-equipped bunch he was leading. The only good thing was that it surely wouldn't occur to those bounty hunters to come looking for him on a wagon train. The thought made him smile and he didn't smile often. He must be loco. Gold and a woman's lips. A woman who sneered and recoiled when he looked into her eyes. She was both a mystery and a challenge.

Ahead of them lay two thousand miles of death and misery, Rider thought. Again, he cursed himself for a fool, and then reassured himself that it was going to be worth it. There must be plenty of gold on this train, carried by men like the banker, Pettigrew, and Carrolton, fleeing the war. Rider would stay with this train only long enough to find it and then desert this bunch of losers. The gold and the girl, and to hell with Oregon and the wagon train!

Emma knew the gunfighter watched her, but she did not look his way. She had noted the way his gaze touched her both brazenly and intimately, and had seen the desire flame in those dark, Indian eyes. She was grateful that Rider had insisted the wagon train include her, but she wasn't grateful enough for what she figured he had in mind. If Rider thought he was going to sleep in her wagon, he was going to be very disappointed.

Behind her, Josh whimpered and she reached back and handed him a piece of cornbread. "It'll be fine now, son," she whispered and smiled at him. "We're going to Oregon — a fresh start for both of us."

"Go?" He took the bread in his chubby fist and her heart melted at the way he looked up at her, so trusting. While she might hate the father, she loved this child with all her heart.

"Yes, go, baby. Everything will be all right now." She turned her attention back to her driving, snapping her little whip over the backs of the lumbering oxen. Up ahead the wagons had stopped. Curious, she got down and walked over to find out what the delay was.

A crowd had gathered to talk. Somewhere up near the front of the train, someone said, a wagon had lost an iron wheel rim. The wagon boss had ridden up front with Stott, the blacksmith, to take care of it.

As they waited, the snooty Millicent Carrolton pointedly ignored her as did the pretty banker's wife, who had stayed out of sight all morning. Francesca Pettigrew's hair looked suspiciously hennaed and she was much younger than her husband. Emma wondered idly if the girl had married the banker for his money. Yet that was hardly Emma's concern, and Emma tried to mind her own business.

Rider came up just then and dismounted.

"Oh," the banker said, "Rider, I don't think you've yet met my wife. This is Mrs. Pettigrew."

Emma watched Rider's face and then Mrs. Pettigrew. They both started and then Rider bowed slightly and touched the brim of his Stetson. "Pleased and honored to make your acquaintance, ma'am."

The pretty redhead's face blanched, and then she recovered and nodded demurely. "I-I am charmed to meet you, sir. My dear husband tells me we have a long and interesting trip ahead of us."

The gunfighter was staring at the pretty redhead. "Long, yes. Interesting? Well, that depends."

Emma watched them both, wondering. Mr. Pettigrew didn't seem aware of the look that had passed between the two, but Emma had seen it. The gunfighter and the red-haired banker's wife had known each other somewhere in the past — Emma was sure of it. Did that have any relationship to the gunfighter deciding to lead this train? One thing was certain: the expression in Francesca Pettigrew's green eyes when she looked at Rider spelled trouble. Well, it was none of Emma's business as long as she got to Oregon.

It look several hours to get the wheel fixed and then they strung out single file again on the prairie trail. The day was hot and long, but Josh played with a toy horse inside the wagon as Emma kept her attention on her driving. The oxen plodded patiently along the road. Up ahead, all Emma could see was the back of the Weeks wagon, their children walking alongside, playing with Josh's shaggy pup that gamboled through the grass.

Rider stayed well away from the Pettigrew's wagon. What a shock! Francie had looked like she would like to kill him. He'd better not turn his back on her. If he'd only known she was on this train . . . oh, hell, maybe he should desert late tonight and go on to Kansas City. Could anything else go wrong?

It was only late afternoon when the elegant Carrolton hailed Rider as he rode past their carriage. "See here, Rider, isn't it about time to set up camp? My wife is awfully tired."

Rider looked at the prim lady under her parasol. Her green silk gown was covered with a thin film of dust. "This trip is just getting started, Carrolton, and believe it or not, this is the best day you'll have. Cave Spring is up ahead and if we push hard, we might make it after dark. We need water, so keep driving."

He could hear spoiled Mrs. Carrolton's sobs and her husband's entreaties as he turned and galloped back along the route, past the girl's wagon. "You doin' all right?" Rider shouted.

She nodded and ran her forearm across her dusty face. "I forgot to thank you back there for making them take me along. Mr. McKade had promised me, but they don't want me. I'm not respectable by their standards."

Rider was mystified. She seemed to be a respectable widow. "They must be loco. You're no saloon girl."

"You don't understand," she began and then hesitated. Once he saw her child, he would know her secret, and he, too, would think the worst. "I-I'll try not to be a bother.

Any excuse will be enough for them to vote to throw me out of the train."

He shook his head, feeling strangely protective of this brave, lone girl. "They won't throw you out of this train — not while I'm leading it."

She almost smiled then and that hint of happiness on her lips lit up her sun-browned face. It made him feel good, the gratitude in those pale blue eyes.

Rider was suddenly ashamed and troubled. She thought he was being kind when he was only out for himself. He glanced away so he wouldn't have to look into those big eyes, touched the brim of his hat to her, and spurred Storm into a lope, regaining his position at the front of the train. He couldn't remember when his body had ached so much for a woman. *Not tonight,* he thought, *but soon she'd be his prize. In the meantime, what the hell was he going to do about Francie? Worse yet, what did Francie intend to do?*

Chapter Three

It was past sundown, the sky turning a pale lavender and pink when Rider finally rode back along the wagons, shouting, "Cave Spring is only a couple of miles ahead. Circle your wagons with your livestock inside the circle when we stop."

Emma sighed and nodded, wiping the perspiration from her face. She was bone tired, but Josh had been good, playing quietly inside the wagon as she drove on.

It was dark when word went up the line they'd reached the spring. Emma slapped her oxen with the reins and began to pull out to make the circle. Funny, she thought, the first part of the day, the gunfighter had seemed to stay near her wagon, watching her. However, later in the afternoon, he often galloped past without looking at her. He was a strange, hard man, all right. *Now just why would a man who was obviously a high-paid gunfighter decide to lead a train like this? Was it the money? Was he on the run? And what was his connection with Mrs. Pettigrew?* Well, none of that mattered to Emma as long as he allowed her to stay in this train.

Still, as she reined her oxen into the widening circle of wagons, she couldn't get him off her mind. Rider seemed so different from her meek, gentle Ethan. This half-breed looked as virile and dangerous as that fancy Appaloosa stallion he rode. As she watched him gallop past her and back up to the lead, shouting orders to the front wagons, she noted the muscle and tendon of him, the breadth of his shoulders, and the strength of those thighs gripping the horse. Sweat ran down his muscular neck, staining the dark shirt. He was all male — dangerous, forbidding, and distrustful. As an isolated and innocent pioneer wife, Emma had been acquainted with so few men, and only one other Indian. The memory made her shudder. Sometimes at night, she still had nightmares.

Josh whimpered in the back of the wagon and she reached back to rumple his black hair as he awakened and looked around. "That's a good boy," she smiled. "Mama will fix you some dinner as soon as she can get the cow milked."

He laughed and sat up, began to play. It had been a long day, Emma thought, and every bone in her body ached, but she would not complain. Maybe Oregon would hold a better future for her half-breed son than the past had held. For the sake of her child, she would accept any challenge.

Rider galloped here and there, motioning to men about turning their wagons into a circle. That accomplished, some of them rushed toward the spring.

"Hey!" Rider yelled, "take care of your animals first. They've got to get you a long way yet."

He noted with satisfaction that Emma Trent was the only one who had immediately begun to unhitch her oxen. Several of the single men hurried over to her. "Here, Miz Trent, let me —"

"I can do it myself." The girl drew herself up stiffly and continued unhitching. She led her oxen and the cow down to the creek with the puppy at her heels. Rider dismounted, watching her. She looked tired, but she wasn't complaining as the other women were. He could hear their shrill, grumbling voices carried by the hot wind. Pity their poor husbands.

Rider dismounted, led Storm to the pool

of the spring, ignored the girl, and watched the stallion bury his muzzle in the cold water a long moment. Then Rider stripped off his shirt, going to his knees and leaning over to get a drink, splashing the cold water on his muscular body. It felt good to him.

Out of the corner of her eye, Emma watched the streams of water run down his scarred, bronzed chest. He had enormous power and strength. Such a strong man could either hurt or protect, take whatever he wanted. The realization unnerved her. Quickly, she turned and led her animals back to the wagons, enclosing them in the circle. She climbed up on the wagon and looked in. Josh smiled at her and waved the toy horse. "Good boy!" she said. "Now you stay here and Mama will get some food ready." She climbed down off the wagon, got a water bucket, and walked back down to the creek. The half-breed gunfighter lounged against a tree, water still dripping down his bare chest as he rolled a cigarette. She hesitated, not liking to feel obligated. "I-I'm much obliged to you for making them include me on this trip."

He didn't answer, only nodded and lit his smoke, reaching to put his shirt on. Emma tried not to look at his scars as he buttoned it.

"Go ahead and ask," he muttered.

"I-I don't know what you're talking about." She averted her eyes as she filled her bucket.

"Yes, you do. They're sun dance scars."

Sun dance. She had heard that the savages had some kind of ritual that only the bravest men endured. "I didn't mean to stare." She staggered as she lifted her bucket.

"Here," he said, and strode toward her.

"I can manage," she insisted and clenched her teeth, gripping the handle with both hands.

"I admire your grit," he said as he shouldered her out of the way and took the bucket from her, "but there's plenty of men around here to do the heavy work."

"I know that, but most of them expect more pay than I'm willin' to give."

He chuckled deep in his throat. "Any man who's got two eyes . . ." He didn't finish the sentence, but she caught the inference.

She wanted to make her position very clear. "Mr. Rider, I'm no slut, no matter what the people on this train think. I can handle a rifle if needed."

"Some men might think it was worth the risk."

Emma didn't answer. She didn't like the way this conversation was headed and she was desperate to change the subject. "You knew Mrs. Pettigrew before."

It wasn't a question, it was a statement. In the shadows of evening, Rider's dark face turned hostile. "What makes you think that?"

His voice was glacier cold and Emma shrugged, sorry now that she had brought it up. "The way she looked at you like she'd like to either kiss you or kill you."

He hefted the bucket and glared down at her from his tall frame. "And now you'll want something for not telling the banker?"

"It's not any of my business," Emma said primly and turned to walk back up the path. It had been stupid to mention it, she thought, and was surprised at herself that she felt so annoyed with Francesca Pettigrew.

"That's right, it's not. Most women would have been eager to spread the gossip." He sounded relieved as he fell in beside her and she almost had to run to keep pace with his long legs.

"I'm different from most women in many ways."

"I've noticed that. The others are already complainin' and harpin' about the trip like a flock of screeching crows."

With everything that had already happened to Emma in her short life, she had learned to endure and keep silent.

They kept walking, Emma struggling to keep up. He seemed to notice her shorter stride and slowed his own. The path narrowed and they were forced to walk so close together, their arms brushed. She drew away from him as if he were a red-hot poker, and in doing so, stumbled. He reached out and caught her arm to steady her and she was amazed at the strength of that grip. "Thank you."

He only nodded and turned her arm loose ever so slowly. She thought that those hard, dark eyes might have softened a little. Rider shrugged and began to walk again. "I don't understand what a lone woman is doing on a wagon train. What the hell do you expect to find in Oregon that you can't find at home?"

"I might ask you the same," she answered as they walked toward the campfires some of the others were building.

He laughed. "Well, since you asked, I've got bounty hunters on my trail. I don't figure you're that desperate."

She looked sideways at him and blinked. "I'm pretty desperate. A widow is fair game, by most men's standards."

"It won't be any easier in Oregon," he said

and set the bucket of water next to her wagon.

"It might be easier for Josh."

"Josh?" He looked down at her, his face puzzled.

About that time, her little son stuck his brown face over the tailgate and laughed, holding out his tiny hands. Emma's heart melted and she smiled and reached for him.

Behind her, she heard Rider's sound of dismay. "A kid? You've got a kid? Well, I'll be damned!"

"No doubt you will be, Mr. Rider." She whirled around, hugging her son to her defensively.

The gunfighter looked both bewildered and upset. "I had no idea you had a son —"

"You never asked now, did you?" she retorted and stood Josh on the grass where he stared up at the half-breed.

The boy took a hesitant step forward. "Daddy?"

Rider backed away from the child as if he were facing down a grizzly bear.

Emma felt her face burn. "Josh has never seen a man who looks like him, so naturally, he thinks —"

"Well, tell him different!" Rider said.

"Uh, Josh, honey, Rider here —"

Before she could finish, Josh toddled over

and threw his arms around Rider's long legs. In the meantime, the shaggy mongrel pup dashed around the three, barking. Emma looked at Rider's expression and felt like weeping.

"Now you know why this crowd doesn't want me," she said softly and bent to unclasp Josh's hands from Rider's legs. She looked up at the gunfighter, furious with herself that she couldn't keep the tears from pooling even though she blinked hard. She didn't care anymore about how people treated her, but she hated anyone who rejected her little son.

"I didn't mean —" Rider began.

"It doesn't matter," she snapped and deliberately turned her back on Rider, reaching for the tin dipper. "Here, Josh, Mama brought you a drink of water."

Behind her, Rider made a sound as if he wanted to say something, hesitated, then turned and strode away, swearing.

If he hadn't been the biggest damned fool! Rider threw down his cigarette when he reached a pile of rocks and stomped it out. He'd been dreaming of enjoying this girl, taking her away with him, and she had a half-breed child. He felt he'd been cheated and played for an idiot. On the other hand, now he could understand what the trouble was between Emma Trent and the others. In their eyes, a white woman who would lie with an Indian was lower than a whore, beneath contempt. Yet Rider remembered how she had shrunk from him the first time he had seen her. She wasn't an easy slut; he knew too many of those. And yet, respectable white women did not lie with Indian men. She was a mystery, all right.

Furious with her and with himself, Rider returned to where he'd tied Storm. That half-breed kid was cute, but a child changed everything. Looked like he could forget about pleasuring himself a little with Emma Trent, then taking the pioneers' gold and skedaddling. Plus there was the problem of Francie. Too much for a man to deal with. Sometimes, as in poker, luck just wasn't with a man. Tonight, he'd better toss in his hand and ride out.

Rider unsaddled Storm and gave him a good rubdown, then staked him out to graze. Then he strode back over to the circle. The settlers had campfires going, cooking food. He looked toward Emma Trent's wagon, but she was milking her little brown Jersey cow, ignoring him. A few of the smallest Weeks and Gray children had gathered around to watch, their faces wistful. Emma gave her son a dipper of milk, turned toward the other children, and hesitated.

From here, he heard her soft voice. "You all go get a dipper and I'll give you each some milk."

About that time, pale little Mrs. Weeks yelled at the children, "You kids, get back over here now! I told you to stay away from that woman!"

Emma's face flushed and she swallowed hard before turning to build her own fire. Rider gritted his teeth. He felt like striding across the circle and shaking Mrs. Weeks until her teeth rattled. There'd been no call to treat Emma like that. Well, it wasn't his place to look out for the lone girl and her half-breed kid.

He started around the circle, inspecting, giving the livestock and equipment a critical look. Some of these families would never make it, even if they had the gumption to go on. Cranky old Mr. Bottom coughed continually and his wife could be heard telling him to be quiet. Consumption, Rider thought; the old man was too ill for this trip and his wife was as mean as a snake. How in the hell had Rider let people like these become his responsibility?

As he neared banker Pettigrew's wagon, red-haired Francie called to him. "Mr. er,

Rider, isn't it? Won't you join us?"

Rider hesitated, but Francie was smiling, albeit a little too sweetly.

"Uh, yes," said the banker, somewhat sourly, "do come eat with us."

Rider noted that Emma Trent had stopped to watch. "Sure, I'd be pleased to." He sat down by the fire and took a tin plate, looking with reluctance at the slightly burned food. As he remembered, Francie's talents weren't in the kitchen. He began to eat. "You folks been married long?"

Francie shot him a warning look, but the banker only took off his derby and grinned. "Not long. Why, I'm just so lucky to have met this fine lady escaping from the war and come to her rescue."

"Yes," Francie simpered, "my poor papa, who was English royalty, got killed and our fortune was wiped out. I had nowhere to go, so I was trying to reach our wealthy friends in the East when I met dear Mr. Pettigrew."

As Rider remembered, Francie's old man had been hanged as a horse thief, but he only smiled. "Isn't it lucky she found you."

Pettigrew nodded proudly. "I never met no royalty before, but I could tell the minute I laid eyes on her that here was a real lady."

Rider managed to keep a straight face as

he sipped his coffee. Francie had burned that, too. Rider glanced longingly over toward Emma's fire. He could smell biscuits baking.

Francie didn't say much — she was too, too sweet, batting her eyes at him and then at her dolt of a husband. Rider wondered what she was up to. The fiery-haired girl who'd entertained him so often at Miss Fancy's bordello wasn't the pioneer type.

The camp was settling down for the night when Rider announced that he would take the first watch, thanked the couple for their hospitality, and returned to his horse. He built a fire up on a little rise, then carried his saddle over, got a blanket and his rifle. He settled down and watched the sky, thinking. Finally he made his decision. After the camp was asleep, he'd saddle up and ride out. It was only a matter of time before Francie spilled the beans on him and he didn't stand a snowflake's chance in hell of taking that yellow-haired girl along when he left, not with her having a kid to look after. Well, to hell with this bunch of whiners and losers! Let them look out for themselves. This was a rough and hostile country and they'd never make it through to Oregon without an expert scout. They were all too weak to stick it out anyway. Let them all go back to their miserable lives in civilization.

Now where was he going from here? He couldn't return to Independence — the bounty hunters might be there waiting for him. It would be cool in Denver with summer coming on, or the mountains of Montana would be nice.

Emma lifted Josh up into her wagon, climbed in herself, and sneaked a look at the gunfighter in the distance. A killer. A hired gun. He had said bounty hunters were looking for him. He was at once dangerously attractive and repelling. At the moment, he looked thoroughly disgusted, sitting on the grass up on that rise, staring into the night. She wondered what he was thinking or planning. Nothing good, no doubt. Mrs. Pettigrew obviously had plans for him; it was evident by the way she had looked at him over by that campfire. Her husband must be a fool not to see it. Well, that wasn't any of Emma's business.

She settled Josh on a faded quilt in the wagon box. "Go to sleep now. Mama will be along in a minute."

She went outside and fed some leftover biscuits to the puppy, watching Rider as she did so. He leaned back against his saddle, staring into the fire. Then his head came up and he regarded her for a long moment. She nodded to him and he touched the brim of his hat with two fingers in a silent greeting. Thus encouraged, she stepped between the wagons and outside the circle. She approached him hesitantly, the puppy dancing around her skirts.

"What do you want?" he asked, and stared into the fire. Looking at her reminded him how much she fired his blood.

"You're thinking of pulling out, aren't you?"

He shrugged and patted the puppy's ears. "So what if I am?"

"This train can't make it through without a good scout."

Rider looked up at her, his dark eyes cold. "You think I give a damn about that? None of these people have the guts to be pioneers and they'll just get killed trying."

She squatted down by the fire. "Maybe if we have to go back to Independence, we'll find another scout."

"Not likely," Rider snapped. "Even McKade was about to back out when he got killed."

Emma sighed and bit her lip. "I-I was hoping to make a fresh start in Oregon, hoping people wouldn't hate my son so."

Rider looked at her, his hand stroking the

puppy absently. "What tribe is he?"

"Cheyenne."

Rider spat into the fire with disdain. "Cheyenne. Cowardly killers who scalped and tortured my father to death. When I grew up, I counted coup on their braves many times and hung their scalps in my lodge."

"So like Josh, you were raised without a father?"

He had never told anyone about his sire, how much it had hurt a small boy to lose him. He looked up into those wide, blue eyes and saw the genuine interest there that broke down his guard. "A French fur trapper. I reckon whites would call him a squaw man."

"Your mother?"

Rider shook his head. "Passing white gold prospectors brought cholera into our camp and I lost her, too."

"I'm sorry," she blurted.

He suddenly felt foolish and vulnerable, revealing his secret pain to a woman, and he wanted to lash out and hurt her in return. "Anyway, what's a respectable white girl doing with a Cheyenne kid?" He glared at her, a sneer on his hard mouth.

"That's hardly your business." She couldn't hold back the tears, but she wasn't going to let this hard killer see her cry. Emma scrambled to her feet and fled across the grass toward her wagon.

The puppy seemed hesitant to leave Rider. It looked from one to the other. She hesitated, turned, and called, "Boots! Here, Boots!"

The puppy seemed to leave Rider reluctantly, running toward her with its clumsy big feet. They both disappeared into the circle of wagons.

Rider stared after her, fighting the urge to run after her. An unfamiliar emotion was coursing through him and he didn't like it. It might be what white people called "shame."

"Rider, you are one mean bastard," he muttered to himself, "and they'll throw her out of this train tomorrow after you're gone." He leaned back against his saddle, torn with his decision. He didn't owe Emma Trent anything, her and her Cheyenne kid. Then why did he feel like such a rotten son of a bitch? He uncorked his canteen and took a long drink of water. Storm snorted and nuzzled his shoulder. Absently, Rider stroked the stallion's velvet muzzle. The horse was the only friend he had in the world, Rider thought. He had never felt so alone as he did at this moment.

Emma wiped away the tears as she climbed into her wagon and pulled the cover over her and Josh.

"Mama?"

"I'm here, baby. Go to sleep and I'll tell you a story." She curled up next to her little son, hugging him to her. Poor Josh, he hadn't had much of a life so far, but maybe things would be different far out on the frontier. "Once upon a time, there was a little boy named Josh who had a puppy named Boots."

The child laughed with delight. In the moonlight, she could see his deep brown eyes light up. "Me, the story's about me!"

"Well, yes." She kissed his chubby cheek. "Little Josh has a long trip ahead of him, but when he gets there, everything will be wonderful."

"Plenty to eat?"

She winced at his innocence. "Plenty!"

"And Daddy will be there and take care of us?"

She could have wept, but she choked back the lump that came to her throat. "I-I hope to get you a daddy, yes."

"And live happily ever after?"

"Yes, like the prince riding off with the princess."

"What's a prince?"

She laughed. "A rich man who goes around on a white horse rescuing mamas and little boys."

"Rider?"

"No, not Rider!" she snapped, and then regretted it. "Just forget about him, all right?"

"Looks like Josh," the toddler said.

"But he's not rich and he's not a Daddy type," Emma insisted, glad the grim gunfighter was not here to catch this discussion. "Look, baby, it's going to be a long day tomorrow, so let's go to sleep." She kissed him again and they settled down.

The child dropped off to sleep immediately but Emma couldn't sleep. The night was too warm and she was just now facing the enormity of her actions. What in God's name had she done, selling the little she had to finance a dangerous trip to a place she'd never seen? Because it might mean a better life for her son; for that, she could endure anything.

From the shadows, Stott watched the yellow-haired girl stride away from Rider and go into her wagon. He pulled his shapeless hat down on his dirty hair, stroked his groin, and thought about her with relish. Yes, she was a purty one, that Emma Trent, and she'd feel good under him. He wanted that red-haired wench, too, and that uppity Carrolton woman. He licked his lips. Yes, he wanted them all, fighting and writhing under him. He liked women to struggle when he took them; it gave him such a heady sense of power. Stott had taken women like that before. They'd sent him to prison for it in Arkansas. In the confusion of the war there this past spring, Stott had managed to break out and escape.

He combed his fingers through his tangled beard and pushed his cap back, grinning with expectation. This was going to be a long trip. Sooner or later, Stott intended to enjoy all three of those women. They'd be too ashamed to tell anyone when it happened. That gave him power. Stott liked power almost as much as he liked a woman crying and whimpering in fear under him. The one he wanted first was the girl with yellow hair. He'd wait and watch for his chance to take her. Now he must be content to spread his blankets and go to sleep, dreaming of the women he'd taken and the power and the pleasure it had given him.

Rider stared after the girl long after she had disappeared into the circle of wagons.

81

He had watched her stride away, her head high, her shoulders back, proud and haughty. She might have had as tough a life as Rider himself, but it hadn't broken her spirit. He liked that in a woman. He watched her long-legged stride and thought about those slender legs opening for him and how that proud mouth would taste. He wanted that woman despite the enemy kid, hungered for her more than the pioneers' gold. Rider always got what he wanted. But maybe not this time.

He had planned to desert the train to-night, but now he reconsidered. Like in poker, maybe his luck would change if he didn't throw in his cards. Hell, he didn't re-ally have anyplace to go anyway, and Francie couldn't tell what she knew about him without messing up her own sweet deal. In Texas, they called this situation a "Mex-ican standoff." Only Francie and Emma Trent knew any of his past. He regretted now that he had told Emma bounty hunters were looking for him. After he thought about it a minute, he shook his head. No, the yellow-haired girl was not the type to spill everything she knew. A man's secrets would be safe with her; he was certain of it.

The knowledge surprised him. He'd never felt safe with anyone. Now Rider's good sense told him he ought to clear out, but his attraction to Emma made him decide he'd stay with the train awhile and see what developed. Rider balanced his rifle across his knees and settled in to guard the sleeping camp. His horse grazed quietly nearby and his fire dwindled to a small flame.

Somewhere to one side, in the bushes, a twig cracked and Rider came to his feet, his rifle ready. "Come out or I'll kill you."

"Shh! You'll wake everyone up." Francie stepped out of the bushes.

He sighed and lowered his weapon. "Are you loco, Francie? I could have shot you. You ought to know better than to come up on a gunfighter without warning. Why aren't you in bed?"

Francie shuddered. "That fat old slug wants to climb all over me."

"He's probably payin' enough for the privilege."

"Don't remind me! Come over here in the shadows where we can talk."

He leaned the rifle against the trunk of a tree. "I don't see that we have anything to talk about."

She caught his hand, pulling him into the shadows. "Don't you remember how good we were together?"

"Me and a hundred other *hombres* around

San Antone," he reminded her with irony. "Is Pettigrew really stupid enough to think you're an elegant lady escaping from the war?"

"A randy old codger wantin' sex will believe anything."

Rider laughed. "Looks like you've got a good life ahead of you if he doesn't find out your past."

"Good life?" The redhead shuddered. "With that old goat always tryin' to get my drawers off? He makes me want to vomit."

"So what are you up to?"

She laughed as she ran her hands up Rider's chest and around his neck. "You know me too well, honey."

He caught her hands and tried to disengage them, but now she pressed her generous breasts against him. "Forget it, Francie."

"You've got a strange set of values," she sneered, looking up at him with pouty, half-open lips. "You're a killer and a thief, but you don't want what I'm offering."

He could feel the heat of her lush body all the way down his and he'd been a long time without a woman. "I didn't say I didn't want it, Francie, it's just that —"

She cut off his protest with her kiss, her mouth hot and demanding, pushing the tip of her tongue between his lips as she molded herself against him. For a long moment, he was almost paralyzed with desire, wanting to throw her down in the shadowy grass and mount her in a frenzy. As hot as he was, he could be finished in three long strokes and she had such generous, creamy breasts that cried out for a man's mouth.

Instead, he took a ragged breath to gain control of his need and stepped away from her.

"I can't believe this," Francie snapped. "You've got another woman — there has to be."

"No." He shook his head.

"It's that blonde, isn't it? The one with the half-breed kid! She's satisfying you — that's the reason you came along."

He only wished it were true. "Now, Francie, you know me pretty well. Would I saddle myself with a woman who has a kid? No strings on me — not now, not ever. Love 'em and leave 'em, that's me."

"Yeah, that's right, isn't it?" She seemed slightly mollified. "I couldn't even hold onto you."

"Sorry about that," Rider said, "but a man was needing a hired gun in El Paso."

"Rider, honey, it could be like it was," she crooned, her eyes as plaintive as her voice.

"We could run off tonight."

"Your husband seems like a pretty decent sort —"

"Husband?" she snorted. "That sorry bastard? He ain't really my husband. Let me tell you about him, Rider. He's deserted his wife and robbed his own bank."

"What?"

"That's right. Cleaned out the safe — figures they'll never track him clear out to Oregon."

"Wonder who gave him the idea." Rider looked down at her and she looked away.

"Okay, so maybe I might have suggested it."

Rider pushed his hat back, considering. "You mean he's got all that money with him?"

She nodded. "Ten thousand in gold, silver, and paper hidden in the false bottom of our wagon. Why don't we take it and leave together? There's enough to last us the rest of our lives."

Rider chuckled. "Sounds like a dream come true, but it'd take some planning."

"Are you stallin' me? That's not like you, Rider. You was always a man of action." She bristled at him. "Just think. You'll have all that money and me to warm your bed. We'll go to San Francisco or Virginia City, live in style."

Rider chewed his lip, thinking. "I didn't say I wouldn't do it. I just said it would take some planning, Francie. You wouldn't want the whole bunch on our trail now, would you?"

She grinned and nodded. "You're smart, honey. I hadn't thought about that. Okay, I'm willing to wait. I've always had a weakness for you, Rider, you know that."

"I know." He slapped her across the fanny. "Now go back to your wagon before he wakes up and finds you gone."

Francie giggled and turned to glide lightly through the shadows back to her own place.

Rider looked around to make sure no one had seen the exchange. The camp was asleep. So far, so good. Then he glanced toward Emma Trent's wagon. She stood by the water bucket, dipper in hand, staring at him wide-eyed.

Rider began to curse under his breath. Evidently Emma had gotten up to get a drink and had seen the whole encounter. What could he do to ensure her silence?

However, before he could move, Emma scrambled back into her wagon. *Now what in the hell was he going to do?*

Chapter Four

Rider started toward the wagon, then hesitated and stopped. He didn't owe Emma Trent any explanation, and she didn't seem the type to tattle. More important, she couldn't know about the money. Rider returned to his fire, thinking. Lusty little Francie and a stolen bank fortune — both his for the taking. No man in his right mind would turn that down. It was much better than the sum the wagon train was going to pay him to get them to Oregon. All Rider had to do was wait 'til the time was right.

It was a hot night, crickets calling. Somewhere far off a lonely coyote howled and it echoed and re-echoed across the land. Mr. Bottoms was coughing again and Rider thought he could hear the man's querulous wife telling him to be quiet. In the middle of the night, Rider let Willie Adams, the sullen, short boy, take over the watch, but Rider didn't sleep much. His body still remembered Francie's hot female flesh pressed against him, the wet mouth exploring his own. However, when he closed his eyes, it wasn't fiery-haired Francie he imagined in his arms, warm and eager, it was the yellow-haired girl. "Sky Eyes," he muttered, "Sky Eyes." He had never wanted a woman as badly as he wanted that one. Small chance. Somehow he knew money couldn't buy her the way it could a slut like Francie.

Maybe that was the reason Sky Eyes was becoming a fever in his blood — because she couldn't be bought and she wouldn't be charmed into his bed. He was certain he would tire of her; he'd never met a woman yet he wanted to keep by his side forever, especially not one with a half-breed kid sired by an enemy brave. Even if the Cheyenne and Shoshoni hadn't been old tribal enemies, he could never forget that he had been orphaned by a Cheyenne dog soldier.

All that was tomorrow's problem, he thought with a weary yawn. He'd work out everything later on the trail.

He awakened in the middle of the night and looked over toward the sentry fire. Willie Adams sat with his head on his knees, sound asleep, the fire burned down to gray ashes. Rider got up, went over, and shook him awake. "Hey, sleeping on guard is a serious offense."

"You bossin' me?" The sullen boy stumbled to his feet, doubling his fists.

Rider sighed. "Don't get touchy with me, kid. I'm the boss on this train. It'll be dawn in another hour and we'll have to begin rousing the camp." He turned and went over to his own blankets and began to build a camp fire to make some coffee.

Willie Adams glared after the half-breed's departing back. *Who did that 'breed think he was anyway?* Rider was tall. Willie hated and envied any man who was tall. Willie doubled his fists and gritted his teeth with rage. He liked to fight, it made him feel good. Other boys had always picked on him because he was a runt, but after he'd hurt two or three of them badly in his rages, they'd learned to leave him alone. He liked to hurt people. It made him feel tall.

Matter of fact, he'd been sentenced to hang back in Virginia for beating a fellow soldier to death with a shovel after a drinking bout. However, the night before he was to die, his outfit had been overrun by Johnny Rebs and in the confusion, Willie had managed to escape. Now he'd make a fresh start in Oregon where the army would never track him down. Rider probably wasn't so tough without his pistol. Sooner or later, Willie would catch him with his guard down and unarmed. He closed his eyes, gritting his teeth and grinning as he imagined hitting Rider across the back of the head. And hitting him and hitting him until the half-breed's skull was a scarlet pulp. Lying on the ground, Rider wouldn't be so tall.

Emma had not slept well, so she was already awake when someone fired a pistol around four o'clock in the morning to awaken the camp. She got up and went outside for a bucket of water, leaving her sleeping child tucked under the quilt. When she looked toward Rider's fire, she saw him watching her. His dark face betrayed no emotion, but the way he looked at her made her uneasy.

She got her bucket of water and returned to her wagon, ignoring him. So the ruthless gunfighter was carrying on a dirty little affair with Francesca Pettigrew. Well, that wasn't Emma's business, unless it imperiled the future of the wagon train. Still, she had felt a sinking emotion that surprised her when she had seen the two in an embrace.

She milked her cow, made some biscuits, and baked them in her small Dutch oven.

She had tied a container of cream to the side of her wagon yesterday and the jostling along had produced some butter. From her precious cache, she got out a jar of home-made strawberry jam. The sky had turned the gray light of pre-dawn when Emma fed Josh milk and biscuits and looked around for the puppy. "Boots? Here, Boots!"

Rider strode past just then, the puppy at his heels. Josh grinned at them both, but she frowned at Rider. "That's our dog."

The gunfighter frowned as he paused. "I didn't steal him."

Josh threw his arms around the dog's neck and smiled up at the half-breed. "Rider and Josh's dog."

Rider hesitated and looked uncomfort-able, a slight smile on his hard mouth. "Sure," he said finally to the child. "He's a good dog." Then he walked on. Emma stared after his broad back. First he had stolen her dog, now he was stealing her son's affections. "Josh, honey, don't get too at-tached to Rider."

Puzzlement filled Josh's dark eyes. "Josh like Rider."

"Well, but he won't always be around. We can't count on him," she said. "It's just us — you and me against the world."

Josh shook his dark head stubbornly. "No,

four of us, Mama, Josh, Boots, and Rider."

She felt a hot flush come to her face, only happy that Rider wasn't around to hear her innocent little son. She fed Boots some left-over biscuits and began to hitch up her oxen.

Rider strode away from Emma Trent's wagon, a little angry with himself. "You can't begin to like that kid," he grumbled under his breath. "You just want to sleep with his mama — remember that. When you tire of her, you'll be gone."

By daylight, the whole camp was packed and ready to roll again. Emma tidied up the inside of her wagon with all its barrels of foodstuffs and household items. There hadn't been much left after she sold the farm and house to pay for the big wagon.

Rider galloped by, shouting, "Line 'em up and move 'em out!"

Josh looked after the big man, smiling. "Rider."

She hated the half-breed for the attraction he held for her little son. "Come on, Josh, call your dog and get in the wagon, honey."

But the clumsy pup was already trailing along behind the big Appaloosa horse. "Traitor!" She called after the dog.

Josh laughed. "Boots go with Rider. Can I go with them, too?"

"No," Emma snapped. "I told you, he's not a Daddy type man."

Josh's dark little face told her he liked him anyway. Without even seeming to care, Rider was stealing both the affections of her child and her pet. She had a feeling Rider always took what he wanted. She thought about Francesca Pettigrew and was disgusted all over again.

She settled Josh in the wagon with some toy soldiers, checked the wooden yokes on her patient oxen, tied the cow on behind and climbed up on the wagon seat. The June sun was already hot as the wagons pulled out on the trail. She put on a faded sunbonnet to protect her sun-tanned face but her arms and neck were turning unfashionably dark. She could hear Millicent Carrolton complaining and weeping, then her husband's plaintive pleading from the fancy buggy just ahead of her as the wagons took the trail.

It was going to be a long day and a trying one until the train fell into some kind of routine, Emma thought. And there would be probably four or five months of this — even more if things didn't go well. Emma shielded her eyes from the sun as the wagons struck out along the dusty trail. At least now, she and Josh had a chance at a new life when there'd been none before, so she'd have to endure dealing with the gunfighter until late in the autumn. For the sake of her son, she could do that.

Rider cantered along, falling in next to her wagon. She looked straight ahead. "Aren't you riding next to the wrong wagon?" she asked pointedly. "The Pettigrews are ahead of us."

"About last night," he began.

"It's really none of my business, now, is it?" She looked straight ahead.

"You're damned sure right about that!" He swore and spurred his horse on down the line.

She saw little of him the rest of the day. They paused in the heat of midday to eat cold leftovers from breakfast, rest a few minutes, and move on. It seemed to Emma the train crawled along like a line of snails, but she knew by anyone's standards that they were making good time. Ahead of them stretched rolling hills and meadows. She knew Elm Grove in Kansas was the next camping spot, then on to the hill called Blue Mound.

Down the line, she heard Mr. Bottoms coughing and his wife's querulous scolding. The Weeks and the Gray children ran alongside the wagons, teasing and chasing each other. In late afternoon, the Adams wagon broke a wheel and the big blacksmith, Stott, jacked up the axle and repaired it while the rest of the people waited. He was a powerful man, Emma thought, watching his muscles ripple, but a bit strange. There was something about the way Stott stared at women that unnerved her. They moved on until dusk when the scout found a good place to camp and shouted for the people to circle their wagons.

Rider disappeared and came riding back into camp with a couple of fat rabbits hanging from his saddle. As she watched, Rider built himself a fire and roasted them. The meat smelled good. Emma had cut up some potatoes and made some cornbread. With some warm milk, it was better than what most of the camp was eating. This time, the dirty urchins of the camp came to her fire, each carrying a battered dipper. "Does your mama know you're here?" she asked and then checked herself. Of course they didn't or Mrs Weeks would be screaming at them all to stay away from her.

Emma smiled and filled each dipper from her milk bucket. The children drank it gratefully and scattered. When she looked up, Rider was watching her. She pretended not to see as she fed her dog and did her chores. Some of the travelers had built a big fire in the center of the camp and were sitting around it, talking and laughing. No one yelled at her to join them, so she only watched from a distance. She heard Francesca Pettigrew call to Rider to come join the gathering. Rider hesitated, then walked over to the fire.

Emma watched for a long moment, then climbed into her wagon, settled down with her child, and told him a story until he dropped off to sleep. Lying there in the darkness, she could hear Mr. Bottoms coughing and Francesca's laughter. She had never felt so lonely in her life. She was part of this group and yet not part of it. Well, it had been this way ever since her husband's death. She might as well get used to it — white settlers would ostracize a woman with a half-breed bastard son.

Rider had hesitated to join the group by the fire, but there were things he needed to clarify with the other men. Otherwise, he wouldn't have bothered. He sure wanted to stay away from Francie, because she was stupid enough to give him away and he'd never get his hands on all that bank money.

He strode over and squatted down by the fire, looked around the circle. "We'll be crossing the northeast corner of Kansas for a few days, passsing south of Lawrence. It'll probably be on the Nebraska prairie that we're liable to run into Indians."

Millicent Carrolton began to cry. "We didn't have Indians at home. Oh, I just hate this awful trip!"

"Now, Millicent, dear," began her husband with a helpless gesture.

"Mrs. Carrolton," Rider snapped, "it's going to get a lot worse before it gets better. You can always go back."

Weatherford B. Carrolton frowned at him. "No, we can't. You see — never mind."

Rider wondered about the secret this elegant pair was hiding, then dismissed the thought. What the hell did he care about any of these losers and misfits? As soon as he could get his hands on that money, he'd be gone. He'd already decided he wouldn't take Francie. A gunfighter traveled light, no responsibilities, no attachments. There was always a hot, eager woman to amuse him in the next town he came to. The only other thing he wanted besides the money now was Emma Trent under him for a night or two until he tired of her. "We'll have to have discipline on this trip, folks helping each other when one has trouble with a wagon or team, maybe some sharing of sup-

98

plies if food gets low."

He watched the hostile glances go around the circle. This bunch had no plans to do anything to help their neighbors. They were a lot like he was, he realized suddenly, not giving a damn about anyone. He didn't like the mental comparison between himself and this bunch of misfits.

"Oh," he said, "the Weekses and the Grays need to keep a closer eye on their kids. There's too many things can happen to them — rattlesnakes, getting run over by a wagon, or even lost out on this prairie. We're behind time now and we can't spare precious days on accidents or breakdowns. To stretch our food, it's not a bad idea for the men to do a little hunting — just don't get too far from the wagons. It's possible we might get some buffalo."

Mr. Bottoms began to cough again and his sour wife scolded him. The man looked weaker today, Rider thought; the Bottomses would never make it to Oregon.

"One more thing," Rider said as he stood up, "we need to keep a lookout every night. All the men will have to take turns standing guard."

"Why?" grumbled banker Pettigrew, taking off his derby to scratch his bald head. "What's the danger? We ain't too far from

Fort Leavenworth, with all those soldiers —"

"Mr. Pettigrew," Rider said with great patience, "I'm not used to people questioning my judgment. Anything can go wrong and it would take a while to get a message to the fort. Animals get out, strangers ridin' into camp, Indians."

Millicent Carrolton began to cry again and the fat farmer's wife, Mrs. Adams, screamed at her to shut up.

"Don't tell my wife to shut up!" Weatherford B. Carrolton snapped. "She's not used to being ordered around by white trash!"

Young Willie Adams stood up, doubling his fists. "You callin' my mama white trash?"

Rider stepped between them. "Look, anyone who wants to fight may get their chance later. Besides Lakota and Cheyenne, we might run into some white bushwhackers."

"What?" Mr. Bottoms asked.

He had their attention now; every face turned toward him. "Sometimes outlaws prey on wagon trains," Rider explained, "figuring travelers might be carryin' something worth stealing."

Banker Pettigrew's fat face suddenly gleamed with sweat in the firelight. He took off his derby, wiped his bald head, and looked toward his wagon. Francie tried to catch Rider's eye, but he ignored her.

"All right, that's about it." Rider stood up. "Now I'll take the first watch and then you men decide among yourselves how we'll split this up in the future."

The Southern gentleman shook his head. "When it's my turn, Liberty can stand guard." He turned and yelled at the black man in the shadows, "You hear that, Liberty?"

"Yes, Boss," Liberty said humbly, but Rider caught the flash of rebellion in the big man's eyes.

"I said *every* man," Rider said. "Carrolton, you may be a big man among the rich planters in Mississippi, but you're just a settler on my train."

Millicent Carrolton's weepy eyes blazed. "The nerve of you, you — you Injun, you! Tell him, Weatherford!"

"Now, my love," the Southern gentleman cooed and made a soothing gesture with his soft, manicured hands.

"I repeat, every man will take a turn at guard duty," Rider said. "Send someone out to relieve me about midnight."

With that, he returned to his fire, sat down, and rolled a cigarette, ignoring the distant circle of wagons. He smoked and watched Emma's wagon. She hadn't come to the center fire but, of course, she wouldn't be welcomed by the other women. He wondered again about her past. She was the only one who wasn't grousing and complaining, a plucky little thing pulling more than her share of the work. *Sky Eyes*. She was as self-sufficient as any Shoshoni girl. Out in the West, with the terrible shortage of women and Emma's beauty, some settler would be only too happy to marry her, even if she did come with a half-Injun kid. He hoped that husband wouldn't be mean to Josh, or throw her past in her face when he was angry. Both thoughts made Rider grit his teeth.

Boots came out from under her wagon, looked toward Rider, wagged his tail. Rider had never owned a dog; a man on the move didn't have time to mess with a pet. Absently, he snapped his fingers and the shaggy pup ran to him, cavorting around him, licking his face.

"Good dog," Rider said, stroking the dog and feeling a little foolish, but no one was around to hear. After a minute, the pup lay down next to him and went to sleep. He had been alone so much of his life with his parents both dead and only an old uncle, now long dead, to look after him. He was not only alone now; he belonged nowhere.

He would not think about his past now, Rider decided, swallowing back the yearning that came to him when he thought of the majestic Shoshoni riding through the mountains of the West, living wild and free. Because of the murder, his mother's people would no longer welcome him into their midst. The fact that his French father had taught him English had enabled him to make a place among the whites. He'd drifted down to Texas and gone to work on the giant Triple D ranch where Trace Durango had taught him to handle a pistol. Then Rider had gotten mixed up with outlaws and left the ranch.

Over at the wagon train, he heard the quarrelsome people arguing among themselves about what was fair and whose turn it was to do what. Rider heaved a sigh of disgust. Well, when the time was right, it wouldn't be his problem anymore. He'd loot Pettigrew's stolen bank hoard and take off, leaving this sour bunch stranded. Hell, it was all they deserved.

As the camp settled down for the night, Rider leaned back against his saddle and listened to the night noises: the coyotes singing far, far away, the wind whispering through the tall prairie grass. Somewhere, a cricket chirped and Mr. Carrolton's fine carriage horse nickered. Emma. No, Sky Eyes. He imagined her asleep, lying on a quilt in that wagon, her hair like puddled moonlight. He tossed a twig into the fire. When he got to Denver, or wherever he decided to go next, first thing he'd do was buy himself a pretty whore for the night. He thought of all the women he had had over the years, but his mind kept returning to the yellow-haired girl asleep on her quilts. He wondered if her mouth was as soft and warm as it looked.

"Stop thinkin' about her, damn it!" He shifted his weight and leaned his arms on his knees. "She's got a kid, remember? You sure as hell can't invite her to run off to Denver or Kansas City with a kid in the picture."

She wasn't the kind to desert a child, he knew that. If she were, she would have already done so, since keeping a half-breed kid only added to her problems. As nervous as she was around men, he wondered for a moment how she had ended up with a Cheyenne son.

After a while, the moon disappeared behind scudding clouds and the night was as dark as the devil's heart. The wind picked up a little, rattling the canvas on the wagons. Next to him, the pup slept peacefully. "I forgot to tell them about thunderstorms and tornados," he said aloud, then decided he'd scared them enough for awhile.

A man came out from between the wagons, a big man. Rider could only see him because of the light-colored shirt the man wore. He walked toward Rider.

"Hello, Boss," Liberty said. "I'll stand guard for a while."

"You got a rifle?"

"Mr. Carrolton gave me his." Liberty sat down by the fire.

"You a pretty good shot?"

"Fair. Shot a lot of squirrels and rabbits for the dinner table back home."

Instinctively, Rider liked the handsome, big black man. "Help yourself to the coffee."

The other hesitated, then poured himself a cup with a good-natured smile. "Thank you much."

Rider shook his head. "The Carroltons don't seem like the type to rough it, not with them used to a soft life."

Liberty started to say something, then seemed to think better of it. "They didn't have much choice," he said finally.

Rider sensed there was something Liberty had been warned not to tell. *Just what were the elegant Southerners hiding?* Well, it wasn't any of his business. "You want a smoke?"

The slave hesitated, as if unsure whether to accept such an offer of friendship, then nodded uncertainly, white teeth gleaming. "Don't mind if I do."

Rider handed him the makings. "You wantin' to go to Oregon?"

The other paused. "Nobody asked me what I wanted; they never do."

"But if they did?"

Liberty hesitated as if wondering whether to trust Rider. "What I'd really like is to join the Buffalo Soldiers in fightin' for the Union."

Rider stood up, stretched. "We're crossing Kansas, just the northeast corner, but it's not that far to Fort Leavenworth."

Liberty paused, still rolling the smoke. "Boss, ain't Kansas a free state?"

Rider smiled. "Sure is; not like Missouri. In Missouri, if a slave escaped, they'd return him to his owners."

Liberty reached for a burning twig to light his smoke and seemed to think it over. "There's a gal I left behind, a real purty, light-skinned gal. Maybe she could get to Kansas when the war ends."

"A woman who loves you and freedom — that'd make you a very rich man, Liberty, a prince among commoners."

"A prince. Yeah, I reckon that's one way to look at it." Liberty grinned and smoked his cigarette.

"Take a little planning is all."

Liberty looked thoughtful. "They got buffalo soldiers at that fort?"

"Maybe," Rider said.

"Thanks, Boss." He stared up at Rider and a look of understanding passed between them. "You ain't goin' all the way to Oregon, either, is you?"

Rider hesitated. "What makes you think that?"

"Boss, you got no reason to stay. You could steal everything the white folks got and take off anytime."

"That's right." Rider flushed. It was the girl, he realized, only his desire for Sky Eyes was holding him. Damn her, she had taken his freedom and made a slave of him.

At that moment as he watched, Emma Trent came out of her wagon and stood there a moment, looking around. Even on this moonless night, her yellow hair shone in the darkness and Rider wondered what it would feel like to twist his hands in those silken strands and pull her close.

Liberty smoked in silence and Rider stared off at the wagons. Even though it was a dark night, the white canvases shone in the blackness. Emma hesitated, then headed for the nearby bushes. He'd have to warn her about snakes.

"Boss, what you thinkin'?"

Liberty's deep voice brought him out of his musings with a start. "Nothing," he lied. He'd been thinking Liberty had more to look forward to than he had. Rider had no woman who loved him — *really* loved him — and he hadn't felt free since he'd joined the white civilization five years ago. A prince? No, he didn't qualify.

The fire crackled and Rider sighed, angry with himself that a woman could make him feel this way. The puppy at his feet raised its head, looked toward the camp, and growled softly.

"What's the matter, boy?" Rider knelt on one knee, stroking the dog's shaggy ears. "You hear a cricket or something?"

The pup continued to growl softly.

Rider picked up his rifle. "I reckon I'll take a look. Liberty, you keep a sharp eye around here."

"Sure, Boss. Let me know if you need help."

Rider started back toward camp, the pup alert and running ahead of him. It occurred to Rider that Emma had never come back from the bushes. He hesitated, then began to walk again. He surely didn't want to walk up on her unannounced and catch her with her skirts up. It would be embarrassing for both of them.

He was not far from the bushes now. The night was so black, he stumbled over a rock. Behind him, when he looked back, he could see the tiny fire where Liberty kept guard. The pup paused ahead of him, looking intently toward the bushes. As black as the night was, Rider couldn't have seen him at all if it weren't for the pup's four white feet and the snowy muzzle.

Long years of surviving, first as a Shoshoni warrior and then as a gunfighter, had kept his senses alert. Now a prickle of warning went up Rider's back. *Indians? A rattlesnake? A bear?*

He hefted his rifle, then changed his course so that he came around on the back side of the grove of bushes. A movement caught Rider's eye deep in the shadows and every nerve in his sinewy body tensed. As the Shoshoni warrior Rides the Thunder, he had learned to move silent as a shadow through the dry grass. Better than any of the other braves, he could sneak up on an enemy and cut his throat before the man even realized he was being stalked. Forgetting caution, Rider raced into the brush.

Emma had adjusted her skirts and was almost out of the bushes when a powerful hand reached out of the darkness and grabbed her. Instinctively, she began to fight, unable to make out anything except the size and strength of her attacker. He was tearing at her gingham dress, ripping the front so that his free hand could reach her bare breast. He made an animal sound deep in his throat and began to drag her farther away from camp.

In sheer terror, Emma managed to bite her attacker's fingers so that he jerked his hand away just long enough for her to make a small cry, an agonized, defiant whimper before his hand clapped over her mouth again.

Rider paused in the brush, listening to the muffled sounds of struggle. Adjusting his eyes to the blackness, all Rider could see was two forms silhouetted in the moonlight, a man tearing at the girl's clothes. Rider grabbed the attacker's shoulder, spun him around, and put all his fury into his blow. "I'll kill you, you son of a bitch!"

The man took off running, crashing through the brush like a crazed moose. In the darkness, Boots began to bark and the girl sobbed a ragged, frightened cry.

Rider had poised to run after the man;

now he turned back to the girl. "Are you all right?"

She appeared shaken. "I-I think so. He grabbed me as I started out of the brush." The moon came out just then and she looked so scared and defenseless in her torn gingham dress and tousled hair that Rider had a crazy urge to take her in his arms, hold her protectively against his wide chest, and tell her she was safe now.

Instead, he blurted, "You see his face?"

She swallowed hard and shook her head. "No, he — he grabbed me from behind. He never said anything." She seemed unaware that her torn dress showed one beautiful breast, pale cream below her sun-tanned throat.

He couldn't stop looking at her. "It could be any one of the men," Rider muttered, "even the married ones."

She swayed as if she might faint and he moved quickly to take her arm. She was standing so close, he could smell the clean scent of her hair, the womanly, warm fragrance of her body. How dare another man put his hands on her? Rider wanted to take her in his arms, hold her very tight, and put his mouth on hers, tasting deep inside while whispering that no one would ever hurt her again. *Who was he fooling? What he really wanted was to make love to her, possess her completely.*

The pup began to bark wildly and Rider cursed under his breath. "He'll wake the whole camp. I was hoping to keep this quiet until I could figure out who the man was." He swung her up in his arms. "I'll carry you back."

She struggled. "I can walk."

"You don't need to as long as I'm around." He could feel her trembling like a small, frightened animal in his protective embrace and he felt an anger he had never felt before. "If I'd caught him, I'd have cut him like a steer!" And he meant it. Her yellow hair was close to his face and he took a deep breath of it and wanted her more than he had ever thought it was possible to want a woman.

He headed back toward the wagon. Around them, the barking pup had aroused the camp. Sleepy, tousled people stuck their heads out of wagons. "What's going on?"

Rider carried her past the gathering crowd. "Someone tried to get too friendly with the lady."

"Lady?" Millicent Carrolton sniffed. "You use that term very lightly."

Fat Mrs. Adams folded her arms across her enormous breasts. "Who can blame the

112

men? The way the hussy's so brazen with her little Injun bastard!"

The banker said, "I knew she'd be nothin' but trouble. We never should have allowed her to come along."

Rider gritted his teeth as he swung toward them, holding her tightly against his big chest. "She's not the one causing the trouble." He looked around at all the men. *Which one was guilty?* They all looked sleepy and puzzled by the confusion. "Now you men hear me and hear me good. I better not catch one of you near Mrs. Trent."

They began to sputter, but Rider cut them short. "Now everyone go back to bed. We got a long day ahead of us!"

They all turned and walked away, muttering.

Rider sighed and set Sky Eyes on the wagon gate. He didn't really want to turn her loose, but he did and stepped back. "You sure you're okay?"

She nodded and crossed her arms over her torn bodice. Her yellow hair fell in a soft cloud about her slight shoulders. The swell of her breasts was visible above the torn blue gingham. "I-I just wanted to thank you," she murmured.

Was she offering what he wanted so badly? Before he could stop himself, he reached

113

out one hand, caught her small shoulder, pulled her to him. His mouth covered hers and her lips were as warm and soft as he had dreamed they would be. She was frozen and stiff for a long moment before she jerked away and slapped him, hard. "You're just like the others after all!"

"Just like all the others." He nodded, and rubbed one hand across his stinging cheek.

"I hoped you might be different!"

"I forgot myself, I'm sorry." Rider felt anger seethe deep inside and he wasn't certain whether it was with himself or with her because she had spurned him. Or maybe he was angry with himself for the disappointment in her blue eyes.

"It's too late for that. Stay away from me, you hear?"

He wished now he hadn't touched her, hated the way her expression had gone from gentleness to a hard fury. Abruptly, she turned and crawled back in her wagon.

Rider stood staring after her a long moment, feeling like a fool. Women always came to him, wanting him. His desire for Emma grew until it seemed to be a pounding in his pulse. He had tried to charm her, protect her, and it hadn't worked. Now he would take her any way he could get her and Rider played a mean hand. He wasn't used to losing and he didn't intend to lose this time. Sky Eyes was going to come to his blankets whether she liked it or not.

With an angry sigh, he turned and left Emma's wagon.

Emma had a difficult time going back to sleep. It began to rain and she pictured Rider huddled under his wet blankets, miserable and cold. Underneath the wagon, safe and dry, she heard Boots scratching at a flea. It would be a while before the pup was much of a watchdog. At least maybe she wouldn't have to worry any more about men trying to sneak into her bed. They were all afraid of Rider. Damn him anyway! Here she had thought he was different, that he intended to protect her. Then he'd grabbed her and kissed her like she'd never been kissed before, his lips telling her how much heat and power was encased in that hard, bronzed body. For a split second, she had wanted to open her lips to him, let his tongue push into her mouth while his hands . . . *What was she thinking?*

Emma sighed at the memory from her past: her sweet husband's awkward thrusting that left her unmoved. She knew that as a wife, she was obliged to let Ethan lie between her thighs every week or so, but she had hoped it would be more interesting than it had turned out to be. Ethan was awkward and embarrassed about his needs and only took a minute or so to finish with her. Often she had lain awake long into the night wondering if it could be any more than this. Well, at least maybe their union would finally produce a child.

It hadn't. Emma shuddered, not wanting to remember the Cheyenne warrior called Angry Wolf.

And tonight, she had softened toward the grim gunfighter who had come to her rescue. Rider's dark eyes had betrayed the hunger and the banked passion deep within him and it had petrified her. For a split second, she had yearned to return that kiss; then she looked up into that dark face and remembered the past. The thought of what that kiss might lead to, the humiliation and the pain of him taking her, dominating her small body, repelled her. Emma had seen the need in his eyes and knew that a mating with that half-breed would be like lightning and thunder across a prairie sky, intense and overwhelming, sweeping over her in a way she had never experienced before.

She had struck out at him in blind terror and the look on his hard face now haunted her. Rider intended to have her — she had seen it in his eyes. *You're mine*, those eyes had said; *you're mine*.

She wasn't sure what the emotion was that now coursed through her, but she didn't sleep for a long, long time. In her imagination, his big, bronzed hands reached out and covered her breasts and then he thrust himself hard into her very being before his hot mouth sought her nipples and molded her to fit against his muscular frame until they were one writhing, sweating being. He would take her, all right; the only question was how and when.

Chapter Five

Josh lay sleeping peacefully, smiling as he held onto the toy horse. Emma's heart melted with tenderness at the sight. Odd that she could hate the father so much, yet love the son. She wondered what had happened to the renegade Cheyenne warrior. Indians. She shuddered, remembering.

She must not think of that. She would think of getting to Oregon. There she would make her own way, or find some gentle man who would marry her and provide well for Josh. A gentle, kind man; yes, that was all she wanted — not the banked, savage passion that she had sensed in Rider's kiss tonight.

Morning came too soon with the sound of the waking pistol before dawn. Outside, the camp was barely stirring. Emma took off her torn dress and put on another. It was also worn and faded, but she didn't own much.

She got her bucket and, followed by Boots, walked to the creek for water.

Rider was there. She wanted to turn and run, but instead, she knelt and began to splash water on her face.

"You all right?"

She glanced up, thought she could still see the marks of her fingers across his dark cheek, or maybe she only imagined it.

She didn't know what to do about the awkward silence so she splashed more water on her face to cool the burning. Then she filled her bucket and struggled to lift it.

This time he didn't even ask. He took it out of her hand before she could protest.

"I've been doin' heavy work for years," she said.

"That's a damned shame, the way white men work their women," he said, and took her elbow.

"Rider," she said, taking a deep breath as they walked, "I don't understand you. Why are you travelin' with this train?"

"I've decided I'd like to go to Oregon."

"You're a liar!" she said before she thought. "You don't have any intention of going all the way to Oregon!"

"Missy," he said, his voice cold, controlled. "I've killed men for less than I've taken off you the last few days."

She was sure it was true.

"I-I didn't mean to pry."

"Then don't." His voice was flat and he looked straight ahead as he walked.

"But you make good money as a hired gun, don't you?" she insisted. "It just doesn't make any sense you'd go cross country with us."

"Less than you know," he laughed without mirth. "If the Shoshoni catch me, I'll be begging for death."

"Why?"

"For killin' a man."

"You're wanted by both the whites and Indians for murder?"

"That's right."

"You must be a very bad *hombre*."

"Some think so. Now stop asking so many questions and let's get this train movin'."

He set the bucket down by her wagon and the pup ran around his boots, wagging its tail.

"Some watchdog!" he said and patted the dog's head.

"I've got to milk the cow before we pull out so Josh can have some."

At the sound of his name, the little boy poked his head out of the wagon. His face lit up at the sight of the half-breed. "Hello, Rider."

120

"Hi, kid." Rider slowly smiled at her child.

"Can I ride your horse?"

Emma felt her face burn. "Josh, honey, Mr. Rider doesn't let anyone ride his horse. Now let's have a bite to eat. Go find your shoes."

The little boy disappeared inside the wagon and she turned to Rider, her face flustered. "You'll have to excuse him. He never knew his father, and other kids are mean to him sometimes because of the Indian blood."

Rider looked at her, a question in his eyes, but she glanced away. She had never told anyone about what had happened that terrible night.

Rider started to say something, then paused. "I've got to get things movin'." With that, he touched his fingers to the brim of his hat and strode away.

Emma stared after him a long moment, then busied herself with getting her child fed, the cow milked and hitching up her oxen. The others stared at her with open curiosity and some of them whispered behind their hands to each other about last night and the men grinned slyly. No doubt most of them figured a white woman who'd breed a son with an Indian was a lowdown slut and deserved what she got.

Rider watched her from a distance as he galloped up and down through the mud, shouting orders to get the train ready to move. He'd seen the way the others stared at her and it angered him. If any man thought she was fair game, he'd have to answer to Rider. He intended to be the man who'd have her in his blankets.

About the time the train was ready to pull out, the Bottoms couple approached him.

"You got your wagon ready?" Rider asked, reining in.

The old man broke into a fit of coughing and his sour wife snapped, "We ain't agoin'."

"What?" Rider leaned on his saddle horn.

"It's too hard goin' for us and we've had second thoughts about a man like you leadin' us. To say nothin' of that blond hussy."

"Watch your mouth," Rider said to the woman. "You really set on turning back?"

Mr. Bottoms nodded as he doubled up with a fit of coughing. Then he choked out, "We can't do no worse takin' our chances back in Independence."

Curious people had gathered around to listen. A murmur went through them.

Sour old Mrs. Bottoms turned to the crowd. "You're all fools if'en you keep goin'. This gunfighter'll get you all killed!"

More muttering and uncertain looks from the crowd.

Rider shrugged. "Anyone who wants to turn back had better go with the Bottomses. I warned you it would be a tough trip and you haven't seen the half of it."

A long pause. Emma Trent looked uncertain and glanced toward her wagon. She was thinking of her son, Rider knew. Finally, she said, "I got nothing to go back to and neither do most of you others. I've got everything I own tied up in this wagon, so I don't know about the rest of you, but I'm going to Oregon!"

An excited murmur ran through the crowd. "She's right, you know, she's right."

Mrs. Bottoms shook her head in a dour prediction. "This gunman will get you all killed, or lead you into an Indian trap, that's what he'll do. You'll be sorry you didn't go with us."

The others looked at each other.

"Well," Rider said and pushed his Stetson back, "you heard Mrs. Trent. Some of us are going to Oregon. Anyone who wants to go, get your wagons moving or turn around like yellow bellies and go back!"

Everyone started for their wagons. Rider sat his horse and watched. In the end, when he yelled, "Head 'em up and move 'em out!" only the Bottoms couple turned their wagon around and started back up the road to Independence.

Last night's rain had made the trail muddy and difficult. The day was warm, but not unpleasant, Emma thought as she sat up on the box and urged her patient oxen forward. Boots trotted behind the wagon, barking occasionally at the heels of the brown cow tied on behind. Josh sat on the seat beside her, sipping his mug of milk, a little white mustache across his small mouth. Like most of the children, he seemed to see this as one big adventure.

Rider rode past, then steadied his spirited stallion to the slow, plodding pace of her oxen. "You doing all right?"

She nodded. "Everything going smooth up ahead?"

Rider shook his head, frowning. "Lot of griping and whining; some of the wagons miring down in the mud. Some of these people have no common sense and others aren't tough enough to make it."

She wondered again why he was riding with this wagon train. Francesca Pettigrew, of course, or maybe it was a good hiding place for a man wanted by both civilizations.

He loped on ahead and she wondered if he were riding alongside the banker's wagon and making conversation with the wife. That thought annoyed her.

More importantly, did he intend to stay with the train all the way? She shook her head; not likely. A chilling thought crossed her mind: what would the pioneers do if Rider should desert them? There wasn't another man here who was capable of leading them.

Rider had meant what he said. They paused only a few minutes at noon to eat and water the livestock, then they were on the move again. Emma put on her sunbonnet, but still the hot sun beat down on her and now as the mud dried, dust swirled up from the oxen's hooves and the wagons ahead of her. Josh had curled up in the back and gone to sleep, lulled by the rhythmic swaying of the wagon.

Finally, near sundown, they came to the Kansas River and Rider allowed them to stop and camp.

"Tomorrow, we'll take the ferry across," he said.

Emma was so weary, it was all she could do to circle up her wagon with the others and lead her oxen into the safety of the circle. She was hoping tonight would pass without any incident.

It was late, the fires burning low. Most of the camp was asleep. Rider was on guard duty, sitting on a big boulder away from the wagons. He studied the landscape, thinking about how long it would be until they reached the Platte River across the flat plains of Nebraska Territory.

Unless they ran across a stray Lakota raiding party or some rustlers tried to run off the stock, there wouldn't be big danger until they reached western Nebraska. That's where they were most apt to run into Cheyenne or Lakota raiders. The Lakotas were old enemies of the Shoshoni, but Rider spoke enough of the various dialects that maybe they wouldn't identify his tribe. Still, he didn't intend to let any braves get that close to the camp because they would take the best of the stock, including his big Appaloosa, and they would steal the prettiest women. He decided at that moment that he'd put a bullet in Sky Eyes's brain before he would let her be raped by an entire war party, then kept as a slave.

Hell, what was he thinking? The girl wasn't his to protect. Yet his threat had kept all the men at bay today, although he'd seen more than one sneaking a glance at the girl up on the wagon box. For a long moment, he wondered which one had dared to attack her in the bushes. There was no way to know for sure, but it had damned well better not happen again. Rider intended to have her for his own . . . until he tired of her.

After that, he'd help himself to Banker Pettigrew's stolen money and clear out. He wouldn't take Francie; he'd tired of her long ago, and besides, she was such a slut. Any man with money could have Francie, while all the gold in the world couldn't buy Emma Trent; he was sure of it. *Then just how was he going to possess the yellow-haired girl?* He smiled as the answer came to him. Yes, that plan would work; he only had to be patient. He could wait a few more days, certain that the pleasure she would bring him was going to be well worth it.

"Rider," he said aloud as he shifted his weight and watched the warm night wear on, "you really are a heartless bastard! But on the other hand, it's not as if she's never had a man. Obviously, she's had more than one, so what's one more?"

An uneasy feeling gnawed at his insides; it

might have been shame. He shrugged it off and remembered the taste of her mouth just before she slapped him. Rider wanted her badly enough to take her any way he could get her. Yes, his plan would work. He only had to wait a few more days until the wagon train was too far out on the Nebraska prairie to turn back.

His muscles were getting cramped and he wished he had a soft bed to stretch out in — her bed. "Damn, Rider," he grumbled, "can't you think of anything else?"

He heard a sound in the distance and looked toward the camp where he saw the big black slave moving quietly out of his blankets where he slept under the wagon. As Rider watched, Liberty sneaked over to the Carroltons' fine horse staked out near the carriage. He untied it, swung up on the horse, and turned to walk it out of the camp. When he saw Rider, he hesitated, apprehension on his dark face.

Rider nodded and touched his fingers against the brim of his hat in a salute. Liberty grinned and looked at him, a question in his eyes.

Rider pointed the direction toward Fort Leavenworth.

The slave gave Rider a respectful salute and rode out of the camp at a walk.

Rider watched him go. There'd be hell to pay when the Carroltons discovered Liberty was missing, but Rider could deal with that. He smiled as he watched the slave disappear into the darkness. "Well, black prince, here's hopin' you get both the girl and your freedom."

For a long moment, he envied Liberty his choice. Living in the restricted white civilization certainly hadn't been what Rider had expected. Many times he had wished he was back among the Shoshoni, riding wild and free through the mountains, his own woman galloping along beside him.

A movement down in the camp caught his eye and Rider glanced around, realizing Emma Trent was watching from inside her wagon. She had probably seen the whole thing. Her expression didn't change, so he looked away, angry with himself. The girl could cause him a lot of trouble tomorrow when she told what she had seen. Well, he'd just have to deal with that; he'd had nothing but trouble for the last five years.

Emma watched in disbelief as Liberty rode out and Rider saluted him. Rider was allowing, no, encouraging the slave to escape. Emma didn't believe in slavery, but she knew there'd be big trouble in the morning when the Carroltons woke up and Rider would have to face them. Funny, she hadn't thought the hired gun, that killer, was a good enough person to help Liberty.

She realized suddenly that Rider was looking at her, his concerned expression showing his awareness that she had seen the little drama. If she told the camp what she'd seen tonight, no doubt she'd be back in everyone's good graces and part of the group. No one had really been kind to Emma in a long, long time. Even the few relatives she had left were no longer speaking to her because she wouldn't give away her bastard child.

What could they do about Rider if they believed her? There wasn't a man in the camp brave enough to stand up to him. Anyway, they needed the gunfighter to guide this train desperately enough that they would grant him anything to keep him from riding out and leaving them helpless and lost.

Emma was right; there was big trouble when the camp awakened in the morning and discovered Liberty was gone. Carrolton strode up and down, swearing in his Southern drawl and urging all the other men to help him track down the runaway. In the meantime, Mrs. Carrolton wrung her nervous little hands and wailed about her carriage. "Mercy me! What shall I do? I can't take my carriage without the horse!"

Rider, leaning against a tree, looked toward Emma. *Was she going to tell what she'd seen?*

She only said, "He must have left very quietly for none of us to hear him."

Mrs. Carrolton's fine, patrician nose drew up in scorn. "No one asked your opinion."

Weatherford Carrolton whirled on Rider. "You! You were supposed to be on guard duty!"

Rider shook his head. "Must have dropped off a minute or two."

The Southern gentleman's expression showed he didn't believe the gunfighter. He hesitated, evidently too afraid of Rider to challenge him. He looked plaintively toward his weeping wife. "Now we have no way to pull the carriage."

Rider sighed in exasperation. "Well, now, I reckon you'll just have to abandon the carriage and ride in your wagon."

Millicent Carrolton wailed even louder. "It's the finest carriage in all Vicksburg and I just can't leave it behind!"

"Suit yourself," Rider shrugged, "but there don't seem to be any extra horses and you'll need all those supplies in your wagon."

Mr. Carrolton paced up and down. "Liberty's a horse thief; that's what he is. We ought to track him down and hang him!"

The thought sent a shiver of fear through Emma, but Rider didn't even blink. "Carrolton, how long was Liberty your slave?"

Carrolton shrugged. "Why, he's belonged to us all his life, but I don't see —"

"Appears to me then that he's worked for free long enough to equal the price of one horse."

"But he's a slave!" Carrolton said.

Rider grinned. "Evidently not anymore."

Carrolton turned toward the gathered crowd. "Let's track that runaway down and hang him. Who's with me, men?"

Willie Adams, Stott, and two or three of the other men stepped forward. "Let's do it!"

Rider swung up on his horse. "Nobody's goin' off on a wild goosechase when we don't have any idea which way he went." He looked toward Emma. He knew she'd seen which way Liberty had headed, but she didn't say anything.

The rest of the people looked uncertain. The aristocratic Carroltons were not very popular with the others.

Banker Pettigrew put on his derby. "The scout's right," he said. "It ain't no skin off our noses if them high-and-mighty Southerners now got to do their own work and ride in a wagon like the rest of us."

A murmur of agreement.

Rider surveyed the crowd. "We're weeks behind schedule now and there'll be snow in those Western mountains before we get there. The sun's gettin' high, so let's roll those wagons. We've got a ferry waiting."

"But —" Carrolton protested and his wife wailed louder.

"You heard me!" Rider snapped. "Carrolton, you and your prissy wife do whatever you think best."

The people scattered as Rider rode to the lead. Emma climbed up on her wagon seat and watched. The Carroltons stood on the prairie in indecision as the wagons began to pass them, the highborn lady wringing her nervous little hands and wailing louder, her husband imploring her to listen to reason. Finally, they headed for their wagon and joined the line moving to the ferry. When Emma looked back, the magnificent buggy with its fancy fringed top and bright red wheels sat under a tree, lonely and abandoned.

Emma checked to make sure Josh was on board and the cow tied on behind. She clucked to the oxen and pulled out in the line, Boots running about and barking. She could hear the half-breed riding up and down, yelling orders, getting the wagons spaced out. At least they were in capable hands, she thought; he'd get them there if anybody could.

But would he? Or would he get tired of these whining, cranky people and desert them somewhere along the way? What was holding him? Was it Francesca Pettigrew or was it the money they were going to pay him for guiding them through? Emma shook her head, certain he could make much more money as a hired gun than a wagon master.

They crossed the Kansas River. It was a hot, dusty ride now, Emma thought wearily as she urged her oxen along the trail. How many miles a day were they expected to make? They had so many, many miles yet ahead of them, but she had no alternatives, nothing to go back to. Josh had curled up inside and dropped off to sleep. Even the pup had tired and walked alongside the wagon, tongue lolling.

Halfway through the morning, Rider cantered back and rode beside her wagon. She didn't even acknowledge him.

Rider cleared his throat. "I expected you'd say something this morning."

"Oh?" She didn't look at him, keeping her gaze on the dusty ruts ahead. "What about?"

"You know what about."

She shrugged and looked up at him. "I figure if Liberty's worked all his life for them for nothing, he's earned the price of one horse. Where's he going?"

Rider hesitated as if trying to decide whether to trust her. "He's gone to join the buffalo soldiers and there's a girl some-where who'll be joining him, he says."

Emma thought about it. "So he's found love and he's got his freedom. That's about as much as a person could ever want, I reckon."

"I reckon," Rider agreed.

Josh awakened, clambered to the front of the wagon and stuck his tousled head out, looking up and smiling at the gunfighter. "Rider, are you my daddy?"

She felt her face flame. "Uh, Josh, honey, I've told you before —"

"It's all right," Rider said. "I've been called worse things." He grinned uncer-tainly at the child.

The little boy looked at the big horse with

envy. "Josh ride Storm and you ride with Mama."

Rider shook his head. "I'm not sure your mama would like that."

Emma didn't answer. She didn't want the half-breed sitting next to her on the wagon seat, his warm thigh pressing against hers. "Josh, honey, Rider has the whole train to look after, not just us." She shot Rider a steely gaze that told him to move on. He took the hint, put the spurs to the big black-and-white Appaloosa, and galloped up the line.

They nooned at Saint Mary's Mission, where a few peaceful Potawatomi Indians watched them curiously. Rider yelled at everyone to fill their water barrels in case they didn't find another source soon. "The Red Vermillion River is somewhere up ahead of us," he yelled, "but I doubt we can make it tonight."

The sun was hot, but Emma found a place in the shade under some cottonwood trees. "Now, Josh, you can go play while Mama rests a minute."

He nodded happily and ran off toward the sounds of other children playing in the grass. *Rest.* She only wished she could. The other women ignored her as Emma got her bucket. She noted Millicent Carrolton slumped on the seat of her wagon, silent and morose. Although the elegant Southerner had been cruel to Emma, she still pitied the woman. She wondered again why such a wealthy couple would suddenly leave the South to take such an uncertain and perilous journey.

Other men were gathered around the spring as Willie Adams pushed his way through. "Get out of my way — I'm goin' to fill my canteen first!"

Meek little Mr. Gray stepped back obediently, but the tall, lanky man named Draper growled, "You can wait, runt."

Draper returned to filling his bucket, turning his back to the younger man. Willie's face turned a furious red; he grabbed a hand scythe off the side of the nearest wagon and ran at the lanky man.

Emma screamed, "Look out!"

Stott managed to take the scythe away from the boy, but Willie snorted and charged at Draper, knocking him down, pummeling the older man with his fists. Emma could only watch in horror, convinced that the angry boy meant to kill Draper.

Francesca began to scream, "Rider! Rider, for God's sake, get over here!"

The half-breed came galloping into the

fray, swung down from his horse, and grabbed the boy by the shoulder. "Hey, that's enough!"

"Get your hands off me, you damned Injun!" Willie swung at Rider.

Quick as a fox, Rider sidestepped the blow, pulled his pistol, and hit Willie across the head.

The short man crumpled with a groan.

Fat Mrs. Adams rushed forward. "You had no call to do that to my poor boy!"

Rider holstered his Colt slowly. "It was better than killin' him. Now throw some cold water on him. He'll have a headache, but he'll be all right by tomorrow."

Francesca smiled up at Rider. If the half-breed noticed the red-haired siren's smile, he gave no sign. "Look, folks, we've got a long, hard trip ahead of us and tempers may get frayed. If there's fights or shootouts, the whole train may fall apart."

Carrolton drew himself up to his full height. "That's what we can expect, traveling with white trash, I reckon."

Mr. Adams bristled. "Who you callin' 'white trash'?"

"I think you know the answer," Weatherford B. Carrolton said. "There's only a few of us who'd be welcome in polite society."

Emma watched him look from Rider to his wife. So the man had noted the way his weepy wife had looked at the half-breed scout.

Rider made a gesture of dismissal. "We can't stand around and fuss all day. Get a bite to eat and you men get your water barrels filled." He looked toward Emma, seemed to make a decision. "Some of you men help Mrs. Trent."

The "respectable" women glared at her, but the men rushed to help. Emma was so busy for the next few minutes that they all forgot about the children.

Rider rode off into the grove of cottonwoods where he could eat a piece of dried jerky and smoke a cigarette in peace. He was sick of all this squabbling and was regretting his decision to stay with the train. Besides, he was beginning to wonder if bedding Emma Trent was worth all the aggravation it was going to cost him.

He smiled ever so slightly at the sound of the children playing in the grass, remembering the happy face of Emma's child. Sudden sounds of discord and squabbling came to his ears. "Hit him! Get the Injun!"

Rider swung up on Storm and crossed through the trees. Half a dozen of the dirty little Weeks and Gray children had ganged up on Josh. The sturdy little boy had his back against a tree, flaying at the bullies with his fists as the bigger boys taunted and struck him. There were tears in his eyes and blood on his mouth, but still the child fought gamely.

"Here, stop that!" Rider shouted. "You kids pick on someone your own size!"

The boys seemed to take one look at Rider's stern face, then scattered, leaving Josh behind.

Rider swung down off his horse. "You all right?"

The child swallowed hard, his big brown eyes full of tears and a trickle of blood in the corner of his mouth. "They — they tore my shirt."

"I know. Here, let me help." Rider got his canteen off his saddle, poured some water on his bandana, and mopped the boy's sweaty face. "Men go one on one, they don't gang up; it ain't fair."

Josh smiled hesitantly. "I fight good?"

"You fight good, Small Warrior." Rider couldn't suppress a grin as he offered the child his canteen. "I reckon they've learned their lesson and won't bother you no more." He must not get attached to this child, he thought with sudden surprise. To do so would obligate Rider and he didn't like obligations. "Let's go back — your mama will be worried."

Little Josh looked up at Storm. "Warriors have ponies."

Rider took the hint. "I tell you what, Small Warrior. You can ride Storm back to camp."

His dark eyes grew round with excitement. "So all the boys can see me?"

Rider nodded. "Here, you can't quite reach the stirrup. Let me give you a hand." He lifted the child up into the saddle.

Josh looked around solemnly. "I like being warrior."

Rider laughed, then realized it had been a long time since he'd laughed. "Come on, Boots, you worthless pup."

Leading the horse with the boy astride and the pup gamboling through the grass chasing butterflies, they went back to the wagons. Everyone turned to look as they approached, but Rider ignored them and led the horse over to Emma's wagon.

She took one look at her child's torn shirt and bloodied lip and paled. "What happened?"

"Not much," Rider said. "You can be proud of your small warrior. He's got grit for such a little guy. All he needs now is a man to teach him about horses, weapons, and such."

Her face flushed and he remembered there was no father to teach Josh. He watched her hurry to lift her child from the saddle and hug him close.

Rider watched a long moment, a sudden yearning in his heart. He had never felt so alone as he did at this moment and he wondered about what kind of man would desert a feisty beauty and a fine son like these two. He should be so lucky as to have such a family.

Rider, are you loco? Wives and kids complicate things, give you obligations you don't want. Sleep with the woman if you can manage it, but it's not going any further than that.

"Of course not!" he said aloud and the girl looked up at him.

"You talkin' to me?"

"No!" he snapped and remounted his horse. "Let's get these wagons movin'. We've wasted enough time already!"

He stayed away from her wagon the rest of the day as the afternoon lengthened. Francesca smiled at him when he passed her wagon, but he only nodded politely. "Maybe things will settle down now," Rider told himself as he scouted out a grove of trees for the night's camping. Sometime in the next few nights, he would steal the banker's gold and light out. "I've just got to pick my time," he reasoned aloud.

They had barely set up camp in the twilight when someone yelled, "Horses comin'!"

Alarmed, Rider reached for the rifle on his saddle. "From which way?"

"The east," one of the men called.

Rider relaxed and swung down off his horse. "Passing travelers," he said, and squatted by the big campfire. "Somebody get the coffee on."

Maybe some visitors would have interesting news from Independence or Fort Leavenworth. He smiled at the thought of conversation with anyone besides this cranky bunch.

However, as the three men rode into camp and swung down from their lathered horses, Rider stopped smiling. Alarmed, he looked toward his horse where his rifle hung. Only a couple of feet. It might as well have been a mile.

The bearded leader held his own rifle on Rider and shook his head. "Don't even think about it, 'breed. We got you cold and the reward's dead or alive, remember?"

"Hello, Dink, long time no see." Rider felt cold sweat make a crooked trail down his muscular back. He recognized the bunch now from past days. They'd just as soon kill him here and now as take him back to Texas. Rider had been dealt a bad hand and his luck had run out. *Dink's gang were bounty hunters.*

Chapter Six

Rider looked up at them, smiling with a cocky exterior he didn't feel. There were three of them — tough, trail-hardened men who'd kill a man with no more emotion than they'd shoot a coyote. "So Dink, how'd you find me?"

The other scratched his dirty beard and grinned. "Some couple named Bottoms had just pulled back into Independence as we rode down the street. They told us you was leadin' this train."

Talk about bad luck! What were the chances that pair would have run into these bounty hunters?

"Smart move on your part, this wagon train." Dink leaned on his saddle horn and grinned. "We'd been tryin' to decide where to look next. We would never have thought about followin' a wagon train."

Banker Pettigrew stepped forward, his chest puffed up importantly. "See here, are you the law?"

The three men guffawed and looked at each other.

Dink said, "Well, you might say that. Luke, Thatcher, and me — we're bounty hunters."

The elegant Mr. Carrolton looked bewildered. "Bounty hunters?"

Rider glanced sideways at him. "They bring in fugitives for the reward. Sometimes the wanted man doesn't make it back alive."

Dink pushed his hat back and grinned. "It's plumb curious how many of them are killed tryin' to escape."

Emma asked, "You mean, our wagon boss is wanted by the law?"

Dink nodded. "Ma'am, it just goes to show, you can't trust nobody these days. Seems Rider killed a rich rancher's son and that rancher has put up a big reward."

A shocked murmur ran through the crowd, but Rider only watched Sky Eyes's lovely face, hating the look of dismay he now saw there. Somehow, it mattered to him that she might think him a cold-blooded killer. "The man drew first, tryin' to make a name for himself as a fast gun. I didn't have any choice."

"Try tellin' that to a judge in a certain Texas county where that rancher owns most of the land and everyone in it," Dink said.

"You can't take him," Francie said.

Dink noticed her for the first time. "Don't I know you, honey?"

Her pretty face paled and the banker snapped, "Don't you address my wife so familiarly, sir. You've mistaken her for someone else."

"I got a memory for pretty faces," Dink said.

"Look here, Mr. Dink or whatever your name is," Weatherford B. Carrolton said, drawing himself up to his full height. "If you take our wagon master, we won't have anyone to lead us to Oregon."

"Listen, you prissy Southern bastard," Dink said with a sneer, "would you believe we don't give a big goddamn? Anyways, why ain't you in the army?"

"I might ask you the same thing," Carrolton said, his face red with humiliation.

Dink laughed. "With our records, I'm not sure either side would want us. Besides, it don't make no never mind to us which side wins." He turned his attention back to Rider. "You're awfully quiet. You thinkin' about how it'll feel to hang?"

Rider had been busy considering which action to take, but Dink and his men were too well armed to risk trying to get to his

147

rifle. He wore his Colt, but with three rifles trained on him, a handgun wasn't enough. "Dink, you ain't got me hung yet. It'll soon be dark. Why don't you and your boys plan on spendin' the night in our camp? The ladies will fix you some food."

"Good idea." Dink dismounted, still keeping his rifle trained on Rider.

Boots came out from under Emma's wagon, wagging his tail and barking.

"Damned dog!" Dink kicked at the pup and it yelped and scurried back toward her wagon.

"My dog!" Little Josh glared up at the big man.

Dink laughed. "I didn't hurt him none. Not much of a watchdog, is he?"

Rider snarled, "You're a sorry son of a bitch for kickin' a kid's dog, Dink."

"Tell me something I don't already know." The big man laughed, keeping his rifle trained on Rider. "Get down, boys. We'll take the man up on his offer of hospitality."

"But Boss," protested the dirtiest-looking one, "I ain't sure that's a good way —"

"Shut up, Luke," Dink snapped. "We got to camp anyways and we can tie Rider up 'til morning. We'll have some drinks and grub." He looked over the women and smiled.

"And maybe we'll have something else, too."

"Now, see here —," Banker Pettigrew began.

"Shut up!" Dink snapped, "before I shut you up. Get down, boys."

The other two dismounted. Rider sized them up. He knew Luke and Thatcher from the past. They were mean as coyotes and they'd kill anyone who crossed them. "Folks, better go along with what they say."

Dink threw back his head and laughed. "Hear him, folks? He knows the smart thing to do. Boys, keep your guns on Rider while I tie him up."

A Colt against three rifles was suicide; still, Rider considered it. At that moment, Emma Trent's little son come to stand next to him, perhaps sensing that Rider was in trouble. He couldn't take a chance on a stray shot hitting the Small Warrior.

Dink looked over the child and then grinned at Rider. "Your kid?"

"No," Rider shook his head.

"Well, some lady likes Injuns, so maybe she won't be so choosy who shares her blankets tonight."

Rider saw the sudden terror on Sky Eyes's face and he lost all caution. He tried to come up off the ground, right at Dink,

149

wanting to kill him with his bare hands.

With an oath, the big man slammed Rider across the head with the butt of his rifle. Fire seemed to explode through his brain and he couldn't make his body work anymore. He fell and lay crumpled by the fire as Dink kicked him with his big boots — kicked him hard. "You damned 'breed! I thought you were smarter than that."

As if from a million miles away, he heard Sky Eyes's angry voice. "You had no cause to do that!"

"He's your man, is he?"

"No," she denied, "no, he's not my man."

He heard Dink chuckle. "The way you're defendin' him, I'd have sworn he was. One of you boys get me a rope and you ladies get some grub goin.' Any of you men got some whiskey? We're bone dry."

Emma watched in dismay as the big man took the rope, bending over to tie up Rider. There was blood in the half-breed's black hair and he seemed barely conscious.

Dink took Rider's fine pistol and holster, nodding in appreciation at the weapon as he stashed it in his bedroll.

Emma glanced around at the others of the train, but they looked uncertain and fearful.

Dink jerked Rider's hands behind his

back and tied them. Then he grabbed that rope and dragged the half-conscious man over under a wagon. "That'll keep you out of our way, 'breed." Now Dink glared at her. "What you standin' there gawkin' at, girl? Go find us some whiskey!"

With the three bounty hunters standing with rifles at the ready, there wasn't much anyone could do but obey. Rider had shot a deer that afternoon and now Emma got out a big iron skillet and her butcher knife and began to cut up the meat.

When the trio looked away, she slipped the knife into the folds of her skirt. She didn't have a plan, but someone had to do something. Emma began to cook the meat while other women made bread. For once, the children were silent and still, sitting on the ground and watching as the bounty hunters took over the camp.

"Luke," Dink growled, "get the horses unsaddled and grab our bedrolls. We got a fun evening ahead of us and after ridin' for weeks, we deserve it."

Dark was coming on as the intruders settled into the camp. Emma glanced toward the still man under the wagon as she cooked. Rider must be unconscious or even dead. Anyway, tied up, he couldn't do anything to protect the people.

Young Willie Adams pushed forward. "Me, I always wanted to be a bounty hunter. Can I join up?"

Dink laughed. "The young pup wants to be one of us."

"Sorry, Shorty," Luke snorted, "we don't need no runts."

The boy's face turned a ruddy red. He doubled up his fists, then seemed to look at the guns and backed away.

Dink flopped down, leaned back against his saddle, and surveyed the fire. "Hey, you!" He yelled at Emma. "What happened to that whiskey?"

Everyone hesitated. Whiskey would only make these three more cantankerous. Nobody said anything.

"You all deaf?" Dink asked. "Or am I gonna have to beat an answer out of you?"

Weatherford B. Carrolton said, "I might have a little Kentucky bourbon, but —"

"Bring it out!" Dink commanded. "Now, the rest of you men got any liquor, you better send your women for it because if I find you was holdin' out on me, I ain't gonna be too happy."

While the men watched in silence, the women, one or two at a time, went to their wagons to get the few bottles of liquor they'd hidden away. Emma gathered it up and brought it to the big bearded man by the fire.

It was dark now as the bounty hunters relaxed a little and helped themselves to the whiskey, not offering any of the wagon men a drink.

Luke scratched himself. "Boss, this is more like it. You was right to camp us here."

Dink grinned and rolled a cigarette. "Liquor, food, and maybe some entertainment later. Anybody play a fiddle?"

Frail little Mr. Gray held up his hand. "I-I do."

"Fine! Now while we eat, you play us some music and then we'll dance with the ladies."

A chill went up Emma's back and she glanced toward the other women. They looked as frightened as she felt, knowing what all this might lead to. Millicent Carrolton began to weep softly.

Dink frowned. "What's the matter with her?"

Fat old Mrs. Adams made a dismissing gesture. "Oh, that's all she does is cry."

The Southern gentleman drew himself up proudly. "My wife is a lady and gently born. It doesn't take much to upset her."

Thatcher sucked his teeth and snickered.

"I ain't never had me no lady before. You, Luke?"

Luke wiped at his sweaty face and shook his head. "Might be fun."

"Now see here —" Carrolton began.

"Oh, shut up!" Dink snapped and took a big drink.

Emma said, "Food's ready."

"Dish it up, blondie," Dink said. "You got coffee?"

"Plenty of coffee," Emma said. If the men stayed sober, maybe the women would be okay.

"Then pour me some, honey." Dink winked at her. "I like my coffee like I like my women, hot and sweet."

Several of the women gasped, but Emma was too busy thinking to react. Although her insides were turning to jelly, she went about serving the food as calmly as if she hadn't heard him. *Maybe she could spill the hot coffee on him, and then grab the rifle.*

However, Dink set his tin cup down at arm's length on a rock. "You don't get any closer with that pot, honey. You look like you might try something brave but stupid."

The three dug into the food as if they hadn't eaten in days. The others watched silently.

154

Finally Emma asked, "Can we feed the children?"

Dink looked up from sopping his bread in the gravy. "Sure, why not? The rest of you can eat, if there's any left. Don't say that Dink and his boys ain't kindhearted." His pair of ruffians laughed at that.

The women rushed to fill tin plates. Emma got Josh a plate and a cup of milk. Then she looked toward the still form under the wagon. "What about him?"

Dink shrugged. "Rider? Let him go hungry. He looks like he might die anyways; I hit him purty hard."

Rider didn't move. For all she knew, he might be dead. Knowing she must keep up her strength for whatever ordeal lay ahead of her, Emma tried to eat a little, but the meat stuck in her throat. Timid Mr. Gray had brought his fiddle to the fire and stood there uncertainly. The trio of bounty hunters had finished their food and were now drinking and belching.

"You, fiddler!" Dink ordered. "Let's have some music, you hear?"

The little man's hands were trembling so badly, he played off-key as he began "Buffalo Gals," but the ruffians didn't seem to notice. They sang along: "Buffalo gals, won't you come out tonight? Come out tonight? Buffalo gals, won't you come out to-night and dance by the light of the moon . . . ?"

What to do? Emma wondered. A butcher knife wasn't much good against three rifles. She had a gun in her wagon as did some of the others. "Can we — can we put the children to bed?"

Dink broke off singing, frowning at the silent, frightened children. Mrs. Gray bounced her baby on her hip to keep it quiet. "Hell," he said, "let them get themselves to bed. The rest of you stay right here where we can keep an eye on you."

Oh, Lord, thought Emma. None of these wagon train men had the gumption or bravery to try to help. Only Rider might save them and he was tied up and might even be dead.

She bent over Josh. "Honey, now you go get in the wagon and go to sleep."

"Where's Rider?" Josh asked.

"Oh, he's resting," she said and blinked back tears. "Now, you go get in the wagon and if you hear any sounds in the night, you just ignore them, you hear?"

Josh looked curious, then nodded as he walked toward her wagon. The other children had also been sent off by the nervous women.

She had to do something. There was no telling what Dink and his men would do if they got drunk enough. She wondered now if the reason Rider had not drawn on Dink was because Josh had come to stand beside him and he wanted to protect the child. Her respect for Rider grew. His concern was going to cost him his neck back in Texas . . . if he wasn't dead already. If only Rider were untied, he would figure something out.

Emma fingered the knife she had hidden in the pocket of her long skirt. What to do? If only she had Rider by her side, she would brave anything, but none of these other men had the backbone to help.

The trio now sat around the fire, laughing and drinking as Mr. Gray sawed out "Turkey in the Straw" on his old fiddle. She could see the sweat gleaming on his pale face from here. The drunken bounty hunters clapped to the music and drank.

Slowly, so as not to be noticed, Emma backed toward the wagon where Rider lay on the ground. Any moment, the trio might notice what she was doing and shout at her to return. Emma's heart was in her mouth as she backed up against the wagon and slowly turned to look down. "Rider?" she whispered.

His dark eyes flickered open.

Abruptly, Dink shouted at her. "Gal, what are you doin' over there?"

She dropped the knife by Rider's hand, turned and hurried toward the fire. "Just checking to see if he was still alive."

"Is he?" Dink turned the bottle up and let the liquor run down into his beard.

"Just barely," she said.

"Hell, it don't make no never mind," Dink belched. "That rancher'll pay us whether we deliver him dead or alive, although I must admit I'd admire to see him swing."

"I seen a man hung once." Luke scratched himself again. "Right entertainin'."

Dink looked at her a long moment. "Gal, come over here by the fire so's I can see you."

She paused, looking around at the settlers in dismay, but the men looked away as if ashamed of their cowardice.

"Gal, damn it, did you hear me?" Dink gestured her closer.

The fiddler stopped playing and now the only sound was the crackle of the fire. Emma took a deep breath and walked slowly toward them. She stood there a long moment while Dink seemed to strip her with his eyes.

"Well," Emma said uncertainly and started to turn away, "I'll just leave you gen-

158

tlemen to enjoy your whiskey."

"Wait, honey." Dink reached up and caught her hand. "The night is young and I feel like dancin'."

"I-I don't dance," she gulped.

"Then old Dink'll teach you." He turned and yelled at the fiddler. "Hey, what happened to our music? We're gonna have us a dance!"

The scruffy pair nearby set up howls of approval and passed the bottle around again.

"Hey, fiddler!" Luke yelled. "You know 'Camptown Races'?"

Gray's pale face gleamed with sweat as he began to play the tune.

"That's more like it!" Thatcher sucked his crooked teeth and looked around at the cowering women. "Which one you want, Luke?"

"Well, I'll tell you one thing," Dink swayed to his feet, still holding onto Emma's hand, "you boys can't have this one. I'll bet she's warm and sweet inside like warm honey."

Oh God, what to do? She glanced toward Rider, but he had not moved. The other women cowered like frightened sheep while Luke and Thatcher looked them over. Francesca Pettigrew's face was defiant while

Millicent Carrolton's eyes were red-rimmed and tearful. The pair of men walked up and down, looking over the women as if buying a horse.

Luke laughed. "I like a little pepper now and then — I'll take the redhead." He grabbed her arm, pulled her toward him.

"Roscoe," Francesca demanded, "you ain't gonna let this bastard touch me —"

"See here now," Banker Pettigrew blustered, "that's my wife —"

"Shut up before I kill you." Luke shoved him back. "Old man, I'm gonna give her what she's been missin' with you. You can even watch if you want." He threw back his head and laughed, but the fat banker only flushed and his shoulders slumped as Luke pulled the pretty redhead into the circle.

"Pick one, Thatcher," Dink said, "any one you want except this blonde."

Thatcher sucked his yellow teeth and looked up and down the frightened women. "This is like a kid in a candy store," he grinned. "I want 'em all."

Some of the women began to cry or cringe.

Dink nodded. "You can have as many as you're man enough to handle. After all, we got all night."

Thatcher paused in front of Millicent

Carrolton. "I always wanted a classy Southern belle. Why, I bet you waltz, don't you, sweetie?"

Millicent began to sob.

"See here," her husband said, "my wife's a high-born lady and should be treated as such."

Thatcher shrugged and pulled her into the circle. "A man what ain't got the balls to protect his woman don't deserve to keep her. How about it, sweetie? You want to ride out tomorrow with old Thatcher?"

Millicent continued to cry, but he paid no attention as he ran his hands over her familiarly.

"Now, fiddler," Dink ordered, "you play us a tune and you men can go on to bed. You ain't got the guts to be dangerous and we don't wanna dance with you."

Mr. Gray began to play again. This time, it was an off-key rendition of "Oh, Susannah." The men of the wagon train paused, then scurried into the shadows like frightened mice.

Emma tried to extract her hand from Dink's but he didn't let go. "Now, honey," he said and swayed a little on his feet, "we ain't through dancin' yet."

All three of the bounty hunters were drunk, Emma thought. If the men on this train had any gumption, they could easily overpower the invaders, but they were too afraid. They'd cower in their wagons and listen to the screams of their women and not do anything to help. Only Rider had any guts. She looked toward the wagon. Rider was gone.

For a moment, she felt relief, wondering what he would do to save them. It occurred to her suddenly that he had no real obligations here. He might sneak out to where his big stallion was tied and ride out. He could be long gone before this trio of drunks ever realized he was missing. She should have known better than to expect nobility from that half-breed. She'd begun to think of him as better than he was. He was only a low-down gunfighter after all.

Dink began to dance her around the fire to the fiddle music, holding her so tightly, her breasts were crushed against his chest. "Honey," he whispered against her hair, "later, I got something better in mind than dancin'."

Oh, Lord. In her mind, she relived the horror of that night almost four years ago. She'd rather die. No, if she were killed, there was no one to look out for her little son. As Dink held her close, planting sloppy wet kisses on her neck as he pawed at her breasts, she felt a new anger at Rider. If he hadn't been on the run and hiding in this wagon train, this rotten trio would never have ridden into this camp.

Rider had lain very still as the girl bent over him. If he moved at all, Dink might notice. A knife. She had dropped a knife by his hand. Rider turned his head ever so slightly as the girl walked back to the fire as she'd been ordered to do. His head seemed to be full of war drums and he was not sure he could make his body move. He lay there, watching what was happening by the fire and struggling to clear his mind, and decide what to do. At last his numb fingers managed to grasp the knife. Gingerly, he slashed at his bonds as Dink grabbed the girl's hand. It was all Rider could do to keep himself from screaming at the *hombre* to get his dirty paws off Sky Eyes.

No, he must not do that yet; a knife wasn't much of a weapon against three rifles, and Dink had taken his pistol. Rider bided his time and lay there as the men demanded more music and women to dance with. Slightly drunk and unsteady on their feet, the bounty hunters had each grabbed a woman and were dancing them around the fire, laughing and singing. Cautiously, Rider rolled out from under the wagon and into the darkness. He stuck the butcher knife in his belt, wishing he knew where Dink might have hidden his Colt.

His rifle. It was in the scabbard on his saddle and he'd not had time to unsaddle Storm. As the men danced and whooped with their unwilling partners, Rider sneaked through the night toward his horse. He could only hope that Storm did not whinny a welcome.

The horse made a soft snort and Rider patted him absently, reaching for the weapon. With it and the knife in his belt, he crept back to the shadows on the edge of the fire where Mr. Gray played his fiddle while the trio danced around the fire. The men of the train might be watching from the safety of their wagons, but they were too cowardly to unite and try to save their women.

Dink had his hand on Emma's back, running his hand up and down her full hips. Thatcher danced Millicent Carrolton around the circle, kissing her face as she wept. Only Francie looked calm although her nose wrinkled in distaste at her disheveled partner. Rider figured Francie had danced and slept with cowboys and outlaws who weren't any better than this one.

Rider hefted the rifle, trying to decide

what to do next. He couldn't start shooting for fear of hitting the women. Sky Eyes looked terrified, but angry and determined. The elegant Southern belle wept, tried to pull away, and begged, "Oh, please, let me go!"

Luke paused. "Hey, boss, what about takin' them off in the bushes for a little — you know."

Dink stopped dancing and laughed. "Good idea. I reckon the men don't have any objections to offering more hospitality, do they?"

No answer from the darkness.

"Well," Luke snickered, "I don't hear no objections from their menfolk."

Millicent began to cry uncontrollably.

Dink looked toward the fiddler. "Hey, farmer, you can stop now. We don't need music for the best part."

Mr. Gray stopped playing. "Can I — can I go?"

"Sure."

As Rider watched from the shadows, the timid little man fled back to his own wagon.

Dink threw back his head and roared with laughter. "Come on, honey, I know you been waitin' all evenin' for what I'm gonna give you. If you're good, I might bring you along when we start back in the mornin'."

He put his hand on Emma's breast and Rider saw the revulsion in her eyes. She looked toward the wagon and Rider held his breath, afraid she would make some sign that he was no longer lying there. Instead, she looked surprised as her gaze darted around the circle as if wondering where he was.

Dink grabbed her by the shoulder, pawing at her breasts, pulling her toward his blankets in the shadows. "Come on, honey, I wanna see what you look like without no dress."

It was all Rider could do then not to charge at the man, beating him in the face, slamming him against a tree in payment for the fear and trembling he saw in her wide blue eyes. The three men walked a little unsteadily away from the fire, each dragging a crying, begging woman, and disappeared into the shadows.

Rider's hand went to the knife in his belt. With any luck, he might be able to lower the odds. As a skilled warrior among the Shoshoni, Rides the Thunder had moved soft as a shadow when he sneaked up behind an enemy. However, tonight, he wore boots, not moccasins, and he was still dizzy from the blow to the head. He reached up to touch the aching place and came away with bright scarlet blood. The odds were long and Rider had no real stake in this drama except to escape. He could mount up, ride out, and be long gone before the bounty hunters ever noticed he was missing. Against three men, he didn't have much of a chance. And then he heard Emma's cry of protest and nothing mattered but protecting her even if it cost him his life.

Emma struggled, but she was no match for Dink as he forced her down to the ground. "Hey," he grinned, his bearded face alive with lust in the glow of the distant camp fire, "you're a feisty one, ain't you? I like that in a woman!"

She made a small cry as Dink put his hand down the front of her dress and squeezed her breast with one dirty hand. No, she must not scream. Josh was asleep and she didn't want her little boy to wake up and come running out to witness this. "Rider will kill you for touching me!" she gasped and tried to bite his hand. Somehow, she knew it was true . . . *or was it?*

"I thought you said you weren't his woman." Dink laughed as he held her down and straddled her lean body while she tried to twist out from under him. "He's got good taste, I'll say that for him. Old Rider's layin' over there out cold. I can hardly wait to tell him in the mornin' how much I enjoyed humpin' his pretty blond squaw."

She closed her eyes to shut out the sight of his grinning face and struggled to twist away from him. She could hear him breathing, his manhood hard and throbbing against her body as he tried to push her long skirt up. Now she remembered the past and the terror came over her again. She had survived once; she could do it again. All that was important was that she live so that she could look after her child.

Dink had her skirt up, running his dirty hands up and down her thighs. "Now, honey," he whispered, "you just hold still until I finish with you, you hear me? You behave yourself and I'll take you with me in the mornin'. I'd like that, old Rider all tied up every night, havin' to watch me takin' his woman."

Dimly, in the background, she could hear the other two women crying and begging. Dink leaned over to kiss her and she spat full in his face.

"You little hellcat!" He slapped her hard. Half stunned, she could taste her own blood. "I'll make you wish you hadn't done that. I'll shove it to you so hard, you —" He cried out in a soft, small way, hesitated, then fell over across her. In the dim light, she could see the silhouette of the knife sticking out of his back.

She couldn't help it — she opened her lips to scream. At that moment, a hand reached out of the darkness and clapped over her mouth. "Damn it, Sky Eyes, keep quiet!"

She almost wept with relief, but she only lay there as the half-breed dragged the dead man off her body. "You all right?"

She couldn't speak, only nodded as he pulled her up and she went into his arms, trembling like a leaf as he held her tight against him.

"That son of a bitch died too easy," Rider said. "If I were still among the Shoshoni, I'd have tortured him until he begged for death."

"The others —"

"I know. Wait here." He pulled the knife from Dink's back and carrying his rifle, crept away. She held her breath and waited, thinking that if one of them killed Rider, she was no better off than before. In the darkness, time seemed to drag past.

Rider crept through the grass. He came upon Luke rutting on Francie, his mouth on her full, pale breasts. Rider reached under the man's head and in one quick motion, cut his throat. Francie screamed as blood sprayed her pale body.

"Hush!" Rider commanded. "You're okay."

Francie scrambled to her feet, cursing under her breath as she straightened her clothes. "The cheap bastard didn't even offer to pay me."

"I thought it was all over when Dink recognized you," Rider said.

"I think he was a customer once in Del Rio."

From the shadows, Thatcher shouted, "What was that scream? Luke? What's happenin'? You okay?"

Rider grabbed Luke's pistol from its holster. Thatcher came staggering out of the woods, his pants around his knees. "Hold it right there, Thatcher!"

Instead, the man went for his gun. Rider shot him dead.

Immediately the camp was in an uproar — Boots barking, children awake and crying, men running. Rider hurried over to where Millicent Carrolton lay sprawled, her delicate lace pantelets torn away, her skirts up to her waist. He caught her wrist and stood her on her feet. She broke into hysterical sobs and went into his arms. "Weatherford didn't come to my aid, but you did! Oh, thank you, thank you!"

He led her out by the fire where the others

were gathering. "It's all right, folks," he said, "everything's all right now!"

Carrolton looked toward his weeping wife. "Did he — ?"

Rider glanced toward Millicent Carrolton's pale face. The proud Southerner wouldn't want a woman who'd lain with an outlaw. "No," he lied. "He didn't have time to touch her before I killed him."

"Francesca!" Banker Pettigrew ran to take the redhead in his arms. "Are you all hurt? Did he — ?"

"No," Francie said and shrugged off his embrace. "Like Rider said, they didn't have time to do anything before he killed them."

Rider took three long strides into the shadows where he knew Emma crouched in fear. He caught her hand and pulled her into the protection of his strong arms. "You're all right now."

For a split second, she relaxed against him, sobbing and shaken. Then she seemed to realize that she was in his embrace and pulled away. "I-I have to see about Josh."

Rider watched her running toward her wagon. He was torn between two emotions — wanting to protect her, yet wanting to make love to her. *Hadn't he earned the right to bed her?* He'd taken her away from an enemy; by Shoshoni law, that made her his woman!

Chapter Seven

The next morning, they buried the bounty hunters before they pulled onto the rutted road. Rider signaled the wagons out onto the trail, ignoring the hostile way the people looked at him. So now they knew what he was. Well, they couldn't fire him; they needed him to get the train to Oregon. Millicent Carrolton and Francie kept giving him secret smiles, but he ignored them. The woman he wanted had thanked him and that was all. He had hoped she'd warm to him, invite him into her wagon, but so far, it hadn't happened. He was losing patience. Maybe he should take the banker's loot and drift on.

That's what he told himself. Instead, he stayed with the train as it crossed the rolling plains.

They came to the Red Vermillion River. Rider reined in and considered. "The water's low; we could ford it and save the ferry fees."

"I'm for that," Emma called.

However, Mrs. Carrolton objected. "And run the risk of getting my fine dress wet?"

Rider shrugged. "It ain't that deep. 'Course, I know most women can't swim —"

"I can swim," Emma said, "and I'll help those who can't if they get in trouble."

Rider looked at her with new respect. She was not only independent, but she wouldn't shrink from possible danger. "Very well, we'll ford right here."

They crossed the river without incident. Now they saw fewer and fewer trees — people were reduced to picking up dried buffalo dung to fuel their campfires. Millicent Carrolton refused to touch the stuff and cried even more. As the days passed, the sun beat down on them mercilessly.

They passed a small herd of buffalo and the men began shooting wildly. Rider cursed and rode up and down the line, shouting, "Stop it, you idiots! We only kill enough to fill our needs."

"But it's so much fun to kill 'em," Willie Adams growled.

Rider glared at him. "The Indians depend on the buffalo and if settlers keep slaughtering them, soon there won't be any left."

Stott yawned. "So who cares?"

"I care," Rider snapped. "When the tribes

173

run out of meat, we'll have trouble on our hands. We only need one to feed the train." He took his rifle from his saddle ring, and aimed it toward the herd galloping madly over the rise. He was an expert shot and a fat one fell, shot cleanly through the heart. "Now some of you men skin it and save the hide; we may need it to wrap oxen's hooves in if they get sore."

That night, they camped at Alcove Spring, and Emma thought she had never been in such a peaceful place.

The next day, however, they were back on their relentless trip, the days a blur as they passed through the tiny hamlet of Marysville and the abandoned Rock Creek Station where the now bankrupt Pony Express had changed horses. Finally, they crossed the Big Blue River and drove toward the Little Blue.

"We'll come to the South Platte pretty soon," Rider said. "Then we'll follow it all the way across Nebraska."

The trip was becoming monotonous, he thought, and was tempted again to desert them when night came. The people didn't change much. Emma Trent struggled valiantly, doing more than her share, even though the others snubbed her. Francie tried to seduce him every chance she got, but he had eyes only for the yellow-haired girl.

She ignored him. He'd made two friends, though. Often Boots followed after him, barking happily, and the Small Warrior waved every time Rider rode past Emma's wagon. Rider nodded to the boy, tipped his hat to the lady. She hesitated, nodded back, but there was no answering warmth. She was both fearful and hesitant. Damn it, what was it going to take to make her his? After a couple of weeks, Rider was losing patience.

The weather was hot, but the trail was dry and dusty, so they made good time. One day as they stopped for noon the settlers gathered in small groups to whisper.

Rider rode into their midst and swung down. "All right, enough of this. What's got a burr under your saddles?"

Mr. Carrolton cleared his throat. "We had no idea when you hired on that you were a wanted man."

Rider shrugged. "Well, you must have been able to tell by lookin' at me that I wasn't a Sunday School teacher."

"Nevertheless," the banker huffed, "you put us all in danger when those ruffians invaded our camp."

"I thought he was wonderful!" Francie sighed, evidently forgetting herself.

Millicent Carrolton looked at Rider with dewy eyes. "If it hadn't been for this hero, I would have been . . . well, you know." Her face flushed crimson.

Both the men turned a flustered red and they glared at Rider.

"Keep in mind, ladies," fat old Mr. Adams groused, "that those renegades wouldn't have come to our camp if they hadn't been looking for this gunman."

Rider shrugged. "If you've all changed your minds, I could just ride on. I got no reason to go to Oregon."

Francie opened her mouth as if to protest, then seemed to realize he was calling their hands and ducked her head to hide her smile.

"No! No!" The people set up a howl of protest. "We're less than halfway there. Outlaw or not, we can't get to Oregon without you!"

"You may not get there at all," Rider reminded them, tipping his hat back. "The worst part lies ahead."

"Then we got to stick with you," said Stott.

Willie Adams looked angry, but he only nodded.

Emma had been standing quietly. Rider looked toward her. "What do you think, Mrs. Trent?"

The pregnant Mrs. Weeks sneered. "Who cares what that tramp thinks?"

Rider felt a rush of anger. "In case you didn't know it, if it hadn't been for her, there's no tellin' what would have happened. She slipped me a knife when no one else, not even the men, had the guts to act."

Emma flushed. "I-I had to do what I could."

The people looked from her to her little boy playing quietly in the grass at her feet. It was plain that with that half-breed child, they would never thank her, never appreciate what a spunky, brave girl she was.

Hell, he couldn't do anything about that. Since they had already judged her, no one was going to object much when Rider made his move to take her. He turned back toward his horse. "Everyone get a cold biscuit and see to your animals. We can put in another ten miles maybe, before dark."

In a few minutes, they were back on the trail, heading across Nebraska, a virtual sea of grass that seemed to stretch on forever toward the west.

Emma put Josh up on the seat beside her as she drove the placid oxen. Rider loped by, the shaggy pup at his heels. Josh waved to him in excitement. "Rider! Hey, Rider!"

"Hello, Small Warrior!" Rider grinned at

the boy as he passed. Rider was almost handsome when he smiled. Emma was so used to seeing his grim, cold countenance that she'd forgotten how virile and magnetic he was. She'd certainly noticed the way Francesca Pettigrew and now even Millicent Carrolton were looking at him. Well, that was to be expected; he'd saved them while their cowardly husbands stood by and trembled. And he'd saved her, too. Why did she suspect he had ulterior motives? At once, she was ashamed of her suspicions.

Josh tugged at her arm. "Did you see? Did you see, Mama? Rider waved to me!"

"I saw." Emma sighed and looked after Rider's departing back. "Honey, don't get too attached to Mr. Rider. He won't be around forever."

"Why?" The child's dark eyes were wide with disappointment.

"Well, because he isn't the type to stay. He's a drifter and he'll be riding out someday and he won't come back." She realized suddenly how she had become so used to having him around, protecting her, making life a little easier.

Josh nodded solemnly. "Then we go with him."

"No," Emma shook her head. "He won't take us with him when he goes. We'll be alone again, just like always."

"Go with Rider." Josh stuck his little chin out stubbornly.

Emma sighed and dropped the subject. There was no way to explain the distant, hard man to a small child. She hated Rider then, knowing that her little boy's heart would be broken when Rider left.

The day stretched long and hot, and the next and the next. The Nebraska plains seemed to stretch on forever, Emma thought, treeless and flat. Eventually, they came to Fort Kearny and the South Platte River. Emma was disappointed that it seemed so shallow and muddy, but at least, they would have plenty of water for a while. They stopped at the fort for a few supplies and camped that night on the bank.

She said to Rider, "I don't call that much of a river."

Rider stared off at the wide, lazy stream. "They say it's too thick to drink and too thin to plow. A mile wide in spots and an inch deep in others."

"Who lives out here, anyhow?"

Rider rolled a cigarette. "A few whites, mostly Indians."

"Indians?" Emma asked in alarm.

"This is buffalo country," Rider explained. "The Plains tribes come here when they're on a buffalo hunt."

One of the men had overheard the conversation. "They friendly?"

Rider looked at him without expression. "Lakota and Cheyenne, mostly. That answer your question?"

Several of the men gathered around. "But you speak Injun, don't you? If we run into trouble, can't you palaver with 'em?"

Rider laughed without mirth. "I'm Shoshoni, a mortal enemy of those tribes. No, I don't think they'll act kindly to any train I'm leadin'."

Weatherford Carrolton cleared his throat. "Are we — are we talking about scalping and burning women and children, and —"

"Shut up!" Rider snapped. "You'll scare the kids."

Emma looked up. A bunch of the dirty little Weeks and Gray children had gathered around. "It's all right," she said gently to them, "you all go run and play."

The children scattered and Emma walked back to her wagon to milk the cow. In the twilight, Rider marveled again at how beautiful she was with her long golden hair under the faded sunbonnet and the pale blue gingham dress. He had to have her. He'd thought of nothing else the last few nights except how she had felt in that brief moment she had been in his arms the night he'd killed the bounty hunters. He'd awaken in the darkness, gasping for air and dreaming that she was under him, reaching for him, eager, warm and giving. Maybe tonight he would give his ultimatum. Emma would hate him for it, but he wanted her badly enough that her opinion of him no longer mattered as long as he could possess her.

Night came on and Francie caught him in the shadows as he went to the river to water his horse. "I been thinking about you, Rider. You and me, and all Roscoe's money."

"Hell, Francie, stay away from me. Aren't you afraid Roscoe will see us together?"

"I don't give a damn anymore, Rider." She put her arms around his neck. "The way that old buzzard paws me makes me sick. He can't do it half the time, you know that?"

Rider tried to pull away from her. "You knew how old he was when you broke up his marriage, and I don't reckon he would have robbed his own bank if it weren't for you."

"How'd you guess? All he could think about was stickin' it to me." Francie laughed and rubbed her voluptuous body against him and he'd been so long without a woman, he couldn't help but be inflamed. She ran her hand down to touch his swollen manhood. "You want me, Rider, you know you do. We could get together some nights on the trail —"

He caught her hand and pushed it away. "And risk the banker catchin' us? Once he gets suspicious, we'll never be able to steal the money."

"Sometimes, I think about havin' you between my thighs and I'm not even sure I care about the money — just havin' you make love to me. I remember how you could make a woman whimper and beg for it." She ran her hands up and down her body and he was too weak to stop her.

"Damn it, Francie," he groaned, "don't do this to me."

She laughed and reached for his hand, put it on her breast. "Remember the taste of these? I can remember the way your tongue touched them, sucked them. Oh, Rider, I want you so bad!" Before he could react, she reached up to kiss him, putting her tongue deep in his mouth, rubbing her hot body up and down his.

For a long moment, he weakened, letting her rub all over him while he kept his hands on her ripe breasts. Then an image came to him of a sturdy, suntanned girl with long yellow hair and abruptly, his desire for Francie died. He took a deep breath and stepped away from her. "Look, you want that money, don't you? If we arouse Roscoe's suspicions, we'll never manage to get away with it."

"Whatever you say, Rider honey." She ran her hands across his wide chest, into the open neck of his shirt. "You tell me what to do."

He caught her hands and pushed them aside. "You'll have to stay calm and be ready. I'm not sure how things will play out, and there's no tellin' what I'll have to do. Old Pettigrew's been lookin' at me with suspicion."

Francie snorted. "Him? He thinks I'm a lady and he's too dumb to see I'm burnin' for you."

"Don't underestimate him," Rider cautioned. "You just keep your mouth shut and let me figure out the best way to get my hands on that money."

"*Our* money," Francie reminded him.

"Sure, *our* money." In the darkness, he was certain she couldn't read his face. He wanted the money, all right, but the woman he wanted to take with him when he left was not Francesca Pettigrew. Would Emma even consider going with him? And what would he do about the kid? "We'd better be gettin' back to camp before anyone misses us."

"I'll go on ahead. You do whatever you think best to keep my old goat from suspectin' anything," Francie said, "and I'll go along with it." With that, she turned and hurried into the darkness.

He waited a few minutes before he returned to the camp, leading his horse. He staked Storm out where there was good grass, unsaddled, and walked into the circle of wagons. Boots met him, barking. "Hey, boy, how you doin'?" He knelt and petted the pup. Josh came running from his mother's fire. "Rider!"

"Hey, Small Warrior."

The child threw himself at Rider, hugging his neck. Rider hesitated, uncertain what to do. He couldn't remember anyone ever hugging him except, of course, drunken whores. "Rider, you eat with us?"

Emma had heard — Rider could tell by her expression. "Honey," she said to the boy, "I'm sure Mr. Rider has already been invited by someone else —"

"I'd love to," Rider said, and took Josh's hand, walking over to her fire. "What are you servin'?"

She hesitated. "People will talk if you eat at my wagon," she said softly.

"They'll talk more before the night's over," he said, looking into her eyes.

She looked puzzled. "What's that supposed to mean?"

He almost reached for her then, the emotion was so overpowering. Francie had built a feeling in him that blazed like a prairie fire, but he could wait another hour or two; he must wait. "Nothing." He sniffed the air. "I hope that's quail frying?"

"You ought to know — you shot them." She turned them over in the frying pan.

"Then it would be inhospitable of me not to accept your kind dinner invitation," Rider said and settled down by her fire.

"People will talk . . ." she began, then looked at her happy child and didn't finish.

Rider leaned back against the wagon wheel, the pup and the boy halfway in his lap, and watched her cook. She was frying potatoes, too, and when she bent over the skillet, he could see the swell of her full breasts straining against the plain gingham dress.

God, how he wanted her and in an hour or two, he would have her. An uneasy feeling crossed his mind. It might have been shame, but he brushed it aside, wanting her as he did. It wasn't as if she were some innocent virgin. With a child as evidence, she must have some acquaintance with passion. That thought made him grit his teeth and he realized it was jealousy that he hadn't been her first, the man who taught her ecstasy. Well, she'd be his tonight and he'd take her to new heights of pleasure.

She dished up the food and he realized she was probably also the best cook on the train. The quail was crispy and juicy, the potatoes delicious, and her biscuits light and fluffy. When she brought out the jam, he shook his head in disbelief. "You're a wonder, Sky Eyes."

"What did you call me?" She looked at him, those blue eyes as wide and deep as two twin lakes.

Rider laughed with embarrassment. "It's a name I thought up for you; it fits you. Indian names mean something."

The little boy yawned noisily and Emma scrambled to her feet. "I'd better get Josh bedded down."

"I'll carry him for you." Before she could object, Rider picked the sleepy child up and started toward the end of the wagon. In the starlight, he could see inside. There was a little pallet of quilts off at the end — for the boy, most likely. In the middle of the wagon was a bed of quilts and some soft feather pillows. After tonight, he intended to be sleeping in that bed.

Emma climbed up in the wagon and held

out her hands. "I'll take him now."

Rider handed the sleepy child over and watched how gently she laid the child down and covered him.

"Tell Josh a story," the little voice yawned.

Emma smiled down at him, combing his black hair with her fingers. "Once there was a prince on a fine horse," she whispered.

"And a princess," Josh volunteered, "but she was unhappy and he put her up on his horse and rode away with her so they could live happily ever after."

Emma laughed. "You're getting ahead of the story."

Rider slunk off into the darkness. She was decent and caring, whatever her past. He was haunted by what he intended to do, but the only thing that mattered to him on this hot, sultry night was the way he wanted to spread her out and kiss her, thrust his hard, throbbing manhood deep within her, possessing her in the most intimate way a man could claim a woman. He paused and rolled a smoke with shaking hands, then looked back toward the wagon. He would have her, by God, he would have her! Hadn't he earned that right when he fought for her?

He strode into the circle where the men sat around smoking and discussing tomorrow's journey. The Pettigrews and the

Carroltons were there, and most of the other men, but the other women were in the wagons, bedding down children. He tossed his cigarette into the big fire. "We need to talk."

Weatherford Carrolton nodded. "We made good time today, didn't we?"

"Your wagon keeps falling behind," Rider complained. "I think it's overloaded."

Mrs. Carrolton said, "It's got some family heirlooms, fine furniture and such, every piece priceless. I'll need every bit of it for our home in Oregon. After all, I've already had to leave my fine buggy." Tears came to her eyes and her husband sighed audibly.

This wasn't the time to discuss wagon train business, Rider decided. "That's not what I want to talk about," he said. "You ladies might want to leave. This is man talk."

The elegant Southern lady's face flamed and she got to her feet, lifting her hoop skirt. "In that case, I'll be in the wagon. You coming, Mrs. Pettigrew?"

Francie shook her head. "Perhaps I'd better hear what this is all about."

"Now, Francesca, dear," old Pettigrew took off his derby and mopped his wet brow, "you just go along now and I'll tell you later —"

"I think your husband is right," Rider said and gave the redhead a long look.

"Well, all right, if you think it's too delicate a subject for a lady's ears." Francie got up reluctantly and headed for her wagon.

The circle of men looked at Rider expectantly. He took a deep breath and glanced around at the wagons. "We've gone too far to go back and you can't possibly make it the rest of the way without me."

They looked at each other, frankly puzzled.

"See here," Carrolton said, "if you're now going to demand more pay —"

"No, not that." Rider shook his head. After all, when he tired of the blonde, there was plenty of money in Banker Pettigrew's wagon to steal and ride out with. "There's one single woman on this train, and well, a man has needs."

Stott and young Willie Adams nodded in agreement. "We been thinkin' we ought to share her around."

Rider scowled at them and Willie doubled up his fists and glared back. "Well, it ain't as if she belonged to anyone."

Rider looked around the circle. "I've decided she belongs to me. I want her as part of my pay."

A flurry of excited talk among the men,

then farmer Adams looked up at him and spat to one side. "She know about this?"

"Hell, no. Anyway, she won't have much to say about it because she's just a lone woman with a kid. I just need to know that it's all right with the rest of the train."

There was a long, shocked silence. The frail little brothers-in-law, Weeks and Gray, shifted their weight uneasily. "I'm not sure that's the right thing to do."

"It ain't fair," Stott and Willie grumbled, "we want her, too."

"I'll kill any man who touches her," Rider said, and he didn't smile.

There was a long, uneasy silence.

"Well, now," Rider said, "we're going to be on this trail another four months or so. A man has needs. Of course, if one of you married men doesn't mind me borrowin' your woman, I reckon I could settle for that."

He was bluffing, of course. He didn't want any woman but the yellow-haired girl, but they didn't know that. They stared at him in shocked silence, each evidently imagining his own woman being forced to satisfy the virile half-breed every night.

Rider put his hand on his holster. "Not one of you can outshoot me," he reminded them.

"Why you?" Willie Adams shouted. "I

been wantin' her ever since this trip started!"

"Me, too," hollered several of the others.

Rider hooked his thumbs in his gun belt. "But I'm the only man this train can't do without and if I ride out tomorrow and leave you stranded, you're in bad trouble."

The men looked at each other in disbelief. "This ain't right," Mr. Weeks whimpered again.

"I don't give a damn if it's right," Rider said. "There's not a man here who hasn't daydreamed of what it would be like to lie between her thighs, if only you could figure out a way to get her."

The men stared at each other, guilt on their faces.

Mr. Carrolton cleared his throat. "Now, let's be practical about this, men. It's not as if she was some innocent virgin. She's got that half-breed kid."

Rider's hand went to his Colt. "Watch your mouth, Carrolton, before you end up on the business end of this forty-five."

"I only meant," Carrolton hastened to add, "that it's all right with me. She won't be any the worse for wear when you tire of her. A woman alone with a kid trying to make it in this world, she's probably pleasured a lot of men."

Rider had to fight the anger building in

him. "No, I don't think she's that kind at all."

The banker looked perplexed. "You think she won't object to this arrangement?"

"I don't know what she'll think," Rider said honestly, "but I want her bad enough that I don't give a damn."

The men looked at each other. Adams chewed his lip. "What'll we tell our women-folk?"

Rider pushed back his Stetson. "Tell 'em it was either this or get stranded out on the prairie without a wagon master. After all, there's no love lost between them and her. They'll probably figure it's good enough for her."

Again silence except for the crackling of the fire. Somewhere in the distance, a coyote howled. The sound echoed across the vast plains and seemed to remind them just how vulnerable and lost they could be out here without Rider.

All eyes turned toward Emma's wagon. Then they looked toward Rider, most eyes full of envy.

Banker Pettigrew cleared his throat. "Who's gonna tell her?"

Rider said, "I need her to know it's a majority decision that she'll have to go along with."

Mr. Gray licked his lips and looked away. "What — what if she won't go along with it?"

"She won't get any choice in the matter," Rider said, "if no one's gonna come to her defense. She's small and slight — I'll just take her." And he wanted her badly enough to do it, he told himself. Charm hadn't worked and she was a fire in his blood. "Well?"

The men looked at each other. Everyone looked shamefaced but no one seemed to have the nerve to stand up to the grim gunfighter. Mr. Gray cleared his throat. "I reckon it's all right with everyone, since your mind's set on it."

"Good," Rider said. "Now one of you go get her."

Again they avoided his eyes. They were losers and whiners, Rider thought, but even at that, none of them was as low as he was, bartering a woman's body as a bonus for the trail boss. "Gray, you go get her."

He looked up at Rider, his face as pale as his name. "I have to tell her?"

Rider shook his head. "Just bring her out here so she can see you're all in agreement."

The little man got to his feet very hesitantly, then turned to walk toward Emma's wagon. The silence hung heavy on the warm air. Rider took a deep breath with mounting excitement. In a few minutes, he would have her in his embrace the way he had in his troubled, restless dreams.

After a moment, Emma came toward the fire with the frail man. She looked bewildered. The firelight caught her hair and turned it into liquid gold. Rider imagined tangling his fingers in that hair and took a shuddering breath. She came into the circle. "What's this about, gentlemen?"

None of them wanted to look at her, not even Rider. They weren't gentlemen; certainly not him. They were miserable cowards, afraid or too indifferent to stand up to him.

"They have something to tell you, Emma," Rider said.

She looked toward Rider, the blue eyes confident, trusting. "If you're talking about putting me out of the train again, Mr. Rider promised me —"

"I'm afraid that's not it," Carrolton said. He looked in agony, Rider thought, the Southern tradition of chivalry bred into his very bones. However, the Mississippi gentleman hadn't been willing to stand up to Rider, either.

In the silence, Emma looked around the circle, then smiled at Rider. "What's this all about?"

Rider bit his lip but stared into her eyes. She must know how he hungered for her; surely she must know. "I've asked for a bonus to stay and they've granted it."

"More money?" Emma asked. "I'm sorry, but I can't —"

"Money's not what I want," Rider interrupted her.

She looked puzzled. "I don't understand."

He could have heard a leaf drop as it hit the grass, the circle was so quiet. Rider said, "I want you, Emma, and they've all agreed."

"What?" She looked both baffled and shocked.

"Mrs. Trent," Banker Pettigrew took off his derby and fiddled with it, not looking at her. "A man has, er, needs, and we'll be a long time on the trail."

Her mouth opened and she began to shake her head. "No, surely you are joking. Surely you haven't all agreed to this —"

"They don't have any choice," Rider said, "and neither do you."

The enormity of her situation seemed to sweep over her. "You mean I'm to — ? And I was just beginning to trust you!"

That hurt him to the quick and he almost wished he could take his words back.

"I won't do it!" Emma said, but she looked uncertain and frightened.

The elegant Southerner shook his head. "I reckon you don't have much choice. We need to keep the gunman happy. Otherwise, he'll desert us."

"I'll leave the train," she said and seemed to be gritting her teeth. "I'll leave the train before I'll submit to being his whore!"

"And what'll happen to your son?" Mr. Weeks asked. "You've got to think of him."

Her face fell apart then, knowing it was the truth. Tears welled up in her eyes and Rider hated himself for her pain but all he could think of was how she would feel soft and warm in his arms.

Willie Adams said, "It'll just be for four or five months, however long it takes to get to Oregon. You can pleasure him for that long, can't you?"

"And after that?"

Rider thought of the money and the hot, eager Francie. "Just the length of the trip," he said.

She looked at him then, drawing herself up proudly, her jaw set, her face a mask of anger and disappointment. "So all I've got to do is play your whore the next four or five months, is that it?"

The men sighed and looked at each other,

shocked that she would make it so plain. The truth was ugly.

"That's it," Rider shrugged.

"You rotten son of a bitch!" She began to curse then, cursing them all, but her shoulders slumped as if she already knew her fate was sealed. She glared at him proudly, not whining and begging like most other women would have.

"Then it's settled," Rider said without smiling. "We'll talk no more and you men make your women understand how practical this is."

"Mrs. Trent," Carrolton said in an apologetic drawl, "we hope you understand that we didn't have much choice —"

"I understand that you're all a bunch of lily-livered cowards who won't stand up when you know something's wrong!"

The banker wiped his sweating jowls. "Now, ma'am, it's more like a business deal, and we've got to be practical."

"Practical?" Emma's eyes blazed like blue fire. "Would you still talk like that if it was your woman he wanted?"

The fat farmer said, "But you ain't nobody's woman and someone was bound to claim you before the trip was over."

Rider walked over to her. "It's done now and you can't do anything about it. Your submitting to me is my price for staying with the train."

"Submit? Submit!" She slapped him hard enough that his head jerked back.

Rider ran his hand across his stinging cheek, then reached out and caught her arm. She tried to pull away from him but his strong grip held her.

"I was beginning to think you might be a decent human being," she screamed at him, "but there's not a decent bone in your body, you — you savage!"

Her words stung as her blow had not. "I'm a savage, all right, and now that you understand how things are going to be, we can go to your wagon. Good night, gentlemen. I suggest you all go to bed." He began to walk into the darkness, pulling her along.

Her slim body was shaking, but he had no mercy.

"Why me?" she asked in desperation. "I've seen the way Francesca looks at you; even the elegant southern belle would —"

"You, Sky Eyes; I want you. I've wanted you since the first minute I saw you — that's why I came on this train."

"Am I supposed to feel flattered?"

He paused at her wagon. "I don't give a damn what you feel as long as I end up in your bed. I've tried charming you and it doesn't work, so now I'll take you any way I can get you." He put his hands on her shoulders, caressing her slight frame.

Her shoulders trembled. "If I'd known how rotten you are, I'd have let Dink take you back to Texas to hang."

"So now you'd be warming his blankets instead of mine," he pointed out. "You're a beautiful woman, Sky Eyes, and some man is bound to bed you. I've decided it will be me."

"You're just like the others, thinking I'm a tramp."

"Get in the wagon." His voice was husky, urgent with need. He put his big hands on her small waist and lifted her up to the wagon gate. His desire was so great that he was past caring what she thought or even if she hated him as long as she was his to possess for all these hot nights under the stars. He climbed up on the gate behind her.

Emma was frantic. She scrambled across the quilts, grabbed up her rifle and turned, pointing it at him with trembling hands. "Don't — don't come any closer."

Rider paused, still squatting on the wagon gate and made a soothing gesture. "Now, let's talk about this, Missy. The noise of that gun goin' off will scare Josh."

She hesitated, looking over at her sleeping child. For a split second, she imagined her son waking up to find his idol sprawled dead in their wagon, his blood dripping from trunks and boxes. "I'm warning you — don't come any closer."

Rider took one step. "Now, Sky Eyes," he said softly, "you don't want to kill me. I'm the only one who knows the way to Oregon."

She hesitated and he took another step.

"Stay back!" she said again, wondering if she could really kill a man.

Rider made another soothing gesture, still talking as he inched closer. Could she kill him?

At that moment, his hand reached out in a lightning move and jerked the weapon from her grasp. "Don't ever let anyone get close enough to grab the gun if you intend to kill him."

Emma wanted to cry, to scream, to hit out at him, but she realized it wouldn't do any good. He was a virile, powerful man who had always taken what he wanted and he wanted her. Hadn't she always known it?

"You bastard," she gritted through her teeth as he tossed the rifle to one side and pulled her close.

Without loosening his grip, he tightened

his embrace, pressing between her thighs as he kissed her.

She struggled to pull away from him, but one of his strong hands went to tangle in her hair, pulling her mouth hard against his. He made a sound of pleasure, low and animal-like as he forced his tongue between her lips, thrusting deep into her mouth. The passion and the heat and the need of the man frightened her, knowing that mating with him would be like lightning flashing with all its heat and power. Emma put her hands on his chest and tried to push him away, but he was strong and his hand tangled in her blond locks pulled her even deeper into his embrace as his free hand wrapped around her waist.

Even though she struggled, his mouth explored hers and she was helpless to resist as his hot tongue ravaged her mouth, sucking her tongue deep into his throat. She managed to pull away from his mouth, breathing hard like a small, frightened animal.

"God, I want you," his voice was a husky whisper. "Get used to the idea, Sky Eyes. You were meant for my pleasure — I knew it the first time I saw you back in Independence."

She shook her head in disbelief as she looked up into his eyes. "You can't mean that. You can't have planned all this when Independence was full of paid —"

"You," he insisted against her lips, devouring her mouth again, "only you!"

It was inevitable, she knew, and yet, she wasn't one to submit meekly. "Are you going to take me right here with Josh lying there asleep?"

"He won't wake up, not unless you scream." He put his big hands on her shoulders.

What he said was true. In the dim moonlight, she could see her little son fast asleep on his quilt. He'd sleep through this, she was sure, so she must not make any noise or cry out.

"I've waited a long time for this." Rider's big hands slid from her shoulders down her arms and across her breasts as he began to unbutton her bodice.

She was trembling with the terrible desire she saw in his dark eyes and tried not to look down, feeling the warmth of his fingers on her skin as he unbuttoned her dress. "You — you should be ashamed."

"I don't have any shame," he whispered, "not where you're concerned." He pulled her dress open and she saw his eyes widen as he stared at her bare flesh. Emma gritted her teeth and closed her eyes as his rough hands cupped her naked breasts. She took a deep, shuddering breath, knowing that tonight, he would claim her as his possession, his love slave, and there was nothing she could do to stop him.

Chapter Eight

He ran his thumbs across her nipples. "Mine," he whispered, "for my mouth only." And then he pulled her to him, lifting her so that his mouth could reach her breasts.

She could feel his tongue teasing her nipple as his rough hands caressed her breasts and she felt a sudden emotion she had never experienced before.

Moonlight poured in through the wagon flap. Emma gasped and looked down at his dark face pressed against her pale skin as he caressed and stroked her. He caught her hand and put it down on his throbbing hardness and she pulled away as it she'd touched a burning sword. "No," she shook her head. "No."

He kissed her mouth, her eyes, and then her lips again. "Tell me you want me, too, Sky Eyes. Tell me you want me deep inside you."

She had no experience with passion and

the feelings that rose to the surface terrified her. All she knew of men were her gentle, dull husband and the brutal Cheyenne who had murdered Ethan. *An Indian.* An Indian, just like this one pulling at her clothing now. Horrifying memories returned from the depths of her soul and overwhelmed her. Abruptly she knew she had to escape from this stallion of a man before he invaded her body and emotions and took what he wanted.

She pushed him suddenly so that he lost his balance and fell onto the quilts. Then she lifted her skirts and clambered down out of the wagon, escaping into the warm summer night, running like a hunted doe across the prairie. If she could make it to the fort, maybe the soldiers would help her. The sand hills were uneven and pulled at her feet. She tripped and fell, then stumbled to her feet again.

Behind her in the darkness, Rider called "Sky Eyes! Where are you? Come back here!"

She turned her head, her heart pounding. Behind her, on the wagon gate, she could see Rider silhouetted in the moonlight. Then he hit the ground with all the grace of a mountain cougar. Oh, God, he was coming after her!

Emma turned and ran blindly through the night, uncertain where to go, what to do. Around her, crickets chirped and night birds called. Behind her, she heard him running easily, as fast as a predator, intent on recapturing his prey. She redoubled her efforts, her heart pounding against her ribs. When she glanced back, she saw he was gaining on her, moving with the easy grace of a warrior. In a panic, she tripped and fell in a tangle of skirts. Even as she tried to get to her feet, he was there, struggling with her. "Are you that scared of me?"

She wouldn't give him the satisfaction of an answer. She fought with him and they both went down, him ending on top of her.

"Stop fighting me," he murmured. "You're going to like it, I promise you that. I've waited a long time for this." His mouth came down on hers hard as he forced his big body between her thighs. His work-rough hands covered her breasts. "Come on, baby," he whispered, "it's not as if you've never had a man before and don't know how this is done. Don't play coy with me."

She bit his mouth, and he pulled back with an oath, a bewildered, angry expression on his dark face. Emma could taste his blood as she took advantage of his surprise and struggled to her feet again, and began to run.

Behind her, she could hear him swearing. "Damn you, Sky Eyes, what kind of game are you playing? You need this as much as I do!"

He was chasing her again. Sheer terror made her stumble on, even though she was exhausted and knew she couldn't win. There was no way to outrun this hardened warrior, and even if she got away, there was no place to go. Besides, she had a child back at the wagon; a child who depended on her. Then she remembered the terror of that long-ago night and promised herself she would never submit to that humiliation again.

Intent on escaping through the night away from the wagons, she barely heard the warning rattle in the grass at her feet. She saw the sudden movement in the moonlight, like liquid silver flashing in the night and in that split second, sharp fangs stung into her ankle and she fell and cried out. "Snake! Rattlesnake!"

In a heartbeat, Rider was there. She saw his pistol flash orange fire in the darkness as he pulled the trigger. The snake writhed for a moment in the grass and was still.

Rider knelt by her. "Damn, I didn't mean —"

"Damn you! I'm going to die," she gasped, "and there'll be no one to look after Josh."

"You're not going to die," Rider said, "not if I can help it."

In the distance, she saw lights flickering on around the wagons as people lit lanterns and came out, yelling questions to each other.

It seemed as though Emma could feel the poison already pumping through her veins toward her heart. "I hate you," she said. "I really hate you!"

He pulled a knife from the scabbard on his belt. She saw it shining in the moonlight and shrank back. "What are you going to do?"

"I'm gonna save your life," he muttered, looking away as if ashamed. "I thought you were playing games. I didn't realize you were really afraid of me."

"Afraid?" She threw back her head and laughed hysterically. "You really don't know, do you? You know how I got Josh? My husband and I saved an injured Cheyenne's life and he repaid us by killing him with an axe and then raping me on our bloody bed next to my husband's dead body!"

She saw the shock in his face. "Good God!"

"You bastard!" she seethed. "Why don't you take me now? I can't get away from you!"

"You're right, I'm a rotten bastard," he mumbled. "I had no idea —"

"Would it have made any difference?" She was crying now, crying and angry that she was going to die and there was no one to look after her child.

Rider didn't answer. Instead, he took off his bandana and tied it around the calf of her leg in a tourniquet. His hands on her bare flesh were strong, warm, and sure. "This is gonna hurt — I'm sorry."

"Sorry?" she spat out, "that's not much help now."

He shrugged. "It's the best I can do. Now hold still until this is over." His big hand encircled her slim ankle.

"What — what are you going to do?" She was mesmerized by the big knife he pulled from his scabbard.

"The only thing I can do, Sky Eyes. I'm sorry as hell about this. Hold still."

"You're not going to cut my leg off!" She was still gasping from exhaustion, but she struggled.

"If you don't hold still, I might," he said. "I'll cut a gash in that bite and suck the blood out."

"No!" She shook her head violently and tried to pull away from him, but he held onto her. "No! I-I want a doctor."

"Baby, we don't have a doctor, you know that. I'm sorry I have to do this. Now hold still."

She was too terrified to move now, knowing that if she winced, the big knife might split her leg open. She was beginning to feel faint and sick; the sweat that drenched her felt ice cold.

He looked deep into her eyes. "I know it doesn't mean much, but I'm sorry. If I'd realized you were that afraid of me —"

"Oh, shut up and do what you have to do!" She gritted her teeth and closed her eyes, already feeling nauseated as the deadly venom seemed to spread through her body.

"I'll be as careful as I can."

By gritting her teeth, she managed to hold back a scream as she felt the knife cut into her ankle. Then she began to sob softly.

"Brave girl. It's okay, baby," he whispered. "It's all over now. I'll take care of you — I promise."

She barely opened her eyes as she felt the warmth of his mouth on her ankle. "What — what are you doing?"

He looked down at her. "I've got to get that poison out."

As she watched, he bent his head to her ankle again, his mouth hot on her skin as he sucked her blood and spit it out. She was feeling sicker by the moment as the poison coursed through her system. She was going to die, she knew it, out here on this forsaken prairie, and be buried in an unmarked grave. That didn't scare her — what scared her was the thought of her little son alone with no one to protect him. "Josh," she mumbled, "someone's got to look after Josh if I don't make it."

Rider glanced up, his face pale, her blood crimson on his sensuous lips. "Don't even talk that way. You're going to be all right."

Emma looked toward the wagon train. Some of the people were walking toward them, carrying lanterns. She had a strange, floating feeling like being in a dream. It couldn't be real; she was out here on this lonely prairie, dying of a snake bite with this half-breed gunfighter sucking her blood, trying to save her life. "I reckon we're even then," she whispered and laughed. "I swallowed some of your blood when I bit you and now you're drinking mine. Does that make us closer than blood brothers?"

"Don't talk loco," he said, and tore away part of her petticoat to wrap her ankle. "Now let's get you back to the wagon." He picked her up and she was startled to realize how easily he carried her as he turned toward the approaching settlers.

"Now," she mumbled and laid her face against his broad shoulder, "now I can't do much about it when you rape me."

She felt him wince. "Damn it, I said I was sorry."

The stars above seemed to be whirling slowly. At least she was going to be unconscious soon. She wouldn't be aware of it when Rider took her. "Josh," she whispered, "someone's got to look after Josh. . . ."

"I'll look after him," Rider promised. "Both of you, I swear it. Now relax and I'll get you back to the wagon."

"Hot," she murmured, "burning up."

"I know," he whispered against her hair as he walked. "It's the fever coming. I'll look after you — I promise."

"Gunfighter's promise no good," she said and tried to keep her eyes open, but she felt so sick.

"Yes, it is," he answered stubbornly. "You'll see."

She didn't believe him but she felt too bad to argue. From what seemed like a long way off, she heard men of the train approaching in the faint glow of lanterns, asking what had happened and Rider's deep, masculine voice telling them about the rattlesnake.

Rider looked down at the semi-conscious girl in his arms. Was she dying? The thought caused fear to twist in his belly. That surprised him. He was afraid of no man or beast, and yet, he was shaking at the thought that the slight blonde in his arms might be dying even as he started back toward the circled wagons.

Old man Adams, Carrolton, and some of the others came toward him, asking questions. He brushed them aside as he kept walking, and they hurried to keep up with his long legs. "She — she was running through the grass and a rattlesnake got her on the ankle," he said.

They all fell silent and seemed to look at him with accusing eyes and then guiltily at each other. Even though no one asked why she'd been running, he figured they knew. Emma Trent had been running from him. The emotion he felt now was a new one for him and he didn't like it; it felt like shame. Without a word, he shouldered his way through the crowd, still carrying the limp girl. She seemed so small and defenseless in his arms and he wanted to protect her from anything that might hurt her. Who was he kidding? He had caused her all this terror and pain. He hated himself then for the overpowering desire that had wiped out his good sense. "Damn you, Rider," he muttered to himself as he strode across the circle, "all you could think of was getting her under you and now see what you've done."

He reached her wagon and others were crowding around, curious as bluejays. "There's been an accident," he said. "I'll look after her. The rest of you go back to bed."

Francie pushed to the foreground. "There's some things only a woman can do for another woman. It ain't fittin' —"

"I said I would look after her." Rider's tone left no question as to his mood and he glared at Francie. "I thank the lady for her concern."

He saw some of them exchange glances, but they were all too afraid of him to argue. Some of the women looked at each other uncertainly. Mrs. Carrolton said, "I'm not certain that's proper —"

"Out here on the plains, we don't follow the rules of proper society, Mrs. Carrolton," Rider said.

Mrs. Gray shifted her baby from one hip to the other. "Maybe they got a doctor at the fort."

He knew army doctors — drunken quacks who couldn't make it in civilization. "I'll take care of her. Now go to bed."

They seemed to disperse reluctantly, curious as to what might happen next. The redhead was giving him looks of jealous hatred, but the chubby banker took her arm and led her away. "There, there, my dear. You offered. A real lady really shouldn't be soiling her hands like that."

Rider hated them at that moment, hated them all. No one seemed really concerned about Emma's fate; they were all concerned with what was proper. He could guess what Francie was concerned about. Gently, he laid the unconscious girl on the wagon bed and climbed up himself. She looked so small and defenseless lying there with her ankle swollen and discolored. Even in the faint moonlight, Rider could see it. He picked her up carefully, carried her in, and laid her on her quilts.

Josh raised his sleepy head.

"Go back to sleep, Josh," Rider assured him. "Everything's fine."

Fine. Sky Eyes might be dying and it was all Rider's fault. The boy lay back down and in seconds was sleeping soundly. The moonlight shone through the opening in the canvas. Rider looked down at the girl. Now what? She moaned softly as he put his hand on her forehead. It seemed burning hot. When he took her wrist in his hand, her pulse seemed too rapid. If he'd been in the Shoshoni village, there would have been medicine men and all sorts of roots and herbs. Here, they only had whiskey and a few worthless white men's tonics. Those wouldn't do any good anyhow with Emma slipping into a coma.

He had to do something; he couldn't just sit here and watch her die. Suddenly she meant more to him than any woman ever had . . . or maybe it was only because he felt so guilty about what had happened. Rider propped her foot higher and tried to decide what to do next. Her plain gingham dress clung to her soft curves as perspiration soaked her. All thoughts of passion were gone now; all he could think of was how sick she was and how Josh's big eyes would accuse him if his mother died. Rider had a sudden vision of a lonely, unmarked grave left behind on the endless prairie as the wagons pulled out. They had already passed a number of them.

"No," he said aloud and shook his head. "No, that's not going to happen, not if I can do anything to stop it."

He dug around in her things until he

found a clean dish towel, then he went outside and got a bucket. The camp was quiet now. The puppy came out from under the wagon, wagging his tail. Rider patted him absently. "Let's go get some cold water, Boots. Maybe I can bring her fever down."

In minutes, Rider was back in the wagon with his bucket of cool water. He put his big hand on her forehead and she seemed to shrink back. He cursed himself under his breath. It hadn't been an act; she was truly terrified of him and now he knew her terrible secret. Rape. Why hadn't she told him before? She hadn't trusted him enough; it was that simple. Well, she had good reason. He had never felt like a rotten, worthless rascal before and he didn't like the feeling. Women had always been delighted to sleep with him, yet this one was so terrified of that, she'd taken her chances on the night-cloaked prairie rather than satisfy his passion.

Rider put the cloth in the cold water, wrung it out, and placed it on her forehead. She seemed to sigh and relax. After a moment, as the rag grew warm, he dipped it again. He would sit here all night if need be, cooling her face. He put his hand on her throat. Her pulse seemed rapid and thready. How fragile her neck seemed under his big hand. Her skin was damp with perspiration. He had to get that fever down. Rider thought about it a moment. He really should get some of the women to do this, but Sky Eyes had no friends among these women. Besides, he didn't like the idea of anyone else looking after her. He hesitated. If she became conscious during this, she'd be terrified and never believe he meant her no harm.

"Well, can you blame her?" he accused himself aloud, "running her down like some crazed stallion?" He'd expected her to accept him, no, even welcome him into her bed, despite her protests. He took one of her small hands in his and examined it. Emma Trent had led a hard life. Though delicate and finely boned, her hands were calloused and scarred from long hours of back-breaking work. Without thinking, he brought her hand up and touched it to his lips, cursing the past life that had worn her down and tried to break her. No one would ever break Sky Eyes's spirit; life might kill her, but she wouldn't surrender without a fight. At that point, her small fingers tightened over his big hand. Something came up into his throat and threatened to choke him and for a minute, his vision blurred. So fragile and so alone with no one to protect her. He patted her hand and laid it gently on the quilt.

Then, very slowly, Rider finished unbuttoning the bodice of her faded, torn dress. His hands trembled as he pulled the dress open, revealing her slight, slim body. Beneath the worn gingham, her skin was creamy pale, in contrast to the suntanned face. Rider hesitated a moment, thinking he had never seen such beauty. Her breasts were small but perfect, with nipples like pale rosebuds. Her small waist flared out to curving hips and her legs were long. For a moment, he imagined what it would be like to make love to her, then cursed himself for his folly and dipped his cloth in the cold water again. Her pale skin shone with perspiration and she muttered in her sleep.

Gently, Rider began to wash her. For a moment, she started, pulling back, but he spoke soothingly to her, assuring her he would not hurt her and she relaxed. Again and again as the hours passed, Rider dipped his cloth and wiped her all over, attempting to bring down her fever. Then she began to shiver uncontrollably. He piled all the quilts he had over her and still she shook. *What to do?*

After a long moment, Rider unbuttoned his shirt and slipped it off, then took off his boots. He hesitated a moment, knowing how terrified she would be if she awakened, but there was no help for it. He crawled in under the covers and took her feverish body in his arms, resting her head on his broad shoulder. Even in her sleep, she tried to pull away from him, but he was strong and he held her, fitting her shaking, naked body into the curves of his dark, hard-muscled length. Funny, he thought, she seemed to fit so perfectly in his arms. He could feel her nipples against his hard chest and her warm breath against his neck.

Damn, he had never wanted a woman as much as he wanted this one. What kind of rotten bastard was he to think such thoughts about an unconscious woman? He could use her now for his passion and she would never know the difference. He bit his lip, cursing himself silently for his need. He'd done a lot of bad things in his past, things he wasn't proud of, but he wasn't low enough to rape an unconscious woman. After a long moment, she stopped shivering and slept. He wished he could sleep, but he was too aware of the naked, heated woman in his arms, her yellow hair spilling like spun gold across the worn quilt in the moonlight.

Toward daylight, she seemed to be better, though she was still unconscious. Quickly,

Rider dressed and inspected her wound. Her ankle and leg were still discolored and swollen. With a sigh, he rebuttoned her dress, covering her slim body. He still wanted her, wanted her as he had never wanted another woman. The council had given her to him for his pleasure, and she'd given him nothing but trouble and a new feeling that might have been guilt. He must not think past getting her well again.

At dawn, Rider, accompanied by the pup, went out on the prairie to search for herbs that he remembered from his years with the Shoshoni. He also checked the snare he had set late yesterday and found a fat rabbit in it. He took the herbs back and brewed them into a poultice over a small fire and returned to the wagon to rewrap her ankle. There was still no way to know whether she would make it or not, but Rider was determined to do everything he could to save her. Emma Trent had been a game girl who never had much luck, but Rider was determined to do whatever he could to change that, if for no other reason, he told himself, than so he wouldn't feel so damned responsible.

The camp was up and stirring as Rider inspected the dressing on her ankle again.

Josh woke up, yawning. "Mama?"

"She's — she's not feeling well," Rider

told the child, avoiding his eyes. "I'll fix you some breakfast and take care of her."

Rider dressed the little boy and took him outside, ignoring the curious stares of the others. As he poked the embers of his fire into flames, Carrolton came over. "We're getting an awfully late start, aren't we?"

Rider shook his head. "We're not moving today. Mrs. Trent is too sick."

"But we're running behind already —"

"I said we're not moving today," Rider snapped. "Now, if any of you think you can get there without a scout, go right ahead."

Mr. Carrolton wrinkled his patrician nose as if he might argue, then seemed to think better of it. He left and soon Rider heard muttering throughout the camp, but no one confronted him and no one asked about Emma's welfare. Most of these people were as rotten and selfish as he was himself, he realized. Nothing but his own needs had ever mattered to him before; now he was concerned with a small boy and a very sick girl. Rider fried part of the rabbit for Josh and made himself some coffee. Later, he said, "Josh, you play with your dog and I'll see about your mother, okay?"

"Mama sick?" the child asked somberly.

"Yes, but don't worry, she'll get well. Now, you go play." Somehow it seemed important that this child not suffer for what Rider had done. He boiled some of the meat to make a rich broth and returned with a bowl of it to the wagon. "Sky Eyes, are you awake?"

No answer. He put his hand on her forehead. Her skin was still hot. "Sky Eyes?"

She muttered something in her sleep and tried to pull away from the touch of his hand. He inspected her ankle. It looked horrible — swollen and discolored. After he got some broth in her, he'd change the dressing and sponge her off again. Mixing a little whiskey in the broth, he tried to lift her by putting one arm under her shoulders.

"No," she muttered and tried to pull away.

"It's okay," he assured her softly. "I'm not going to hurt you. I'm just going to feed you some broth."

No answer. Thus encouraged, he picked up a spoon and held the broth to her lips. By putting the spoon between her lips, he let a little of it run down her throat. "There, that's the way. You've got to eat."

For a minute, she seemed to struggle, but she was too weak against his great strength. Finally, as he continued, she stopped fighting and let him drip a spoonful of broth between her lips. Very slowly and patiently he fed her, one small spoonful at a time. He'd put most of the broth in her before her eyes fluttered open weakly and she seemed to realize who he was. She gave a cry and began to struggle.

"Shh! Shh!" He held her firmly but gently. "I'm not going to hurt you — I'm trying to help you. You were bit by a rattler last night, remember?"

Her beautiful face furrowed as if searching for the memory; then she frowned as she must have remembered why she'd been running through the dark. "Josh," she managed to gasp. "Josh?"

"He's okay," Rider said and set the bowl to one side. "He's been fed and he's outside playing."

"Hate you," she muttered and dropped back off to sleep.

"I know and I deserve that, I reckon," Rider agreed. Somehow her words hurt more than any wound he'd ever suffered as a warrior or a gunfighter. He held onto her a moment longer, relishing the softness of her in his arms, remembering how she had felt naked and soft against him last night. With a sigh, he laid her back on her pillows and inspected her swollen leg. It looked bad. There was no way to know if she'd survive this or not. He'd seen more than one man die in writhing agony after a snake bite.

"Sky Eyes," he whispered, "you can't die. Josh needs you, I need you." His confession startled him. *What the hell was he saying?* Rider didn't need her; he didn't need anyone. He was a lone wolf — always had been, always would be. He used women for his pleasure and theirs, then deserted them without a backward glance. He'd planned to steal the banker's money soon and move on, riding alone like always. Yet now he felt obligated to stay because of this sick girl who hated him.

She was moving and muttering, a slight sheen of perspiration on her sun-browned face. Rider put his hand on her forehead. She was burning with fever. He got up and took his bucket, went outside, walked toward the river.

Francie caught up with him. "Well, is she gonna live?"

Rider paused and looked at her. "What do you care?"

"I don't," the redhead snapped, "but you seem to care too much!"

Rider sighed. He was more than a little weary of Francie and her jealousy. Why had he ever thought she was pretty and desirable with those hard lines around her mouth and all that makeup? "Look, we can't be seen together — you know that."

"I wanna know what's goin' on in that wagon." She glared up at him.

"Nothing. The girl's unconscious, maybe dying. I swear nothing's happened between us."

"Then why'd you ask the council to give her to you like she was a slave or a pet?"

He could not admit his need for the yellow-haired girl. "I had to throw them off the track, right? I wouldn't want anyone to suspect there was something between you and me."

She smiled. "So nothin's changed?"

He had changed, but he wasn't certain how or when or what. He avoided Francie's eyes, almost fearful that she could see the difference in him. "We'll talk later. In the meantime, stay away from me."

Francie tried to drape her arms around his neck, rub her ripe body against him. "I don't wanna stay away from you, Big Boy. I want you to take me down in the grass and . . ." She whispered in his ear what she'd like him to do to her.

Trying not to show his disgust, Rider broke her grip and stepped away from her. "Stop it, Francie. Old Pettigrew is going to notice if you keep this up."

"I don't give a damn," she pouted.

"You'll mess up the whole plan if he suspects anything," Rider reminded her.

"You're right. Okay, I can wait a little while longer." She walked away, swinging her hips suggestively.

Rider watched her go, his groin swelling at the thought of what she was offering. Then he remembered a frail, sick girl who was his responsibility and he forgot about Francie and knelt to fill his bucket at the river.

When he returned to the camp, Josh still played with his puppy. Rider climbed up into the wagon and watched Emma's face a long moment. She was so different from Francie or any of the women Rider had ever known. "Damn you," he muttered, "for making me want you. I could take old Pettigrew's loot and skedaddle if it weren't for the hold you've got on me."

It was lust, that was all it was. Once he'd had her, he'd know she was just like any other woman after all. He felt like a rotten bastard because he still wanted her, even though she was sick and helpless. Well, he wasn't the kind who would take advantage of an unconscious woman.

With a sigh, Rider unbuttoned her dress and tried not to look at those two perfect breasts as he sponged her heated body with cool water. He wiped her down over and over until her temperature dropped and she slept soundly. Carefully, he covered her and left the wagon. He was bone weary. Rider checked on Josh, then found himself a shady spot under some trees and caught a quick nap, the pup curled up by his side. "Look, you," he said to the dog, "I don't need a pet or any responsibilities."

The pup seemed to grin at him and licked his face with a rough, pink tongue as if it didn't believe him.

In the afternoon, Rider ignored the grumbling people and went to check on Emma. She was feverish and thrashing about, her ankle still swollen and miscolored, but it looked a little better. He sponged her off again, humming an old Shoshoni chant that seemed to soothe her until she dropped off to sleep. Well, he had done all he could to help her; now it was up to her own strong spirit.

That night, little Josh looked up at him anxiously as he ate the food Rider prepared. "Is Mama still sick?"

Rider had always thought of himself as a hard man, yet now he put his arm around the toddler's small shoulders and looked down into the anxious little face, as dark as his own. "She'll be all right. You need to go to bed."

"Do you know a story? Mama tells stories."

"Stories about what?"

Josh wrinkled his handsome face in thought. " 'Bout princes on fine horses that rescue people."

Rider shrugged. "I'm afraid I don't know much about princes, but I know some stories." He began to tell old, old Shoshoni tales about how the world began and how the warriors fought and won great battles.

The little boy seemed charmed and smiled up at him. "Good as Mama's," he decided, yawning sleepily.

"Now you're going to bed." Rider picked him up and carried him to the wagon. He put Josh down in his quilts and then went outside and rolled a cigarette. The camp was quiet and asleep. Even Stott, who was on guard duty up on the rise, appeared to be asleep with his shapeless hat pulled down on his head. Rider frowned. He was having a difficult time keeping the sentries awake because they didn't realize how quickly a war party could sneak up on a sleeping camp. And if it weren't a war party, there were always white outlaws roaming the trails, ready to kill or plunder an unsuspecting train. Well, he was going to be awake most of the night himself, so he'd keep a lookout. Rider didn't want to talk to anyone right now, certainly not the strange Stott.

He put out his smoke and got a towel and a sliver of soap from Emma's wagon. With the dog trailing at his heels, Rider headed down to the river to wash up. He stripped down, hanging his holster on a tree. The dog lay down to watch as Rider began to splash himself.

Abruptly, the puppy growled and Rider came alert. The pup was looking into the bushes, his ears up. Rider froze in place, then scrambled for his pistol. "Whoever the hell you are, come out with your hands up!"

Millicent Carrolton stepped out of the bushes, a hesitant smile on her lips. "I-I've been waiting to get you alone." He could only blink in stunned surprise as she put her arms around him and kissed him hesitantly.

Chapter Nine

Her mouth was hot and wet and she pressed her breasts against him and ran her elegant hands down his bare hips. For a long moment, he reacted as only a virile man who has been a long time without a woman could react. He pulled her against him hard, letting her mold herself all the way down his virile, lean frame. Then his good sense took over and he pulled away from her, jerked her hands off his neck. "What the hell are you doing?"

Millicent Carrolton hesitated, twisting her hands together nervously. "I-I'm not sure how a woman goes about appealing to a man like you."

"You mean a lowdown gunfighter?" Rider shoved the pistol back in its holster and grabbed for his pants. "Mrs. Carrolton, you shock me and I'm not an easy man to shock."

She turned away from the sight of him

putting on his pants. "I-I don't know what came over me."

Rider shook his head as he dressed. "Look, lady, I don't know what your game is, but it's a dangerous one."

Her elegant features showed surprise as she turned. "You're not afraid of my husband?"

Rider paused, scowling at her. "Do I look like I'd be afraid of any man walking?"

"No, and that's what attracted me to you." She caught his arm in desperate appeal. "Weatherford is a coward, you know that? He's running away from 'The Noble Cause', too lily-livered to fight. The other planters ran us out of the county and burned our plantation because he was con- sorting with Yankees."

So now he knew why the Carroltons had come along on this ill-fated wagon train. "Look, Mrs. Carrolton, I have no interest in politics, but I do know messing with a mar- ried woman on a wagon train will lead to trouble."

"Oh?" She smiled with a smug, superior mouth. "Funny, you don't seem to feel that way about Francesca Pettigrew."

Rider paused in putting on his shirt to give her a questioning look.

"Oh, don't try to play innocent with me." Her patrician drawl became annoyed, frustrated. "I saw you and that red-haired hussy together. She seemed to be begging you to take her down right there in the dirt."

He could feel sweat breaking out on his muscled back. "Maybe you misunderstood what you saw."

She laughed again, a look of triumph on her beautiful features. "I don't think so — women know about such things."

Rider didn't answer, but his hands were shaking as he rolled a cigarette. "So what do you intend to do with all this knowledge? Blackmail?"

"Oh, goodness me, no. A gently bred Southern lady would never do such a thing."

He gave her a direct look. "So what is it you want?"

"I hate this trip!" she said with sudden fury. "I hate everything about it. I want to go back home, or at least to New Orleans or Atlanta. I'll sleep with you if you'll desert this train and escort me south." She came to him suddenly and put her arms around his neck, running her hands over his muscled back under his shirt.

Roughly this time, Rider pulled away from her, tossing away his unlit cigarette. "Mrs. Carrolton, the South you knew is gone and will never be again. All you're going to find if you go back is burned-out plantations and misery."

"No," she shook her head, "that cannot be. Things can't change, they must not change." She put her face in her hands and began to weep.

Very gently, Rider put his hand on her shoulder. "Forget the past. Maybe you and your husband can build a new life in Oregon."

"That horrid, uncivilized place!" Her lovely eyes glittered with fury. "Live with a man who turned his back on our Noble Cause and fled like a cowardly cur?"

Rider didn't say anything for a long moment. "I'm sorry," he said finally. "I wish I knew what to tell you, but I won't leave this train to take you back south."

Her pretty face turned ugly as she sneered, "It's that blonde, isn't it? That slut with the half-breed kid —"

Rider reached out and grabbed her by the throat. "Don't say it," he snarled. "Don't you even let her name cross your lips."

She pulled away, obviously frightened as he relaxed his grip. "All right, so I deserved that. I could be as good in bed as she is — you'd see. If you don't do as I ask, I'll tell everyone about you and that Pettigrew woman."

"Are you threatening me?" His voice was as cold as his heart. "Mrs. Carrolton, if you tell, I'll tell him what a conniving slut you are and the offer you made me. You don't want to put your silly, weak husband in a position where he has to challenge me to a duel, do you?"

"I-I hadn't thought of that. I reckon Weatherford is gallant enough to challenge you."

Rider nodded. "I'd hate to kill him and leave you traveling alone. Not much future for a woman alone in Oregon if word gets around her husband was killed defending her honor."

With that, he turned and headed back to Emma's wagon, wondering if Millicent Carrolton would call his hand. What he didn't need right now was having to deal with a jealous husband.

From the shadow of the trees, Stott had watched the encounter between the two while stroking himself with frustration. That Carrolton woman was a high-class bitch who needed tending to. If her husband couldn't and Rider wouldn't, old Stott might have to step in and pleasure the lady. But not yet, no, not tonight. He watched the lady returning to her wagon. He'd give her more man than she could handle, but not yet. Like the other ones back in Baltimore, Cincinnati, and Arkansas, Stott would have to catch her unexpectedly. Until then, he'd have to pleasure himself.

Rider catnapped all night, awaking often to sponge Emma down with a wet rag. Toward dawn, he noted with satisfaction that the swelling in her ankle seemed to have gone down.

After he forced some broth down his unwilling patient and looked after Josh, Rider tried milking the cow. He didn't do a good job of it; he was no farmer. The patient cow kept turning her big brown eyes to look back at him. Rider finally got a small pail of milk and gave it to Josh and a cup to Emma. Her eyes flickered open and she sipped it.

"What'll I do with the rest?" he asked.

"You're — you're milking the cow?"

He felt foolish. "Somebody had to. You were so damned worried about her."

Her face softened. "Share it with the children of the camp," she murmured.

"After the way these people treat you?"

"The children need the milk."

He stood up. "Okay, whatever you say. It's your cow."

Later, he sat beside his campfire drinking

coffee as the morning lengthened.

The grumbling pioneers gathered around the big campfire.

The fat banker shook his head. "It's no good, our wastin' time like this."

The others muttered agreement.

"Look," Rider snapped, "you wouldn't get a hundred miles without me and you know it. I'll say when we move on and that will be when Emma is better."

Francie shot him a black look, but he ignored it.

One of the sisters, Mrs. Weeks, gestured toward her wagon. "But what about all these young'uns? You said yourself we're behind schedule and if we don't get through the mountains before the winter snows, we might be just like that Donner Party in California."

Rider scowled and nodded, torn between those indisputable facts and caring for the girl whose life was in his hands. Everyone knew about the ill-fated Donner Party. They had taken too long getting through the mountains on the California Trail and become marooned in the snow. Before they were finally rescued, many of them died and the survivors grew so desperate, they resorted to cannibalism.

Rider also knew something these others

might not know. Only two years ago on the Oregon Trail west of here, there'd been a worse disaster, the Utter Party. Which was another reason a man had to be loco to go to Oregon. He might be stupid, he reasoned, but he was not loco.

He said, "We'll pull out this afternoon."

The young Adams approached him, doubling up his fists. "And I say we pull out right now."

Rider sighed and rolled his eyes, looking toward Willie's father. "Do something with the kid before I have to kill him."

"Now, son," the older Adams caught his son's arm, "let's not get into no fight."

"Yeah," agreed one of the other single men, Draper. "We don't need no more trouble right now."

The Adams boy whirled on Draper. "Who asked you to mix in?"

The taller man doubled his fists. "I don't have to take that from no short, wet-nosed boy like you."

The Adams boy went for him and they went tumbling, rolling end over end as they fought.

Rider watched and didn't move. "Somebody stop that fight because if I have to, I'll break both their heads."

Several of the men moved in to separate

the pair, but the Adams boy was red-faced and muttering curses as he backed off.

"Now," said Rider as he threw the dregs of his coffee into the fire, "we got Windlass Hill ahead of us soon, and it will take all the energy you've got. Also, let's spend some of that energy repairing wagons and cleaning weapons. The farther west we get, the more apt we are to run into a war party."

That had the desired effect. The men paled and scattered to their wagons.

Rider leaned against a tree and watched them. Things were getting too complicated. Maybe he was loco. Here he was in bad need of a woman and the only one who made his blood run hot not only didn't want him, but had gambled her life to escape his embrace. In the meantime, two beauties had offered to pleasure him. He only had to choose Francie or Millicent and stall them along until he stole the banker's gold, pulled out, and abandoned the train.

About that time, Josh came over and put his hand on Rider's arm. "Can I see Mama?"

Rider hesitated, trying not to let the big, brown eyes pull at his heart. "Sure, kid." He picked Josh up and went to check on Emma. She was asleep, but her eyes flickered open when she saw her son and she smiled.

Josh reached to pat her hand. "Me and Rider doin' fine," he assured her.

She looked at Rider, giving him a withering look that said if she had the strength and the opportunity, she'd kill him.

He could live with that, if she'd only get well. "You feeling better?"

"Thirsty," she murmured.

Rider got a dipper of cold water and held her head up so she could drink. She gulped the water and it ran down both sides of her mouth, dripping onto her breasts. He watched her drinking, wanting to kiss the drops off her face, but he did not touch her. She looked up at him, hatred and fear in her eyes. "Send — send Josh out."

"Okay." He turned to the boy. "Hey, Small Warrior, go outside and play awhile."

"Anything you say, Rider." The little boy crawled over the end of the wagon gate and disappeared.

"You bastard," she whispered. "Did you — did you . . . ?"

"Did I what?"

Her face turned crimson and he realized suddenly what she was asking.

"No, I didn't," he said. "I'm not as rotten as you think, but believe me, I wanted to. The council gave you to me, remember?"

"Never," she said and shook her head.

240

He reached out and brushed a blond curl from her eyes, his pride hurt that she hated him so much. "We'll see," he answered gently. "All you've got to do right now is gain some strength so we can move on."

She tried to raise up on one elbow. "I-I've been holding up the train?"

"It can't be helped. It was my fault. I chased you out into the night." It was the closest he could come to an apology.

She looked worried. "They'll abandon me and move on."

Rider shook his head. "Not as long as I'm in charge. Now you get some rest — we're pulling out this afternoon now that you're better."

Tears came to her big blue eyes. "I-I'm not certain I'll be able to drive."

He reached out and caught the tear, wiping it away gently. "Let me do the worrying for both of us, okay?"

And I still want you as much as ever, he thought, but didn't say it. *And I'll have you yet,* he promised himself silently as he rose and went outside. He must be the world's biggest fool, he thought with frustration, hungering for a woman who hated him. His fascination with the blonde could only be because she didn't want him; yes, that had to be it. He couldn't think much past her getting well. Then he'd deal with what to do with this woman who was his property and yet wasn't.

Later that day, the train made ready to pull out.

Several of the men looked toward Emma's wagon, young Adams and Stott among them. "What about her? Is she in any condition to handle a team?"

Rider scowled at the men. He had a feeling he didn't like — a protective, jealous feeling. "I'll drive her team myself."

They all looked disappointed, but they scattered to their own wagons. Young Adams and Draper had angry words over lining up the wagons and Rider had to shove them apart and threaten to whip them both. That Adams kid was going to kill somebody before this long trip was over. "Listen, kid, if you want to fight, we may run across some Indians in the next few weeks that'll give you all the fight you want."

The Adams boy swaggered away. "I ain't afeard of no Injuns," he flung back over his shoulder.

"Then you're a damned fool!" Rider yelled. "I don't want any more trouble, you hear? We're a long way from sheriffs and judges and jails."

Mr. Carrolton drew himself up proudly. "We'll take civilization with us to Oregon."

"Uh-huh," Rider said doubtfully. "If we get there."

He hitched up Emma's team of oxen and tied his fine horse next to the cow behind the wagon. Then he put Josh inside and whistled to the pup to follow along as he climbed up on the wagon seat. "Move 'em out!" he shouted.

Emma came awake and tried to sit up. "What — what do you think you're doing?"

"Driving your team, Missy. Someone's got to do it."

"I'll not have you —"

"Shut up and lie back down," Rider ordered. "I'm not used to people defying me and you've defied me every step of the way."

Which was why she was so appealing, he thought to himself as he pulled out on the trail at the head of the train. Emma Trent had both spirit and guts, every bit as much as a Shoshoni woman.

There was nothing she could do but lie back down and obey Rider. She lay on her quilt, watching Josh play with a toy horse, and glared at Rider's broad back. The rhythmic swaying of the wagon finally lulled her back to sleep.

She awakened with a start. "Why have we stopped?"

"We're at Windlass Hill — you want to see? For safety, you and Josh will have to get out of the wagon anyway."

She didn't want him touching her. "I — can get myself out, thank you." She tried to stand up, but her body made a liar of her. She stumbled and grabbed at the canvas cover.

In a split second, Rider was beside her. "Damn it, let me help you." Despite her denial, he swung her up in his arms and lifted her out of the wagon, depositing her under a straggly bush at the top of the hill. Then he went back for Josh.

Emma looked around and gasped. The wagons were lined up at the top of a steep incline. It looked too steep to take a wagon down. Rider came back and set Josh next to her. "Take care of your mama."

He clutched his barking dog and smiled happily up at the big man. "Anything you say."

Emma looked at the steep hill again. "Can't we go around this thing?"

Rider shook his head. "If we can get down it without wrecking the wagons, Ash Hollow is down there at the foot, all nice and green with good water."

The others had gathered around. "We can't take those wagons down that slope," Adams whined. "Why, it's almost straight down."

Rider pushed his hat back and surveyed the hill. "Other trains have done it. All it takes is patience and some guts."

Millicent Carrolton's nose went up in the air. "It isn't polite to use that word in front of ladies."

"Lady, I may say a lot worse before this day is over," Rider snapped. "All right, everyone listen to me. We'll all work together to get each of these wagons down."

Emma watched him explain how they would run a rope around a sturdy stump, then tie it onto the back axle of each wagon to send it slowly down the hill without losing it in a runaway fall that would crush the wagons and kill the oxen.

Carrolton had sweat on his upper lip. "Who's going to drive each wagon down the hill? Looks pretty dangerous."

Rider regarded him with ill-concealed contempt. "If you're not man enough to do it, Carrolton, I'll drive yours."

Thus challenged, Carrolton said he'd drive his own.

It took most of the afternoon to get the wagons down the hill. Rider had to drive most of them. Even the men handling the rope watched in nervous silence knowing if the rope broke, the wagon would plunge down the sharp slope, out of control, and kill the driver and oxen.

Finally all the wagons were down and Rider came up to retrieve Emma. She didn't want him to touch her, but she was certain she couldn't get down the hill alone. She would have to suffer his hands on her body. She could only marvel at how gentle those big hands were as he carried her to her wagon and rounded up Josh and his barking pup.

"Ash Hollow ahead," he said as he put her in the back and climbed up on the wagon seat.

She didn't argue with him as he drove toward the camping place. Soon he reined in and climbed down, reaching for her. She knew better than to argue with him, so she didn't object as he carried her outside, set her under the shade of tall trees, and handed her a canteen. "I'll take care of the stock."

She sat there sipping the cold water, enjoying the lush grass and cool shade near the creek as Rider left to unyoke her oxen and water all the animals. The banker's wife and the elegant Southern lady passed her and their noses wrinkled in distaste. So they thought of her as Rider's slut. She couldn't do anything about that at the moment. They wouldn't believe her if she denied it.

She watched Rider strip down to the barest of loincloths and take Josh out into the creek to splash. She started to call out to him to be careful, then hesitated, knowing it would be foolish. Besides, Rider seemed to be watching out for her child with great care while the puppy ran up and down the bank and barked.

Many of the men and most of the children had joined Rider in the water, splashing and washing. Wistfully, Emma imagined how cold and good the water would feel on her perspiring body, but then, of course, white women didn't shed their clothes or even show an ankle when men were around. Still, Rider and Josh seemed to be having the time of their lives splashing in the water. The sunlight reflected off Rider's dark, muscular body. There was no denying he was the most handsome, virile man on the train.

Others thought so, too. When she looked up suddenly, she saw many of the women looking him over with more than a little interest. The looks on Francesca Pettigrew and Mrs. Carrolton's faces were almost torrid. They both caught her looking at them and seemed to tear their gazes away from Rider reluctantly, while returning her gaze with hostile anger. Both women wanted Rider; Emma realized that now if she hadn't known it before. Well, they were welcome to him.

Rider came up out of the water and, carrying the laughing child, came over and stood over her. She wouldn't look at him. "You're dripping water on me."

He flopped down next to her on the grass and let go of Josh, who promptly ran back to play in the mud on the bank. "You must be feeling better — you're fussing at me."

She didn't answer him for a long moment. "I feel a lot better, so I'll drive my own team tomorrow and you can get out of my wagon."

"No," he shook his head and leaned back against the tree, reaching for his shirt. "You're still weak as a kitten. If you feel like it, you can sit on the seat next to me."

"You know I won't like that."

"But I would," he answered and gathered her up in his arms. She struggled only a moment, then realized people were watching and stopped as he lifted her. She still had some pride, even though she was sure the whole bunch now thought of her as Rider's toy.

He strode back to the wagon, his naked,

wet chest against her face. She was tempted to sink her teeth into his flesh, but decided he might howl and drop her. No, Rider wouldn't do that. She wasn't sure what he would do. Rider was a strange, complex man and she was more than a little afraid of him. She was his toy and his possession. Sometime soon, he would take her and she wasn't strong enough to stop him. No one in the train would raise a hand; they had given her to him as a gift and a bribe to make sure they all got to Oregon. Damn them for it.

He set her up on the wagon gate and began to button his shirt. "I'll get a fire going."

"I can fix my own food," she insisted and almost toppled off the seat.

"Sure you can." He reached up and steadied her. Then he turned and yelled to the others. "Let's get the camp organized. It'll be dark soon."

She watched him stride away to start a fire. He picked up Josh and gave him a ride on his broad shoulders as he busied himself with a fishing pole, the puppy jumping and barking around his feet. In less than thirty minutes, he had catfish cooking, potatoes fried, and the camp tidied up. He brought her a plate. "You doing okay?"

She thought about turning it down, but it smelled so delicious. "I don't like being obligated to you."

"Then we're even, lady." He shrugged and put the plate on the wagon gate. "The proper thing to say is 'thank you'."

She didn't like the way he was looking at her, like he'd like to take her in his arms and kiss her. "I hate you," she said and picked up the plate.

"The proper response is 'thank you,' Missy."

"I still hate you."

He shrugged. "I know. I deserve that, but sooner or later, I'll get you anyway and I don't give a damn if you hate me or not."

"Have you no shame?" This man was impossible.

"Not where you're concerned." With that, he turned and went to find Josh and fix him a plate.

Sooner or later. She shivered at the thought.

That night, she lay awake a long time, holding her breath and listening to the gentle breathing of her son. Was Rider coming to her tonight? She crawled to the end of the wagon and looked out. The camp was quiet. Rider lay asleep in his blankets on the ground at the foot of her wagon, a rifle within easy reach, the pup curled up next to him, his big stallion grazing peacefully next to her oxen. She breathed a little easier, knowing he was there; her personal guard as if she were a princess to be protected. Protected, hell! He was the one she was going to need to be protected from.

But not tonight. With a sigh of relief, Emma crawled back into her blankets and closed her eyes. The gunfighter was determined to have her; she knew that. She remembered the taste of his kisses. Maybe it wouldn't be so bad. Then she remembered that other savage and shuddered, torn and puzzled by her emotions. It was a long, long time before Emma dropped off to sleep.

The next morning, Rider still insisted on doing her chores and driving her wagon, even though she objected that she was perfectly well now. Rider ignored her as he yelled back at the others, "Head 'em up! Move 'em out!"

The train fell into line behind her wagon, following the rutted trail, continuing across the dry plains of western Nebraska. Up ahead on the far horizon she could see a giant rock and a smaller one. "What's that?"

"Courthouse Rock and the smaller one is Jailhouse Rock. They're a lot farther away than you think. After that we'll get into Wildcat Hills."

She tried to put as much space as possible between them on the seat, but the jostling kept throwing her against him.

"Make it easy on yourself, Missy," he said softly and reached out, pulling her to lean against him. She tried to pull away, but he was strong. After a moment, she gave up and leaned her slim body against his muscular one as they drove. She watched how he controlled the team, the strength of his hands as he handled the reins. This was a man to be reckoned with, sure and determined. The warmth of him, the strength of him, was almost welcome at this moment. She'd been alone so long, fighting her way through a hostile world to protect her little son.

Who was she kidding? she thought suddenly. The first chance he got, Rider was going to use her for his pleasure. She was nothing but a toy for him, a toy the council had given him to keep the virile stud away from their women and leading the train. She couldn't win against this powerful male, but she wouldn't give in easily.

"I-I'm not feeling too well," she confessed.

Rider looked down at her, concern etched on his dark, chiseled features. "Crawl in the back and take a nap with Josh. I'll handle things up here."

"But this is my team and I'm responsible —"

"Missy, stop arguing with me every time I offer a suggestion."

"I've been taking care of myself ever since my husband died."

"Then it's time you let a man take over again. Now hush and do what I tell you."

She had a sudden feeling that she couldn't win an argument with this man. With a shrug, Emma crawled in back, lay down next to Josh, and dropped off to sleep with the rhythmic sway of the wagon.

When she awakened, the late sun was slanting through the wagon but it was still moving. She crept to the front and looked past Rider at the landscape. It was flat and treeless in the hot summer sun as they moved slowly along the muddy North Platte. Rider was staring off in the distance.

"What do you see?"

"Nothing. Stop worrying."

There was something in his tone that gave her pause. She managed to pull herself up on the seat and stared off into the direction where Rider looked. There was a slight rise of hills in the distance with small clouds touching the tops. "Are those clouds? If they are, they're funny-looking clouds."

"Yeah, clouds," Rider said, but something about the tone of his voice made her take another look.

As she squinted, a small puff of white went up into the air, then another. "What is that?"

"Hush," he cautioned. "You'll wake Josh."

"Indians?" she whispered and her heart seemed to stop. "Could it — could it be Indians?"

Rider's mouth was a hard slash across his dark face. "Okay, so now you know. Smoke signals."

"Friendly Indians?"

"What do you think?"

She didn't answer. Rider's grim expression told her everything she needed to know.

Chapter Ten

"Oh, my God!" Without thinking, her hand went to her mouth.

He must have felt her tremble because he glanced over, his dark brow furrowed. "You okay?"

She managed to regain control of herself, even though the terrifying memories of being raped by a savage came rushing back to her. "Yes, I-I'm okay."

"You don't sound like it," Rider said. He pulled his pistol, checked its load, reholstered it. "Can you handle a rifle if need be?"

She nodded. "I'm a fair shot."

"Good girl." He patted her hand, his gaze on the distant horizon. "There's no way of knowing if they're friendly or not."

She put her hand on his arm. "What can I do to help?"

He looked over at her with satisfaction in his dark face. "I should have known you weren't the kind to whimper and panic."

Was he complimenting her? That made her feel warm, somehow. "I'll back you up the best I can," she said, "just tell me what to do."

He kept driving, nodding toward a distant grove of trees. "I think I'll call for an early camp without scaring the others. Some of those women would go into hysterics."

"Like Francie and Millicent?"

He actually grinned. "Like Francie and Millicent."

"Damn you, Rider. Does every woman in the world want you?"

He shook his head. "Every one but the one I want."

"Let's keep our mind on the Indians."

Rider kept driving toward the straggly cottonwood trees, his gaze on the smoke signals. "I don't know if it's a war party or they're just wanting to trade. They've been with us all afternoon."

"All afternoon? I didn't see —"

"I'm the only one who's spotted them. You have to be alert to survive out here. What do you think has kept me alive this long?"

"I figured the devil looked after his own."

"That's probably right, too."

"So what happens next?" She gripped the

seat until her knuckles turned white as the wagon swayed along, but she couldn't keep her gaze from straying to the distant puffs of smoke.

Rider shook his head. "No way to tell yet. The next move is up to them. They may be peaceful or they may be deciding whether we're strong enough to hold off an attack."

Emma bit her lip, staring at the far horizon. "When will we know?"

"Soon enough."

"That's not a cheering thought."

"Sorry. I figured you were brave enough to face the truth."

He was putting her on an equal basis. "I'm not brave," she admitted, "not brave at all."

"Well, at least I don't think you'll start screaming and carrying on like most white women. I like that in you, Sky Eyes."

"My name is Emma," she answered stiffly.

He shrugged and didn't look at her. "If you were among the Shoshoni, Sky Eyes would be a perfect name for you."

"We're not among the Shoshoni," she reminded him and watched the puffs of smoke on the horizon. "Unless that war party's Shoshoni. That's your tribe?"

He nodded. "Half. My father was a

French fur trapper."

She brightened. "Well, then, if they're Shoshoni, we'll be safe because of you."

Rider threw back his head and laughed. "I'm gonna tell you a little secret, but don't tell the others."

She got a sense of dread deep in her belly. "You trust me not to tell?"

He looked down at her as if judging her, then nodded. "I'm no safeguard against the Shoshoni — just the opposite. They catch me, they kill me as slowly and painfully as possible. They exiled me."

She looked into his dark eyes. No, he wasn't joking. She was almost afraid to ask. "Why?"

"Murder."

She was both horrified and disappointed. Somehow, she couldn't think of him as a cold-blooded killer. "So the Shoshoni want you dead and those bounty hunters did, too. Don't you have a friend in the world?"

"No, 'fraid not." Rider shook his head.

"Then I reckon we're more alike than I thought."

"You're not alone — you've got Josh."

"He likes you, Rider. Little kids have a lot of trust."

He scowled. "That's because they haven't been around long enough to find out what people are really like. He'll learn not to trust anyone."

"I hope not." She looked toward the smoke signals drifting up against the clear, hot sky. "Oh God, Rider, I'm scared."

He reached out and put his big hand over her small one. "Would it make you feel better to know I'm scared, too?"

"You?" She scoffed and pulled her hand away. "Why, you'd spit in the devil's eye and call his bluff. If anyone can get us out of this mess, it'll be you."

"Thanks for the vote of confidence. Now get in the back with Josh."

"Why — ?"

"Don't ask questions, just do as you're told," he snapped.

"I believe I've got a right to know —"

"Because if they get a look at that yellow hair, they'll want you and I don't intend to let go of you. Now get in the back."

The images his words brought to mind unnerved her. Without another word, she scrambled into the back of the wagon. She watched his broad, strong back as he drove. "Why don't they attack us? What are they waiting for?"

He shook his head, patted the Colt at his waist, and kicked the rifle at his feet with his boot. "If they were going to ambush us, they wouldn't have let us see their smoke. They may follow us for days before they decide what they're going to do."

She was shaking now, but she kept silent. Rider was strong and capable, she knew that. Probably the only man on this train who'd know what to do. She lay down with Josh, wondering how she could protect her child in case the Indians attacked.

Rider said, "I'm going to circle the wagons now so we can make some plans in case they turn out to be hostiles. Those trees will offer a little cover."

Emma crawled up and peered over the seat, staring off toward the distant sand dunes to the north. Shimmering heat waves rose off the hot, sun-baked land. "If they don't intend to attack us, what do you suppose they want?"

Rider shrugged. "They may just be following us out of curiosity. Or could be, they'll try to run off our stock later tonight. Indians are very patient — whites could learn something from them."

"You sound as if you miss the Indian way of life."

"Sometimes." He sounded wistful, but he said no more as he began to turn the wagon, shouting at the oxen as they pulled toward the ragged grove of cottonwood trees.

She remembered all the horrible stories she had heard about Indians attacking wagon trains, remembered again the terror she had lived through. More importantly, she had a small son to protect. "Might they wait for dark and attack us tonight?"

"No," Rider shook his head as he cracked his whip, "Indians, whatever tribe, hardly ever attack at night. They're afraid if they're killed after dark, their souls won't find their way to the Place Beyond the Stars."

She looked over the seat. "They aren't doing anything — just watching us from that distant rise. It gets on my nerves."

Rider laughed without mirth. "You think this is tough? If they're hostiles, the war drums going all night while they make medicine will drive you loco."

They were making a circle now, the wagon creaking as it moved under the trees.

"Rider, why do they hate us so much?"

Rider reined in his oxen. "Why shouldn't they? Who can blame any of the tribes? Hundreds of thousands of whites are crossing their lands, killing their game, using up the grass and water they need for their own horses. No wonder they're beginning to attack wagon trains. The tribes aren't stupid; they realize all these wagon trains will crowd in on the land and send them to reservations."

He climbed down from the wagon seat, signaling the wagon behind him that they would camp in the grove and to circle up. She looked out the back flap. The wagons began to make a tight circle behind them.

Rider looked up at Sky Eyes. She appeared pale and a little scared, but she wasn't sobbing or going into hysterics. He liked that in her; she had grit. Some of the Shoshoni women could take lessons from this white girl.

Now, Carrolton, the banker, and several of the others hurried to confront him.

"See here," Carrolton said, "just why are we stopping? We could get in another four or maybe five miles before dark if —"

Rider turned and pointed toward the distant smoke signals. "You folks must all be blind. If it weren't for me, you might be driving into an ambush."

"Oh, my God," said Mr. Weeks and he turned pale enough to faint.

The others set up an angry, excited buzz. "Injuns! What'll we do?"

"Do? Why, right now, nothing." Rider said. "Corral your livestock so they can't run them off and we'll set two guards tonight in case there's trouble. They might have a scout come close to check us out, see how many of us there are, and whether our horses are worth taking."

"The women," the banker wiped the sweat from his pink jowls. "What'll we do about the women?"

Rider shook his head. "Some of them are bound to see the smoke now that we're camping. Tell them as gently as possible. After all, the Indians may be harmless and just want to do some trading."

The banker looked upset, no doubt thinking about his hoard of gold. "They'll rob us?"

Rider laughed. "It's usually the other way around."

"I'm not joking," sputtered the banker.

"Neither am I," Rider said.

The two brothers-in-law, Gray and Weeks, had big drops of perspiration on their thin faces. "When will we know if they're hostiles?"

Rider shrugged. "Believe me, we'll know soon enough. Now let's get these wagons set up. We don't want to be caught off guard." Emma's little son climbed over the end of the wagon and Rider caught him. "Here, Small Warrior, you stay close to your mama and don't get away from the wagons, hear?"

The child nodded and ran to play inside the circle with his dog.

Emma started to climb down out of the wagon.

"Sky Eyes, you shouldn't put any weight on that ankle for a few days."

"I'm okay."

"I say you're not." He reached for her, swung her up easily in his arms, and carried her over to sit her on a fallen log. "You watch and I'll milk the cow and take care of the stock."

"I'm not used to being waited on."

"I know you're not. Sit still, and that's an order."

"Does anyone ever buck you?" she snapped.

"Not usually. Now behave yourself and obey me. I've got a lot to take care of right now."

She decided from the tone of his voice that Rider wasn't a man to argue with. She was weary and it felt good for a change to sit down while he handled the chores. She couldn't help but feel the annoyed and jealous gazes of some of the other women.

"Well," said Francesca Pettigrew sarcastically as she passed by, carrying a bucket of water, "what have we here, some kind of princess?"

Millicent Carrolton swished her fine skirts as she passed. "Not a princess, just that half-breed's bed toy."

"Rider's never touched me." Emma came up off the log, fuming.

"Mercy me, of course not," drawled the elegant Mrs. Carrolton. "He just carries you around like fine china because you make such great conversation."

Rider came back just then, carrying Josh on his broad shoulders. "What was that all about?"

"Nothing," she answered. "People are calling me your toy."

He lifted Josh to the ground. "That bother you?"

"Of course it does. It's a lie."

He looked deep into her eyes. "Not for long. But right now, I've got bigger problems."

"Rider, what did you tell the men?"

He shrugged. "That the Indians just might want to do some trading."

"Like what?"

"Oh, trinkets, beads, mirrors. Maybe some flour and cornmeal."

"That's all?"

He looked down at her and for the first time she saw uneasiness in his dark face. "They haven't seen many yellow-haired women."

"Rider, you wouldn't let them — ?"

"You'll be okay, baby, I promise you that. No one takes anything that belongs to Rider away from him."

There was no point in arguing with the stubborn half-breed, she decided, not when they might be facing a common enemy later.

He roasted a haunch of antelope and while she and Josh ate, he checked out the grove. Under a tree, he found two crudely made grave markers, the writing already faded from sun and rain. "Well, there's two pioneers who never made it to Oregon," he grunted to himself. These weren't the first graves they had seen as they moved across Nebraska, and he was sure they wouldn't be the last. Disease and accidents took many more lives than Indian war parties, but that wasn't much comfort right now.

He walked from campsite to campsite. "Everyone make sure their guns are loaded," he warned, "and be careful. They may not show themselves again for a couple of days or maybe not at all."

The Gray woman began to wail as she hugged her baby. "We're all gonna be massacred!"

That set a number of the women sobbing and weeping.

"Stop it!" Rider ordered. "You'll scare the kids."

Emma, despite her bad ankle, hobbled around, soothing everyone and reassuring them that everything would be all right. "Rider will take care of things," she said. "Hasn't he done a good job so far?"

That seemed to quiet most of the women and children. They all settled down for an uneasy sleep as Rider checked the camp, told every man to keep his rifle at the ready, and set up a double guard. "Young Adams, you and Stott take the first watch. Gray and Weeks, you take the second watch."

It was dark as Rider headed back to Emma's wagon. She was just heading outside the circle, into the shadow of the trees. "Where do you think you're going?"

"I need to . . . well, you know." She blushed furiously. "Please don't follow me."

"Okay, I'll put Josh to bed. Don't get too far out from the circle."

"Don't worry, I won't."

Emma limped slowly and carefully through the darkness to the bushes. Funny, she had the strangest feeling that someone was watching her. Maybe she was only imagining it. With her heart in her throat, she rearranged her clothing hurriedly and almost ran back to her wagon. She was out of breath when she got there.

Rider caught her as she fell. "What the hell — ?"

She pulled away from him, feeling a little silly now. "I-I felt someone watching me."

"You see anything?"

She shook her head.

"Let me rebandage your ankle. Then you go to bed and I'll take a look out there."

"I can change my own bandage."

"I'll do it." He sat her up on the wagon bed, then reached down and caught her small foot. His big hand neatly encircled her slim ankle.

"You just like putting your hands on me," she snapped.

"I can't deny that." He studied her wound. "It's looking better. Here, I'll put a fresh bandage on it."

He began to wrap her wound, thinking how trim her ankles were, how long her legs were. For a split second, he imagined those long legs wrapped around his hips as he came into her — bare flesh slamming against bare flesh in a heated, wild mating.

"Is something wrong? Your hands are shaking."

"What?" Rider came back to reality with a start. "Never mind, I'm finished. Now go to bed."

"You go see what scared me?"

"Sure, although it was probably a rabbit or a coyote."

"Who's on guard duty?"

Rider looked out on the plain for reassurance. "The Adams kid on one side of the circle and Stott around on the far side. Adams is angry enough all the time that I think he'll stay awake. Stott's a strange one, but he seems to be a good sentry."

"You won't go too far?" She seemed to need reassurance.

"I'll be back in a minute," he promised. With a sigh, he strode away from the wagon, stopping here and there to make sure the horses were hobbled securely, checking on Adams and Stott to make certain they were alert and had their rifles ready.

Stott seemed short of breath as he pulled his shapeless hat down on his bald head. "I don't like it," he grumbled. "I can feel them out there, prowling around in the darkness."

"Just don't take any wild shots," Rider cautioned. "You might scare the whole camp over a prairie dog."

He continued his rounds, heading for the grove of trees Emma had been so uneasy about. There wasn't anyone else in the camp awake, Rider decided. At least, they were all in their wagons. Some of the people had almost gone into a panic when Rider had told them about the Indians. These people didn't have the guts to be pioneers, he thought in disgust. No wonder no other wagon train wanted them. All the fires were burning low and nothing moved in the camp. Somewhere in the distance, a coyote howled and the sound echoed and reechoed through the darkness. *If it was a coyote,* Rider thought. Indians used many animal and bird calls to send messages to each other.

Aware of every night sound, Rider walked softly out to the bushes and stood there a long moment. There was no noise except a frog somewhere and the breeze rustling through the dried grass. The moon had gone behind some clouds. Abruptly he sensed he was not alone. He knew it with all the keen instincts that had kept him alive so long. The hair went up on the back of his neck as he heard a twig snap behind him. His hand hit leather and his Colt was in his hand as he whirled. "Who's there? Come out or I'll kill you!"

Francie stepped out of the shadows. "Good God, Rider, you about scared me out of my drawers!"

Rider relaxed and sighed with relief as he holstered his weapon. "As I remember, Francie, you don't generally wear under-wear."

She grinned at him in the moonlight. "And as I remember, you were pretty skilled at getting it off if a lady was wearin' it."

He was tired and his interest wasn't the red-haired slut. "Francie, you been out here awhile?"

"No, I just came out when I saw you headin' this way."

That mystified him. Emma wasn't the type of silly woman who panicked for no reason. "Well, just what the hell are you doing out here in the dark alone?"

"You know the answer — waitin' for you."

Oh damn. "Look, Francie, we've been over this before."

"It's her, ain't it? That blond slut satisfying you?"

Rider grabbed her roughly. "Don't call her a slut."

"Oh, so you're defending her like she was a lady."

"She's more of a lady than you'll ever be."

"She any good in the sack?" Her tone was jealous.

"That isn't a proper question and none of your damned business anyway." He wanted to get her off that subject. "Look, Francie, this is a dangerous place to be, away from the wagons. You saw those smoke signals. There could be a warrior waiting out here in the darkness to carry you off."

She laughed. "I already got a warrior who's gonna carry me off. Me and ten thousand dollars, remember?"

"Yeah," he said, but he wasn't thinking about Francie or even the money. He was thinking about a sturdy, suntanned girl with pale blue eyes. "Go back to your wagon, Mrs. Pettigrew."

As he turned to go, she caught his arm. "Stop callin' me that. It's drivin' me loco, thinkin' about you and her together while I sleep with old Roscoe."

"It ain't like that, Francie. She's different." He tried to pull away from her but she rubbed her big breasts against his chest.

"Do it to me!" she demanded. "Take me right here in the grass, here and now. I want to feel you in me, deep in me. We was good together, Rider, good and hot!"

For a long moment, he didn't pull away, remembering the heat and the passion of this woman. She knew how to satisfy a man, all right. She should; she'd satisfied enough of them when she worked at all those whorehouses. For a split second, he weakened, letting her paw at him, rub up against him. He needed a woman so badly.

Francie paused and looked up at him. "What is it with you?" she asked, her voice plaintive. "What's that blonde got that I ain't got?"

The blonde. Sky Eyes. Her small, sun-tanned face came to his mind. "Integrity and character, Francie."

She looked up at him, puzzled. "I don't know what the hell that is."

"I didn't figure you did. Neither one of us has any." He managed to break her grip and step away from her. "Francie, you must be loco. If anyone sees us out here, it will mess up all our plans."

"I'm gettin' impatient. You got a smoke?"

"Pettigrew ever seen you smoke?" He reached into his pocket for makin's and papers.

"Of course not," she laughed. "There's lots of things old Roscoe don't know about me."

He watched her roll a cigarette expertly. She had done it a million times for cowboys, no doubt after she took them to bed. "If you need a man, you got one waiting in your own wagon."

"Him?" She paused. "He makes me want to puke. It's his money — that's all I ever wanted from him."

The money and a hot redhead. Too big a temptation for any man. Rider pulled out his little match safe and lit her cigarette.

When the flame flared, he saw the lust in her green eyes. She needed him as bad as he needed a woman. All it would take was five minutes in the grass. His groin was aching just thinking about how passionate that five minutes would be.

Her sultry eyes looked up into his as she smoked. "I've been waitin' for you to give me the signal. When we gonna pull out? What about tonight?"

"Tonight?"

"Sure, leave the wagon train to the savages."

"Francie, you're a hard-hearted bitch."

She shrugged. "The old Rider would have done it without a second thought."

She was right about that. There was no good reason for him to stay and yet . . .

"I haven't decided yet when we should pull out, but tonight, everyone will be on the alert. Be patient, Francie."

"I'm damned tired of being patient. I want you, Rider, just like it used to be. I need a real man to take me down in the dirt like some squaw or slave and ride me hard. You want it, too. I can see it in your eyes. If that blond dame ain't takin' care of you, I sure can."

He was angry with her and with himself. Her for seeing the need in his eyes, himself

for wanting to do just what she suggested —
take her here and now with half a dozen
hard strokes.

He shook his head. "Get back to your
wagon, Francie, this can wait. We don't
want to botch this thing up now, do we?"
Without waiting for an answer, he turned
and strode away, back toward Emma's
wagon. Damn Francie. Damn Emma Trent,
too. One was a slut, the other as cold as
stone. The blonde was his possession, yet
he'd never possessed her. Francie had built a
fire in him. If he was going to get killed in an
Indian attack tomorrow, it was a shame to
pass up the temptation of Sky Eyes's ripe
body tonight. She was his, the wagon train
had given her to him for his amusement and
pleasure. He was letting a woman make a
fool of him and he didn't like that thought.
Tonight, he was going to take what was his
and the devil take the hindmost. Tomorrow,
when this crisis with the Indians was over,
he was going to wish all women to hell, steal
the banker's gold, and ride out without a
backward glance!

Francie leaned against a tree and smoked
her cigarette. Damn that half-breed anyhow.
She wasn't sure what was happening to
Rider, but he seemed to be changing

somehow. She wanted the old Rider back. Well, she'd get him yet. He was only a man, after all, with a man's weakness. She sighed wistfully and watched the smoke from her cigarette drift in the moonlight. That stupid Emma Trent was missing a real treat. Rider was the best and most skilled lover Francie had ever had. He was not only big enough to make a gal gasp when he came into her, he was never in a hurry and he knew just how to stroke and caress, where to kiss to make a woman dig her nails into that muscled back and beg for more.

The moon went behind clouds again and it was as dark as the inside of a well. Rider had disappeared. She pictured him lying in his blankets, staring into the darkness and thinking about what Francie could give him out here in the bushes. Her own need was great enough that she was willing to wait a few minutes to find out if he'd think it over and return.

She ground out the cigarette under her heel. At that moment, she heard a slight noise behind her and identified it as a man's heavy breathing. "Rider?"

Rider couldn't have gotten behind her; she'd watched him leave. It had to be someone else. Indians? She opened her lips to scream and a hand clapped over her mouth and pulled her up against a big male body. She could feel his arousal against her back and all thoughts of passion fled. She began to fight, but one big hand had gone around her waist and was now clawing at her breasts. Even as she struggled, her unknown assailant dragged her deeper into the brush.

Rider had hesitated at Emma's wagon. She'd thrown his blankets under her wagon. That independent gesture angered him. Who did she think she was? He took off his gun belt, climbed over the tailgate, and looked around. In the moonlight, he could see Josh asleep on his little pallet in the front of the wagon bed. Sky Eyes lay spread out, her yellow hair spilling across the quilt like gold. The temptation was too great.

Softly, so as not to wake her, Rider lay down beside her, watching her. The swell of her breasts moved gently as she breathed. He put out his hand and touched her hair. It was soft as golden cornsilk. God, how he wanted her.

Her eyes flickered open and he saw the alarm in her face. "Hush," he whispered. "You'll wake Josh."

"Get out of here," she said and he heard the tension in her voice.

"You belong to me," he said softly, "and

I've yet to claim you." He reached out and caught her small shoulder, pulling her to him.

He wasn't sure what he expected, whether it was that she might come into his arms with eager heat, or fight him like a hellcat as he put his mouth on hers, forcing her lips apart. Instead, as he put his tongue in her mouth, caressing its velvet interior, she simply lay there without moving.

Puzzled, he kissed her deeper still, his hand moving to caress her breast outside her clothing, pressing his swollen manhood against her. His need was throbbing, urgent, but she lay there almost limp and lifeless. "What's wrong with you?" he muttered. "Kiss me back or fight me, but don't lie there like a dead woman."

She didn't move. "I'm yours to use as you wish, so use me."

He kissed her again, hungrily, his hands roaming her body, tangling in her hair, but she did not respond except to tremble slightly. "Damn you!" he muttered. "This isn't what I want! I want more than this!"

She looked up at him calmly as he hovered over her. "That's all you'll get. Now if that's enough, take it."

He sat up, angry enough to strike her. "This isn't the way I want it, Sky Eyes, you lyin' there like a paid whore."

"That's what you're making of me." Only then did the moon shine on her face and he saw the tears pooling there and the fear. At that moment, he wanted to gather her into his arms, kiss her gently, hold her close and protect her. Hell, he was the one she needed protection from.

He'd sworn to kill any man who touched her and he was that man. With an oath, he stumbled out of the wagon, leaned against the wagon gate and tried to roll a cigarette with shaking hands. Damn her for tying him in knots like this. He wanted more than she was willing to give; he wanted . . . hell, he didn't know what he wanted. No woman had ever made him feel like this before. He didn't like this confusion of feelings, didn't like it at all.

Abruptly, from the distant grove, a woman screamed. *Francie*. He'd know that voice anywhere. Throwing down his cigarette and grabbing up his gun belt, Rider took off at a run.

Chapter Eleven

Francie fought like she had never fought before, trying to break free of the unseen hands that had reached out of the darkness to grab her. *Injuns,* she thought. *They're gonna rape and scalp me.*

The thought terrorized her into greater action. She twisted her head, wrenching her mouth so that she got the hand that imprisoned her between her teeth and bit down hard.

The man shouted and hit her across the face even as she screamed. When she screamed again, he turned her loose and fled. She heard him crashing through the bushes as she screamed and screamed. In the camp, she saw lanterns light up as sleepy people came out of their wagons and grabbed weapons.

Rider's heart was in his throat as he gripped his gun belt and ran through the dry grass toward the screams. If the Lakota

managed to surround them in the darkness
. . . Behind him, men were shouting questions to each other, women's voices cracked
with hysteria, and newly awakened children
cried.

The moonlight revealed Francie in a heap
on the ground, her dress torn and her face
bloody. "Are you all right? What happened?"

She didn't answer for a long moment,
only sobbed as she stumbled to her feet.
"Injuns! An Injun reached out of the dark
and grabbed me, tried to carry me off!"

Rider remembered abruptly how Sky
Eyes had been spooked. It could have been
the blonde who'd been grabbed rather than
tough little Francie.

Now they were surrounded by men of the
wagon train, all shouting questions.

"My Lord," swore the banker, "Francesca, darling, are you hurt? What were you
doing out here alone?"

Rider made a gesture of dismissal. "Never
mind all that — she's not hurt."

"But the blood —" protested the banker.

"I bit him," Francie said. "He tore my
pretty dress."

"You poor dear," the banker said and
gathered her into his ample arms. "I'll buy
you ten dresses when we get to Oregon. As

for that war party —"

"They've fled by now, if it was Indians," Rider said. "I'll take a look around."

The Adams boy and Stott ran up just then.

Stott asked, "What happened?"

"You two see anything?" Rider asked. "Someone tried to grab Mrs. Pettigrew."

Under the shapeless hat, Stott's eyes grew round with fright. "Injuns? We got Injuns?"

Rider ran his hand through his black hair in frustration. "You sentries didn't see a thing?"

They both shook their heads.

"Well, try to keep a little better lookout the rest of the night — and you women don't venture outside the circle, no matter what."

The banker handed his handkerchief to the sobbing Francie. "Dear, what were you doing so far from the wagons?"

"I-I was doing something personal," Francie said and looked away modestly.

"Never mind." Roscoe patted her shoulder. "You come back to the wagon now. I think I may have some brandy. You've had quite a scare for a lady."

"I could use a stiff belt," Francie said.

"What?"

"I-I mean, a sip of sherry might revive me."

Rider motioned the men back toward the camp. "I'll take a look around and see if I find anything. You sentries return to your posts and keep a closer watch."

"I wasn't asleep," big, clumsy Stott said.

"I wasn't either," young Adams declared, but he yawned and blinked.

"I wasn't accusing you of anything," Rider said. "Go on back to your posts."

Everyone returned to the wagons and Rider made a wide circle, pausing to listen now and then. If there was a war party out here in the brush, he couldn't imagine them sending one man in to carry off a woman; it didn't make any sense. The whole thing was a puzzle. Finally he shook his head and headed back to Emma's wagon.

She was sitting up, a quilt around her shoulders. "Was it Indians?"

"Somehow I don't think so, but I'm not sure. You were right — there was someone lurking out there. He grabbed Francie."

"Francie?"

"Uh, Mrs. Pettigrew."

"So you do know her much better than you admit. Is she all right?"

Rider nodded. "Fine — just shaken up. I don't think anyone will get much sleep.

They all see Indians in every shadow."

She looked around and shivered. "You don't think they'll come in at night?"

He shook his head. "Probably not." He turned away.

"Where are you going?" She sounded alarmed. "You aren't leaving?"

Rider shrugged. "You made it pretty clear I wasn't welcome."

"Could you — could you maybe sleep underneath my wagon?"

He started to say something curt and arrogant, but saw the fear in her eyes and sighed. "Okay, I'll sleep under your wagon so if there's any trouble, I'll be here."

"Thank you for that." Her voice was soft, gentle.

He must be loco to play by her rules. Always before, Rider had made the rules. "Think nothing of it," he snapped.

"Thank you anyway," she whispered. "Josh and I are much obliged."

"I'd rather you were grateful in a different way." He felt testy, thinking about sleeping on the hard ground with her in a featherbed just a couple of feet above his head.

"What?"

"Never mind." Cursing under his breath, he stalked off to get his blankets and weapons, then curled up under her wagon with the dog. The pup snuggled up against him and wagged its tail. "Boots, you definitely weren't the member of this family I expected to share a bed with, but I suppose you'll have to do."

The pup curled up and dropped off to sleep. Rider didn't sleep much. He must be the world's biggest damned fool. He heard her turn over above him and imagined how soft and warm it must be in her bed. He closed his eyes, imagining the scene, imagining her kissing him.

Rider came awake suddenly and realized that it was the pup's wet tongue on his face. "Quit hogging the blanket, Boots," he grumbled. "You ain't what I had in mind."

Emma had lain awake a long, long time, imagining Rider lying just under her wagon. The thought of him so close made her feel both uneasy and at the same time, safe. She hadn't felt safe in a long, long time. Safe? She threw back her head and laughed. This gunfighter had made it very clear that he intended to have her body, sooner or later. Yet tonight, it was reassuring to have him sleeping so close by. Once she heard him talking to the pup and smiled. In spite of his rough, hard ways, he was kind to dogs and children.

She reminded herself that when they reached Oregon, or even before, Rider would drift on and she and her son would be on their own as they had always been. She remembered his kiss and the way she had felt when his big, rough hands caressed her skin. Her own unaccustomed feelings had scared her almost as much as his touch.

The next morning, when she woke before dawn, Rider was already out from under her wagon. *Indians,* she remembered with sudden dread, *today we'll have to deal with those Indians.* The thought made her hands shake with fear, remembering the ugly Cheyenne brave who had raped her and murdered her gentle husband.

She got up, helped Josh into a clean shirt, and limped outside. Her ankle was healing fast, although she'd always have that small scar where Rider's knife had cut her. The others were stirring, too, cooking breakfast, feeding livestock, glancing nervously toward the sandy hills.

Emma poked up her fire and began to make coffee as Rider emerged from the bushes and came between wagons to her fire. "I was wondering where you were."

He shrugged and sat down on a rock near her fire. "I went out to see the area where

Mrs. Pettigrew was attacked."

"Find anything interesting?"

"Tracks."

She poured a cup of coffee and handed it to him. "Well?"

Rider shook his head and sipped the coffee. "No tribe that I'm aware of wears boots."

She paused in dishing up some bacon and biscuits. "Every man on this train wears boots."

"That's true. Don't mention this, okay?" He took the plate.

Emma nodded. "You know you can trust me, Rider."

He looked at her thoughtfully and nodded. "I know that." He drank his coffee.

Josh toddled over and sat down next to Rider, the puppy panting at his feet. "We go today?"

Rider smiled and patted his shoulder. "Sorry, Small Warrior, we're expecting company. We'd better stay forted up."

He and Emma exchanged glances.

"Can I ride your horse?"

"Storm? He's hard to handle, but you can ride behind me when we leave out."

Josh chortled with delight and ran off to brag to the other children.

Emma poured Rider some more coffee.

"Thank you for being kind to him — he's not used to it."

Rider shrugged. "Damned shame. He's a gritty little kid. Any man ought to be proud to have him for a son."

She sipped her coffee and didn't look at him. "That's what I'm hoping — that some man in Oregon will marry me and help me raise him."

Rider snorted. "Some prissy shopkeeper or farmer? White families don't want a half-breed kid."

She caught the bitterness in his voice that betrayed what a hard, lonely time Rider had had in the white world. "I'll settle for any man who'll be kind to him."

"What about yourself? Don't you want anything for yourself?" He looked at her over his coffee cup.

"Once I hoped . . ." She paused, shook her head. "Little girls dream of handsome princes on fine steeds who'll romance them and carry them off, but I've grown more realistic with everything that's happened."

Rider frowned.

"What's the matter?"

He shook his head. "Nothing." How could he admit to her that the image of some fat shopkeeper claiming her as his bride at the end of this trip upset and annoyed him

288

very much? "You won't have any trouble getting a man. You're pretty and there's a shortage of women in Oregon."

"Farmer Adams says his brother has a big general store and is looking —"

"Spare me the details," Rider snapped. He stood up abruptly, tossed the last few drops of coffee into the fire, and handed the cup to her without a word. Then he turned and strode away, leaving her puzzled and annoyed at his rudeness. She begin to gather up the tin dishes, thinking that though he seemed a complex, troubled man, at least the wagon train was in strong, capable hands under his leadership.

The sun moved relentlessly across the sky and still the warriors had not shown themselves. Rider insisted the train stay forted up and the animals contained within the circle. Everyone's nerves were frayed.

"Look," said the banker, "we ought to be moving on. Nobody's seen any Injuns this morning — they've ridden away."

Rider watched the horizon and shook his head. "They're out there, watching us."

The Adams boy's face turned an angry red. "Then why in the hell don't they show themselves?"

"Easy, Shorty," Draper laughed. "You'll get to kill some Injuns sooner —"

"Who you callin' 'Shorty'?" The boy went for the taller man, but Rider caught his arm. "If you want to fight, kid, save it for later. A war party may bring you all the fight you need."

Stott pulled his shapeless hat down over his bald head. "This drives me crazy, doin' nothing."

Rider shrugged. "It's meant to. White men need to learn patience — that's why they have so much trouble dealing with Indians."

Weatherford B. Carrolton adjusted his fine silk cravat. "But we're losing time," he drawled, "waiting for them to show themselves —"

"Would you rather lose your life or have your woman — ?" He didn't finish the sentence; there was no need to.

Emma saw the women exchange glances and in her mind, she was lying across a bloody bed again, being mounted by a sweating savage. "I'd rather die than go through that again," she said softly.

Rider reached out and put his hand on her shoulder. "Are you okay?"

"I-I — sure." She swallowed hard and shook his hand off.

The hot July day dragged by slowly.

Mr. Weeks cleared his throat. "Maybe

Pettigrew's right. Maybe they're not out there," he said. "Maybe —"

"They're out there," Rider said with certainty as his dark eyes scanned the horizon. "They may be playing a waiting game, hoping we'll break and run. A wagon train's much more vulnerable if it's strung out along the trail."

The banker paced up and down, taking off his derby occasionally to wipe his florid face. "We can't just sit here —"

"Yes, we can," Rider said stoically. "We have to wait. The next move is theirs."

It was late afternoon before the Indians finally showed themselves again, strung out on a distant ridge, watching the circled wagons. There must have been several dozen of them.

Rider sat his horse. "I was afraid of that — they're Lakota, all right. I was hoping for Pawnee or Kaw. Now we'll find out what they want."

The young Adams boy raised his rifle. "I don't give a damn what they want! I want to kill me an Injun!"

Rider galloped over, freed one boot from his stirrup, and kicked the rifle away. "Are you loco? Can't you see they're out of range? Besides, we're outnumbered. Now everyone hush and listen! Don't show any fear and don't make any sudden moves they might see as hostile."

Emma was scared as anyone, but she only pulled her little boy close and watched the silent riders in the distance. Around her, women began to sob.

The riders came toward them at a lope, drew up a few hundred yards out, and studied the wagons. They were handsome, big specimens on mostly spotted horses, Emma noted. Feathers and bright brass coins reflected the light from their lances. She looked over at Rider, who studied the group.

"Lakota, all right," he muttered. "At least they aren't wearing war paint. Maybe they just want to trade. I'll go out and palaver."

Emma caught his stirrup as he passed. "Aren't they liable to kill you?"

He shrugged. "They can try. Shoshoni and Lakota are not on good terms, even if the Laramie Treaty tried to fix things."

"Don't you want to take some men with you?"

Rider looked around at his men and sighed. "I think I'll be better off alone. Some of these hotheads are liable to panic and start shooting."

He was the bravest, coolest man she had ever known and she was suddenly afraid for him, afraid of what they would do without him. She hadn't realized how much she had come to depend on him. "Rider, what do we do if you don't come back?"

"You can handle a rifle, can't you?"

She nodded.

"Then hold them off as long as you can — try to kill their leader. They'll think it's a bad omen and maybe ride out."

"And if they don't?"

He looked dead serious now as he un-buckled his gun belt and tossed it to her. "Sky Eyes, save two bullets." He paused as if to let his words sink in. "Do you under-stand?"

One for herself, one for Josh. Oh, dear God. The gun belt was heavy in her hands. "I-I understand."

"That's my good girl." Now he turned his horse and trotted slowly out to meet the si-lent Indians while the wagon train watched.

Rider felt as tense as a wired trap as he rode toward the group, his hand in the air by way of greeting. They were Lakota, all right. Their painted ponies and the decorations on their weapons and buckskin moccasins told him that. He noted with relief that they wore no war paint, though old scalps flut-tered in the wind from their ponies' bridles.

He reined in a few yards from where their

leader sat a fine pinto stallion. The warrior's face was immobile, curious, and his warbonnet carried numerous eagle feathers, denoting his rank and many brave deeds.

Rider held up his hand again and waited.

The other looked him over, nodded with satisfaction, and said in a mix of broken English and border Spanish, "You face us alone?"

Rider took a deep breath. "A brave man needs no help when he faces another brave and honorable man."

"Well spoken. What tribe are you?"

Rider hesitated. He could lie, of course, but his horse wore a beaded bridle of Shoshoni make and he was certain the Lakota had noted it. "My mother was Shoshoni."

The other nodded silently, but around him, his men muttered and moved restlessly.

"I am Wolf's Eyes," said the leader.

Rider nodded. "I have heard of your many feats. I am called Rider."

A murmur through the Lakota braves.

"Rider?" said Wolf's Eyes.

Rider nodded. "My deeds are not so famous as yours."

The other gestured. "All tribes know of the exiled dog soldier, Rides the Thunder, who now rides the white trail."

Rider took a deep breath. "Tell me, great chieftain, Why do you come this far west?"

"We seek buffalo and have seen none," the leader said and looked toward the wagon train. "The white men, with their wagons and farms, have killed all the game or caused it to scatter."

"What you say is true," Rider said. "That is why I lead this bunch far, far away." He gestured toward the west.

The Lakota warriors looked toward the wagon train again and Rider noted how lean some of them looked. From somewhere over the rise, he heard a baby crying. "You travel with your women?"

"A few," the other said. "We have been hunting many suns and have seen little meat."

They were hungry, Rider realized suddenly — hungry, but proud. They also knew the wagon trains would have food. "We would be most honored if you and your people would feast with us tonight," Rider said solemnly.

The other considered a long moment, then smiled a slow smile. "We will smoke a pipe and talk of the olden days."

Rider nodded. "When the only white men in the West were the few like my father who trapped the beaver and otter, and was always a friend to all red men," Rider said. His father had become Shoshoni in his heart and customs. Where he had been taken by the Cheyenne, they found his final, defiant gesture: his knife plunged to the hilt in the ground and broken off so he could not be disgraced by being scalped with his own knife when enemy warriors overran his position.

"It is good," Wolf's Eyes said finally. "We will come at sundown." He turned and translated and the braves smiled and nodded, talking among themselves.

"Until tonight." Rider touched the brim of his Stetson in salute, turned, and galloped back to the wagon train. *Tonight,* he thought, *tonight we must make the Lakota happy, or we'll all be slaughtered before daylight.*

Chapter Twelve

"Everyone break out all the food you've got, and sugar, especially sugar," he shouted, swinging down off his horse.

Weatherford B. Carrolton drew himself up proudly. "We're not going to feed those red devils, are we?"

"You'd better believe we are," Rider said. "Now everyone gather round and listen. I don't know how many of them there are, but we've got to put on a feast with plenty of coffee and anything else we can rustle up."

Fat Mrs. Adams shook her head. "We've barely got enough food for ourselves, much less a bunch of thieving —"

"If you want to live through the night," Rider warned, "treat them with respect and give them as much food as we can spare. You men gather up your tobacco."

The banker blinked. "You don't mean my fine, expensive cigars — ?"

"And any other tobacco you've got,"

Rider said. "We've got to send them away happy."

Draper said, "What about whiskey?"

Rider shook his head. "Hide the whiskey — it'll only bring us trouble. Maybe they'll be happy with sugared coffee."

Emma felt herself blanch. "Must they come into our camp? What if something goes wrong?"

He looked at her pale face and immediately understood. "Stay out of their way and close to me."

Mrs. Carrolton began to weep. "We're going to be massacred, I just know it!"

"Oh, shut up," Emma snapped, "and start cooking!"

"Put away the weapons, too," Rider said. "We want to appear friendly."

Willie Adams scowled. "I'd like to take me an Injun scalp."

Draper sneered. "Shorty, you ain't takin' nobody's scalp 'less you become a barber."

"Don't call me Shorty!" He lunged at the taller man.

Rider tripped Adams and grabbed him as the boy stumbled to his feet. "Look, you two, you can beat each other senseless later in the trip. Right now, we've got to entertain some Lakotas." He turned and pointed.

The Lakotas were gathering up on the

hill, women and children among them.

Stott took off his hat and stared, licking his lips. "They got some pretty women."

"Leave their women alone," Rider ordered, "unless you want to lose your hair. What happened to your hand?"

Stott looked down at his swollen finger. "Mashed it with the butt of my rifle when I tripped and fell."

It looked more like a bite, but Rider didn't say so. He had plenty to deal with right now.

Within the hour, the Lakotas rode in. They looked weary and thin, but it was obvious they had worn their best to impress the whites. Quill work and colorful feathers decorated their buckskin clothing. Behind the braves came a dozen or so women, serious wives carrying babies slung in cradleboards on their horses. Here and there rode a pretty, younger girl, all shy smiles and flirtatious dark eyes.

Rider stepped forward and, in his best border Spanish and sign language, welcomed the somber leader and his men to the encampment as they dismounted. Although he smiled, Rider felt uneasy at allowing this many Indians inside the perimeters of the camp. He had put his holster and pistol within easy reach under a blanket next to Emma's wagon, but he knew they didn't have a chance if something went wrong.

With great ceremony, he ushered Wolf's Eyes and his men to the best spots by the fire. The women hung back in the shadows, uncertain and nervous. Rider brought out Banker Pettigrew's fine cigars with a flourish. "Good smoke," he said.

The older warrior's serious face brightened. "Much smoke," he agreed.

Rider passed the cigars around to the braves and they lit them with a burning branch from the fire. The other white men watched, fidgeting. Rider gestured to them to sit and have a cigar. The banker frowned. "Do you know how much those cigars cost?"

"What's your life worth?" Rider muttered and nodded to Wolf's Eyes, who smiled and blew a puff of smoke.

"Whiskey?" grunted a brave.

Rider took a deep breath. "No whiskey, but plenty of coffee and sugar." He motioned to Emma to begin pouring the coffee, made the way the tribes liked it — strong and very sweet.

The white men sat sullenly; the white women seemed to be as withdrawn as the Indian wives. The white women came forward reluctantly, pouring the coffee for the group around the fire.

One of the younger warriors looked Sky Eyes over appreciatively as she poured his coffee and said in broken English to Rider, "I would give ten ponies for this yellow-haired woman."

Emma blanched and stepped back.

Rider paused. "I am deeply honored that my woman pleases your eyes."

The younger man looked disappointed. "She is your woman?"

Rider nodded. "That is my fine son standing by her."

Emma looked at him in surprise, but he gave her just the slightest shake of his head.

Pettigrew came close and whispered in Rider's ear. "Do they have anything we'd like to trade for?"

Rider sighed and smoked his cigar. "Don't be in such a rush — you'll offend them. Indians are never in a hurry and they consider haste to be bad manners."

The old chief, Wolf's Eyes, looked toward Mrs. Carrolton and Francie and said in broken English, "He talks of trade? Some of our braves would trade fine horses or good weapons for white wives."

Mrs. Carrolton blanched. "Why, the nerve of him. Me sleep with some filthy —"

"Carrolton," Rider commanded, "control

your wife before she creates big trouble for us."

"Millicent, dear," the elegant gentleman caught her arm, "Please don't —"

She jerked out of his grasp and fled to her wagon. The air was tense again. Rider looked around at the whites. "Everyone smile and bring out food, anything you can spare."

The old chief tasted the heavily sweetened coffee and licked his lips. "Much good." To Rider, he said, "Are you staying in our land or moving on?"

"We are moving on," Rider assured him. "We do not intend to trespass on your buffalo lands."

The handsome young one grumbled, "Even the whites who pass through cause trouble. Their livestock eats up all the grass so there is none left for the buffalo and they either use up or foul the water — besides the diseases they bring."

Rider nodded. "I agree. However, we do not stay. Tomorrow, we move on and I pray your hunt will find luck from having supped at our fire."

"Well spoken!" the old chief said and smoked his cigar. Emma hurried to pour him more coffee and he looked her over critically. "She is young and strong, Rider, and your son is big. It is past time for you to put another child in her belly."

Rider held back a grin as he looked at her flushed face. "I quite agree, Wolf's Eyes, and I intend to do just that." He signaled the women to begin serving big kettles of boiled mush covered with molasses and salted pork cooked with beans.

The nerve of Rider! Emma had been fearful, but now the gunfighter's arrogant words almost made her protest. Then she remembered that one of the braves had offered to trade for her and that only Rider's claim of ownership had protected her.

The tension lessened now as the white women finished filling tin plates for the men and began to serve the Lakota women. The prettiest of those girls, a maiden probably not as old as herself, reached out in wonder to touch Emma's yellow hair. Instead of pulling away with an oath as the red-haired banker's wife did, Emma managed to smile. The Lakota girl smiled back.

As the evening wore on, the tension relaxed. Soon the braves and Rider were laughing and talking, sometimes about hunting, as little as Emma could understand, or battles they had fought. Scrawny Mr. Gray brought out his fiddle and began to play. Wolf's Eyes listened for a long moment before he turned to Rider. "It sounds like an animal in pain."

Rider laughed and handed him another cigar, but he frowned slightly as young Adams, Stott, Draper, and some of the others grabbed Indian girls and began to dance them around the circle. The Lakota men watched somberly.

"Whiskey!" yelled one of the white men. "We got whiskey! Let's celebrate a little!"

Rider came up off the ground, but the damage was already done. Stott stumbled into the circle, carrying a jug under his arm. It was evident he had already been drinking. "I got whiskey." The braves smiled and nodded approval.

"It is a fine celebration," Wolf's Eyes said and reached for the liquor. He took a long pull and passed it to Rider.

He must not insult his guest, but he needed all his wits about him. Rider only pretended to drink and then passed the bottle on. There was no way to put the bottle away now without insulting the Lakota and maybe there was only enough for everyone to have a sip or two.

Just then, a brave stumbled into the fire-light, holding up two bottles he'd found hidden. Rider cursed under his breath. Things could get ugly now and the settlers were outnumbered. Any hopes he'd had for merely feeding the Indians and then ushering them out of the camp faded fast. The celebration began to build and get louder.

It was going to be a long night, Emma thought as she left for a few minutes to put Josh to sleep. Josh complained loudly. He wanted to stay by the fire and play with the Lakota children. It occurred to Emma that besides Rider, her son had not seen many people as brown-skinned as himself. Behind her, the feast seemed to be getting more boisterous.

With a sense of uneasiness, Emma returned to the fire. Fueled both by whiskey and maybe relief that the Indians were friendly, little Mr. Gray was playing fast and furious. The white men and the Lakota were drinking freely and she could see the strain on Rider's face. He was expecting the worst. Emma knew that he couldn't very well take the liquor away once it had been offered without offending the guests. Most of the white women had left the scene and gone to their wagons, but many of the men, white and brown, seemed to be drunk, except Rider. Even some of the Lakota women were sipping from the bottles as they were passed around.

Rider looked toward Emma and caught

her eye. His expression was grim and worried. "Sky Eyes, go to bed," he ordered.

"But —"

"I said go to bed."

She paused, then realized the younger brave who had tried to trade for her was staring at her and Rider had seen it. Perhaps Rider figured with liquor flowing, she'd be safer out of sight. She nodded, turned, and returned to her wagon. She didn't sleep. From inside as she settled down, the celebration sounded louder with much music and laughter. Maybe soon the whiskey would be exhausted and the Lakota would all ride out. There was nothing she could do but lie here and hope that Rider could stay in control of the situation.

Stott took another swig from the bottle and wiped his mouth on his sleeve, looking around. Men and women drank and danced around the fire, some of the Lakota women as drunk as the men. Only Rider looked sober, sitting by the fire as if expecting trouble.

Stott swayed on his feet. A woman was what he needed now. He hadn't had a woman in months and it was always on his mind. The two he'd wanted most, the yellow-haired one and the fire-haired one, had managed to escape from him when he went after them and he was afraid that half-breed scout, Rider, suspected him. That damned savage would probably geld him for even looking at his woman.

Off toward the farthest part of the firelit circle, the prettiest of the young Indian girls caught Stott's eye: Wolf's Eyes's daughter.

The thought made Stott's groin tighten. Shoving his shapeless hat low on his bald head, he circled around through the darkness to her and smiled.

She was timid, smiling as if not sure what he wanted. He gave her his warmest grin and held up a bottle of whiskey and a cheap necklace. She was entranced with the beads and tried to take it from him. Stott shook his head. Then tapping his chest and pointing to her, he indicated that they should go off in the darkness together.

The girl hesitated, looking with longing at the beads. Stott smiled again, holding the prize just out of her reach. Again he made motions they should go sit somewhere and he would give her the present.

Again she hesitated, looking toward the fire as if she should ask permission or advice. At that moment, Stott handed her the bottle and indicated she should taste the whiskey. It made her choke and cough, but she smiled at Stott and looked at the necklace again.

He took another drink and offered her the bottle. This time, she took a long drink. He looked toward the fire. The old chief was drinking and telling stories with Rider. Most of the other Lakota women seemed to have left, maybe ridden back to their camp.

The girl indicated that she should go, too. Stott shook his head, smiled, and held up the necklace so that the glass beads caught the firelight. He took another drink and offered her one. When she tried to refuse, he held it to her mouth until she swallowed. She swayed on her feet, looking up at him with a shy smile, and reached for the beads.

Stott grinned and shook his head. "You must give me a gift in return," he said, breathing heavily.

She indicated she didn't understand. He took her hand and led her into a grove of trees behind the farthest of the wagons. They passed that Trent woman's wagon and that damned pup came out from under the wagon and barked at the couple as they passed. Stott aimed a kick at the dog, intending to kill it, but then he remembered the pup was a favorite of Rider's and there was no telling what he'd do to the man who hurt it. He heard the Trent woman call to the mutt to be quiet.

Damn, if he'd known that yellow-haired wench was alone in her wagon, he would have gone after her. Stott thought about it for a split second, then decided Rider would do more than kill him if Stott touched her. Well, the Trent slut and her half-breed brat could go to hell; this pretty Injun squaw would serve his purpose.

Stott led the girl to a little wash half-hidden by tall weeds, sat down, and patted the soft grass beside him. The girl swayed on her feet a little, looking behind her toward the campfire now out of sight. Evidently she sensed danger or had been warned about how white men treated Indian girls. Stott gave her his most disarming smile and patted the ground beside him again, holding out the necklace. She hesitated and he caught her wrist, pulled her down, and offered her the bottle.

The girl took a drink and looked longingly toward the beads in Stott's hand. Very slowly, he dropped it over her head, his fingers touching the swell of her breasts under the bright glass. She looked up at him, smiling and happy.

"Now, honey," he whispered, "you're gonna pay ol' Stott for them beads." He leaned over, tangled his hands in her braids, and kissed her.

She reacted with a surprised start, but Stott didn't let go; instead, he reached for her with both hands, deepening the kiss, forcing his tongue between her lips. She made a sound of dismay, but with the laughter and the music from the big campfire, it sounded no louder than a sigh.

"You're gonna take me, honey," Stott said against her mouth and began to fumble with the top of her doeskin dress. She tried to pull away from him, but he had his mouth on hers so she couldn't cry out. One of his big hands, the one with the bite marks still visible, jerked her even closer as his other hand tore the top of her dress, his dirty paw fumbling to cover and squeeze her breasts.

She was fighting to get away now but Stott had been frustrated by women long enough. They never wanted to let him do it to them — never. Hadn't he served time in prison for trying? She was only an Injun squaw and who'd care if Stott dipped into her warm honey?

Easily, he forced her to the ground, his hot, wet mouth still on hers, his big hand ripping at her shift until she was naked and vulnerable under him. She was fighting him now, clawing at his face as he unbuttoned his pants, but she was a small thing, no match for him. His shapeless hat tumbled off and she raked his bald head with her nails, so he slapped her.

He grunted his satisfaction when he saw her bare body in the moonlight, soft and full with breasts to make a man want to suck and bite them. He fought to get between her thighs, his hand over her mouth. "Only a minute," he grunted. "Let me have you once or by God — !"

She was fighting him but he was determined. She managed to pull her face away and tried to scream. In response, he cursed and twisted the string of beads around her neck, desperate to shut her up. "Damn you, red wench, don't you understand I'm tradin' the beads for a little lovin'?"

Obviously she didn't, because she continued to struggle even as he tightened the twisted beads around her throat. He had to have her; he just had to. She was fighting him, making gasping sounds, but he twisted the necklace even tighter as he forced himself between her thighs. She must not scream out until he was finished with her and then, who'd believe a drunken squaw?

"Stop it, damn you," he muttered through gritted teeth as he tightened his hold. "Don't you understand what I want? Lay still and let me do it to you!"

Maybe she understood now because she gradually stopped fighting. He tore at her buckskin shift, desperate to take her — too desperate. Even as he freed his throbbing manhood from his pants and it brushed against her warm thigh, he lost his seed all over her buckskin dress.

Cursing mightily, he staggered to his feet. "Hell, you can get up now. I didn't even get in — and you can keep the damned necklace."

She didn't answer or move.

Uneasy, Stott stared down at her. The moon came out from behind clouds and Stott took a good look at his captive. Her eyes were open in terror and her mouth was formed in a silent scream, the cheap string of beads cutting deep into her neck. He could only stare, the whiskey clouding his mind as he tried to understand what the moonlight revealed. There was no mistake; the pretty Lakota girl was dead.

Chapter Thirteen

Rider kept a watchful eye as the party grew louder and more drunken. He tried to stop the flow of whiskey, but it was already out among the settler men and the Lakota. *Who could he trust among the wagon train men to help him if things got worse?* He looked around, realizing that he had no faith in any of them.

He kept his rifle and his six-shooter within easy reach and stayed on the alert as the evening wore on and the dancing and feasting got louder. Most of the white women had sneaked off to their wagons and many of the white men were stumbling drunk along with the warriors. Gradually people began to slump on the ground in a drunken stupor. Finally the food and the liquor ran out and the Lakota mounted their horses and rode out into the night.

With a sigh of relief, Rider looked around to see if any of the white men were sober enough to help him guard the camp, but they all seemed either drunk or asleep. He stood guard the rest of the night alone, waiting for the dawn. He wouldn't feel easy until the wagon train was far away from here.

Finally, the sky turned lavender gray and he began to rouse the camp. Everyone moved slowly this morning, some of them suffering from last night's liquor, some just weary. He saw Sky Eyes making coffee and he walked over and helped her poke up her fire.

"Sit down," she said, almost kindly. "You look exhausted. Did you get any sleep at all?"

He accepted a cup of coffee and shook his head. "I'm gonna beat hell out of whoever brought that liquor out last night. Anything could have happened."

"Is that why you sent me to bed?" She paused in frying bacon.

Rider nodded. "That one young buck wanted to trade me a bunch of ponies for you."

She actually smiled. "Did you tell him I didn't belong to you?"

"And make you fair game?" Rider sipped his coffee. "I told him you were my favorite wife and I wouldn't part with you for any number of ponies."

She looked at him a long moment. "Well, thanks — I think."

"No need," Rider said. "I'd have killed him if he'd tried to take you."

"Wouldn't that have started a massacre?" She held out a plate of bacon and biscuits to him.

"Yes. I still would have done it." He took the plate. "Where's the Small Warrior?"

The boy stuck his head out of the wagon. "Here I am, Rider."

Rider grinned at him in spite of himself. The child was beginning to mean something to him and that wasn't good. Rambling gunfighters couldn't afford any emotional ties. "Let's get some breakfast, Small Warrior, then get the cow milked and the oxen hitched."

"All right. Can I ride your horse this morning?"

Rider nodded and reached for more coffee. "Sure. Now get moving."

The boy disappeared back in the wagon and the woman looked at Rider with gentle eyes. "Thank you for being kind to him."

Rider shrugged. "He's a nice kid. If I had a . . ." He didn't finish, knowing he had almost said *I'd want him to be just like Josh.* He must stop thinking about this little family as his responsibility. It seemed to be getting more difficult to remember that his only stake in this adventure was that gold of Pettigrew's and getting the blonde into his blankets for a few nights' amusement.

They were late getting the train ready to move, but it couldn't be helped with most of the men sick and sullen from last night's celebration. Finally all the people had eaten, doused their fires, and were harnessing their animals.

"Let's get a move on!" Rider ordered. "We need to clear this place before the Lakota pay us another visit."

Little Josh turned on the wagon seat and pointed. "Too late. The Injuns are back."

Rider felt his stomach churn as he whirled his horse around to look. The Lakota warriors rode slowly over the top of a rise toward them.

Millicent Carrolton made a small sound of dismay.

Fat farmer Adams muttered, "What do you suppose them redskins want?" He reached for his rifle.

"Leave that weapon alone," Rider ordered. "We're outnumbered and we don't want trouble if we can avoid it." Still, he kept his own weapons within easy reach. If the Lakota decided to make trouble, the wagon train didn't have a chance in hell and he knew it. "Everyone keep a cool head and don't make any sudden moves." He spurred his stallion and rode out to meet the Lakota, holding up his hand in greeting. "Ah, Wolf's Eyes — it was a good feast."

The other nodded somberly. "It has been a long time since I have enjoyed so much food."

Rider wondered what it was the chief wanted. It was not good manners to hurry a talk. In dealing with Indians, one must always have patience. "Would Wolf's Eyes wish to come sit by my fire and have coffee and smoke?"

The other's dark eyes seemed remote and hostile as he shook his head. "This morning, we noted that my daughter was not among the women."

"Perhaps she is asleep in some gully from last night's celebration."

Wolf's Eyes shook his head. "It is not like her to do such a thing. We wonder if she hasn't taken up with some white man and is leaving with your wagons."

Rider was truly mystified. He took off his Stetson and scratched his head. "I have heard nothing of this."

"She is promised to one of my best and bravest warriors," Wolf's Eyes said. "I would take it as an insult if some white man tried to take her."

Sweat began to break out between Rider's shoulder blades. He had no idea what had happened to the girl, but it was not good to anger her father. "I do not think this is true, Wolf's Eyes, but we will ride into my camp together and see what my people have to say."

The Lakota chief signaled his warriors. Very slowly, they began to fan out in a large circle, surrounding the wagons. Rider pretended not to notice this hostile gesture as he wheeled his horse and he and Wolf's Eyes rode back into the center of the wagon circle.

The banker wiped his pink face. "What's the matter?"

Rider dismounted while the Lakota sat his paint horse stoically. "His daughter is missing. She didn't come home from our party last night. I hope none of you men are loco enough to try to take her with us."

Everyone looked at each other blankly. It seemed evident to Rider that no one knew anything. "Does anyone even remember seeing the girl?"

"Real pretty?" Willie Adams asked.

"I reckon so," Rider said.

Willie turned toward Stott. "I saw her with him."

"Hey, that's right," Draper nodded. "I saw her sharin' a bottle with the black-smith."

Everyone turned toward Stott.

Sweat made his ugly face shiny wet and his bald head gleamed in the sun.

For the first time, Rider noticed the scratches on the man's face and arms. "What happened to you? You look like you fought with a bobcat."

The other hesitated, then looked away. "I-I got tangled in some bushes last night, scratched me up."

Rider began to get a sick feeling in the pit of his stomach. "You seen that girl, Stott?"

The other shrugged. "I might have had a drink with her — I was plenty drunk. But that's all. I swear I didn't hurt her none."

"Nobody accused you of that." Rider chewed his lip, thinking and remembering the attacks on the women of the train, the footprints of big boots. "Where's your hat?"

The other felt his head absently. "I-I don't know. I must have dropped it someplace."

Rider glanced around at the grim-faced Lakota warriors encircling the train. "Unless we find her fast, we're in big trouble. Maybe she's passed out somewhere. Everyone search their wagons and the surrounding brush."

Sky Eyes frowned suddenly. "I — no, I reckon it's nothing." She shook her head.

Rider looked at her troubled face. "What?"

"I-I heard something last night near my wagon."

All eyes turned toward her.

Rider walked over to her. "Tell me, Sky Eyes. We've got to find that girl."

"I figured it was a coyote or something," the blonde shrugged. "I'm not sure what the sound was. It was probably a bobcat or maybe a wolf — kind of a cry."

A bobcat's cry. Could it have been a woman's scream? Sweat broke out on Rider's face and he looked toward Wolf's Eyes. The Lakota chief had dismounted and come over to join them. "Wolf's Eyes, we are not sure what happened to your daughter, but we'll find her."

He took Sky Eyes's arm. "Show us where you think the sound might have come from." The settlers followed the pair silently. Rider yelled to the men, "Spread out and start looking. Maybe she's asleep under a bush somewhere."

Somehow, even as they spread out and began to search the tall grass, Rider knew something was terribly wrong. An obedient

Lakota girl would not disappear without her father's consent.

Emma walked next to Rider, her eyes searching the grass. *What was it she had heard last night?* She'd been sleepy and she was no longer certain if she'd heard anything; maybe she'd only dreamed it. Uncertainly, Emma stopped before her wagon and looked around, trying to remember. She pulled away from Rider and walked out into the tall grass. It made a soft swishing sound like a woman's silk skirts as the prairie wind blew through it. Overhead, a hawk circled, throwing a dark shadow across the sunburnt grass around her. She looked back toward Rider. "I-I'm not sure."

"Try to remember," the gunfighter urged. She looked toward the Lakota chief. His expression was chiseled in brown stone. Emma closed her eyes and tried to relive last night. Maybe . . . no, it might have come from farther to the west. She took a deep breath and started walking. Up ahead, she could see a small, protected clearing. It was almost noon — she could tell from the overhead sun beating down on her with its relentless July heat. She began to walk again. When she reached the edge, she noticed how trampled the grass was. Behind her, the people were moving forward, although the silent, hostile warriors still ringed the camp.

Emma glanced down at a clear spot in the trampled grass. Something pale brown . . . In that split second, she recognized it as a human hand. Even as she saw the crumpled body, she screamed and stepped backward, stumbling in her haste to escape the horrid sight.

She closed her eyes against the nightmare before her, shaking and sobbing as Rider ran up and put his hands on her shoulders. "What is it, Sky Eyes? What did you — ? Oh, my God," he whispered and she wasn't sure whether that was a prayer or a curse.

Emma opened her eyes slowly as Rider moved her to one side and squatted down.

The pretty Indian girl lay with a string of beads pulled tight around her neck, her mouth and eyes open wide as if she were screaming silently. Her clothing was torn and pushed up, her legs spread. In one clenched fist, she held onto a shapeless cloth object. Emma knew immediately what had happened. In that instant, she relived her own terrible rape. She stumbled away, sobbing.

Rider yelled at the men, "Keep the women and kids back."

They pushed forward anyway, each driven by morbid curiosity. Rider cursed long and loud. "What son of a bitch did this?"

Emma watched as Wolf's Eyes strode toward the scene. No father should have to see his daughter this way, she thought. She took off her shawl and spread it over the poor, disgraced body. The chief strode to the scene, pulled away the shawl. He stared down a long moment but the only emotion he showed was a quick intake of breath and his jaw trembled. "Who — who has done this thing?"

"I don't know, but I intend to find out." Rider leaned over and took the shapeless object from the girl's clenched hand and held it up. It was a hat. Wordlessly, he turned toward Stott.

"I didn't do it," Stott babbled. "We only had a drink, that's all, someone else must have —"

"And the scratches?" Rider's eyes turned deadly cold as his expression.

"I-I was tradin' a little lovin' for some beads," Stott babbled. "I never meant —"

"You scum." Rider spat out his words as he glared at the blacksmith. "You rotten, filthy scum!"

The chief turned slowly and stared at Stott. He said nothing, only stared with eyes full of black anger.

"She offered to trade for a drink," Stott

said. "I gave her some whiskey, and then she changed her mind —"

"You rotten son of a bitch!" Rider said. "You're the one who's tried to grab the women on this train."

Stott shook his head and began to back away. "They keep temptin' me, just like the sluts back home. I didn't mean to hurt any of them — I just wanted to lie with them —"

"Grab him!" Rider ordered and Draper and young Adams rushed forward.

The giant blacksmith fought the two. He broke away and took off running across the prairie. The chief gave a sharp command; two warriors rode him down and he stumbled and fell, lying in the grass, cursing and kicking. "It was the Injun slut's fault! She shouldn't have fought me!"

Rider turned toward Wolf's Eyes. "Chief, I cannot tell you how much sorrow this brings me. What do you want to do?"

The banker took off his derby and wiped his sweating face. "What're you asking him for? Stott's one of us. We'll try him and —"

"Chief," Rider ignored Pettigrew, "what is your choice in this matter?"

"Give him to us!" Wolf's Eyes thundered. "We will handle this in the Lakota way."

Rider nodded. "It is as you wish."

One of the warriors threw a lasso around

the kicking, screaming man as he stumbled to his feet.

Some of the white people looked alarmed. "You're gonna turn him over to the savages?"

Rider shrugged. "I'd say Stott's the savage."

Draper and some of the others set up a protest. "Turn a white man over to Injuns? It don't seem right —"

Rider looked toward the silent warriors ringing them. "It's just," he said, "he's guilty of murder. We'll let the Lakota set the punishment."

Emma glanced at Rider's set face. The gunfighter was right; Stott deserved whatever he got. And even if the whites wanted to stop this, they were vastly outnumbered.

The warrior who had lassoed Stott began to drag him, fighting and screaming, across the dirt as Rider gestured to Emma. "I need a woman to help with the girl."

She swallowed hard. He was right; protecting the girl's dignity was woman's work. "Yes, I'll find a blanket to wrap her in if someone will look after Josh."

"I'll do that." The very pregnant Mrs. Weeks turned and headed back to the wagons.

Rider turned to the others. "The rest of

you get back to camp."

Carrolton's mouth trembled. "What's going to happen now?"

Rider shook his head and looked toward Wolf's Eyes. The Lakota stared straight ahead, watching his warriors drag the protesting Stott across the rocky ground toward the distant Indian encampment. "I think we'd better stay circled up."

Emma bit her lip and looked into Rider's eyes. She knew what he was thinking; the Lakota might decide to wreak vengeance on the whole train. "I'll get a blanket. Tell her father to bring a travois."

As she hurried away, she looked back. Stott yelled in protest and tried to get to his feet, but he stumbled and fell. The warrior didn't stop, but continued to drag him through the briars and across the rocks while the burly blacksmith fought the rope and cursed.

Emma took a deep breath and returned to her wagon for a quilt. When she got back to the scene, a brave had brought up a travois. She tried not to look at the poor dead girl as she rearranged her clothing and wrapped her in the faded quilt. Rider came over, lifted the body almost tenderly, and laid it on the travois. He said some gentle words to the old chief in his own language and the chief nodded and motioned to the brave pulling the travois to move out. The travois started for the Indian camp, the bereaved father riding along behind it.

In the distance, the Lakota warrior jerked Stott across more rocks, the white man cursing and fighting to get to his feet.

"What will they do with him?" she said under her breath.

Rider shook his head. "You don't want to know."

The settlers stared silently after the Indians as they rode away. They could see Stott being dragged along the ground, kicking and screaming. Behind that rider came the little group with the travois. Slowly the warriors who ringed the wagons turned their horses to follow the sad little procession. Rider signaled everyone to return to the circled wagons and they did so silently; all but Emma.

She stood silently, clenching and unclenching her hands.

"Are you all right?" Rider asked.

"I-I think so."

"You've got guts, Sky Eyes. I notice no one else offered to help."

"Some of the settlers will be angry that we turned Stott over to the Indians."

"That can't be helped," Rider shrugged.

"I reckon he's raped enough women that he deserves whatever he gets."

The ugly word made her gasp and Rider reached out and put his hand on her shoulder. "I'm sorry," he said. "Let's go back to camp."

"I-I'm fine," she lied.

He took her elbow and they started back. Emma suddenly felt so weak and sick that she stumbled and went to her knees. Immediately, Rider swung her up into his strong arms. "I thought you said you were fine."

"I reckon I'm not." She sighed and laid her face against his shirt as he walked with strong, sure strides. His shirt smelled of sun and dust and the warm scent of a man. She felt safe in his big arms somehow, in spite of what she knew about him — and what he was demanding from her.

Behind them, faintly in the distance, they could still hear Stott cursing and yelling as the Lakota dragged him away.

Rider looked down at the woman in his arms. Her face was pale and her eyes were closed. He shouldn't have asked her to help wrap the body, but he'd needed a woman's aid and Emma Trent was the only one of the bunch he trusted. He felt very protective of her and had a terrible impulse to kiss those soft pink lips, but he managed to resist that urge. Instead, he carried her to the camp circle and set her down gently on a log.

The settlers were white-faced, terrified, and defiant.

The banker said, "What will they do to him?"

"That's not our problem," Rider said, although he knew with a terrible certainty what the Lakota intended for the killer.

"It is our problem," young Adams snarled. "We can't just turn over a white man to a bunch of savages to —"

"That's right," Millicent Carrolton interrupted. "It's just not civilized."

"In case you folks haven't noticed," Rider sighed and began to roll a smoke, "we're not in civilization anymore. Besides, they outnumber us." He looked around the circle as he lit his smoke. "How many of you are willing to die to go rescue Stott?"

Dead silence. Everyone avoided his eyes.

"Well, now that we have that settled, we'd better stay on the alert." Rider blew a cloud of smoke in the air. "I think old Wolf's Eyes will be satisfied and let us leave, but I'm afraid to gamble on it until they finish with Stott."

They heard a cry then, a long, very faint cry carried on the hot wind.

Some of the settlers' faces went pale.

"Oh, my God," gasped Mrs. Adams. "Oh, my God."

In the distance, Stott screamed again.

The elegant Southerner's hand shook as he poured himself a dipper of water. "How long will this take?"

Rider shook his head and smoked his cigarette. "As long as they can keep him alive and breathing. Maybe tomorrow."

The faces around him looked horrified. "Tomorrow?"

Rider nodded, remembering his own father's death. "There's an art to killing a man by inches."

In the distance, Stott screamed again.

Emma Trent's face turned pale but she didn't say anything. Rider wondered what was going through her mind. Millicent and Francie began to cry.

Rider turned to the frail Mr. Gray. "Why don't you get your fiddle and play some good, loud music that the children can all dance to?"

Mrs. Adams snarled at him. "How can you think of dancing at a time like this — ?"

"I'm thinking about the children," Rider snapped. "Or do you want them to hear him scream all night?"

Gray's face turned grayer than dust. "I'll get my fiddle."

It was the most ghastly day Emma had ever spent and it crawled past. Almost woodenly, she went about her tasks of feeding Rider and Josh, keeping her fire going. The fiddle music played and played and played until she wanted to shout for silence but she knew that if Mr. Gray stopped playing, they'd be able to hear Stott's screams from the distance.

Finally the day passed. She was exhausted and sick at heart, but she knew she wouldn't be able to sleep, not with all she'd seen today, not when she could imagine what was happening in the Lakota camp.

As darkness came on, Gray stopped playing, exhausted. There was only silence from the Lakota camp. The settlers ate and fed their stock, listening apprehensively. Rider sat at her fire, staring into the flames as everyone began to bed down.

Josh looked up at Rider with anxious eyes. "I'm scared to go to bed."

Emma held her breath, waiting for the tough gunfighter to scold her little son, but Rider smiled and touched Josh's shoulder. "You want to know a secret? I'm scared, too."

"You, Rider?" the child grew big-eyed, then shook his head. "No, Rider is brave, never scared."

The half-breed laughed and picked him

up. "Small Warrior, being brave is being scared and acting anyway. I promise no one is gonna hurt you. Maybe Boots is scared, too. I think he ought to sleep with you tonight."

Josh grinned and looked toward her. "Can he, Mama?"

She thought about how dirty the pup might be, and looked into her child's eyes. "Oh, I reckon it's all right if Rider thinks it's a good idea."

"Then it's settled." The gunfighter carried the child over and set him on the wagon gate, then picked up the pup and put him in the wagon. Boots licked the little boy's face.

Josh looked up at Rider. "You look after Mama?"

"You know I will."

Satisfied, Josh turned and clambered into the wagon, the excited puppy going with him.

Rider sighed and returned to the fire where Emma had just sat down on a log. The camp was deserted now, everyone seeking the shelter of their own wagons.

She didn't look at him. "You want some more coffee?"

He sat down on the log next to her as he shook his head. "I'm bone tired — I was up all last night."

"Why don't you get on my feather bed and go to sleep?" she asked. "You got someone on guard duty?"

Rider yawned and nodded. "Carrolton, young Adams, and Draper. We'll pull out at first light."

"This trip has become a nightmare," she said.

"I told everyone it would," Rider reminded her. "Why don't we leave this train? You and me and Josh? We could head for California and —"

"You'd just abandon these people?" She looked aghast as she stood up.

"Don't be so shocked," he said with a shrug. "This bunch is the dregs of humanity and they sure haven't been nice to you." He, too, got to his feet. They were standing close together and he reached out and caught one of her long curls in his big, dark hand.

She knew she should pull away, but she couldn't seem to move. She stood looking up at him, feeling the warmth and closeness of his big body. "You were wonderful today. We were all scared to death."

"I'm not going to let anything happen to you," he answered softly as his hand played with her hair.

"You're a strange man, Rider," she answered softly.

"I'm a lonely man," he whispered.

"If so, it's your own choosing. I've seen the women trying to seduce you."

"I'm sick of that kind of woman." He put his hand on her shoulder.

She could feel the strength of him though his hand was gentle. "You could take me by force anytime — we both know that."

He shook his head. "That's not how I want you."

She looked up at him. "You want me to be willing?"

"Lady," he whispered, "you don't know how badly I want you to be willing."

"No," she shook her head. "No." The old fears came crowding back in on her and images flashed through her mind of a bloody bed and a brown face.

He seemed to read her mind. "Forget the past," he murmured and put both big hands on her small shoulders. She noted his hands trembled. "I must be the biggest damn fool in the world," he murmured. "I've never wanted a woman as much as I want you, Sky Eyes."

She looked up into his dark eyes, not trusting him, not trusting herself.

About that time in the distance, Stott screamed again.

"Oh, God!" She squeezed her eyes shut

and clapped both hands over her ears, then began to cry softly.

Rider gathered her into his arms and held her tightly against his muscular chest. "It's okay, Sky Eyes," he whispered against her hair. "It's okay. I won't let anything hurt you."

She was aware that her body shook and that he was kissing her hair, but she didn't pull out of his embrace.

"Sky Eyes," he whispered. "Sky Eyes."

She only trembled against him and let him hold her. His arms felt so protective as he held her close and stroked her hair. She needed his strength and some tenderness. She'd been alone and on her own, fighting the whole world so long. She didn't mean to, but she looked up into his eyes, blinking back tears.

One of his big hands cupped her chin and brought her face up to his. When his mouth claimed hers, she surrendered to the emotion for a split second as his mouth caressed her lips, gently opening them so he could slip his tongue inside.

She let him mold her body against his hard one as his hand went down to clasp her buttocks, pulling her against his hard manhood while his mouth possessed hers and his tongue searched and tasted and caressed. His arousal throbbing against her brought her to her senses and she jerked her face away, gasping. "No, please, no."

He was breathing hard as he looked down into her eyes and shook his head. "Don't stop me, Sky Eyes, let me. I want you so bad, I can't think of anything else —"

"No." She managed to pull out of his arms, then stepped away from him, shaking visibly. All she could remember at this moment was a bloody bed with her gentle husband lying dead on it while a big, virile savage forced himself between her thighs. It had been both brutal and terrifying.

In the distance, Stott screamed again, more faintly now. She wanted to flee back into the safety of Rider's strong arms, but she could see the need in those dark eyes, know what he wanted so terribly at this moment: a chance to lose himself in the softness of her. Instead, Emma turned and ran blindly toward her wagon, too confused to know or care whether Rider was coming after her.

Chapter Fourteen

It was a sleepless, tense night for Rider. Before dawn, he had the train up and moving. The settlers pulled out with guards posted along its route.

Rider drew a deep sigh of relief as they put distance between themselves and the Lakota camp, but there were no smoke signals or signs of trouble. Evidently, Wolf's Eyes was satisfied that justice had been done.

The landscape was flat, hot, and dry with few trees as they moved slowly west. They passed Courthouse and Jailhouse Rocks, looming huge over the desolate plains, their shadows black across the moving wagons. In the distance, Chimney Rock seemed small on the horizon. It seemed to grow taller, like a thin needle of stone in the three days it took to reach it.

He avoided Emma Trent as much as he could because she troubled his mind and he'd never met a woman quite like her, a woman he wasn't sure how to handle. Francie constantly tried to seduce him and talked of when they should steal the money and flee. Rider gave her evasive answers, no longer certain himself of what he intended to do.

Rider wanted to avoid the gigantic Scott's Bluff, so he led the train through Mitchell Pass. It was here they came upon the four wagons out on the prairie: one with a broken wheel, one full of sick people. The other two looked as if their oxen were weak or starving.

Rider rode up ahead and dismounted. "What's going on here?"

The people looked at him, mostly too weak to move. "Cholera and bad luck," one of the men gasped. "The rest of the train moved on, deserted us; told us to catch up if we could."

Cholera. Rider shuddered and stepped back. It was one of those dread diseases that swept through wagon trains and Indian camps, leaving dead and dying in its wake. It had taken his mother.

One of the sick women looked toward his canteen. "Can you help us?"

Rider reached for his canteen and signaled his wagons to pull on up. "How long you folks been here?"

"A week, maybe," the man said. "We run out of food and nobody was strong enough to fix the wagon."

The children looked at Rider, all hollow-eyed. "You got food, mister?"

"We'll get you some food," Rider promised gently. He turned and looked toward the fresh graves nearby.

"Couldn't dig 'em too deep," the older man apologized, "Nobody's got the strength."

Rider shrugged. "They don't know the difference. You folks bound for Oregon?"

One of the women nodded. "We'd about give up hope. With us all sick, our train left us behind — told us to catch up if we got better."

"That's almost a death sentence," Rider scowled. "Where you from?"

"Mostly Baltimore," said the man.

"You city folks don't have any business out here," Rider grumbled. "There's hundreds just like you dyin' on this trail."

The other man shook his head. "We got no choice, mister. We got to get to Oregon for the children's sake."

He heard Emma come up behind him. "What's happened?"

"Stay back," Rider ordered. "They're just gettin' over cholera. Bring them a bucket of water out of your barrel and see if everybody can spare them some food."

"Don't boss me around," she said with spirit. "We're gonna help these folks."

He'd learned by now that Emma Trent could be stubborn, so he didn't argue with her.

Carrolton and Pettigrew joined him as Emma headed back to her wagon. "What's holding us up? We could get in another five miles today."

Rider gestured around. He didn't need to say anything. The disabled wagon, the fresh graves, the hungry faces said it all.

"Well," said the fat farmer, Adams, "we ain't gonna delay to help these folks, are we?"

Rider made a sound of disgust. "What would you suggest?"

Mrs. Adams and her son came up just then. "We hardly got enough food to finish the trip. If we share, we might not have enough for ourselves."

Before Rider could say anything, Emma rejoined them. "Now what kind of attitude is that?" she demanded. "Of course we're gonna help these folks. Let's camp for the night."

Millicent Carrolton walked up, silk skirts swishing. She took one look and recoiled in horror. "We aren't going to stop just for this poor white trash, are we?"

Emma's blue eyes flashed fire. "But of course we are."

Pettigrew blustered, "Can't we just give them a little food and water and move on? We're losin' time here."

Everyone looked toward Rider. He looked into Emma's eyes and it was abruptly important to him that she think well of him. "We'll stop the night as Mrs. Trent suggested. Some of you ladies get some soup cooking and some water for their oxen. You men see what you can do about that busted wheel."

For the first time, hope flared in the strangers' tired faces. "Much obliged, mister. My name's McGinnis and these in the other wagon are my neighbors from back home — Jones and some of his kinfolk."

Gratitude made Rider uncomfortable. "You can move on with us as soon as we can get your wagons fixed and your people are well enough to travel. There may be Indians ahead and there's safety in numbers."

The others grumbled, but everyone seemed afraid to confront Rider. Later, Emma came by and brought him a tin cup full of soup. "You're a nicer person than you let on."

"No, I'm not," he said and shook his head. "I've survived by looking out for myself first. There's safety in numbers and if we run into more Indians, we'll be glad to have the extra help."

She handed him the cup. "Somehow I don't believe that, but you say whatever you want." She turned and left.

Rider took a taste of the soup. The woman could cook. In the past, roaming the country, he'd lived off whatever he could roast over a fire himself or sometimes in a greasy roadside saloon.

They lost several precious days, but finally the train took to the road again with the new people added, although some of Rider's bunch grumbled about having to share supplies with the newcomers.

The trip was hot and monotonous as July ended and August began. They reached Fort Laramie and paused only overnight. The soldiers warned them to expect Indian trouble ahead. Then they moved on into the hills, pausing at Register Cliff just long enough for some of the people to scratch their names into the red sandstone beside the many names of those who had already passed.

Emma was weary and dusty when they finally reached Warm Springs. Here there was a natural heated pool where they could bathe and wash clothes; then they were on the trail again, headed for Platte Bridge Station, a grimy little army post. All this time, they had been following the North Platte River.

Rider rode alongside her. "Just ahead is Bessemer Bend. We'll cross the Platte there. After that, we've got three or four days of rough, dry country, so pass the word before we leave the river to fill the water barrels and water the animals good."

She was so very tired and weary. "And after that, what?"

"The Sweetwater," he said. "It'll be worth the trip — you'll see."

Emma was beginning to think nothing was worth the trip as she urged her oxen into the muddy river. No, Josh was worth it; maybe he'd have a better chance out west.

Rider was right about one thing — that dry stretch as they left the Platte and headed across the desolate wasteland toward the Sweetwater was as dry and hot as a stovetop. The weather was unmercifully warm, the animals growing thinner, the querulous settlers bickering over petty things.

It was during this time that young Willie Adams murdered Draper. It was noon and they had stopped on the bald prairie for a bite of food. The sun blazed down, the heat waves making the flat, treeless landscape fuzzy. The only water was tepid and warm from the barrels.

Rider rode along the line of wagons, inspecting each with growing concern. Some of the oxen were weak and might not make it to fresh water, then on to Fort Bridger where the settlers might buy fresh stock. Many of the wagons needed repairs but the people were too lazy to do anything until an axle broke, a wheel fell off, or Rider insisted they fix it.

The second morning after they left Bessemer Bend, Rider passed the Carroltons' wagon, drew in and frowned. "Your load is way too heavy. If you don't abandon some of it, you'll lose some oxen."

Millicent Carrolton threw up her hands in dismay. "You aren't suggesting I throw away some of my things?"

"Lady," Rider snapped, "you do what you want with all that fancy furniture and dishes, but I'm telling you that if you don't lighten your wagon, when your oxen die, you'll end up leaving all of it on the side of the road.

Millicent began to cry and her husband handed her a handkerchief. "I can't!" she wailed. "I just can't set up housekeeping without all my silver and fine things."

"Now, Millicent," her husband began. "be reasonable —"

"Reasonable?" she shrieked. "I wouldn't be in this godforsaken place if it weren't for you."

Weatherford B. Carrolton turned on Rider in a fury. "Now see what you've caused, upsetting my wife this way?"

"Look," Rider said, "it don't make me no never mind what you two decide to do. I'm just warning you what will happen in the next fifty miles."

As he turned and rode away, he could still hear her wailing and her husband pleading. The woman didn't have any common sense and didn't want to sacrifice in any way to make it to Oregon. Her husband was gutless in more ways than just fleeing the war.

Hell, he was sick and tired of this wagon train. And there was all that money in Pettigrew's wagon, just waiting for Rider to help himself. And every mile he stayed with the settlers brought him that much closer to Shoshoni country and mortal danger. Yet he made excuses to himself about why he stayed on.

It had been a long, luckless morning and the train had stopped to eat at high noon. He rode up to Emma Trent's wagon. There was no shade and she looked exhausted and deeply tanned as she and her son shared a cold biscuit. She smiled up at him in a way that made his insides feel all soft. "You hungry?"

He swung down and reached for a bucket to water his horse. "You're the only woman on this train who isn't complaining and belly-aching."

Emma shrugged as she held out some cold biscuits. "My grandmother used to say 'what cannot be cured must be endured.' Things are bound to get better because they can't get any worse."

"I wouldn't bet on it." He took the biscuit and munched it. It was lathered with butter from the Jersey cow and some tart, home-made grape jelly. From the other wagons came the sound of men grumbling and women whining. "You're better than most white women. You're almost as easy to have around as an Indian girl."

A shadow crossed her lovely face. "You've got a woman among the Indians?"

He shook his head. "Her name was *Chosro,* but —"

She looked up at him expectantly, but he paused. "Never mind."

"What does it mean?"

"Blue Bird."

Emma swallowed hard. "A girl with that name must be very beautiful."

He didn't answer.

"Did you — did you love her?"

For a long minute, there was only silence. "Chosro is the reason the Shoshoni want me for murder."

"Murder? What — ?"

"No questions." He broke off abruptly, his expression betraying that he'd already told her more than anyone else knew about his past. "After I water my horse, I'm going to ride ahead and see if I can find a decent place to camp tonight."

"With some trees?" she asked hopefully, looking around at the barren landscape.

He shook his head. "Reckon not. Things won't get better until we reach the Sweetwater. We'll be getting into hills and some pretty rough terrain."

Her shoulders slumped. "The worst of the trip is still ahead of us, isn't it?"

But not for me, he thought. *Any day now, I'll take old Pettigrew's money and light out.* "It'll be tough, all right."

She gave him a dazzling smile. "We'll make it — we have to."

Rider only grunted and went off to water his horse. Then he left the wagon train people resting and grumbling while he rode ahead, scouting out a camp for the night.

Emma watched him ride out and wondered about the hard, hostile man. For a long moment, as he faded into the distance, she wondered about Blue Bird. Had he loved her? Had he killed her? Rider seemed a very complicated, very private man with many emotional conflicts behind that stern mask. He seemed dangerous, yet she had seen his gentle, protective side. Yes indeed, he was a puzzle.

It was while Rider was away that afternoon that trouble broke out again between Willie Adams and Draper. Conflict had been brewing between the young hothead and the older man for a long time. She would remember later that it began over some small thing, and the merciless heat and the tension pushed tempers to a breaking point. It escalated into name-calling and then shoving. Finally, they were into a fistfight, with people gathering around to watch.

"Stop it!" Emma demanded. "Can't some of you men stop this?"

They ignored her, enjoying the fight.

Oh God, if only Rider were here to take charge. Everyone followed his orders and he didn't believe in wasting energy over trivial things. But tensions had been building over the past weeks and nothing was trivial anymore.

The two fought and went down, rolling over and over in the dust. Adam's mouth was bleeding and it caused dirt to stick to his face. They rolled under a wagon, turning over pans and equipment. Horses neighed and reared.

"Stop it!" Emma shouted. "Stop it, I say!"

The men paid no attention to her and no one moved to separate the two. Amusements were far between on this trail and the crowd was entertained by the fight.

Where were old farmer Adams and his wife? They might stop this. Emma ran toward their wagon. Behind her, she heard cursing and blows as the two fought. She looked back over her shoulder. Draper knocked young Adams down and the man didn't get up. "There, Shorty," Draper said. "You've annoyed me too long."

He dusted off his hands and turned to walk away. Young Adams stumbled to his feet, wiping at the blood on his mouth and cursing as he grabbed up a rifle.

A woman screamed and Draper whirled around. He was unarmed. "Now, kid, let's talk this over!"

"I'm done talkin', you bastard!" And

Willie Adams shot him down.

For a split second, there was only the surprised look on Draper's face as his hands went to his shirt where blood suddenly spurted warm and red between his fingers. Then there was stunned silence and the sudden scent of acrid powder. Draper crumpled into the dirt and women began to scream.

Young Adams only grinned. "That son of a bitch is done callin' me names. He thought I was a coward, but he ain't the first man I've kilt. Anyone else wanna call me 'Shorty'?"

There was a long silence. Emma looked into his pale eyes, alight with a maniacal rage. They were dealing with a madman, Emma thought as the boy waved the rifle menacingly at the crowd. They all shrank back. No one had the nerve to try to take it away from him.

Farmer Adams had come running at the sounds of shots. He took in the scene. "What happened, son?"

"He was insultin' me," the boy whined and gripped the rifle even tighter.

The farmer wiped his perspiring face. "Well, then Draper deserved what he got."

Emma took a deep breath. "He shot an unarmed man." A murmur of agreement ran through the gathered crowd.

Farmer Adams chewed his lip. "Let's just bury this man and forget about it."

Everyone looked confused and uncertain. Willie Adams was a maniac, and who knew who his next victim might be? Emma wished Rider were here to take charge.

At that moment, Rider galloped into camp. "I was on my way back and heard the shot. What the hell happened?"

All eyes turned toward Willie Adams, but no one said anything.

Rider turned in his saddle to see the dead man on the ground. He began to swear under his breath as he dismounted and strode over to inspect the body. Finally he took off his hat and wiped his dark forehead. "He's dead. Draper wasn't armed." He looked toward young Adams.

"I don't give a damn!" the kid yelled defiantly. "He's had that comin' for a long time!"

Rider walked slowly toward him, his hand outstretched. "Willie, give me the rifle."

"No," the man said and backed away. "Don't you come any closer."

The whole crowd seemed to be holding their breath. Emma watched Rider take a step, still holding out his hand. "Willie, give me the rifle."

"I had a right to kill him," Willie babbled, "just like that soldier I killed with a shovel. The army was goin' to hang me for that, but I got away. I didn't come all this way to die out here."

No one moved. None of the other men were making a move to do anything to help. Boots barked suddenly in the silence and the angry young man whirled toward the dog, rifle cocked. "I'm sick and tired of that mutt! I'm gonna finish him!"

Josh cried out and threw himself across the puppy. Emma screamed even as Rider charged Adams, struck him hard in the jaw, and grabbed for the weapon. He wrestled it out of Willie's hands and shoved him to the ground.

"By God," grumbled old Adams. "You can't do that to my boy —"

"Adams," Rider said, "did you know the army was going to hang your boy?"

Mrs. Adams was crying defiantly. " 'Course we did. That's why we was takin' him to Oregon for a fresh start."

Rider sighed and nodded to Carrolton and a couple of the new men. "Tie him up — we'll have to have a trial."

"Out here?" asked Francie, her voice incredulous. "Can't we wait 'til we get to the next fort?"

Rider shook his head. "We've got to be our own law out here; we're far from civilization. You men choose a jury. Looks like we're here for the rest of the day."

Emma couldn't believe this was happening. Out here on this isolated, treeless prairie, a man was going on trial for his life with the father and mother protesting that the dead man deserved to be killed. Jones, one of the newcomers, had some background in law and offered to take charge. Rider took no part in the proceedings, only watching as the men chose a jury from among their members and waited for the sun to set as they began the trial. Willie's parents swore and cursed at all the others, threatening to kill anyone who tried to harm their boy. The children were fed and sent to their wagons by Rider's orders.

Emma watched Rider's face as the trial began. His face was a cold mask and he looked as if he'd rather be anywhere but here. She wondered if he had ever seen a man executed. No doubt he'd seen many men die.

At the end, the settlers' jury agreed that there'd been a fight over something trivial and that young Adams had grabbed a rifle and shot down an unarmed man in cold blood. As the day turned to dusk, the jury brought in a verdict of guilty with a death sentence.

Willie began to curse and threaten everyone in the wagon train.

Mrs. Adams began to cry. "No, you can't do this to my poor boy!"

The fat old farmer grabbed a rifle and pointed it at the jurors, but Rider overpowered him and took away his weapon.

"I'm sorry for you," Rider said gently, "but he should have gotten justice when he killed that soldier with a shovel. If he had, Draper might be alive now."

"He's our only child," the old woman wept. "We always overlooked every bad thing he done."

Rider shook his head. "Then maybe you're to blame for what's become of him." He looked at Emma. "Would you take her to her wagon and stay with her?"

Emma wiped tears from her eyes and nodded, but as she started toward the woman, the woman spat at her. "You! I'll not have some Injun's slut comfortin' me!" She turned and walked toward her wagon.

The old farmer had slumped down on a rock. Willie continued to curse and threaten everyone on the wagon train with bodily harm.

Weatherford Carrolton had been one of

the jurors. Now he looked at Rider. "We've condemned him, but what's to be done now?"

Rider took off his hat and wiped his dark face with a resigned sigh. "The easiest thing is a firing squad."

The other men began to shake their heads. None of them had the stomach to be on a firing squad, Emma thought.

"I see," Rider said. "You condemn him and nobody's got the guts to carry out the sentence."

"If we was back home," said McGinnis, one of the newcomers, "he'd be hanged, proper-like, but out here . . ." His voice trailed off as he looked around. There wasn't a tree for miles.

Pettigrew looked to Rider. "You're the wagon boss. What do other wagon trains do in a fix like this?"

"I know what they do." Rider stood up. "So as wagon boss, you want me to assume this responsibility, too?"

There was a murmur of assent.

Rider spat on the ground in distaste. "I don't know how any of you gutless cowards are gonna make it in Oregon, but that's not today's problem. We can't let a man get away with cold-blooded murder."

"You're a fine one to talk!" Old Adams

shouted and tried to attack Rider with his fists. "You gunfighter — you've killed more men than my son ever did!"

"But I never killed them in cold blood," Rider said. He held off the old man's attacks without hitting him back. "The jury has passed sentence — now it must be carried out."

"You can't hang my son," old Adams shouted. "You ain't got no trees!"

Rider gestured to two of the men to hold the fat farmer's arms. "I'm sorry, old man, but we're gonna hang him. He's murdered two men, so we're just finishing up what the army meant to do."

Young Adams began to curse and yell threats again.

Hang him? Everyone looked around and Emma knew immediately what they were thinking. There wasn't a tree for miles on these flat, hot plains.

Rider looked toward the wagons. "We use wagon tongues."

"What?" Pettigrew asked.

Rider nodded. "You pull two wagons so that their tongues form an 'A' frame in the air and lash them together. Let's get it over with."

Willie Adams had fallen to his knees and was begging for his life while his father fought and cursed and swore vengeance. "I am really sorry about this," Rider said gently and gestured to some of the other men to tie the old farmer up. "Take him back to his wagon," he said. "He shouldn't have to watch this."

Now he turned to Emma. "This isn't going to be a pretty sight. Get all the women and take them back to their wagons. Let the men handle this."

"But Rider —"

"Sky Eyes, don't argue with me," he thundered. "This isn't something I want you to see."

Emma took a deep breath and motioned to the other women. Their eyes were full of dread and fear as they gathered up their children and went to their wagons.

Rider watched her go. He hadn't meant to speak so harshly to her, but she was a gentle soul and what she would witness would give her nightmares. He'd seen a hanging once — one of the few friends he had among the white people. What was ironic was that Whitt was no outlaw. Innocent or not, he'd been lynched and they hadn't done a good job of it. Rider had tried to rescue him, but the mob had held him back while Whitt slowly strangled and gasped for air from that beam in an old barn. That had been the final step in putting Rider on the outlaw trail.

He shuddered at the memory, never wanting to witness another hanging, but as wagon boss, this carrying out of the sentence was now his responsibility. He knew it had to be done or all discipline would break down on this train. Besides, Willie Adams was such a furious, crazed man that he might kill someone else before the train reached Oregon.

The day was dying, turning the sky the color of pale blood as Rider mounted up, riding around and giving instructions as the men pulled two wagons close enough to lash the tongues together up in the air. One of the men threw a sturdy rope up over the beams and someone brought a horse around.

Rider had never hated anything as much in his life as he hated being a part of this. He looked down into the angry, terrified face of Willie Adams. "You want time to pray?"

Instead, Willie let loose with a string of oaths. "You bastards! You got no right to kill me!"

"A jury of your peers has found you guilty of cold-blooded murder," Rider said softly. "And you were already under a death sentence. Society has a right to protect itself from men like you. That's all that keeps civilization from breaking down completely."

Young Adams spat at him. "If I could get loose, I'd kill you first of all, you half-breed Injun bastard! I'd kill the rest of you, too!"

The other men looked uncertainly at Rider. He took a deep breath and tried not to think of Whitt. "If we must do this, let's do it right."

Two of the men wrestled the defiant one onto a bay horse, then led him under the makeshift gallows.

As they put the rope around his neck, the young tough was shouting curses and was so terrified, he wet his clothes.

Rider looked around. "You men want to draw straws to see who whips the horse?"

The others shook their heads and began backing away.

Rider frowned. "Somebody connected with the jury ought to do it."

Pettigrew took off his derby and wiped his red jowls. "You're the wagon boss — we figure it's your job."

Rider sighed. Dusk was turning pale lavender with only a few faint bloody streaks to the west. There wasn't enough guts in this whole bunch to make one real man. He rode Storm over behind the bay horse.

Young Adams twisted in the saddle, cursing and weeping, threatening what he would do to everyone if he could get loose.

"Willie, I'm sorry it came to this," Rider whispered.

"You go to hell!" Willie shouted, "You Injun bastard and the rest of you sons of bitches —"

Rider slapped the bay across the rear with a quirt and the horse half-reared, then galloped out from under the condemned man. For less than a heartbeat, Willie fell and then the rope jerked taut. It almost seemed to Rider that he heard the man's neck snap and the agonized sigh of the others as they watched. Willie went limp, swinging from the end of the rope between two wagon tongues. Rider closed his eyes and tried not to think of Whitt. When he opened them, Willie was silhouetted in the dying light, swinging gently at the end of the rope on a treeless prairie.

"Oh, my God," Carrolton said.

Banker Pettigrew stumbled away into the darkness. Rider could hear him vomiting in the grass.

He was suddenly sick himself and he swallowed hard and looked away. "All right, it's done. Someone cut him down and bury him. At dawn, we'll move on."

He wheeled his stallion and rode away without looking back. Rider found a big outcrop of rocks a few hundred feet away from the wagons, unsaddled, and staked out his horse. Then he took his bedroll and climbed up there, spreading it out. He didn't want to spend tonight among the wagons. He rolled a cigarette and watched the coming night. His soul was in turmoil, but the sky seemed so peaceful.

He was anything but peaceful himself. He thought of the life he had led for the past five years, a life of violence and carousing. Once he had had a warrior's heart. Now he felt as dead and lifeless inside as Willie Adams. The sounds of the prairie and the wind comforted him and he remembered his life among the Shoshoni and wished for that freedom in the mountains again.

A noise. He turned, drawing his pistol. Emma Trent's small face appeared below him. "You took a chance coming out here, Sky Eyes. I might have killed you. What do you want?"

"I-I brought you some food."

He shook his head. "I'm not hungry. What I'd really like is a drink."

"Sorry, I don't have that."

He ignored her and stared into space. When he looked down, she was still there, waiting patiently. "Go to bed. We've got a long day ahead of us tomorrow."

"You don't want some company? It's mighty lonely out here."

Rider shrugged. "I'm a lonely man. Now go back to your wagon."

Emma watched his profile in the moonlight as he rolled a cigarette. When the match flared, she realized his hands were shaking as badly as his voice. She hesitated, then climbed up on the rocks and settled on the blanket next to him.

"Didn't you hear me?" he muttered.

"I heard you." She put her hand on his arm. "Rider, what you did just now was a hard thing, but it had to be done."

"Damn it, I don't want to talk about it!" He ground out the smoke without ever taking a puff. In the moonlight, she saw him look down and notice her hand on his arm. "What is it you want, Sky Eyes?"

She shook her head. "I don't want anything. I just felt sorry for you because —"

"I don't need anyone to feel sorry for me," he thundered and jerked away from her touch. "I'm doing just fine, lady."

"Are you?" She looked up at him and with a muttered curse, he reached for her, pulling her hard against him as his hungry mouth sought hers. The terrible conflict, the need of him, was more overpowering than her own fear, and she didn't pull away as he kissed her deeply, passionately. He was pawing at her bodice, pushing up her skirts. Although her heart pounded with uncertainty, she didn't move or fight him.

"Don't you understand?" he panted. "You stay here and I'm gonna take you so hard . . ."

Perhaps he expected her to scream or scramble away from him, but she looked up into his tortured face and saw the terrible need there and his need was greater than her fear. "Oh, Rider." Gently, she took his weathered, dark face between her two hands and brushed her lips across his.

He hesitated, perhaps unsure what message she was sending him. Then with a groan, he gathered her to him, kissing her deeply. She was trembling as she slipped her arms around his neck. "Yes, Rider, yes. . . ."

She took a deep breath and didn't stop him as his mouth kissed wildly down her throat and he tore at her bodice. He needed comfort and she could give him that.

He seemed wild in his desperate hurt as his dark face found her pale breast. She ran her hands through his black hair as he sucked her hungrily and let her thighs fall apart. His hands shook with need as he pushed up her skirt and tore her pantelets away. For a split second, she hesitated, terrible memories flooding over her. Then she closed her eyes and reached to unbutton his pants. She put her arms around his big frame, pulling him toward her. He made a sound like a wounded animal as he came down on her. "Sky Eyes . . . Sky Eyes. . . ."

She opened to him and he came into her, hard and big as a stallion, his flesh slamming against hers. He was too big for her, bigger than she had known a man could be and violent with his need. She reached up under his shirt, feeling the scars and the hard muscle there as he rode her in a frenzy, like a wild stallion mounting a mare. Flesh slammed against flesh as he rose and came down on her with all the power of his hard-driving, lean hips.

"You," he whispered against her lips, "wanted you from the first moment I saw you. . . ."

He had not said he loved her, but that didn't matter. All that mattered was his need and the comfort her body could give his. Emma wrapped her long legs about his hard-driving hips, bucking with him as he mated with her. It was fierce and primitive and yet somehow gentle because of the protective way he enfolded her in his arms and kissed her lips.

At that moment, he came hard and long, his whole big body quivering as he gave up his seed to her deepest place. She could feel him throbbing deep within her as he gasped and came again, his hands moving under her hips, pulling her against him as he filled her. She held him close, stroked his hair, and kissed his face.

For a long moment, he lay there gasping and shuddering. Then he rose up slowly on his elbows, his dark face bewildered. "What? Why?"

"You needed me, Rider," she whispered.

"Need?" He pulled out of her and sat up, swearing. "By God, I need no one and I take no pity, least of all a woman's!"

"But Rider —"

"You felt sorry for me? Is that it? You let me have you because you felt sorry for me?"

For a moment, she thought he would strike her; his face was a mask of fury and she drew back.

"Look, lady, I don't need your pity and I don't need you." He climbed down off the rocks, buttoning his pants. "Just stay the hell away from me from now on!"

"But Rider, you don't understand —" However, he had already unstaked his horse and headed toward the wagons in long, angry strides. Emma watched him go, torn with conflict. Now that she had given in to him, he was angry with her. Rider was a proud man and he took charity from no one, not even the brief comfort of a woman's arms.

Emma looked down at her bare breasts and remembered the image of his dark face against her pale skin, the sensation of his hot mouth caressing there. She could smell the male scent of him on her skin. The memory of him in her arms stirred an emotion that she didn't recognize. It had not been fear. Even at the moment of his most primitive, rough consummation, she had not feared Rider. He had stirred something deep within her that almost made her want to be one with him. Puzzled at her feelings and his hostile reactions, she walked slowly back to her wagon.

Returning to camp, Rider went out into an isolated place in the grass to bed down. Somehow tonight, he didn't want to sleep under her wagon and think about her lying right above him. *What was he so angry about?* He'd finally possessed her and wasn't that what he'd been after all the long weeks of this trip? No, he hadn't possessed her, he told himself grimly; she'd let him use her body. By God, there was a difference. He wanted more from her than a whore would give — much more. What was it he wanted? He'd never experienced this feeling before so he wasn't quite certain. Damn it, it wasn't pity.

He lay there sleepless, watching her return to her wagon and remembering the softness of her mouth and the taste of her breasts. She'd aroused something in him so overpowering that he couldn't get enough of her, not nearly enough. Damn her for that. He didn't need her charity. Hell, he'd show her. Lying there sleepless, Rider vowed that at the next opportune moment, he was finally going to steal the banker's gold and ride away. To hell with them all. He'd seen enough of Emma Trent and this wagon train to last him a lifetime!

Chapter Fifteen

They pulled out at dawn past the fresh grave of Willie Adams. Rider ordered the men to take all the older Adamses' weapons because the man had threatened to kill Rider the first chance he got.

Rider didn't look at Emma Trent as he galloped past her wagon. He would not be beholden to anyone, especially a slim girl who had now exposed the most vulnerable, loneliest core of his inner soul.

Emma had not slept well herself. Again and again in her troubled dreams, she had been locked in the gunfighter's hot embrace, giving herself to him to soothe his deep, terrible need. She couldn't stop remembering his hot mouth on her breast, the strength of his embrace, the surprising tenderness that he hid behind that hard exterior.

They reached the Sweetwater none too soon. The animals, crazed for water, ran the last few hundred yards to the river, dragging the wagons so fast, buckets and tools fell from the sides. The people were almost as crazy with relief, splashing in the water and drinking their fill. Some wanted to linger, but Rider insisted they fill their water barrels and take the trail again. Emma began to lose track of time. It seemed one day was just like the day before, monotonous and miserable. Rider ignored her, and she'd reached a point that she didn't care anymore.

Then in the distance loomed Independence Rock — she could concentrate on moving closer to it each day. Like many of the others, Emma and her son climbed up to add their names to its scarred sides. She wondered how many of the names scratched in the rock had actually made it through this wilderness to Oregon. She didn't want to think about that. From here, she could see Rider sitting his Appaloosa and staring at her. She couldn't fathom his expression.

Rider turned away from watching the girl and muttered to the fat banker. "We're running behind."

McGinnis wiped his sweating face. "How much?"

"Well," Rider said, "they call it Independence Rock because most successful trains reach it around the Fourth of July. We're just reaching it in the middle of August. We're liable to be caught in the high country when it snows."

The next day, they moved on. The terrain was much rougher now, the Sweetwater slicing through the granite hills of Devil's Gate. The pass was too narrow so the wagons went south of it; in the distance, they could see Split Rock like a beacon beckoning them toward the Rocky Mountains.

Rider let the train stop overnight at the Ice Spring Slough where even in the summer, ice was protected by the peat bog. He smiled as he watched Josh marvel at the ice floating in his tin cup of water, but when Emma looked his way, he ignored her. He would be deserting the train soon, and looking into those trusting blue eyes troubled him.

They passed through the South Pass of the Rockies, such a gentle rise that most never realized they had crossed the Continental Divide until they noted the streams now ran toward the Pacific. They were halfway to their destination and the worst still lay ahead.

The hills got steeper and some days, the train didn't make five miles. During the struggle to get the Carroltons' heavy wagon up a slope, one of their oxen fell dead.

Rider rode up, rubbed his forehead, and cursed. "I told you to lighten your load."

"No!" Millicent wailed, "I've got to have my walnut chest and Grandmother's chair, and the dishes — oh, I can't leave my china for some savage to destroy!"

"Now, Millicent," her husband began, "the man's right, you know."

"He's a savage — he doesn't know anything!" Millicent shrieked. "I won't leave my things!"

The rest of the wagons had stopped to watch the little drama out of curiosity.

Rider shrugged and took the canteen off his saddle for a long drink. "Suit yourself, Mrs. Carrolton, but I'm telling you that your remaining oxen can't make it another two days with that load. Some of you men cut up that dead ox. At least we've got beef for supper."

Emma's heart went out to the distressed woman as she watched the Carroltons argue. She herself had never owned such fine things, but she could see how much each treasure meant to the aristocratic southern belle. She swung down off her wagon and walked back. "Perhaps," she said gently, "perhaps me and some of the ladies

371

could help her decide what to take and what to leave."

"No!" shrieked Millicent and burst into a storm of weeping. "I'll not have a gun-fighter's slut pawing through my things. She might take something!"

Rider's mouth hardened into a grim line. "Watch your mouth, Mrs. Carrolton, before I forget you're a woman. Mrs. Trent is trying to help. There's no call to treat her like that."

Emma gestured him away. "It's all right," she said, "she's upset."

Rider looked at her. "I don't give a damn how upset she is, nobody talks to you like that."

No one had ever protected or defended her before. She liked the feeling. "Thank you," she whispered.

Rider didn't look at her. He shrugged as if it were a small thing. "Well?" he said to the elegant Southerner. "What's it going to be, Carrolton?"

The man sighed. "I'll have to help her choose the things to leave behind. I'm afraid it'll take awhile."

Grumbling reverberated through the crowd.

"Okay, then we'll camp for the day," Rider said, more than a little annoyed.

The banker frowned. "But we'll lose half a day."

"I know." Rider nodded agreement. "But the oxen are tired after making this hill and so are the people. We'll leave at sunrise."

They set up camp and ate, then everyone sat around and stared glumly into the fire. Josh climbed up on Rider's lap, but Rider brusquely told the little boy he was busy and chased him away. He told himself that it wasn't good that the boy get too attached to a roaming gunfighter who would leave soon. There was no place in Rider's life for the responsibilities of this woman, her kid, and the dog. Still he didn't like the hurt look in Josh's big, dark eyes as the child ran for his mother's wagon. It made Rider feel like a villain.

Most of the night, the Carroltons argued while Millicent wept. It kept the whole camp awake. Each piece her husband tried to leave behind, Millicent put back on the load. "You can't expect me to set up housekeeping without my mother's trunk? How can I entertain properly if I don't have my silver punch bowl?"

"My dear, I'm sorry, but we must leave most of this behind."

Millicent broke into a storm of weeping. "You!" she sneered at her husband. "If you hadn't been such a yellow belly, afraid to fight, they wouldn't have run us out of the county. I could still be in my big, fine home. I hate you for your cowardice, you hear me? I hate you, Weatherford!"

"Millicent, please! Do you want the whole world to know — ?"

"I don't care what the world knows!" she shouted, "Hey, everyone, my husband is a coward who's running from the war and now it's going to cost me my beautiful things!"

It went on all night, but finally, at dawn, when Rider went over to inspect, the Carroltons' wagon was almost empty; a huge pile of dishes and furniture was stacked by the side of the road. Millicent Carrolton sat on a rock, weeping silently. Rider cleared his throat. "We're ready to move on."

"I won't go!" Millicent came to her feet. "I'm going to stay right here with my things, Weatherford, until you decide how I can take them with us."

"But my love," the aristocratic Southerner wrung his hands, "we've got to go or be left behind."

"No," she shrieked and stomped her fine little shoe. "I will not leave my things on the road so some traveling white trash can pick through and take them."

The husband looked up at Rider helplessly. Rider leaned on his saddle horn. "She's your problem to deal with," he said.

Just ahead of the Carroltons' wagon, Emma Trent turned on the wagon seat and looked back at him as if asking what she could do to help. Rider made a helpless gesture.

Weatherford B. Carrolton must have realized the whole train was waiting and watching. He grew flushed and flustered. "Millicent, dear, I am your husband and I'm telling you to get in that wagon and let's go."

She drew herself up proudly. "I will not do it."

"Very well then, I'll put you in the the wagon myself." The Southern gentleman got down, went over, and picked her up, kicking and screaming. He set her up on the seat of the wagon while she surrendered to a storm of weeping. Then she slapped him hard, clambered down off the seat, and returned to sit on the furniture and boxes piled by the roadside.

Her husband looked at Rider in frustration. "Let's just leave her," he said in a loud, embarrassed voice.

Rider paused. "Whatever you think — she's your wife." He turned his stallion and galloped back up to the front of the train. "Wagons ho!"

They pulled out, Emma craning her neck to see behind her. As the trail curved, she could see Millicent in her fine blue silk gown and parasol sitting on top of her abandoned pile of things. Surely Rider wasn't going to allow Millicent to be left behind? However, the train kept moving. When they had gone nearly a mile, Rider cantered by and she hailed him. "What are you going to do about Mrs. Carrolton?"

He reined in, shrugged. "She's not mine to do anything about. If Carrolton can't control her, that's his problem."

"But we can't just go off and leave her!"

Rider sighed. "I imagine in a few minutes, she'll get scared and start following us or Carrolton will lose his nerve and go back and beg her on bended knee."

His arrogance annoyed her. "And what would you do?"

"If she were my woman, I'd whip her bottom and throw her across my saddle. She puts more value on things than people. Besides, she's making her man look like a fool."

She just surveyed him without speaking, thinking about Rider's pride and wondering about a beautiful Shoshoni girl named Blue Bird.

In another hour, Weatherford B. Carrolton begged the wagon train to halt, and borrowed a horse. Humiliated and angry, he took Rider with him to go back after his wife. She was still sitting on her pile of boxes. "If you've come to apologize, Weatherford, it isn't enough."

"Look, lady," Rider snapped, "you've held up this train long enough. Now I'm telling you we're moving on and if you won't go with us, we're leaving you here. You and your silver punch bowl will be quite a prize to a passing Indian war party."

Her face blanched but she did not move.

"Please, Millicent," her husband begged.

"No, not without my things."

Rider's dark face turned grim. "Act like a man, Weatherford. Pick her up and put her on your horse."

The gentleman dismounted hesitantly. "Please, Millicent, you heard the man."

"No." She drew herself up proudly. "You haven't got the guts, Weatherford, to man-handle me like that gunfighter might do a woman."

Carrolton hesitated.

Rider glared at him. "We're wasting time. Take her."

Carrolton approached her hesitantly and she kicked and scratched and yelled at him like a common saloon tart. Her husband struggled to pick her up, full silk skirts and all, and put her on the horse. With her shrieking and fighting, they turned back up the trail to the train.

When they reached the wagons, Carrolton managed to get her up on the seat behind the three oxen and the train started off again. Millicent collapsed on the seat, sobbing her eyes out as the wagons began a steep, rocky ascent. "My things!" she wailed. "My beautiful things!"

"I'll buy you some new things. My sister will know how to order from San Francisco —"

"Your sister!" Millicent sneered. "Why, she has no taste — she ran off with some poor sharecropper. The Carroltons are white trash compared to my family, do you hear? White trash!"

"Please, Millicent, everyone is listening!" Her husband tried to quiet her, but every wagon heard her screeching.

"We're going to a godforsaken place where the yokels won't even know how to use a finger bowl. I hate you, Weatherford! I hate you as much as I did the day the county ran you out as a coward!"

Rider shook his head at the man's humiliation and rode up ahead to check out the trail. There were lots of rocks and deep ravines along the path and he needed to keep a sharp lookout. They would soon be in Shoshoni country and the air was turning cooler with August advancing.

Finally they camped for the night. At first light, as they hitched the oxen and made ready to leave, Carrolton came running. "It's Millicent — she's disappeared!"

Rider began to curse. "How long's she been gone?"

The other shook his head. "Sometime in the night, I reckon."

"She's putting the whole train at risk with these delays."

Emma listened, then cleared her throat. "You know she's gone back to get her things. Maybe some of us could make a little room for the best of it, the things that mean the most to her."

Rider smiled at her in spite of himself. "You're a generous soul, Emma Trent." Then he remembered how generous she had been with him and stopped smiling. He turned to the distraught husband. "We'll go back and look for her. It's a dangerous trail after dark."

They halted the train and went back. Rider spotted the blue silk blowing in the early morning wind long before he realized what he was looking at. Millicent Carrolton had fallen down the side of a gully and lay still as a broken doll. "Oh, my God," Rider said and dismounted.

"No!" Weatherford B. Carrolton's patrician face turned pale as clay as he turned and saw what Rider was staring at. "No, this can't be."

Rider didn't say anything. He climbed down the side of the crevice and knelt by the body. "Carrolton, go get some of the others."

Carrolton peered over the side of the rock, shaking his head. "Millicent? Millicent dear, don't play tricks on me. I'm sorry. Do you hear me? We'll make room for all your things and —"

"She can't hear you now," Rider called. "Go get help."

The other man began to sob and shake violently. "This is your fault! You were the one who insisted she couldn't take her things. This is all your fault!"

"Carrolton," Rider spoke gently as if to an injured child, "go get help. You don't want to leave her here, do you?"

That seemed to bring him to his senses. Sobbing aloud, the man mounted up and galloped away.

Rider squatted down beside her. Her head lay at an odd angle, her swollen eyes staring into the vast prairie sky. Gently, he wiped the dust from her pretty face. "You selfish little bitch," he whispered. "Now just see what you've done over some damned dishes."

In a few minutes, many curious faces peered at him over the edge of the rocks.

"Throw me a rope," he ordered.

McGinnis said, "It's pretty dangerous for you to try to bring her up."

"Yeah," Francie peered over the edge, "and after all, she's dead. Why don't you leave her lay?"

"Have some feelings for her husband," Rider scolded the redhead. "Now, damn it, someone get me a rope."

Emma's face appeared over the top, her eyes wide with worry. "What can I do to help?"

He could count on her — he could always count on her. "Wait'll I get her up," he said.

It was harrowing work, but Rider took the dead woman in his arms, and with the help of a rope, worked his way up the rocky hillside.

Weatherford B. Carrolton rushed forward as Rider laid the woman carefully on the ground and smoothed her skirts to protect her dignity. The husband fell beside her, helpless with grief, but screaming curses at

Rider and blaming him for Millicent's death.

Rider stood up and sighed. Emma handed him a canteen and put her hand on his arm. "The women will take over from here."

He nodded and went over and sat down on a rock, watching Emma wash the dead woman's face ever so gently.

They buried Millicent Carrolton of the Vicksburg Carroltons on the side of a nameless hill somewhere in the Wyoming country. Her grieving husband returned to their abandoned things, got her silver punch bowl, and put it on the grave. "It was the kind of marker she would like," he explained, "since there's no elaborate granite works hereabouts."

No one said anything as he looked toward Rider with hate in his eyes. "All your fault," he mumbled. Rider didn't answer or try to defend himself.

After Jones had said a few words and the people had sung a hymn, Rider said, "Well, I reckon we'd better be moving on."

The Southerner turned toward him with a numb expression. "You mean, just go off and leave her here a thousand miles from anywhere? No, I-I can't do that."

Emma put her hand on his arm. "Mr.

Carrolton, we have to go on. She's dead."

He shook his head. "I can't leave her. She'd hate this desolate hillside."

Emma said gently, "She's in a better place now."

His shoulders slumped. "I never should have taken her from Mississippi," he wept. "She was not a pioneer sort."

No one said anything.

Emma took his arm. "Come on, Mr. Carrolton, you were going to Oregon, remember?"

He didn't seem to remember anything at all, but he let Emma lead him to his wagon and climbed up on the seat.

Mr. Weeks said, "I'll ride with him awhile and drive."

The wagons pulled away in the late afternoon across the hostile, rocky landscape. When Emma looked back, she could see the sun reflecting on the silver punch bowl marking the grave of a highborn lady thousands of miles from home.

Only a day later, as they traveled, Rider saw two riders in the distance. He reached for his rifle and held up his hand to stop the wagons.

A voice called, "Hello, the train!"

White men. Rider motioned them to approach and two grizzled miners leading a donkey came down the trail and reined up. Rider looked at the gold pans hanging from their burro. "Where you hombres heading?"

The one with the battered hat and yellow teeth said, "Ain't you heard? There's been a gold strike up on Grasshopper Creek."

"That's right," said his bearded partner, "we've made a poke full of dust and we're headed back to civilization for a good time. It's supposed to be richer than the Blue Bucket mine."

Rider almost groaned aloud. Gold meant many more greedy prospectors pouring into the area and more trouble for the Shoshoni. Trouble for the Shoshoni meant trouble for white settlers.

In the meantime, the men on the other wagons had passed the word and were scrambling to surround the pair. "Gold? did you say gold?"

The yellow-toothed one nodded. "Yep, plenty of gold."

The settlers looked at each other. "Let's set a spell and hear about it."

Rider leaned on his saddle horn. "We're losin' time."

"But gold's important." Gray's eyes lit up along with the others.

He wasn't going to move this train any

farther today, Rider decided. "All right, tell the women to make some coffee."

The bearded one looked around. "Women? You got white women with you?"

Rider frowned, thinking of Emma. "Not your kind of women."

The two laughed. "Listen, stranger, we got plenty of gold in our pokes. Any kind of woman likes that."

They all got down and built a fire. Tobacco was passed around as the settlers eagerly pressed the miners for details. Rider knew without asking that when they got close to the gold fields, some of these people would no longer be bound for Oregon.

Emma came over, followed by Josh and the barking pup. One of the newcomers looked at Emma with ill-disguised interest, then at the half-breed child. "Your woman?"

"My woman," Rider said flatly.

He saw that she started to argue that point, then seemed to think better of it. "Rider," she asked, "will you be going to the gold fields?"

He saw the fear in her eyes that he might be about to abandon them. "Too much work, that and farming." Besides, he thought, there's plenty of gold in Pettigrew's wagon.

The others crowded around, asking about news of the gold, their excitement growing as the prospectors talked.

Rider rolled a cigarette. "You see any sign of Indians?"

The newcomers shook their heads. "Everyone behind us is talkin' about trouble, but all we seen is some fire somewhere up the canyon."

"You go have a look?"

Yellow Teeth shook his head. "Never go lookin' for trouble," he said. "If it's Injuns, we might find them and they say Bear Hunter and Man Lost is out for blood. Besides, the fire might just be some trees lightning set fire to."

"In Shoshoni country?" He didn't say anything else, but got up, walked over, and leaned against a tree a few hundred yards away from the others. Bear Hunter. His old enemy, *Potoptuah*, might be riding with Bear Hunter's band. *Wasp*. It was a fitting name for that warrior.

Emma Trent followed him out there. "What is it?"

He shook his head. "I might as well be honest with you. We're getting deeper into Shoshoni country. We're late in the season, short on everything but trouble. I've got old man Adams waiting for a chance to shoot me in the back and Millicent's half-crazed husband wanting to help him. I'd be loco not to clear out tonight."

"And go to the gold country?"

"Anyplace but here." He laughed. "Besides, we've got gold with us, stolen from old Pettigrew's bank."

"How do you know that?" She looked up at him with those deep blue eyes, deep enough for a man to lose himself in.

"Because Francie wants me to take it and the two of us vamoose."

She drew in a small breath. "Why — why are you telling me this?"

"I don't know," and he really didn't, except that he trusted her. "I'm loco not to have cleared out already."

"Don't you have a care about the people on this train?"

He snorted. "About as much as they do for me." He didn't want her to think she might have come to mean anything at all to him.

"This train can't make it to Oregon without you, Rider."

"You think I give a big goddamn?" He threw his smoke in the dirt and ground it out.

"You're a hard man, Rider."

He turned away. It was difficult to be cynical and bitter while looking into those sky-blue eyes.

"What about Josh and the other kids?"

"I didn't sire them — they ain't my responsibility."

"I can't believe you said that," she whispered and her tone sounded both betrayed and angry. "Josh loves you. We both depend on you."

"By God, you'd better stop depending on me, you hear?" he lashed out at her. "Because you can't. Just because I want your body doesn't mean I want the responsibilities of a woman, a kid, and a mongrel dog."

"I see." She whirled and strode back to the wagons.

He watched her proud, angry silhouette as she left him. Her small shoulders shook as if she might be crying. He hated himself at that moment for making her cry and hated her for the emotional hold she seemed to be putting on him. Damn, things were getting complicated. He'd only come along to use her as a plaything. Now that he'd had her once, it wasn't enough. He wanted more from her and he wasn't quite sure what it was. He felt a terrible need to run after her and apologize for hurting her.

No, he shook his head. Rider never apologized. There was no need to care what she thought, not when he'd be riding out soon. Let this damned wagon train look after itself; these losers deserved to be stranded.

Somehow, that didn't make him feel any better.

The next morning, the two prospectors headed out, riding east, and the train took to the trail again. Emma didn't speak to Rider all day as they drove and that suited him just fine because he'd already decided that tonight was the night. When everyone was asleep, he was going to knock Pettigrew unconscious, take the gold, and leave. Maybe he'd take Francie with him just because there was no way to leave her behind without her raising a ruckus. He'd have plenty of opportunities to dump her on the way to San Francisco. She was pretty and fun to sleep with, but girls like Francie were a dime a dozen, not like Emma Trent.

Well, to hell with Emma Trent, too. Tonight, he'd abandon them to their own foolishness.

What changed his plans was that late in the afternoon, they topped a rise and spotted a curl of smoke rising up through the trees. Rider called a halt, and taking some of the men with him, rode over to investigate. When they topped a rise and looked down, the hair on the back of his neck rose in warning prickles as he realized the silent, twisted wreckage below was the remains of a burned-out wagon train.

Chapter Sixteen

They stared down at the smoldering wreckage a long moment.

McGinnis took a deep breath. "Good Lord," he whispered, "I-I think it might be the train that deserted us. I recognize some of the wagons."

Rider stood up in his stirrups and looked around, listening. He wanted to make sure they weren't riding into an ambush. "All right," he said finally, "let's go down and see."

The scent was what he remembered most as they descended the trail — the scent of smoke and burned bodies and rotting oxen. Around him, the others gagged and retched, but Rider had seen too much death to sicken at it anymore. "Hello, the train!" he yelled. "Anyone here?"

He paused to listen, but there was no answer. He hadn't really expected to find survivors after he'd first seen the burned destruction. Rider wended his way on down to the site and dismounted. A buzzard flew up suddenly from what was left of an ox lying dead in its traces, feathered arrows sticking from its bloated hide at odd angles. He leaned over and pulled one of the arrows, studied the markings.

Behind him, Jones said, "Oh, my God, it is our train."

"*Was* your train," Rider corrected. "Looks like Shoshoni got 'em." He didn't say that he recognized the personal mark on the arrow as *Potoptuah*'s. To do so would invite all sorts of questions. "Have a look around," he said. "There might be someone still alive, but I doubt it."

A quick walk around the site confirmed his worse suspicions. The train appeared to have attempted to circle up and then tried to hold off a war party. The few weapons found at the scene were empty. The dead lay scattered across the landscape in their burned wagons, war lances sticking from bodies and sacks of grain. Wasp had evidently come out of nowhere with his fast and deadly sting. He was aptly named. The train had never had a chance.

Behind him, men cursed as they walked around, surveying the scene. "Let's get them buried," Rider ordered, "then see if there's anything left we can use."

Pettigrew wiped his red jowls and frowned. "It don't seem quite right to rob the dead."

Rider shrugged as he leaned against a wagon wheel. "They don't need the stuff anymore and we do. However, the Shoshoni are pretty hungry themselves — they may not have left much."

A quick inventory proved him right. Although some foodstuffs and clothing were scattered, it appeared the Indians had looted most of the food, weapons, and blankets.

Jones reached for a shovel and wiped tears from his eyes. "We gonna go after those red devils?"

"Are you loco?" Rider snorted. "We're outnumbered, short on food and cartridges, and soon to get snowed in in the mountains."

The others looked outraged. "We ain't gonna just let them go unpunished?"

Rider pushed his hat back. "We're approaching Fort Bridger. We'll report it to the army and they'll send out patrols of soldiers who can't find their butts with both hands."

"But the savages have killed all these innocent people!" McGinnis raised his voice as if talking to an idiot.

"This is war, mister," Rider said, holding his temper, "and innocent people always die in war. These wagon trains coming through are pushing the Shoshoni and the other tribes deeper into the mountains. There's a lot of innocent women and children among them, too."

Pettigrew sneered. "Half-breed Injun lover."

Rider almost lost his temper, then decided it would do no good. "Do like I tell you — get these folks buried fast, pick up what we can use, and let's clear out."

Carrolton looked bewildered. "Why is there a rush?"

"Because," Rider said patiently, "the Shoshoni always have scouts out. They might have spotted our train by now and we'll have to fight our way to Fort Bridger."

His words galvanized the others into action. Quickly, they buried the dead and picked up whatever they thought was useable. It wasn't much. The Shoshoni war party had obviously been in dire need of supplies.

It was almost dusk when they returned to the train. The women hurried to meet them. "What was it?"

Rider gave the other men a warning shake

of the head. There was no point in pan-
icking the camp, especially the children.
"Nothing," he said, "just the remains of a
fire probably started by lightning. We found
a few usable things a train might have abandoned when their loads got too heavy. We'll
camp here tonight."

Rider tossed Emma Trent sacks of beans,
rice, and cornmeal. Then he ordered the
men to set a double guard. He tied up his
horse, walked away from the camp, and sat
down with his back against a pine tree. He
took out the arrow he had stuffed in his shirt
and stared at it. There was no doubt it was
Wasp's mark. Rider had pulled it from the
back of an old lady. How like that brave to
kill the helpless. Old memories came
flooding back. Wasp had been his enemy
since they were young boys. It was the
murder of Wasp's brother, Porcupine, that
had caused Rider to be exiled from his tribe.
The beautiful maiden, Blue Bird, had been
promised to Porcupine.

It was growing dark. Rider heard foot-
steps from the camp. Quickly, he slipped the
arrow inside his shirt.

Emma Trent walked toward him. "I
brought you some food."

He took the plate, still sick with the
memory of the carnage he'd seen this after-

noon, but he ate a few bites.

Her trusting blue eyes watched him. "What did you men really find out there today?"

He hesitated. "Like I told you."

"Rider, I've gotten to know you well enough that I can tell when you're lying."

He shrugged. "I don't like people getting that close."

"I know that. What did you find?"

He sighed. "You don't want to know."

"That bad?"

He nodded. "Shoshoni war party led by a dog soldier named Wasp. They could be anywhere within a couple of hundred miles."

"I see." There was tension on her suntanned face, but she did not sob or grow hysterical. "Are these friends or enemies of yours?"

Rider laughed without mirth. "I don't have any friends."

"But you know this brave?"

"Too well. He's the brother of *Muinyan*."

"Which means?" she prompted.

"Porcupine, the warrior I'm under a death sentence for killing."

She sat down on the ground and surveyed him calmly. "Then you're in big danger the further you get into Shoshoni country?"

"Yes."

She chewed her lip. "Then I reckon no one could blame you if you cleared out."

"That's just what I intend to do, Sky Eyes — take Pettigrew's gold and skedaddle." He reached out and caught her hand. "Go with me."

"What about Francie?"

"To hell with her," he snapped as she drew her hand away. "I owe her nothing. Francie's a whore I knew in the old days."

"You — you slept with her?" She looked away.

"That isn't a proper question."

She looked at him. "Did you sleep with her?"

"Hell, yes, and so did every other cowpoke and prospector from Texas to Canada. Now, does that answer your question?" He leaned back against the tree.

"I mean, on this trip?"

"Now why should that interest you? You haven't been panting to share my blankets."

She didn't say anything, just kept looking at him with those wide blue eyes.

"No, I haven't been sleeping with her, although she keeps offering. I must be the world's biggest damn fool."

"Rider," she reached out and put her hand on his arm, "are you really going to desert this train?"

He shook her hand off, angry with himself because she made him feel guilty. "I said I was, didn't I? You and Josh go with me?"

She sighed and shook her head. "It isn't right, leaving all these folks to fend for themselves. They can't make it through alone."

"After the way they've treated you? Why, you should be glad they're all going to get their just deserts."

"You're a better man than that, Rider."

He stood up. "By God, don't lecture me, lady. You got me into this mess in the first place."

"Me?" she touched her chest in surprise.

He looked at the swell of her breasts at the neck of her simple gingham dress. "You. I came because I wanted your body. I still want it." He reached out and took her arm, tried to pull her to him, but she tensed and did not let him fit her body against his.

She looked up at him, her lips slightly parted, tense. "I don't like this side of you, Rider."

He shrugged. "I told you the truth without sugar-coating it. Go with me, Sky Eyes. We can have a lot of high livin' on ten thousand dollars."

She shook her head. "I couldn't — not stolen money."

"Hell, old Pettigrew stole it himself. I don't know if you can steal stolen money."

She tried to pull away from him but he held onto her. "Oh, Rider, I-I was beginning to care about you, but —"

He cut off her words with his lips, molding her against him, his strong arms holding her close as he kissed her deeply, hotly. His insistent mouth parted her lips, explored within. She gasped at the sensation and he slipped his tongue inside. She wasn't afraid of him; what scared her was her own emotions, the way her body leaned toward him, pressed against him. His hot mouth sucked the tip of her tongue and she hesitated, then sighed, her pulse pounding harder as she let him suck her tongue into his mouth. Against her belly, she felt the hard mound of his arousal.

"Sky Eyes," he whispered insistently against her lips, "you — I'd do anything to possess you, really own you. Let me . . ." His hand went to cup her breast and for a long moment, she let the sensation sweep over her, wanting his hand to stroke and caress even more.

What was she thinking? This blackguard was getting ready to desert all of them, steal money, and run like a common, cowardly thief.

"No," she said and managed to break away from him. "No." She pulled from his grasp and fled into the darkness.

Rider looked after her, cursing. Time after time, he'd let this woman drive him almost loco with unquenched desire. He'd be a fool to stay.

Emma fled out onto the prairie, realizing how close she'd come again to letting the gunfighter possess her. What surprised her was the fact that her body had almost wanted that. She sat there in the darkness thinking. By morning, Rider might have deserted the camp if he could get his hands on that money. She and the rest of the train couldn't get through without his help. What could she do to make sure Rider stayed with the train? What was it he might want more than gold? She knew the answer to that; hadn't he told her often enough?

When she got back to camp, Rider had everyone yoking their oxen.

"We're moving in the darkness?" she asked.

"I'd like to put some distance between us and this place," he said.

Some wanted to bicker and gripe, but even they seemed to sense there was some kind of trouble and they needed to put this place far behind them. The moon came out big and bright and they traveled a number of miles before dawn.

Rider said, "With the sun coming up, let's camp among these pines. We'll be hard to see there."

There was a wide creek and Emma was only too glad to call a halt. Rider had instructed that they were to keep their fires low so no smoke would drift above the horizon. Some of the settlers took advantage of the the clear creek to bathe and wash a few clothes. Josh and his puppy played in the water while Rider sat up on a rock above them, keeping guard. She watched him as she carried Josh back to camp, a plan forming in her mind. Rider had to stay with this train; they'd be lost without him. She would do whatever it took to keep him with the train.

When she went back to the water, the others had returned to their wagons. The place was quiet in the late afternoon sun. Rider looked down at her from his guard post. "You shouldn't be out here alone."

"I'm not alone, you're here, so I figure no Indian's gonna sneak up on me."

He laughed. "You've got a lot of faith in me."

She nodded and began to unbutton her dress. "I could use a bath."

"You gonna take that off in front of me?"

She hesitated. "Well, you could turn your back."

He raised one eyebrow. "And if I don't?"

"I-I'll take it off anyhow." She stepped behind a tree, pulled off the dress, and hung it over a limb. She stood there a long moment, trying to decide if she had the nerve to do what she'd planned. If she seduced the gunfighter, let him have as much pleasure as he wanted, would he stay with the train so they could all get to Oregon?

She made a quick run and immersed herself in the stream, going down on her knees so that only her shoulders were out of the water. He watched her without speaking and she couldn't read his expression. Emma took a deep breath for courage. "Rider, wouldn't you like to join me?"

He frowned and shook his head. "Stop it, Sky Eyes. You don't know how to play this game."

He was right; she was ashamed at flaunting herself so brazenly. She didn't look at him. "I don't know what you're talking about."

"Sure you do. You're too innocent to play the whore." He strode over, got her towel off the limb, brought it to her, and held it out. "Now get out and get your clothes on before

401

I change my mind."

He had turned her down. Humiliated, tears began to gather and threatened to overflow. She took the towel, wrapping it around herself as she came up out of the stream. "I guess I'm not as attractive as Francesca Pettigrew —"

"Attractive?" He sounded angry. "Lady, you do try my patience and my will power."

She was sobbing now, looking up at him. "Oh, Rider, I'm bone tired and we're running short of food and without you, I'll never make it to Oregon."

He swore softly. "So this is what this is all about? You think you can bribe me with your body?"

"Obviously not." When she raised one small trembling hand to wipe away her tears, the towel half fell from the curves of her breast.

He reached out and jerked her hard against him, his hands going under the towel to hold her, his mouth claiming hers. His hands felt like fire on her wet skin as he molded her against him. "You already belong to me, remember?" he whispered with an oath. "The council gave you to me — I just wish you'd do the same."

She pulled her face away. "I'm offering."

"Hell," he muttered and shoved her away from him. "You're too naive to understand. Not this way, damn it. I don't want it this way." He turned on his heel and strode back to camp.

He brushed past Francie standing by her wagon. "Well, stud, where you goin' in such a hurry?"

"None of your damned business!" He waved her off brusquely. "When you want to clear out of here?"

Francie smiled and tried to take his arm, but he pulled away from her. "Oh, Rider, honey, I was hopin' you'd finally say that. We'll have such good times in San Francisco."

"Yeah, sure." He didn't look at her. He'd dump the coarse redhead the first chance he got and move on. Ten thousand dollars would take him a long, long way from the little blonde who was haunting his dreams and keeping him in a state of agitation. "Fort Bridger is only a day or two ahead of us — lots of people there. Maybe in all the excitement, we'll have a chance to clear out."

"Right." She grinned. "Until then, we'll act casual. Funny, I thought you had a thing for that blonde."

"Her?" Rider snorted. "You're the one,

baby. A man always knows where he stands with you."

With that settled, he went to see about his horse.

Emma had stared after him for a long moment, puzzled. Humiliated, she dried off, dressed and returned to camp. She was beginning to feel differently toward Rider and it unnerved her. She wasn't afraid of him anymore and she didn't hate him. She wasn't sure what the feeling was, but it kept her dreams in turmoil. Well, he'd be riding out soon and the train would have to do the best it could to survive. Emma sighed. She didn't have much hope that any of the other men could lead them all the way to Oregon. Maybe no new emergencies would happen.

That night, Mrs. Weeks went into early labor. Emma and some of the other women gathered around her to help. When Emma went back to the fire to get some hot water, Rider looked up at her. "How's it going? You look tired."

Emma pushed a yellow curl back. "I don't know — it's a hard labor."

From the Weeks wagon, a cry of pain.

Francie had just walked past. "Can't anyone make that dame shut up? Nobody can get any sleep."

"Francie," said Rider, "you're all heart."

Emma took the pan of hot water. "Rider, will you look out for Josh tonight?"

He nodded, "Sure."

Reassured, she returned to her task.

Rider stared after her. "That Weeks woman hasn't been too nice to Emma."

"She's a fool to help," Francie sneered. "I sure wouldn't bother. I'm surprised the Trent woman asked you to look after her half-breed brat. He ain't your problem."

"Don't call Josh that," Rider said and he didn't smile.

"Well," Francie looked him over, surprise in her green eyes, "ain't you the noble one all of a sudden? She got you thinkin' you're some kind of knight in shining armor?"

Rider looked at her a long moment and abruptly, he didn't like himself or Francie very much. "She just makes me wish I were a better hombre than I am," he said softly.

"Don't give me that shit!" Francie snapped. "We're two of a kind, out for ourselves, remember? Me and all my old geezer's gold is yours once we get to the fort."

"Sure." He stared into the fire.

"Well, you could sound a little more excited about it."

"I'm just tired, Francie. You'd better go to

your wagon before old Roscoe suspects something."

"Hey, you're right about that. But the fat bastard will want to climb on me."

Rider shrugged. "You knew what you were getting into."

She made a face. "Sometimes, I almost think the money ain't worth it. I'll close my eyes and pretend it's you, baby. You was the best I ever had." She turned and flounced away and he watched her go.

The best I ever had. The best he'd ever had was on a blanket up on a boulder under the stars the night they hanged Willie Adams. It could have been better. If Emma Trent had responded with passion instead of passive gentleness, it could have been so much better.

"Rider, you're a damned fool," he muttered as he poured himself a cup of coffee and stared into the fire. "Emma offered herself a while ago and you wrapped a towel around her instead. You could have enjoyed her, promised to stay with the train. You've lied before to get what you wanted, especially to women."

He found it impossible to lie to Emma. She was different and he knew it. Well, damn her to hell anyway for what she was doing to his mind. He got up, went to check on Josh. The little boy was curled up with his puppy in the wagon.

"When's my mama coming to bed?"

Rider reached out, brushing the dark hair from his eyes. "She's busy helpin' a lady in trouble."

Josh smiled shyly. "She's good with people in trouble."

"Yeah, she is," he said, remembering how she had reached out to his tortured soul the night they'd hanged Willie Adams. "You go to sleep now. Tomorrow, we'll move on and soon, we'll be at the fort. There'll be lots of people there and lemon drops in the store."

"What?"

"It's candy. Don't you know what candy is?"

Josh's small face wrinkled in thought. "I think I had some once."

Jesus. Times had been much worse for Sky Eyes and her son than Rider had thought. "If you could have anything in the world, what would it be?"

"A pony. A spotted one."

Rider nodded. "Well, maybe somewhere down the line, that can happen. A pony out west shouldn't be too hard to come by."

Josh's dark eyes lit up with excitement. "A pony? You promise?"

"I don't make promises. Besides, don't

ever believe in people too much. They'll break your heart like they break their promises."

"Would you do that, Rider?"

The child's innocence suddenly annoyed him. "Hell, kid, if I was going to, I wouldn't tell you."

"Oh."

He sounded crestfallen and Rider cursed himself for dashing the child's hopes. He'd try changing the subject. "You lookin' forward to Oregon?"

Josh nodded. "That's where we'll find the prince."

"The prince?" Rider scratched his head.

"Uh-huh. He'll carry us off on his big, fine horse and we'll live happily ever after."

Rider bit his lip. "Look, Josh, I wouldn't get my hopes up if I were you. Sometimes things don't work out the way they do in storybooks."

The child looked up at him confidently. "They do if you believe."

"Sure. Go to sleep now."

"Whatever you say, Rider."

Rider turned and walked away from the wagon. *Believe.* His lip curled with derision. Rider didn't believe in much of anything anymore, not storybooks, certainly not people. People always disappointed you and let you down. He had no doubt Francie would double-cross him in a minute if she got a better offer, just as he would her.

He sat by the fire most of the night, waiting to see if Emma Trent would need any help. Mrs. Weeks moaned and screamed every now and then. It was a hard thing to bring a child into the world, he thought, and remembered his own gentle mother and the love she had had for his father.

Finally, just before dawn, he heard the sudden wailing of a baby and grinned in spite of himself.

In a moment, Emma emerged from the Weeks wagon, carrying the tiny bundle. She showed it to the father, who waited by the wagon, then brought the infant over to the fire. "Isn't he cute? A little boy."

Rider glanced at the tiny, helpless bundle, then at Emma. Her face glowed with tenderness and he thought he had never seen such beauty. He pictured her suddenly holding his baby in her arms, smiling at him across the tiny little head as she was doing now. The thought made him feel all soft inside and he frowned. Softness was bad. Any bit of weakness could get a man killed in this dog-eat-dog world.

"Yeah, he's nice. Now can we move on in the morning?" He yawned and stretched.

She looked disappointed. "Yes, I reckon so."

"Good. We've had enough delays already."

"You're a hard man, Rider." She turned and carried the baby back to the Weeks wagon.

She'd know just how hard when he and Francie left them all stranded at the fort. Hot, passionate Francie would warm his bed as long as he wanted her, and there'd be other pretty women like her in San Francisco. Ten thousand in gold would buy him a lot of good times with no strings attached.

Chapter Seventeen

The early days of October were turning the trees yellow as the wagon train finally pulled into Fort Bridger. Rider signaled the wagons to pull up outside the fort's gates. "We'll be here several days, folks, enough time to repair wagons and buy supplies."

Boots ran around Emma's wagon, barking with excitement while Josh waved at Rider. "Rider! Hey, Rider!"

"Hey, Small Warrior!" He tipped his hat to Emma, but she only stared back at him. *This is where he leaves us,* she thought in desperation, *and we'll never make it through without him.* She'd barely spoken to Rider the last several days and he seemed to be avoiding her, too. Josh's feelings had seemed hurt over the neglect, but she could only tell him that Rider was very busy with his duties as wagon boss. *What to do?* Even if she told the others what Rider and Francesca Pettigrew planned and they believed her, what could they do? They couldn't tie Rider up and force him to lead them.

"Rider," her son yelled, "can I ride with you?"

"Josh, I don't think —" Emma began.

"Sure, kid."

Before she could stop him, Rider loped up and lifted her child to sit before him on the saddle. As the wagons formed their circle and stopped, curious people from the fort gathered — solders, trappers, and shop-keepers. Dogs ran everywhere and in the distance, commands to soldiers drilling on the parade ground rang through the woods. Weary people piled out of the wagons, eager to see the sights and visit with those at the fort.

A very handsome lieutenant in a blue uni-form came out of the gates and up to her wagon. He saluted smartly. "Lieutenant Foss at your service," he said to Rider, but he was looking at Emma.

She blushed at his frank appraisal. Rider's vision seemed to follow the young officer's gaze and he frowned. "We'll be here a couple of days, Lieutenant, with the com-mander's approval, of course."

He stroked his mustache and frowned. "Your train's awfully late coming through. We haven't seen one in some weeks now."

Rider nodded. "We found one of those that didn't make it in a canyon a few days ago."

Lieutenant Foss sighed. "Indians?"

"Shoshoni." Rider dismounted, put Josh on the ground.

The other man's patrician features wrinkled in arrogance. "And just how would you know it was Shoshoni — ?"

"Believe me, Lieutenant, I know. I even recognized some of the arrows. That war party was led by Wasp."

"We need to talk," the officer said. "We've been having a lot of trouble with the Shoshoni lately — Bear Hunter's clan and Man Lost's."

Rider shrugged. "All the tribes are starving. Can't you keep the whites off their lands?"

"The army is here to protect the settlers, not the Indians," Foss sniffed.

Rider frowned and patted his horse. "In the long run, I think it's the Indians who need protection."

"Now you sound like those damned Mormons," the officer scoffed, then tipped his hat to Emma. "Sorry for the profanity, ma'am, but it's annoying. The Mormons use this trail, then branch off for Salt Lake City. They say they'd rather feed the In-

413

dians than fight them."

"Maybe that's not a bad idea. Hungry people have nothing to lose by attacking wagon trains," Rider said.

The elegant officer looked hot and annoyed. "Policy making is not my problem," he snapped. "I'm sure the colonel will want your full report." He spoke to Rider, but she noted he was looking at her. She nodded politely and he smiled.

"There'll be a dance tomorrow night."

She saw Rider frown. "We may not be staying that long, Lieutenant."

"That's only one more day," Emma protested. "Surely we can spare an extra day?"

"I don't think so," Rider snapped.

The handsome officer hadn't taken his eyes off Emma as he stroked his mustache. "That'd be a shame. We don't get many women, especially pretty ones, through here very often."

Emma blushed and turned away. When she looked back, Rider was glaring at her. He put his hand on Josh's head. "Climb up there, son, and help your mother circle her wagon."

The lieutenant's mouth opened, then closed as he looked from Rider to the child. Before he could say anything, Rider gestured. "It's hot out here in the sun, Lieutenant, and I'd like a drink. Let's go see your commander."

Emma glared after him as the pair walked away. Here an eligible man had expressed noticeable interest in her and Rider seemed to be trying to run him off. He had plenty of nerve, especially since he was planning on deserting the train here. She put her arm around Josh as he climbed up on the wagon seat.

"Did you hear Rider? He called me 'son.' "

How could she tell him the hostile gunfighter was only trying to discourage the handsome young officer's attention? "I'm sure that if Rider had a son, he'd want him to be just like you, dear."

They couldn't get all the repairs made and new supplies bought, so the train was still there the next afternoon, parked out in the shade of tall trees near the fort's walls. The fort teemed with settlers, fur traders, soldiers. Many people came and went from this place, a crossroads of civilization before the final and most difficult stretch of the Oregon Trail. Some of the single men in the train departed, heading to California from the Hudspeth Cutoff or up to Grasshopper Creek and the new gold fields.

She saw nothing of Rider; he seemed to be avoiding her. On the other hand, the handsome and dapper Lieutenant Foss had found several occasions to ride past her wagon and tip his hat.

Now he stopped to chat. "Your husband seems to be a very able wagon boss."

Damn Rider for that. "He's not my husband."

"Oh?" The man's hazel eyes brightened.

"I — my husband is dead," she said. "I'm on my way to Oregon, hoping to start a new life for me and my son."

"Long way to Oregon — pretty dangerous."

She nodded. "I know, but I don't seem to have many alternatives. The war, you know."

"I know," he nodded. "My parents are having a difficult time keeping their shoe factory running in Massachusetts — no men to do the work."

That only confirmed what Emma had already guessed — the lieutenant came from an educated and privileged background. "How terrible for them," she said.

"A pretty widow should have many suitors." He smiled, showing perfect white teeth.

"So far I haven't found anyone who wants

the responsibility of my son."

He cleared his throat. "I don't know why. He strikes me as a fine little tyke. Will you be at the dance tonight, Mrs. Trent?"

She nodded, her heart beating a little faster at his intense gaze. He was such as gentleman, not like the rough and hostile wagon boss. "All the ladies are excited about it."

"Not as pleased as the soldiers," he said and smiled at her. "We don't see many women out here. May I have the privilege of escorting you?"

She hesitated. Rider was the man she longed to dance with, but the lieutenant might be a husband for her. He was well-spoken, handsome, and polite. "I'd be delighted."

"Wonderful! I'll be looking forward to it. See you at eight." And tipping his hat politely, he rode away.

Josh, sitting beside her, frowned after the man. "Don't like him."

"Now, Josh, you haven't given him a chance."

Rider galloped up just then. "What did the prissy officer want?"

"Now what is that to you? He asked me to save him a dance tonight. And by the way, I didn't appreciate your making him think

I belonged to you."

The gunfighter glared after the other man's departing back. "Watch out for him, Sky Eyes. Soldiers are just out for what they can get."

"Not like gunfighters, who have such noble intentions." Her voice dripped with sarcasm.

Josh climbed down from the wagon and took off running, the pup barking at his heels. She turned to look at Rider. "When are you and that red-haired slut skipping out?"

Rider leaned on his saddle horn and shrugged. "Waitin' for the time to be right. You gonna spread the alarm?"

She drew herself up proudly. "Would it do any good? You don't care about anybody but yourself."

"I've survived this long by looking out for me and me alone. I reckon you should do the same."

"Fine, I'll do that. Maybe Lieutenant Foss would like a wife."

Rider glared at her. "I've got a sixth sense about people, Sky Eyes, and I don't like Lieutenant Foss."

"Then I like him even better." She glared at him.

Rider glared back. "He just wants to sleep

with you, not marry you."

"Sounds familiar." Her voice was icy cold.

"Okay, so I deserved that," he acknowledged. "I'll see you at the dance tonight."

She watched him gallop on down the line of wagons toward the Pettigrews. There was no telling what he and that redhead were plotting, but of course, there wasn't anything she could do about it. The thought of him in that woman's arms made her grit her teeth, which puzzled her because she knew she shouldn't care who he was sleeping with as long as he stayed out of her own blankets.

Emma decided right then and there to dazzle the young officer tonight. Mrs. Weeks had offered to watch Josh while she attended the dance. Emma walked him over there, then returned to her wagon and began to dress. She had a tiny bit of fragrance saved and one good dress from her marriage, a light blue watered silk just the color of her eyes. She intended to make Lieutenant Foss sit up and take notice. If she were looking for a husband, he was as good a choice as any.

After he left Emma, Rider had ridden down to the Pettigrew wagon. Francie poked her head out. "Well, it's about time. You've been avoiding me."

Rider didn't look at her. "I didn't want to make your husband suspicious."

"Good thought," she agreed. "Roscoe's at the trading post playing cards. By the way, I heard the men talkin'. They intend to beat you out of your fee."

"Figures. I don't feel so bad now for taking Roscoe's money."

She smiled up at him, running the tip of her tongue along her full lips. "We clearing out tonight?"

Rider shrugged and hesitated. "Haven't decided yet."

"Haven't decided yet?" She put her hands on her hips. "What's wrong with you, Rider? We could go anytime — there's no reason to wait."

"I wanted to make sure."

Francie said something obscene. "Look, with the dance tonight, there'll be a lot of confusion and excitement. Everyone will be there. We could make a quick appearance at the dance, then sneak out and come back here. My old geezer will probably drink himself senseless and most of the wagons will be deserted. Roscoe's already bought me a saddle horse at the fort so I can go ridin' when we get to Oregon. We can load the gold in our saddlebags and clear out."

Rider nodded. "Good idea. With all the

partying and drinking, no one will miss us 'til tomorrow."

"Then it's settled." She smiled up at him, putting her hand on his booted foot. "When we reach a safe place, I'm gonna be all over you, Rider. I ain't forgot how good you was. I been aching for a good man between my legs and you was always the best." She began to describe in erotic detail what she wanted to do to Rider.

"Sure, Francie. See you at the dance." He turned and cantered away, his mind troubled and confused. Francie knew how to satisfy a man in ways the innocent Mrs. Trent had never heard of. He was a virile man and he'd been without a woman for a long time except for that incident the night they had hanged Willie Adams. In his mind, he held the yellow-haired girl again, and she was warm and innocent in her giving. Damn her for dogging his thoughts.

He rode past her wagon — she was beautiful in that blue dress. Impulsively, he called, "Want me to escort you to the dance?"

She shook her head and her voice was cold. "Lieutenant Foss has asked to escort me."

Rider slapped his quirt against his leg. "You watch out for that guy."

"I need a husband," she shrugged.

"What that dandy's got in mind isn't marriage."

"Now, that's hardly your concern, is it?" She tossed her head. "I might have a lovely, civilized life in Massachusetts."

"He won't want Josh." His temper was rising and he wasn't certain why.

"You don't know that," she snapped. "Probably like you, the lieutenant wants to get between my legs, but I'll bet he'd be willing to marry me to get it."

The thought of the dapper young officer lying on Emma's belly made him madder still. "Don't count on it!" He spurred Storm and galloped away, angry with himself that he cared. After all, he was leaving tonight with the sultry redhead who knew how to please a man.

The elegant young officer had brought a buggy to Emma's wagon. When she stepped out on the back gate, his eyes widened and he took a deep breath. "My, don't you look nice!"

She blushed furiously, trying to remember the last time a gentleman had paid her a compliment. "Thank you. I had to make do with a dress I owned before I married."

"Just the color of your pretty eyes," he gushed. "Here, let me help you down." He held up his hands, clad in fine white gloves, and put them on her small waist.

She let him lift her to the ground. The heat of his fingers seemed to burn through his spotless white gloves and the blue silk of her dress. *Was this her prince?*

"Lieutenant, do you intend to stay in the army?" She took his arm and they walked to the buggy.

"Hardly." He laughed. "I've left my younger brother trying to help Father run all the family businesses, but I hope to go into politics, so a few medals would help."

"Oh. Of course." Well, perhaps it was expecting too much for the prince to also have high ideals.

He assisted her up into the buggy and they drove inside the gates to the big hall and reined in. "I'm afraid what we offer a pretty lady tonight is pretty primitive." He got down and came around to help her out.

Emma had seen little of the finer things, having married at seventeen to a frontier farmer. The officers' hall looked like a palace to her. "I'm sure it will be delightful."

He looped her arm over his, patting her hand intimately. "Only because you're here, my dear. The other officers will be green with envy, but I shan't spare you for a single dance."

He kept that promise, waving off any eager young officer who approached and tried for an introduction. The hall was small and crowded with humanity. All the ladies had worn their best and even the trappers had washed and combed their long hair. There was a refreshment table at one end and a small army band at the other playing mostly Stephen Foster tunes.

The lieutenant took her down the receiving line, introducing her to the colonel and other senior officers. Out of the corner of her eye, she saw Francesca Pettigrew come in on proud Roscoe's arm. Francesca wore a bright green taffeta, cut shockingly low at the bodice. Rider was nowhere to be seen.

Lieutenant Foss insisted on dancing almost every dance, holding Emma very close and ignoring any eager shopkeeper, trapper, or officer who tried to cut in. As they finished a fast reel, she saw Rider enter the hall. He was dressed all in black, his hair long and his boots polished. He looked like what he was, a handsome, deadly gunfighter. At least he wasn't wearing a pistol.

Emma fanned herself with her dainty lace fan. "Oh, my dear Lieutenant, you must let me catch my breath."

"How thoughtless of me! I'll get you some punch." He disappeared into the crowd gathered about the refreshment table as the little band began a slow waltz. Rider came up and caught her arm. "I believe this is my dance."

Before she could object, he whirled her out onto the floor, holding her close as they moved. He was as graceful as a black panther and probably just as deadly.

"You surprise me," she said. "I didn't think you could dance."

"On the contrary," he said against her hair and pulled her closer still, "all the saloon girls love a gunman who can waltz."

"I'm sure you know many saloon girls." She tried to put more distance between them, but he held her in an iron grip.

"Dozens."

Somehow, that annoyed her. On the sidelines, the lieutenant had returned with the two cups of punch and stood there looking annoyed. "I'm surprised you aren't dancing with Francie."

They whirled past her and the fiery-haired girl glared at Emma. Rider laughed deep in his throat. "With Francie, a man can do other things besides dance."

Emma felt a terrible urge to kick his shins,

then decided it would not be wise. "Are you leaving tonight?"

"That's hardly your business. Will you miss me?"

"You know I won't. You're messing up my chances with the lieutenant."

Rider laughed. "Ain't that too bad?"

The music ended. He bowed low and returned her to her escort. "I'm sure the officer did not mind sharing."

Young Foss looked like he minded very much, but he only blustered, "To be sure. Here's your punch, Mrs. Trent."

"You're so kind," she purred as she took his arm and gave Rider one last dirty look. Rider grinned and moved over to strike up a conversation with the Pettigrews. When Emma looked back, he was dancing with Francie, holding her very close while the woman looked up at him with evident adoration. Emma gritted her teeth.

"Mrs. Trent?"

"What?" She brought her attention back to her escort.

"I asked if you've ever been to Massachusetts?" He was peering at her over his punch cup.

"Uh, no, but I'd love to visit sometime." She sipped her punch and gave him her most dazzling smile.

"Perhaps that could be arranged. It's terribly warm in here. Would you like to go for a stroll?"

"Of course." She set down her cup on a tray beside his and took his arm. He opened the door and they went outside into the moonlight. Would he try to kiss her? Of course not. Lieutenant Foss was an aristocrat, a perfect gentleman. She might have to linger at the fort, perhaps get a job clerking in the sutler's store for awhile. With his fine sensibilities, it might take the young officer many months to finally ask for her hand in marriage.

"Let's go out under the trees," the lieutenant said. "The moonlight is beautiful and we can see the Uinta Mountains south of the fort from there."

"That would be lovely." Behind her, the faint strains of "Jeannie with the Light Brown Hair" drifted on the night breeze.

Back at the hall, Rider frowned as he looked up from whirling Francie to see Emma Trent leaving with her escort.

"Ow, Rider," she scolded, "you just stepped on my foot, which ain't like you. Where's your mind tonight?"

"I don't know," he muttered.

"Well, start thinkin' about our trip,"

Francie scolded. "Old Roscoe looks pretty drunk right now, but he could be drunker. I don't want him to miss me 'til morning."

"Good idea." He led her off the floor.

"Rider, you could go ahead and get things ready. I'll join you back at the wagon after a while."

"Sure." He started toward the door. Francie was right, of course; everything was working out just the way they'd planned. By morning, he and Francie and all that money should be many miles from here. All he had to do was get his stuff together and meet the redhead. Somewhere in the distance, he heard Boots barking mournfully and smiled. He'd gotten used to having that little boy and his dog around. He wouldn't be seeing them anymore after tonight. Nor the mother, either. Tied to the hitching post, Storm whinnied a welcome. In the moonlit distance, he could just barely see the light blue silk of Emma's dress as she disappeared into the woods with her escort. To hell with her. All he had to do was mount up and wait for Francie at her wagon. From now on, it was good times, gold, and a hot redhead at his beck and call. He didn't need the frustrations of dealing with the stubborn blonde.

Emma paused under a giant tree as the

lieutenant stopped and took both her hands. The way he was looking at her made her uneasy. "Lieutenant, don't you think we should be getting back to the dance?"

"Oh, do call me Howard," he said and put both hands on her small shoulders. He smiled at her and his beautiful white teeth made him twice as handsome.

She wanted to pull away, but to do so would insult him. "All right, Howard."

"You are beautiful," he whispered huskily.

"Lieutenant, this is hardly appropriate —"

"It's been a long time since I've seen such a lovely woman," he whispered. "We don't get that many pretty ones on the passing wagon trains. It's very lonely out here, my dear." He took both her hands in his white-gloved ones, kissed her fingertips.

"Lieutenant —"

"Howard," he prompted, kissing her hands again. "Howard," she said, "I appreciate your compliments, but I really think we should be returning —"

"Not until I do something I've wanted to do all evening." He reached out, pulled her to him, and kissed her. His mouth was wet and cold.

She pulled back in distaste. "Really, Howard, this is very forward behavior —"

"Oh, don't play the innocent with me!"

His tone turned annoyed, arrogant. "You're a widow, aren't you? You know what this is all about!"

She slapped him and he grabbed her, pulled her hard against his mouth. "You teasing slut! I saw that half-breed kid. You've slept with some dirty Injun!"

She struggled to get away from him, but his mouth came down on hers as one hand pawed at her bodice. "I'm gonna have you, bitch, and you won't tell anyone. No one would believe a woman who's slept with Injuns!"

Their struggles took them to the ground and he was like a madman, ripping at her dress, trying to get on top of her. "It won't do you any good to fight me. I want you and by God, I'll have you!"

She clawed at his face and he struck her, hard. "Lay still, you bitch! I intend to have you here and now!"

Emma fought him, trying not to let the tears overflow. She tasted blood from her cut lip and her head rang, but she had been raped once and she would die before she would let it happen again. *Why hadn't she listened to Rider?* He had recognized this predator for what he was.

Despite her struggle, the man had her down in the grass, pulling at her clothing.

She could hear him breathing hard as he fought her. Her pride wouldn't allow her to scream and she wasn't sure there was anyone about to hear her anyway.

She sank her teeth into his white-gloved hand and he swore and pulled back, striking her hard across the face. "You'll pay for that, bitch! You Injun's slut, you!"

His mouth covered hers again and she fought to get out from under him.

Abruptly, a hand reached out of the darkness, grabbed young Foss by the shoulder, and pulled him to his feet. When she looked up, half-dazed, she saw Rider's big frame looming out of the darkness and the fury in his dark eyes was terrible to see.

"She — she was trying to seduce me," the officer babbled, "and me a married man! I—"

He never got to finish the sentence. Rider's big fist connected with the lieutenant's beautiful white teeth as he threw Foss against the nearest tree.

Emma stumbled to her feet, trying to rearrange her clothing as the two fought.

Rider hadn't felt such rage in a long, long time. He grabbed the other man by the front of his jacket, hit him again. Some of the officer's fine white teeth broke out as Rider's fist slammed into his mouth. He made a weak effort to defend himself, putting his hands up in a formal boxer's stance. Rider, used to fighting rough frontiersmen, dodged under Foss's arm and slugged him again.

The man stumbled and fell with a groan. Rider charged in and kicked him in the groin.

"Rider, stop! You'll kill him!" Emma grabbed his arm.

"Good enough for the rotten bastard! He'll attack no more women." His rage was too overpowering to control.

Emma grabbed his arm, pulling him away as the other man stumbled to his feet, blubbering, "My teeth! You've knocked out some of my teeth!"

Rider went after him again, but the officer staggered backward, turned, and lurched away, the silver bars on his uniform reflecting the moonlight as he ran. Rider started to go after the man, but Emma held onto his arm. "Let him go."

He turned toward her and began to swear anew as he saw her discolored face and torn dress. "I should have killed him. Are you all right?"

She managed to nod, afraid that if she spoke, she would burst into tears. She took a step and hesitated, swaying. Rider swept her up into his arms. "You're okay now," he murmured. "I'll take care of you."

At that point, she broke down and wept against his shirt. "I-I feel like such a fool! You were right."

He sighed and kissed the tears off her face. "You're too trusting, Sky Eyes."

She slipped her arms around his neck and held onto him tightly while he murmured to her and held her against his chest. "I can't go back there to the dance."

"You don't have to, baby," he assured her as he sat her on the grass under a tree. "I'll wash your face and take you back to your wagon."

She looked up at him with anxious eyes. "He might tell — you'll be in trouble."

He wiped the tears off her face with one big hand. "You let me worry about that. If he tells, he'll have a lot of embarrassing questions to answer and he wouldn't want this gossip to get back home since he's married."

"I'm such a fool." She buried her face in her hands. Rider leaned back on his heels and watched her. She was valiant and brave, but alone; she and her child would always be at a disadvantage in a man's world.

"Are you all right?" he asked softly.

She took her hands away. "What are you doing here anyway? I thought you were leaving with Francie."

"Shut up about Francie," he snapped.

She looked up into his hard face. "You aren't going with her?"

"Damn it, I didn't say that." He sounded annoyed, but his eyes betrayed the truth. Instead of leaving with the redhead, he was here with her.

"Then you are leaving with her?"

"Maybe. Hell, how can I when every time I turn around, I've got to come to your rescue?"

She smiled up at him. "You'd fight a dragon for me, wouldn't you?"

"Damn it, I don't know what a dragon is. Anyway, I'm not making any commitments. Just because I rescued —"

"Then I'll take whatever I can get," she whispered and she reached up and put her arms around his neck.

He started as she pulled him to her, then his arms went around her and she found herself locked in a protective, strong embrace as he kissed her deeply, thoroughly. She had never felt so much at peace, so safe. She deepened the kiss, pulling his body against her own.

He let her, but he breathed harder and his hands roamed up and down her back.

She lay down in the grass, pulling him with her.

"Watch it, baby," he warned her. "Who knows where this might lead?"

"I know." And she kissed him again. "Make love to me."

He hesitated. "No strings attached?"

"None," she assured him and then she kissed him again. Tonight, she thought suddenly, tonight, for the first time in her life, she wanted a man to take her, possess her, teach her what love was all about. No, not just a man. She wanted Rider.

Chapter Eighteen

His hands caressed her breasts gently, turning her nipples into hard peaks of desire as his mouth kissed her swollen face ever so tenderly. "Sky Eyes, oh, Sky Eyes, what you do to me."

She reached up and ran her hand into the open neck of his shirt, feeling the muscles cording like steel there.

"Unbutton it," he ordered.

Her gaze on his, she unbuttoned his shirt, running her hands over the scars on his dark chest. He had survived many wounds. She raised up and put her tongue to his nipple. He gasped and pulled her hard against his chest, his eyes burning like black coals as he looked down at her. "Don't tease me, baby. I can't take much of this."

"I'm not teasing you, Rider, honest." She unbuttoned her bodice, freed her breasts. "These are for you alone."

He groaned and cupped them in his two

big hands, stroking and caressing them before his tongue worked its way down her
throat and tasted each one. She whimpered
at the sensation. Her husband had been
awkward and quick taking her, while Rider
was stroking her skin and playing with her as
if he intended it to last all night. His hand
went down to work up her skirt. She tried to
close her thighs.

"Open to me, baby," he commanded.
"Open to me."

She took a deep breath and let her thighs
fall apart. Rider's hand stroked up her thigh.
She wore pantelets with the opening in the
middle seam. Rider's hand moved to touch
her most private place. She reached down
and caught his wrist, intending to stop him,
but the way he was touching her made her
forget everything but the dizzying sensation
his fingers were causing. Instead, she pulled
his hand harder against her body so that he
could stroke her insides even as his mouth
went to her breast again. "Oh, Rider."

"All night," he whispered, his breath
warm against her breast, "I'm going to pleasure you all night."

She encouraged him by putting her
tongue into his mouth, pushing against his
hand, wanting still more.

"Touch me," he gasped, "touch me." He

unbuttoned his pants and reached to put her hand on his throbbing maleness. It was hot and hard as an iron rod fresh from the blacksmith's forge and wet with his need.

Their kisses deepened even as Rider slid down her body. Surely he wasn't going to — ?

And then he put his mouth on her, invading her most private place with the hot blade of his tongue. She gasped and tried to close her thighs, afraid of this overpowering sensation, but he was strong and he wouldn't let her pull away from his seeking mouth. She couldn't seem to get enough air, taking big gasps at the heat that seemed to be enveloping her. "Rider, oh, Rider, please."

She wasn't sure what it was she wanted because with her husband, she had only lain there, waiting for him to finish in his quick, clumsy way. Now her need was as great as Rider's and she caught his head in her hands, pressing it against her as she began to go into convulsions. This new sensation was almost scary as it roared through her body like an overflowing volcano. For a long moment, she thought she must be unconscious and then she gradually opened her eyes.

Rider lay looking down at her and smiled. "You like that?"

"I-I never felt anything like it before."

"Get used to it, baby. It will be like that from now on." He kissed her again, her own taste on his lips and his manhood hard with need against her body. In seconds, he had her clutching him to her again, wanting him yet again, pulling him down on her, aching for his hard male body to fill the emptiness within her. He was big and she tilted up to take every inch of him, locking her legs around his hard-driving hips so he couldn't escape until he had quenched the fire that roared through her being again.

"Rider, I'm going, I'm going . . ."

"And this time, Sky Eyes, I'm going with you," he promised and thrust into her one last time. She could feel every inch of him as he began to come. She welcomed the oneness it made of them, straining together as they both reached that ultimate peak of fulfillment.

Afterward, they lay in each other's arms in the moonlight. She had never felt so happy and peaceful as she did at this moment.

"Rider, I think I love you." She kissed him again.

He didn't answer, but he began to kiss her again and she could feel his maleness already hard and throbbing against her thigh. This was a virile male animal, one who needed a lot of coupling with a chosen woman and she was that woman. He hadn't said he loved her, but at this moment, the only thing that mattered was that she was in his arms and she was safe.

He made love to her twice more under the stars and then she lay with her head on his shoulder. "I suppose I ought to go back to the wagon, but I'm too tired to move."

"I'll carry you." He rearranged her clothing and swung her up in his arms like a doll. "Mrs. Weeks prepared to keep Josh all night?"

"Yes." She reached up and touched his face gently as he walked with her. "What about Francie?"

She could tell by his expression that he had totally forgotten about Francie. He cursed under his breath. "Damn, she'll be mad as a wet hen."

She swallowed hard. "You can always leave with her tomorrow night."

"Yeah, I could do that." He didn't say anything else as he strode back to her wagon. "Let me stay with you tonight, Sky Eyes. I want to wake up with you in my arms."

"I'd like that." She would not try to force a commitment; Rider was as wild and untamed as the mustangs that roamed the West. He belonged in that free and hostile land, not cooped up in some tiny shop or on a farm. "I'll accept whatever you're willing to give and ask no questions."

"You're one in a million, baby," he whispered as he sat her up on her wagon gate.

She crawled inside and stripped her clothes off. Rider joined her and the moonlight threw his shadow across her bare body. She held out her arms in invitation and he came down on top of her, eager and virile as he kissed her. Their lovemaking was as torrid as if he'd hadn't already taken her tonight.

Finally, he dropped off to sleep still in her arms, his body meshed with hers. She kissed his dark face and stared into the night, wishing she could keep him with her forever, but it would be like lassoing the wind. She would have to settle for whatever he would give her before he moved on. The thought of losing him brought big tears to her eyes, but she managed to stifle them so she would not wake the man in her arms. He must not ever know how much she'd come to care for him.

When she awakened, it was dawn and she realized she was naked and alone. Quickly, she dressed and stuck her head out the canvas. "Rider?" No answer. Now that he'd finally satisfied his need, had he left with Francie?

Her hands shook as she pulled on her little shoes and untied the pup. The two of them walked down to retrieve her son.

Josh threw himself into her arms. "We going today, Mama?"

"I reckon so." She looked around at the others readying their wagons. "You want some breakfast?"

He nodded and when they reached her wagon, she built a fire, put on the coffee pot, began to fry bacon.

Josh watched her cook. "Where's Rider?"

"I don't know." She didn't look at her son, not wanting to tell him that now that she'd finally served the gunman's lust, he and Francie were probably long gone.

A big shadow fell across her and she looked up. Rider leaned against her wagon. "Can a man get a cup of coffee?"

Astounded, all she could do was stare. When she didn't answer, he walked past her, poured himself a cup. "Hey, Small Warrior, how are you this morning?"

"Fine, we goin' to Oregon?"

"Well, if your mother ever gets us fed, I reckon."

At that, she came to life. "I thought you —"

"Well, you thought wrong. Here, I talked a storekeeper out of four eggs." He handed the delicacy over. "You milk the cow yet?"

She wanted to shout and hug him, but she only accepted the eggs in wonderment. "No, I haven't had time to milk."

"Then Josh and I will take care of that. Come on, partner."

He motioned to Josh. Emma wiped tears from her eyes as she broke the eggs into the skillet.

Rider looked up as he grabbed the bucket. "What's wrong with you?"

"Nothing, I just got smoke in my eyes, that's all."

"I like my eggs over easy," he said, and he and her son went off to milk the cow, the puppy barking at their heels.

She didn't dare hope or even ask. She could only watch him eat and talk to Josh. The gunfighter seemed to be in a rare good humor this morning.

Afterward, Rider was everywhere on his big Appaloosa, giving orders, lining up the wagons. Before the sun was over the eastern horizons, the train pulled out toward the mountains looming to the west. Emma knew they were about to begin the most hostile, dangerous part of their trip.

Rider was too busy getting the wagons out on the trail to give Emma Trent any attention. He knew she was surprised to find him still here. *Damn,* he thought, *I'm surprised myself.* She had given of herself last night expecting nothing and it had touched something deep inside him that he didn't know was there. More than that, as many women as he had had, he had never before experienced the pleasure he'd found in her arms. It had been a wonder.

He must not think too deeply about all this and he sure as hell didn't want to talk to Francie, who sat her wagon seat, glaring at him as he rode past. Roscoe was sitting next to her, his head in his hands, groaning loudly.

However, when they stopped at noon for rest and to water the stock, Francie cornered him behind a wagon. "I want to know what the hell happened last night?"

He smiled absently, remembering his night in Sky Eyes's arms.

"Damn it, Rider, ain't you gonna answer me? I stood by the wagon all night, waitin' for you to come."

"Let's say I changed my mind."

"Changed your mind?" Her jaw dropped. "You're not the man I used to know, Rider. That man would have walked across hell to get that much gold."

"Gold doesn't seem that important to me anymore."

"Are you loco?" she almost screamed at him. "There ain't nothin' more important than gold — men steal and lie and die for it. I sleep with a fat old slug I hate for it."

"Well now, Francie, that was your decision. We all have to live with the choices we make."

"I knew it — it's her, ain't it?" She blocked his way as he started to leave.

"I don't know what you're talking about."

"Oh, yes, you do." She put her hands on her hips. "Was you sleeping with her last night and she bribed you to stay with the train?"

Had Emma bribed him with her body? If so, he didn't care. All he could think of was making love to the blonde night after night after night. "She's different, Francie, real different."

Horror crossed Francie's hard little face. "You're in love with her — that's it. The big tough, gunfighter's fallen in love."

He shook his head. "Love's for weaklings — makes a man vulnerable. I'm not even sure what it is."

"It's what I've always felt for you, you half-breed bastard, and you've never returned it."

He looked into her tear-streaked face and felt something he had not felt before. Maybe it was pity. Being around Emma Trent was making him sensitive to others' emotions. "I'm sorry if I've hurt you, Francie."

"I hate you, you know that? You ain't the man I knew. Next thing you know, she'll have you farming and raising chickens and cows."

Rider tipped his Stetson back, remembering the wonder of last night. "With her, maybe that wouldn't be so bad."

She ran at him and pummeled him with her fists. "I don't need you, you hear that? I don't need anybody. When I get to Oregon, I'll run off all by myself with that gold and catch a boat down to San Francisco. I'll find a better man than you and live like a queen."

He threw up his hands to protect his face, but he didn't hit her. Rider would never strike a woman.

With a sob, Francie turned and ran back to her wagon.

Rider stood staring after her, feeling sorry for her. He hoped all the banker's gold bought her the life she wanted. As for himself, he wasn't certain what he wanted or what he intended to do except that tonight he would sleep in Emma Trent's arms and tomorrow night and the night after. It was payment enough for taking this train on to Oregon. He looked at the mountains in the distance. The weather was growing cooler and they were approaching the heart of Shoshoni country. *Ee-dah-how. The sun coming down the mountain.* The whites pronounced the Shoshoni word as "Idaho." He was gambling with his life to travel there, but Emma and her child couldn't make it through safely without him. For her, he would risk it; that and the heaven he'd discovered in her arms.

That afternoon, they faced the grim challenge known as "the big hill," one of the steepest hills on the trail. They lost one wagon over the side. When Rider ran to the edge of the incline, he watched it bounce crazily, its wheels falling and rolling as if they had a life of their own. The hapless Jones family trudged on, now completely without supplies. Only a few offered to share with them and Emma was one of those.

They camped late at Soda Springs, where the waters bubbled and fizzed. The joyful children added precious sugar and flavoring to cups of the water and enjoyed a rare treat. After dark, Rider came to Emma's wagon. He stood there, looking at her, waiting.

She bit her lip. "I saw you talking to Francie today."

He shrugged. "What of it?"

"She was crying and she looked upset."

"She is."

Emma took a deep breath. "Want to tell me about it?"

"No." He couldn't admit, even to himself, the hold this woman now held on him.

Emma shook her head. "I love you, Rider, and I trust you."

"Don't trust me, Sky Eyes. I've left a hundred women behind me with tears in their eyes."

She wanted to scream out, *And will I be next?* She didn't. "I'll take whatever you want to give me and then cherish the memory when you leave." She motioned him in.

He glanced over to where Josh slept heavily, then climbed up and sat down on her quilt. "I've never met anyone quite like you — giving, asking nothing. I'm a bad hombre."

"I don't think so." She put her hand on his arm. "I think love can change a person."

He laughed without mirth. "That would take more than love — it would take a miracle."

"Love is a kind of miracle," she replied earnestly.

"You're naive, you know that? I'm a wanted man in half a dozen territories. Even the Shoshoni want me for murder."

"Did you do it?" She looked up at him in the dim light.

"Will you believe me if I say I didn't?"

"I would believe anything you tell me, Rider. I love you."

"Stop saying that, damn it." Yet he looked down into her honest face and wanted to be the kind of man she thought he was. "I can't promise you anything."

"Did I ask for anything?"

"By God, I never met a woman like you before." He took her in his arms and kissed her tenderly, sweetly. She laid her face against his wide chest and let him make love to her, answering with a passion that surprised them both.

Afterwards, they lay in each other's arms and he stroked her hair. She closed her eyes, content just to be in his arms. If he decided to ride away tomorrow or the next day, she would have these hours to remember the rest of her life.

So the days passed and the weeks as the train crawled slowly through country that became more rough and hostile with each passing mile. They were following the treacherous Snake River, which twisted and turned through the rocks like a writhing serpent. Yet they were moving along the rim of its canyon, its cold water far below them where they could only stare at it as they did without water, or drank from pools so alkaline that it made people and cattle sick.

The Moon of Falling Leaves gave way to the month the whites called November and Rider's people called the Mad Moon. The wind grew sharper and while before they had sweltered in the heat, now the pioneers shivered in the early morning frosts. The wagon train moved at a snail's pace. One day, an axle would break and stop them for hours; another, an ox would stray and have to be found. Always, there was Indian sign and Rider felt certain they were being watched as they moved across the hostile terrain toward the rocks called the Gate of Death and the City of Rocks, a perfect place for an ambush.

Weatherford B. Carrolton seemed to be losing his mind. He looked dazed and went about looking for his wife. Sometimes he would wander off into the brush and they would lose precious time looking for him. Old farmer Adams grew silent and stoic with his hatred, but Rider was sure the man would not try to kill him . . . yet. He must know that only Rider could get the train through to Oregon. Once there, he might try to kill the wagon boss, but Rider couldn't worry about that now.

Francie no longer spoke to him, but he didn't care; even the fact that he might not be able to collect what the pioneers owed him didn't matter. All that mattered were the looks Sky Eyes gave him when he rode past her wagon and the way she opened her arms to him after the camp was asleep. They made love three or four times every night and still it was not enough. He would never get enough of her, he realized suddenly as he held her close and kissed her hair.

Eventually, they came to the place known as A Thousand Springs, water gushing through the rocks in many small waterfalls that caught the light and changed them to rainbows. And just ahead as the Snake tamed itself through low hills, they arrived at the Three Island Crossing.

The river was running full with a strong current. Rider brought the wagons to a halt and shook his head. "Still getting runoff from melted snows or maybe there's been some rain. This is gonna be the devil to cross."

The others looked at him, then at the water. The cold, rushing river created a terrible roar.

Pettigrew took off his derby and mopped his jowls. "Is there a way around it?"

Rider shook his head. "This is the safest crossing of the Snake." He pointed. "We'll go from one island to the next, but there's a wide stretch of river between that last island and the bank."

McGinnis blinked. "In that current? We'll lose them all."

"What do you suggest?" Rider leaned on his saddle horn, "There is no ferry in this isolated spot and no bridge, either."

They all looked at each other and seemed to know he was right.

"It's settled then," Rider said. "Get the tar bucket and try to make the wagons waterproof. Throw away anything heavy."

Mrs. Weeks looked horrified, holding her new baby close to her breast. "We've done about thrown away everything we own along the way. Besides food, all we got left is my trunk and our plow."

"It's your decision to make," Rider said. "The plow won't do you much good if you aren't alive to use it."

He saw Francie and Roscoe Pettigrew exchanging looks. The gold in the bottom of their wagon was heavy. Well, that was their problem. "Let's get busy — we're burnin' daylight."

It was nearly dark before he determined the wagons were ready to attempt the stream. "I'll take Mrs. Trent's wagon across. The rest of you wait until I get to the bank."

He tied Storm on in front of her oxen, hoping the stupid brutes would take courage from the horse. "You ready?" He looked at Emma. She took a deep breath, her knuckles white as she clenched her fingers around the wagon seat and glanced back at her son and the pup in the back. "We're ready."

Rider urged Storm into the cold, fast-moving stream. The Appaloosa hesitated, but he seemed to have confidence in his owner's ability. Rider urged him again and Storm plunged forward into the water and started for the first island, swimming strongly.

Emma held her breath as they fought the current. Then they were driving up on the spit of sand in the water, the oxen lowing in relief.

"One down, two to go," Rider murmured and urged the horse forward again.

After a tense minute, the wagon pulled up, dripping, on the second island. The oxen moved across the sand, then plunged into the water again, swimming strongly. They bawled loudly in protest as they swam toward the third island, then came up on the sand. The worst lay ahead.

Rider paused to let the team rest a minute, then patted Emma's hand. "We're almost there now. Small Warrior, are you and Boots okay?"

The child laughed. He seemed to think it was a great adventure.

"Rider," she said under her breath, "if something goes wrong, let everything else go and save Josh."

He nodded. "Don't worry, Sky Eyes. I said I'd take care of you and I will." Rider didn't tell her that he lowered his head and said a quick prayer to *Tobats,* the Great Spirit, before he drove the team into the wide and dangerous current between the third island and the far bank.

Emma was saying a few prayers of her own as she clung to the seat and bit her lip. She had great faith in Rider, but she knew the river was a killer without conscience as she felt the strong current pull at the wagon. "We're starting to drift!" she yelled.

Rider yelled at the team, demanding it to put all its strength into getting the wagon across. Storm's great heart answered his master's voice and he fought the current for the next few heart-stopping moments until the wagon pulled ashore, dripping from the cold water. The Snake had reluctantly let them live.

Rider drove the team up the bank and out of the way. "You all right?"

Emma took a deep breath and nodded. "I was never really afraid, not with you at the reins."

He laughed. "I was scared as hell, Sky Eyes. You've got more confidence in me than I deserve."

"Fun!" Josh giggled from in back. "Me and Boots want to do that again."

Rider shook his head. "I think once is enough, Small Warrior. You and your mama can watch the others cross."

He strode back to the river bank and looked over at the others on the far bank. "All right," he yelled over the roaring water, "who's next?"

The men looked at each other uncertainly, then at the deadly stream that threw a cold spray across their faces.

"Well," said McGinnis doubtfully, "I reckon I'll be the next to try."

The two brothers-in-law, Weeks and Gray, shook their heads. "There has to be a better way."

Rider spat in disgust. "Believe me, there isn't."

Pettigrew took off his derby and wiped his balding head. "Maybe tomorrow or the next day, the water will go down."

"I don't think so," Rider said, "and time is our enemy. The longer we wait here, the better chance of getting caught in the snows of the Blue Mountains."

"You mean, like the Donner Party?" Adams yelled.

The others looked at each other. Drowning was a better choice than slowly starving and resorting to cannibalism.

Reluctantly, the men began to position their wagons behind McGinnis.

"Get up there!" McGinnis cracked his whip and the oxen hesitated at the water's edge. "Ho there! Giddyap!" He cracked his whip over their heads and the oxen entered the stream, clumsy in the water. After a moment, they began to swim and the light wagon floated. They made it to the first island, hesitated, plunged in again. The current threatened to sweep them downstream.

Rider yelled advice. "Don't let them head downstream! You'll lose the whole shebang!"

McGinnis followed instructions and in a few heart-stopping minutes, his wagon pulled up next to Emma's, his team dripping and exhausted.

Rider pushed his hat back and yelled to those on the other side. "It'll be dark soon.

You coming or shall I lead just two wagons to Oregon?"

"Don't leave us!" The ones on the far bank set up a howl of protest.

"Then get those wagons moving!" Rider yelled over the roar of the rushing water.

One at a time, they entered the river and chanced the crossing. A few things floated away when one wagon tangled with a floating tree trunk, but finally, every wagon except the Pettigrews' was safely across.

It was dusk. In only a few minutes, it would be too dark for further attempts. The banker took off his derby and wiped his red jowls. "I don't know about this."

"You'll have to try," Rider yelled.

Francie glared back at him from the wagon seat. Abruptly, Rider remembered the heavy gold in the bottom of the wagon. "I'm afraid you'll have to leave anything heavy behind."

Pettigrew looked undecided, but Francie yelled back, "No, I won't! I've gone to a lot of trouble for that cargo."

"Is it worth your life?"

Pettigrew looked uncertain. "I've sacrificed everything for what I'm carrying."

"Is it worth your life?" Rider yelled again. "I'm telling you your wagon is overloaded."

Francie grabbed the whip from her paramour's hands with an oath. "I ain't leavin' one single bit of it behind." She lashed the oxen with her whip and the startled animals lurched into the stream. The wagon only made it a few feet before it began to sink as the current caught the heavily-loaded wagon, pulling it farther downstream. Francie tried to guide the oxen, but she knew little about crossing rivers. As the heavy wagon bobbed, trying to stay afloat, it tilted and began to float away. Both people fell into the water, shouting and fighting to stay afloat.

Rider pulled off his boots, stuck a knife between his teeth, running forward to help. The heavy wagon was pulling the terrified oxen under.

"No, Rider," Emma yelled, "you'll drown!"

He paid no attention, swimming strongly against the current, skillfully avoiding the frightened animals' churning hooves. The dying light flashed on his blade as he cut the oxen free. At that moment, the wagon over-turned and began to drift downstream in the icy, foaming water.

The banker was almost to the second island.

"Roscoe!" Francie yelled as she floundered in the water. "You got to save the money! I need that money!"

The fat man hesitated, then turned to swim after the wagon.

"No!" Rider shouted as he swam toward Francie. "Let the damned money go!"

"The gold!" Francie screamed again, "Roscoe, I'll leave you if you don't save the gold!"

The man seemed to be listening only to Francie's voice because he kept swimming toward the upside down wagon that bobbed in the water. Greenbacks floated on the surface in the white foam. The banker went under, re-surfaced, grabbing for the dollars as they floated past him.

Rider shouted at him. "Let the money go!"

The other man didn't seem to hear anything. He kept swimming after the floating paper.

Rider managed to reach Francie and grab her, but Pettigrew was being swept downstream in a swirl of white foam and green paper money. In the meantime, the heavy gold had pulled the wagon completely under and it was half-submerged as it disappeared downstream and over the rapids to be broken up in small pieces. The banker seemed intent on grabbing the money as it floated past. He went under, then re-surfaced, gasping and choking. Women on the shore screamed, but no one moved.

Rider held onto Francie and turned toward the shore. The current pulled at him, but he would not give in to it. The girl's heavy, wet skirts jerked them under and she hung onto him, her long nails digging into his flesh. He knew he could make it if he let go of her and let her drown. Instead, he fought the current, determined to save her.

Finally, he touched bottom and stood up, staggering under the weight of her dripping skirts as she swung from his arms. "My money! Rider, save the money!"

"To hell with the money!" He dumped her on the ground unceremoniously and turned back toward the water, intent on rescuing the man, but there was no sign of him. Only a handful of paper money floated on the foamy, fast-moving surface. His gaze searched the water, but there was no sign of anything but the wagon disappearing in the distance over the rapids in a swirl of cold foam and green paper. Banker Pettigrew had died trying to save his wealth.

"My money!" Francie screamed. "I've lost all my money!"

Rider looked at her a long moment and didn't know whether to hate her or pity her. He took a deep breath and staggered away from the water.

Sky Eyes caught his arm. "That was a brave thing."

He collapsed on the ground against a tree, still trying to wipe out the image in his mind of the fat man frantically trying to retrieve the money for Francie. Her greed, and maybe Pettigrew's, too, had killed him.

Sky Eyes knelt by him and wrapped a warm blanket around his shoulders. "I'll get some coffee going and then fix some food. I feel so sorry for Francie."

"Don't," Rider snapped. "She sent him to his death over that damned gold."

Emma looked at him. "I thought that gold was important to you, too."

He sighed. "Once I thought it was. It doesn't seem that important anymore."

She waited for him to continue, but he only leaned back against the tree and closed his eyes.

"I'll get you some coffee," she said softly.

The wagon train pulled out again the next morning, still following the Snake River and moving still deeper into Shoshoni country. Francie Pettigrew, now penniless and alone, was taken into the McGinnis wagon. Weatherford B. Carrolton's madness seemed to be worsening, Emma thought. He often talked to himself and wandered off into the endless wilderness. They would have to stop the train and search for him. He said he was looking for his wife. Adams said little, but the hatred on his face as he watched Rider worried Emma. She knew he was plotting something and was only biding his time.

The weather grew colder as the train moved farther west. Oxen sickened and died, wagons broke down, and the people, tired and hungry, quarreled over small things.

One morning while they were still in camp, Rider said, "I'm going hunting. Our supplies are low and we've got to have some meat besides an occasional rabbit and waiting for an ox to die."

"Be careful," Emma said. She loved this man, she knew it now, but she didn't speak the words, knowing he feared commitment. Trying to bind Rider to her would be like roping the wind.

After Rider had ridden out, Emma got a basket from her wagon. "I thought I saw a few berries back there the bears haven't gotten," she mused. "It'll give us something to do."

The fear of bears caused her to tie the puppy to her wagon wheel and leave him behind. Boots was just young and stupid enough to go chasing after a bear and end up as the bruin's dinner. She carried one of Rider's pistols, so she felt safe enough. "Anyone want to join us?"

Francie only glared at her; Carrolton looked at her with blank eyes. The others shook their heads, too weary and lethargic to move.

She took Josh's hand and her basket. "This is going to be fun," she told him a little more brightly than she felt. "Rider will bring in a pronghorn and maybe we'll find enough berries to make a pie. That would be good, wouldn't it?"

Josh nodded. "I'm hungry and cold."

Emma sighed. "I know you are, honey, but we'll build a big fire when we get back to camp and think of the good supper we'll have. In a few more days, we'll be in Oregon."

"With Rider?"

She looked down into his trusting face. "Well, I don't know about that," she said. "Rider hasn't told me what he's going to do." The thought made her heart lurch. She had a sinking feeling that even though the gunfighter had been sharing her blankets and making passionate love to her every night, when Rider reached Oregon, he'd collect whatever pay he could from the survivors and ride out. She took a deep breath, not even wanting to think about it. Rider was the only man she wanted to touch her, make love to her, but she had a child to feed, so she must face the reality that soon the half-breed would ride out of her life forever.

The berries were scarce near the wagons. She motioned to Josh and they moved deeper into the brush, hunting the juiciest ones. She laughed at her small son, busy eating more than he was putting in the basket, his face smeared with purple juice. They were out of sight of the wagons now, but she'd been breaking off branches as she moved. The thought of becoming lost out here in the endless forest gave her pause. She'd heard that it had happened with other trains — people wandering off never to be seen again.

Ahead of her were several bushes with big, plump berries. Eagerly, she moved through the dense brush, her mind on the pie she would bake Rider tonight.

Josh made a small noise of dismay.

"What's the matter, honey — ?"

She never finished that sentence. She saw only the flash of a dark, war-painted face. She started to scream, but a big hand reached out and clasped over her mouth. As she fought, she saw that one of the braves had Josh in his arms, throwing him across a war-painted black pony.

Her son. These savages might kill her, but she would save her son. She tried to reach her pistol, but the savage wrestled it away from her, tossing it into the grass. Then with a cruel laugh at her terrified struggles, he threw her across his horse and mounted up behind her. She bit his fingers, trying to free her mouth so she could scream a warning. At that, her captor hit her hard, again and again. Half-stunned, she was only vaguely aware that she hung across the horse with his hand grasping her breast as the war party galloped away.

Chapter Nineteen

Rider returned from his hunting trip at mid-morning with a fat pronghorn buck slung across the back of his horse. He found Boots tied up and barking frantically. Puzzled, he untied the dog and began to look for Emma. No one could remember seeing her since early that morning. When he realized Josh was also missing, he knew something was wrong.

He began searching the area around the wagons. Boots began to bark. "What's the matter, boy?"

Rider walked over to the dog. The ground was churned up by horses' hooves and the horses were unshod. *Indians.* He grew both angry and uneasy as he studied the scene and found one of Emma's shoes and her basket, overturned, berries strewn across the ground.

Quickly, he returned to the others. "Mrs. Trent and her son have been taken by a war party." His words created a panic, but none had heard or seen anything suspicious.

Rider chewed his lip, thinking aloud. "They're probably Shoshoni," he said. "Which means they're as silent as ghosts. They got Josh, too."

Francie yawned. "Now ain't that too bad? Well, there's a couple more who won't make it to Oregon."

Rider gritted his teeth, wanting to slap her. "I'm going after them."

A long silence. None of the men offered to go with him.

"You can't do that," Gray whined. "Who'll guide us the rest of the way if you don't come back?"

The others set up a clamor of agreement.

Rider stared at them in angry disbelief. "You'd just abandon her and go on?"

No one said anything. The men avoided his furious glare, cowardly and ashamed.

"She's probably dead now anyway," the fat Mrs. Adams said. "We got to think of ourselves."

These people were as selfish as he'd always been, Rider realized suddenly. "No," he shook his head. "I'll bring them back or die trying."

Death was a real possibility, Rider thought as he searched through his saddlebags. Inside, he had some of his clothes he had worn as a dog soldier: a leather breech cloth, moccasins, beaded bracelets. He went into Emma's wagon to change. When he emerged, he looked so much like a warrior that the people drew shocked breaths of surprise.

"I'm going after Emma," he said again. "If I don't come back by tomorrow, move on without me."

"We don't know the trail," Francie cried.

"Just move west and follow the wagon tracks, but be on the lookout. The Shoshoni know we're here now."

He checked to make sure his weapons were loaded, untied the pup, and then mounted up. "Come on, Boots, let's see if you can help me follow that war party."

The pup wagged its tail and took off running. Rider followed him, his mood grim. He was under a death sentence among his mother's people, but he could not leave the girl behind, even if it cost him his life. Rides the Thunder realized suddenly that he cared enough to die attempting to save Sky Eyes and her little son.

Every once in a while, he dismounted to check the trail. Sometimes when he lost it, Boots sniffed it out and led him forward. The terrain looked more and more familiar to him now and he took a deep breath for courage. He was heading into a favorite camping spot of old Chief Washakie, the very clan that had banished him for murder. He was riding to his death, and he knew it because any warrior who saw him would certainly shoot on sight. Everything in him warned him to forget the white girl and leave her to her fate, return to the wagon train, and get out of this country as fast as possible. No, he couldn't do that because the pair meant so much to him. He had found a love worth dying for.

In the late afternoon, he saw smoke curling up from the campfires of a village ahead and knew he was reaching the end of his search. The sounds and the sights seemed as familiar to him as if he'd never left and old memories came crowding back. The thin veneer of civilization fell away and he rode into the camp boldly as the honored dog soldier, Rides the Thunder.

Dogs barked and people ran out of their lodges to stare at him as he passed. Here and there, a warrior gaped in open-mouthed amazement without blocking his way. It was almost as if they could not believe his temerity in returning.

So far, so good. He had expected to be

shot down as he reached the camp without any chance to explain. Ahead of him in the big circle blazed a fire before the lodge he knew as Washakie's. Near that fire, one slender ankle tied to a stake in the ground, was Emma Trent, her dress torn so that one beautiful breast peeked from the faded gingham.

She looked up slowly and he saw the sudden hope in the big, blue eyes. "Rider! Oh, Rider, I knew you'd come!"

He had to fight his impulse to keep from dismounting and running to sweep her up in his arms. Instead, he pretended not to notice her, dismounting proudly and speaking in the native tongue to the irate men who blocked him. "I come to see Washakie."

Curious people gathered around the circle in the late-afternoon shadows. The great chief himself came out of his lodge and stood there a long moment. "How dare Rides the Thunder enter this camp when he has been banished?"

He looked about with a bold, careless gaze. "I come to bargain for the woman and child."

"She is mine!" Out of the crowd stepped his old enemy, Wasp — tall, lithe, and deadly. "You murder my brother, Porcupine, and then return to this camp? Are you

470

prepared to die?"

A large, silent crowd of Shoshoni had gathered in a circle, ringing the two. Rider glanced toward Emma. She was looking at him now with doubt and terror.

"Rider?" she asked. "Are you returning to the Indians again? I thought you had come for me."

He ignored her as if the cries of a woman were of little importance to a brave of many coups and war honors.

A beautiful Indian girl ran out of the crowd and paused, looking at Rider. Anyone could see by the look on her face that she loved him. "Rides the Thunder! You have returned!"

Wasp grabbed the girl's arm in a rage and threw her to the ground. "It is not enough that you murder my brother — you have my wife's heart, too."

Rider shook his head. "I have no interest in Blue Bird. I have come for the yellow-haired captive."

The other brave's cruel mouth smiled without mirth. "She is your woman? Good, I will enjoy her twice as much. Blue Bird has given me no children, but your woman will."

"Not as long as I draw breath," Rider vowed.

"Silence!" the chief roared. "You, Rides

the Thunder, you come boldly into this camp under a death sentence to retrieve a mere woman?"

Rider nodded. "She holds this warrior's heart," he declared and knew for certain it was true. "I will exchange my life for hers."

"Never!" Wasp raged and stepped between Rider and the blond girl. "She is mine by right of capture and I intend to enjoy her this very night."

Blue Bird's pretty face turned ugly with jealous rage. "You hear this, Rides the Thunder? Take me! I will gladly leave with you. Let Wasp have the white slut."

Rider shook his head and turned toward Washakie. "Your people have always lived at peace with the white man, not like Man Lost or Bear Hunter's band."

The chief nodded. "What you say is true."

"Then let me take this woman and child and go unharmed."

"No!" Wasp brandished a lance. "She is mine by right of capture and I will not give her up without a fight!" An excited murmur ran through the crowd.

The old chief nodded. "She belongs to Wasp and you cannot take her without giving him something in trade."

Rider hesitated. "Wasp, you have always

472

wanted my fine stallion, Storm. I offer him now in trade."

A louder murmur. Everyone knew this was a fine horse, one of the best ever trained by the Shoshoni. Rides the Thunder must value the yellow-haired one very much to offer his stallion for her life.

Wasp smiled and shook his head slowly. "I want you to think tonight when you lie down to sleep how your little son is now my slave and how much I will be enjoying your woman. The thought that you care for her will make it twice as good."

Rider clenched his fists, but he only looked toward Washakie for a decision.

The chief considered. "It is Wasp's choice to make since he captured her. Because we admire your bravery, you may ride out of here unharmed."

Rider shook his head. "I will not leave without her if I die on this spot."

Blue Bird spat on the ground. "If only you had cared so much for me!"

Wasp looked at his woman and the jealousy and hatred for his rival was there for all to see. "I would see you dead, Rides the Thunder, revenge for the death of my brother. I challenge you to the death."

A loud murmur ran through the crowd. All knew that Wasp was a skilled fighter in hand-to-hand combat. The old chief considered for a long moment. "Rides the Thunder is under a death sentence and Wasp has never received vengeance for Porcupine's death. What say you, Rides the Thunder? Would you risk your life in hand-to-hand combat for your honor and this woman?"

Rider looked at her a long moment, at the love in those pale blue eyes for him and him alone. "I say again that I did not kill Porcupine — he was my friend. But I will risk my honor and my life to save this woman."

His enemy threw back his head and laughed. "I will spill your blood in the dust, and before the evening is finished, I will mount both your horse and your woman."

The images the other dog soldier's words brought to mind made Rider grind his teeth with rage, but he only nodded calmly. "So be it. We will battle to the death then."

"At sunset," the chief announced, "here in the circle." He made a gesture of dismissal and returned to his lodge.

The others, seeing there would be no action until later, began to disperse.

Rider stood staring at Emma, wanting to run to her, take her in his arms, but it was not seemly conduct for a warrior.

Wasp walked to his captive and kicked

dirt at her. Then he leaned over, caught her long hair in his hand, and twisted her face up to his. "Did you hear, bitch?" he said in missionary school English. "I am to fight this half-breed for possession of your body."

Rider strode toward them. "Don't touch her — don't you dare touch her."

The other made a threatening gesture toward her with his lance. "After I spill your blood tonight, I intend to do more than touch her. By tomorrow morning, she will be carrying my child. Your small son will be my slave."

Blue Bird looked from one to the other. "What about me?"

Wasp shook his head and yawned. "I tire of you, bitch. Because of you, my brother is dead. I cannot forget that."

And Wasp had killed his own brother, Rider thought, *in a jealous fight over Blue Bird.* No one had believed Rides the Thunder when he had told that truth five years ago because Blue Bird, angry because Rider did not want her, had backed up Wasp's vow before the Council that Rider had killed his friend in a dispute over her.

"Enjoy your last few hours of life," Wasp gloated before he turned and stalked away.

Rider walked over and stared. Emma's clothes were torn and dirty, her blond hair hanging down to hide her breasts.

She looked up at him. "Is that true or can we leave?"

Rider shook his head. "There is to be a battle," he said. "The winner is to get you and Josh. They think he's my son. Where is he?"

She bit her lip. "He doesn't understand enough to be afraid. He's playing with the Indian children. It's the first time he's ever seen children like himself."

"He'll be all right then until tonight."

She reached out to him. "You're risking your life?"

He nodded. "I must."

"I can't bear to see you hurt. And if you lose?"

He took a deep breath. "Then Josh will be Wasp's slave and you will warm his blankets. He intends to breed you since Blue Bird has given him no sons. For that reason, I must not lose."

"Oh, Rider, I'm so afraid for you!"

"No, I am afraid for you," he answered. "Now I must go and make medicine, pray to the Spirits to help me in this coming fight and, perhaps, clear my name. I did not murder Porcupine. He was my friend."

She smiled up at him. "I never thought you did, Rider."

He nodded and strode away.

Emma wanted to scream after him not to leave her. She yearned for the safety of his arms. In a few minutes, Josh and Boots joined her. She hid her tied ankle under a fold of her faded dress.

"I saw Storm," Josh said, his dark eyes wide with excitement. "Is Rider here to take us away?"

"Yes," she said with calm certainty.

"I knew he would come," Josh said and patted his dog, "but Mama, I'm happy here."

She took a deep breath. "We've got to get to Oregon, remember? Rider's come for us. We have to wait awhile, that's all." She was afraid — not for herself, but for Rider and her little son. In only a few hours, Rider might be dead, Josh a slave, and she enduring Wasp's touch.

The sun was high as Rides the Thunder went to a hilltop to make medicine and pray to his personal protector, the God of Thunder and Lightning, *Talawi Piki*. Too long he had lived as a white man, he thought, and had not prayed for his power since he had danced the *Dagoo Wiode*, the Dance of Thirst other Plains tribes called the sun dance. Now he called upon his dead ancestors in the Home of the Departed Spirits, *Thigunawat,* to show him the way to victory or brave death. Deep in his heart, he was not white, he was *Saydocarah,* Shoshoni, the conquerors. How well his tribe's enemies, the dog-eating Arapaho, Cheyenne, and Lakota, knew this truth.

He knew word of the coming combat must have spread though the drums echoing across the *Ochoco,* the Land of the Red Willow; that was the soul of their people. Warriors from across the wilderness would hear that message and come to the big campfire in the center of the village. In the meantime, he knew Wasp would be praying to his own protector, *Paluna,* the Spirit of War.

Finally, he was ready. As a final gesture, he took bright yellow war paint and marked across the bridge of his nose and high cheekbones. This advertised to all his people that he fought for a beloved woman and he would rescue her or die in the attempt.

The air had turned cold with a hint of snow. Emma, still staked out by Wasp's lodge, shivered and watched the preparations with growing uneasiness as she clutched her son to her and tried to cover her nakedness. She saw many warriors give her admiring looks. Blue Bird came out, kicked dust at her, and struck her with a quirt.

Emma came up off the ground fighting, grabbing for the whip, sending the sullen Shoshoni girl stumbling backward.

The other Shoshonis smiled and nodded approval. Evidently, they admired courage and did not like the sullen brown beauty. The village drums continued a steady rhythm as darkness deepened and the people gathered. Emma held her breath and put a comforting hand on Josh's arm. Thank goodness, she thought, that her son, playing happily with his puppy, had no idea what was being decided here tonight.

Finally, the drums ceased abruptly and Washakie came out of his lodge. The old chief was resplendent with hammered silver coins in his braided hair and the finest of furs. He was joined by other older men who took their seats cross-legged on blankets before his lodge. Emma knew by the way the others deferred to them that these were well-respected warriors and leaders of the Shoshoni tribe.

At that moment, Wasp rode into the camp on a fine black stallion. A murmur of admiration rippled through the gathering throng. The handsome warrior was dressed in his finest, heavily beaded moccasins and buckskin pants. War paint red as blood slashed across the bridge of his nose and his cheeks. As he dismounted and handed the reins of his stallion to another warrior, he said to Emma in English, "Tonight you will see me kill your man and after that, you will share my blankets."

"Never!" Emma spat at him, but he only smiled and went to stand with his feet apart and his arms crossed before the council. There was silence in the camp now, broken only by the whinny of horses, a baby crying somewhere in the camp, and the crackle of the big fire.

The air was cold and tense as the Indians waited. Emma, too, strained her neck, looking about for Rides the Thunder. Blue Bird had come to sit in the circle to watch. She gave Emma a jealous frown, then ignored her.

For a few minutes that seemed centuries long, there was only silence. Slowly a murmur ran through the crowd as if they wondered if the challenger would come.

The thought came suddenly to Emma that under the circumstances, no one could blame the half-breed if he should change his mind and ride out. Emma had unshakable faith in Rider. He was more than a brave man; he would not shirk his duty and he would never abandon her and her child.

There were so many people gathered in the great circle that Emma, tied as she was to a stake in the ground, could not see all that was happening, but she saw the crowd beginning to part and a murmur of admiration running through the Shoshoni. Rider rode slowly into the circle. No, she gasped in awe, he was no longer Rider, the white man's gunfighter; he was truly Rides the Thunder, a renowned Shoshoni warrior of many battles and coups, with an aura of nobility about him.

He was naked save for the brief loincloth and his mighty brown body showed its many scars and battle wounds. He had stripped off all his beadwork and braided up his black hair. Across his face, bright yellow paint contrasted sharply with his dark skin. His horse had been brushed until its coat shone and there were symbols of old honors painted on its shoulders and spotted flanks. Feathers and fancy beadwork hung from Storm's bridle.

She heard a murmur of admiration as people pointed to the stallion. Storm was indeed a worthy prize for the winner. Rides the Thunder dismounted with dignity, led the horse over, and tied it to the stake where she was tied. Emma stared up at him and as his gaze caught hers, he gave her the slightest nod of recognition. "Tonight, you will truly become my woman."

"I was always your woman," she whispered, "always."

Her words gave Rider courage as he turned and walked to the council to stand beside Wasp. He noted that the other dog soldier wore crimson paint, the gesture telling all that he was there to avenge another Shoshoni warrior.

In the circle, he saw the beautiful Blue Bird watching the little drama; her dark eyes told him that her love belonged to him and always had. Rides the Thunder ignored her as he bowed his head in recognition before the council.

Washakie stood up and raised a hand. Immediately all chatter ceased. It was silent enough to hear the small, lonely cry of a night bird flying through the forest.

"Rides the Thunder," the chief said solemnly, "you have been banished from this camp for the murder of your friend and Wasp's brother, Porcupine, yet today you defy us and return."

"I deny again that I killed my friend," Rider said solemnly in a voice loud enough for all to hear. "Tonight I throw myself on the mercy of the Great Spirit to prove my innocence. If I lie, may my blood soak this ground."

The council looked at each other and whispered.

Washakie said, "Remember there was a witness, Blue Bird."

Rider looked toward the beautiful Indian girl and sneered. "She lied because she was angry that I would not take her as my woman."

"And what of the noted dog soldier Wasp's testimony?"

Rider took a deep breath. "I say that Wasp lied also because he lusted for the woman and would have her even if he had to murder his own brother."

A horrified murmur ran through the crowd and Wasp's face darkened with fury. "I saw him stab my brother — I swear this on my honor."

Washakie raised his hand to silence the excited buzz that went through the crowd. "Rides the Thunder, you have said strong words against a noted warrior."

Rider held up his hand in an oath. "May the Great Spirit take my life if I speak with a forked tongue."

The old chief folded his arms and

nodded. "Very well. The Shoshoni do not usually allow a fight to the death between its warriors, but this is a terrible thing that only blood can cleanse." He looked toward Emma with her half-torn dress. "The winner of this fight proves his innocence and gets both the fine stallion and the woman and her whelp. The loser's blood will spill across the dust of this circle."

So saying, Washakie took a big knife from his robes. He held it up to the evening sky, singing a chant while the people waited. The starlight and the fire flashed on the sharp blade. Rides the Thunder recognized that knife from the marks on its bone handle; it had belonged to Porcupine. Washakie looked at each of the combatants. "You both know the custom."

They nodded and Washakie gestured to the people to move back and give the pair a large circle around the fire for their battle. Then he walked to the center near the campfire and drove the knife to the hilt in the ground. Now he motioned to the two men to move to the outer edges of the circle.

Rider crouched, glaring at Wasp across the circle. This would be the only weapon and the most agile and fastest would own it; the other would be armed only with his wits and his fighting skills.

"Are you ready?" Washakie asked.

They both nodded. Rider glanced toward Blue Bird, who watched impassively as if she did not care who won or lost, even though her own man would be fighting for his life tonight. She was a cold bitch who had plotted to put the two brothers at each other's throat while she tried to charm Rides the Thunder into wanting her.

He glanced toward Sky Eyes. Her beautiful face was pale, but her lips moved and formed the words: *I love you.*

He made no sign that he understood, although his heart was full to overflowing with his love for her.

Washakie raised his arm and the two crouched, waiting. Rider focused his attention on the knife, the firelight reflecting off its bone handle.

The old chief dropped his hand suddenly and both men charged in, grabbing for the knife. Rider got there first, but even as he reached for it, Wasp collided with him, caught him by the throat, and smashed his fist into Rider's mouth. Stunned and choking, Rider broke that hold with sheer brute strength and staggered backward. Around him, he heard the rumble of dismay. Wasp had never been well liked among this band.

Even as the other tried to wrench the knife from the ground, Rider stumbled to his feet, ran over, and kicked Wasp's hands away. The other man grabbed his ankle and jerked him to the ground. They locked and rolled over and over across the dirt. They came up near the big fire. Wasp kicked Rider in the head and as he fell, he was on top of the half-breed, catching his arm and bending it toward the flames. Rider could feel the heat as he struggled to keep his hand from being forced into the fire. He felt the pain and smelled the singed flesh even as Emma screamed.

Startled, Wasp's attention was diverted; quick as a cat, Rider tossed him to one side. They both made a dive for the knife again. The other man wrenched it from the ground and crouched, his eyes shining. "Now, you half-breed who pretends to be Shoshoni, now will I cut your heart out and smear your woman with your blood before I rape her!"

"No!" Rider shouted. In the circle, a great murmur went up as he feinted, then made a dive for the other's legs. Wasp stumbled and went down, the knife flying from his hand. They locked in combat, rolling over and over as they both tried to reach the knife. It lay on the edge of the circle, its blade gleaming in the firelight.

Wasp moved suddenly and grabbed for the knife again. In one quick move, he slashed across Rider's arm even as Rider ducked and moved agilely away. Bright blood ran down his arm now as he faced the other, scarlet as the paint on Wasp's cruel face. Both men were shiny with sweat even though the night air was turning colder. Rider could smell his own warm blood and see the gleam of triumph in Wasp's dark eyes. They both knew that if this fight continued much longer, Rider would lose enough blood that he would be too weak to continue. Everyone else must know it, too, because a muted roar swept through the crowd.

They clenched and Wasp whispered in his ear. "Tonight as you lie dying, I will mount your woman and put my son in her belly!"

"No!" Rider shouted. "No man touches her but me!"

Wasp's mocking words gave him new strength and he grappled with the other, both struggling for the knife, both slippery with Rider's blood. He could smell the hot, coppery scent of it, knew he was growing weaker. Then he glanced toward Sky Eyes, saw the fear in her face and knew he must save her from this terrible fate, no matter if it cost him his life.

Wasp had the knife, but Rider tripped him and as the man sprawled, Rider grabbed up the blade. He crouched, moving toward Wasp. He saw the fear in the other man's eyes even as he charged in and took him to the ground.

The circle was so silent, Rides the Thunder could hear his own tortured breathing. Wasp began to shriek, begging for mercy as Rider put the sharp dagger against his throat. Around him, the people murmured in disgust at this show of cowardice. Rider pressed the knife to the other's throat. "You offend the Gods and this tribe with your forked tongue. Tell the council what really happened the night my friend Porcupine died."

Wasp hesitated. Rider put the sharp edge of the blade against the veins. A tiny drop of blood ran from the cut. "Tell them!"

Wasp was sobbing with fear. "It's true!" he whimpered. "It's true. My brother and I fought over the girl and in a fit of jealousy, I killed him."

Rider stood up and tossed the knife into the fire. It was over; his friend was avenged. He turned toward the council. "I give the coward his life. You have heard the truth."

The old chief looked toward Blue Bird. "Is this true?"

She hesitated.

"For once," Rider thundered, "tell the truth."

Blue Bird began to sob. "It — it is true. I pitted the brothers against each other until they fought. Then I was angry that Rides the Thunder did not want me, so in a fit of jealous rage, I spoke with a forked tongue to get him exiled from the camp."

There was an excited mutter from around the hundreds of people surrounding the circle even as Wasp stumbled to his feet, wiping at the cut on his neck.

Washakie stood up and his face was as black as a summer storm. "Wasp, you have lied and have no honor. You are hereby banished from our band."

"No!" The dog soldier held out his hands in a plea. "Where shall I go?"

"Go?" Washakie sneered. "Go join the Shoshonis who make war on the whites, Man Lost or Bear Hunter."

Blue Bird ran out into the circle. "What about me? What shall become of me?"

The old chief looked at her with utter contempt and disgust. "You will go with your man."

"No," she said and fell on her knees before the council. "No, I never cared for this man. I only loved Rides the Thunder!"

Rider shook his head. "You are responsible for one brother killing another. Now you bear the consequences."

The two guilty ones looked around the circle and seemed to see only hostile faces.

Wasp begged, "The weather is turning cold. We risk death by trying to reach the warring bands."

Washakie held up his hand for silence, his face cold as stone. "You gave no mercy nor shall you receive any. Leave this camp and take your faithless woman with you. Never show yourself among us again on pain of death."

A group of grim warriors surrounded Wasp and Blue Bird and led them away, both of them protesting as they were put on horses. The horses were whipped into a gallop as the pair were driven out into the cold night.

Washakie held up his hand for silence. "Rides the Thunder, you are restored to your place of honor among my warriors. We will feast in celebration and in the morning, you may take the woman and child and do as you wish."

Rider nodded modestly. Sky Eyes smiled up at him but it was unseemly to notice a mere woman even though in his heart, his warrior's heart, he longed to sweep her up into his embrace and hold her close. He must not display such adoration before the others. He strode over to Emma and said haughtily, "Woman, you are a prize for the winner. You will be fed and made ready for my pleasure. After I smoke the pipe with the council, I will return to the lodge and claim my reward."

Chapter Twenty

Sky Eyes and her son were led away to be fed and washed while Rider went to eat and smoke with the tribal elders.

Washakie said, "We are sorry you have been treated so badly. Would you wish to return and live among us?"

Rider paused and stared into the fire in the center of the lodge. "I'm not sure," he said. "I miss the freedom of living among the Shoshoni and my life among the white men has not been a happy one." He hesitated and didn't continue. *The girl,* he thought, *he couldn't lose the girl. She was the beat of this warrior's heart and she was determined to go to Oregon.*

Washakie nodded and took a deep puff of the pipe before passing it around the circle. "Our lives with the whites invading our land grows harder, still we manage to stay at peace by moving farther into the mountains, not like Man Lost and Bear Hunter's bands, who attack wagon trains and soldier patrols."

Rider shook his head. "Sooner or later, the army will come and many will die," he said. "The whites are as many as grains of sand and they will not permit such attacks to continue. Wasp has been sneaking off to join their war parties."

Washakie looked grim. "He lied to us, telling us the booty he brought was found in abandoned wagons on the trail."

The old warriors nodded agreement; they smoked and ate and talked of the good days of hunting and riding through the mountains. Life among the Shoshoni was the height of freedom and Rider missed it.

Finally, Washakie said, "If you will not stay, go to your woman and take the pleasure you have won. Tomorrow at first light, you may return to the wagon train."

The council broke up and Rider washed himself in a clear stream that ran near the camp and bound up the cut on his arm. Then he went to the lodge the council had provided. The weather was growing colder, he thought; it might begin snowing by morning.

Inside the lodge, Sky Eyes looked up from her place beside the fire. She had been dressed in a fine beaded doeskin outfit. He thought he had never seen any woman so beautiful as she was with her long golden hair and the Shoshoni dress and moccasins.

For a long moment, Emma could only stare up at the brave. He did not seem to be Rider, the man she knew. This man looked every inch the Shoshoni warrior from his braided hair down to his beaded moccasins. On his lithe, brown, muscular body, all he wore was the briefest of loincloths, fine beaded jewelry and silver ornaments in his black hair. He was truly Rides the Thunder, the honored dog soldier.

She rose from her place by the fire. For a heartbeat, she could only stare at him; then he opened his arms without speaking. Such a gesture needed no words. With a glad cry, she ran into his embrace. He held her so tightly that she could scarcely breathe, then he swung her up in his big arms and kissed her ever so tenderly. "My Sky Eyes."

"They have given me to you?"

He held her close as he nodded. "You are my captive. I have won you and you are mine to do with as I please."

She had a split second of apprehension, then smiled up at him. "And what pleases you, my master?"

"Make love to me all night long," he said and carried her to the pile of soft furs by the fire. "Where is Josh?"

She nodded toward the child curled up fast asleep with his dog in a corner of the lodge and Rider smiled. "Was he frightened?"

Emma shook her head. "I think he's rather enjoyed himself. It's a much more free and different life, and the children he played with looked like him."

Outside, the wind blew, shaking the lodge and when she looked out, she could see a stray snowflake against the blackness of the night. "The wagon train? I've got to get to Oregon."

Rider shook his head. "At dawn, we leave here, but tonight, you are here for my pleasure."

Even as he spoke, he reached down and pulled the doeskin shift from her body, leaving her naked to his sight against the pile of soft furs. She tried to hide her nakedness with her hands, but he pulled them away with a frown. "You are very beautiful and I would feast my eyes on what I risked my life for."

"All right then." She sat up, boldly displaying her proud, pert breasts and silken thighs.

Rider took a deep breath and his eyes turned intense with need. Wordlessly he reached down and ripped off his loincloth. He stood there, strong, naked, and beautiful as a bronze statue, his manhood rigid. "Tonight I will love you as you have never been loved before."

She came up on her knees and put her arms around his thighs, pressing her naked breasts against his legs as she kissed the scepter of his manhood in deference. "I am awaiting your pleasure, Rides the Thunder."

He stood there a long moment, trembling with his need as she kissed his manhood with hot, wet lips. Then he tangled his fingers in her long hair, pulling her mouth against him to tease and taste him with her tongue.

Finally, with a groan of surrender, he went to his knees and gathered her into his strong arms. "You make me want you as I have never desired another woman," he whispered against her lips. Then he kissed her, thoroughly, deeply, expertly, exploring her mouth with his tongue as he crushed her breasts against him. She felt her pulse quicken as his hand came down to clutch her buttocks, molding her hard against his own powerful body. Her hands went around him, too, exploring his back, every sinew and scar and muscular fiber of him as they fell to the furs.

The furs were soft and sensual against her naked skin; then he rolled over on his back, positioning her above him. "You make love to me," he demanded.

"I-I don't know how."

"This is not the time to be shy," he said as he reached up and caught her breasts in his two big hands. "You know what I like. I am your master, so pleasure me."

Her own desire was building and she was suddenly shameless. She began to kiss every inch of him, moving with deliberate, agonizing slowness with her hot tongue.

He writhed under her. "I can't take much more of this."

"Oh, but you must," she laughed. "I may do this for hours yet."

"I think not!" He pulled her on top of him, lifting her to where his mouth could reach her breasts. Emma closed her eyes and took a deep breath as he caressed and tasted.

She wanted him with a need that could not be denied. Against her thigh she could feel his manhood, hard and insistent. "I'm going to ride you, my stallion," she whispered.

"I'm waiting."

She spread her thighs and mounted him

ever so slowly, letting his big maleness slip in an inch at a time with excruciating, delicious slowness.

He moaned and moved restlessly under her, but she would not be hurried.

"Enough!" he murmured as he reached and grabbed her waist, slamming her body hard against him so that he entered her to the hilt. Deep inside, she felt him throbbing with his need. She began to ride him very deliberately, her own desire building.

"More!" he gasped. "More!"

"Such pleasant torture," she smiled. "Let's see how long I can make this last."

But Rider grabbed her waist, arching up into her as he pulled her body down on his, slamming her against him, their two bodies slapping, flesh against flesh.

At that moment, she could take no more. She arched, took a deep breath as her body went into convulsion, squeezing the seed from his. Beneath her, he paused, breathing hard; then he pulled her down on him one final time and held her there as he poured his seed deep within her.

"Rider, my Rider . . ." She kissed him even as they both reached a final pinnacle of pleasure.

Afterwards, they slept curled up in each

other's arms by the fire.

In the middle of the night, he reached for her again. She opened her eyes and looked up into his dark ones, smoky with renewed desire. There was no need for words. She offered her breasts to him and opened her thighs. It was a hurried, intense mating and he dropped off to sleep still lying on her.

Just before dawn, he made love to her again and held her close. At peace with the world, they looked out and watched the snow fall in the coming Shoshoni sunrise.

"It is the most beautiful sunrise I ever saw," she murmured, "because I spent it in your arms."

They ate and dressed warmly in furs that the chief had sent them. Josh awakened and ran to Rider's arms with a glad cry. "I knew you'd come for us."

Rider held the boy close, not wanting to think about how much this child and his mother had come to mean to him. "Were you scared, Small Warrior?"

The little boy shook his head as his mother dressed him in furs. "I knew you and Boots would come for us. Some of the Shoshoni boys have ponies. I always wanted a pony."

"We'll talk about that later," Rider smiled. "Now eat and feed your dog so we can leave.

We've got to get back to the wagon train. They're probably all wondering what they're going to do about now."

They rode out of the Shoshoni camp, Emma and Josh riding with him on his great stallion, Boots barking and gamboling in the falling snow as they waved good-bye and rode away.

"You know," Emma said and looked back, "after I got over being afraid, I almost envied their freedom."

Rider nodded. "They roam the mountains, moving the camp when they feel like it, and they have no clocks."

She remembered last night. "What about Wasp and Blue Bird?"

Rider shrugged. "They have been exiled from this camp. No doubt they will go join up with a warring bunch. Bear Hunter camps many miles from here up on Bear River. They are not a peaceful band."

And so they rejoined the train. The people ran to meet them, relieved they would not have to try to find their own way across treacherous streams and mountains.

The next few weeks were full of peril as the weather worsened and they ran low on food, but there was nothing they could do but keep going. Once they found a burned-out wagon train with no survivors; Rider's face was grim as he inspected the smoldering remains. He leaned over and picked up an arrow from the smoking canvas.

"This is Wasp's — I recognize his mark. No doubt he rides now with either Man Lost or Bear Hunter. Sooner or later, the army will attack those bands."

The Southerner, Carrolton, kept wandering off, his mind deteriorating. They would have to stop and search for him. When they did find him, he would tell them he was looking for Millicent. It seemed to do no good to tell him that she was dead. The others still watched Rider with suspicion and hatred. They needed him, but they hated him, which was probably the only reason Adams or one of the others didn't try to murder Rider. Emma thought when they reached Oregon, the people still might plot against him. Francie rode in the McGinnis wagon, but there was squabbling and ill will. Emma had never been so weary of anybody as she was of this bunch of misfits.

They had to leave another wagon behind because it was too worn to be repaired. Once a Weeks child wandered off and they were delayed for hours while Rider searched until he found her. Emma's cow died, so they had fresh meat for several days. Sometimes the weather was rainy and other times, biting cold, the wind cutting through her worn clothes like a straight razor. She had given her warm furs to one of the women who was sick.

Finally one day, in the early winter, they topped a hill and a treeless, arid valley lay below them.

"There you are," Rider reined in next to her wagon, "there's Oregon."

The tired, ragged people set up a cheer and Emma smiled with relief, hugging Josh to her. "Did you hear him, honey? Now we'll have a nice house, plenty to eat, and a daddy."

"Rider?" Josh asked.

Her heart lurched and she turned and looked wordlessly at the big half-breed sitting his horse. He didn't say anything, only looked at her.

Well, she had her answer. Not that Rider had been anything but honest with her. From the first, he had told her he wanted her as a convenience and his pleasure to warm his blankets until they reached Oregon and now they were here. Now he would try to collect his money and ride out of her life. She would not beg for his affections, not that it would do any good. Hadn't he told her how much he valued his freedom and hated commitment?

Rider rode on ahead and Emma snapped her whip over her weary oxen, wishing she could be happier. She had reached Oregon but now she would be losing the man she loved.

People ran out to greet them as they pulled into town. Josh shouted and waved, but the people seemed to notice his dark little face and frowned. Emma's heart sank. It wasn't going to be any different here, she thought; her half-breed child wouldn't be welcome. Surely there was one man in the settlement who'd be kind enough to her child that she could marry him. She had a problem, though, that she wasn't sure how to deal with. She wouldn't think about that now.

People crowded around, but seemed to frown and draw back as they looked over her son. Weatherford B. Carrolton's sister came to claim him and took the dazed man away.

Emma parked her wagon under a tree and unhitched her oxen, staking them out to graze.

Near dark, Rider rode up and dismounted. "Well, you're here at last. You happy?"

She nodded, not wanting to admit that

what she wanted was to be his forever. "A whole new start."

Rider frowned. "You think you'll find the kind of husband you want here?"

What she wanted was Rider, but of course, there was no point in telling him that. She might as well try to rope the wind. "There's bound to be some nice farmer or shopkeeper who won't mind taking on a woman with a little boy. I'm strong and I can work hard."

He looked even more annoyed. "I can't imagine you stuck with some dirt grubber who works you like a slave. I hope you find one who'll look after you and protect you."

She shrugged. "Sometimes you can't have everything. Did you manage to collect your money?"

Rider laughed and shook his head. "Of course not. Now that they're safely here, I got all sorts of excuses as to why they couldn't pay me. That's okay — with Pettigrew dead, the others don't have much. Anyway, there's good money to be made as a hired gun for some of the big ranchers in Texas or California."

He sat his horse, looking down at her, thinking he would never care so much for another woman. She wanted roots, some sweating dirt farmer who would bend his back in all kinds of weather forcing a poor living from the land. *Could Rider give up his precious freedom for her?* He wavered.

"Rider," she said, interrupting his thoughts, "there's something I need to tell you." She paused and looked away.

"So tell me," he snapped, annoyed with her because she had made a captive of his heart and he wasn't sure he could break it and ride out.

"Are you going to be around a while?" She wasn't looking at him, wetting her lips nervously.

"I reckon." He pushed his Stetson to the back of his head. "Maybe I'll ride out tomorrow."

"You're dead set on going?"

Rider laughed. "You think a hired gun would be welcome in this town for long?"

"Never mind. I've got to go into the general store before it closes for the night." She turned away from him. "Maybe we can talk before you leave."

"Sure. I'll be camped in that grove over there past your wagon."

She took Josh's hand and, followed by Boots, headed for the store. *Why didn't you tell him?* she scolded herself. Because she was afraid he wouldn't care, that he would still ride out without a backward glance.

Well, she was a strong woman. She could deal with this as she had dealt with everything else, with courage and determination.

It was dark as she walked toward the general store.

"Psst!"

Emma paused and looked around. "Who's there?"

Timid little Mrs. Weeks, carrying her young baby wrapped in a blanket, stepped out from between the buildings. "You care about that Injun as much as I think you do?"

Emma bristled at the word. "What is that to you?"

"We don't have time to stand here and argue." Mrs. Weeks smiled and her homely face was etched with concern. "I just heard something you'd want to know if you love him."

"He's out of my life." *Or soon would be,* she thought.

The other caught her arm. "You were good to me and I'm grateful, or I wouldn't do this. My husband will be angry with me if he finds out I warned you."

"Warned me?" She had a sudden feeling of alarm.

Behind them, in the general store, she heard the sound of angry voices rising.

The other gestured. "That's what I mean.

The town is gettin' together a lynch party. That fat old farmer, Adams, is behind it all."

"A lynch party?" She felt a cold chill run down her back. "But Rider got them here — they ought to be grateful —"

"They aren't," Mrs. Weeks said. "And old man Adams holds a grudge over hanging his son."

"But the settlers made up the jury that found Willie Adams guilty," Emma protested.

"You think they care about that now that they're safely here?"

Behind them, the doors to the general store opened. Men came out on the wooden sidewalks, shouting and angry.

Rider had to be warned. "Thanks, Mrs. Weeks. Look after Josh a minute." She turned and, lifting her skirts, took off up the street toward the grove where she knew Rider camped. When she looked back, she saw men lighting torches and one throwing a rope over the beam holding the big sign in front of the livery stable. There was not a moment to lose.

She was breathless as she ran. She tripped and fell once, then scrambled to her feet and kept running. When she looked back, the men had lit a dozen torches that glowed in the night. Now an angry mob, they were marching up the muddy street.

She ran past her wagon and into Rider's camp.

"What the hell?" He came up off his blanket, pistol in hand.

"It's me, Rider."

He relaxed, smiling. "I've been thinking about what you said about farming — been thinking a lot, Sky Eyes."

"No time to talk," she gasped. "They're coming!"

"Who?"

She was breathless, motioning behind her. "A mob — a lynch mob led by some of the wagon train bunch."

Rider cursed. "That's gratitude for you. I ought to kill some of them."

She shook her head. "There's too many of them. Now get out of here unless you want to hang from that rope in front of the lively stable."

He grabbed up his bridle and began to saddle his horse.

"Hurry!" she urged, looking down the road at the mob with their torches marching toward them.

He picked up his weapons. "What about you? They won't like it that you warned me."

"As cowardly as they are, they still won't harm a woman," she said. "Now get out of here while you still can!"

He hesitated as if there was something he wanted to say, then only touched his fingers to the brim of his hat as he mounted up. "Thanks, Sky Eyes. Best of luck to you."

She didn't want him to see her cry so she merely nodded and waved as he rode out at a gallop. Tears blinded her then and she could no longer see him as he faded into the night, but she could hear the fading hoofbeats and the mob behind her coming closer. Later, she would cry her heart out, but she could not enjoy that luxury now.

He was gone, riding out of her life just as he had ridden in. Now it was too late to tell him the secret she had been hiding so many weeks. Maybe it wouldn't have made any difference to the gunfighter anyway. He liked his freedom and didn't want to be tied down. Still, she wished she had had the chance to tell him she was expecting his child.

Chapter Twenty-one

In the weeks that followed after Rider rode out, things didn't go well for Emma. With her half-breed son and the knowledge that she had helped the gunfighter escape, she was less than welcome in the dirty little settlement.

Most of the wagon train survivors had stayed on, too cowardly to chance the dangerous Blue Mountains, although Weeks and Gray had moved toward Baker City, searching for the lost Blue Bucket mine. The McGinnis and Jones families had forged on, hoping to make it through to the Dalles, the Decision Point where they would have to decide whether to chance the treacherous Columbia River or take the dangerous Barlow Road to the rich Willamette Valley.

At first, Emma thought she would have good luck finding a husband, even though she was expecting the half-breed's child.

There were plenty of single men and very few women in this miserable little town of Gold Nugget but besides Herman Adams, old man Adams's younger brother, no other man approached her. Herman had made it clear he was not only the richest man in the area, but very interested in marriage. However, there was something about him that repelled her besides his looks — and Emma rebuffed him.

As winter came on and weeks passed, Emma tried desperately to find a job. No one would hire her. She tried the dairy, the feed store, the cafe, the fabric store. Each owner avoided her eyes and told her how sorry he was, but times were hard and they weren't hiring.

Emma traded her oxen to Herman Adams, who not only owned the general store but the bank. While she tried to ration her supplies, they were slowly running out. She didn't have enough food to make it through the winter and the wagon was not going to be much shelter against the snows.

What to do? Perhaps her only recourse was to find a husband. The thought repulsed her because sharing a bed with any man but Rider now seemed unthinkable. She had never known passion until he had seduced her with his skillful lovemaking, and the thought of another man touching her made her cringe. However, with one child to feed and another due in early summer, she had to do something. However, when she smiled at men on the street, they retreated from her almost with alarm.

Desperate now and with winter deepening, one day she decided she would ask Herman Adams for credit and went to his store.

"Credit?" He lowered his glasses and peered at her. The kerosene lamp hanging overhead reflected off his bald head. "Mrs. Trent, I haven't become the richest man in Gold Nugget by extending credit."

"Then perhaps you could offer me a job?" she said. "I could clerk and help stock shelves."

He came around the counter and took her hand in his fat one. "Really, my dear, I'm not good with words, so let me put it this way. I don't need a clerk, I need a wife."

Emma looked down into his round face, thinking of allowing this homely, fat man to mount her, kiss her. The thought made her sick. "You don't understand, Mr. Adams —"

"Please call me Herman." His hand on hers felt sweaty.

"Herman," she said and swallowed hard.

"I'm a widow with one child and another on the way."

"I understand how it was," he said in a soothing voice. "My brother told me how that rotten gunfighter forced himself on you."

She hesitated, remembering the wonder of Rider's arms, the way he had made love to her. She wouldn't have traded that memory for the world and all she would have to remember him by was his child.

"Not many men would want to raise two children that weren't his own." He licked his lips and his eyes behind his spectacles were shiny with desire. "I could be a father to your children, a wonderful husband, if you'd just be mine."

She pulled out of his grasp, trying not to shudder. "Let me think about it."

Behind her, Josh and Boots entered the store.

Herman Adams smiled and patted Josh's head. "Oh, this is your little tot and his pet, isn't it?" He held out a candy stick. "Sonny, I just love dogs."

Josh took the candy skeptically and the dog growled at the store owner.

Emma gasped. "Boots! What's wrong with you? I'm so sorry, Mr. Adams —"

"Herman," he prompted with an oily smile.

"Honestly, Herman, he's never growled at anyone before."

"Well, the pup doesn't know me. We all need to get to know each other better."

"Of course." She backed away from him.

"Don't take my offer lightly, my dear," his face smiled but his voice held a threat. "You'll not get a better one and remember, I'm the richest man in town. I own everything and everybody. You could be my queen in a fine mansion with the best of things shipped in by boat from San Francisco."

"I-I'll think about it," she stuttered and turned and fled the store, taking Josh and his dog with her.

Outside, she heaved a sigh of relief. Herman Adams might be rich, but surely there was another man who might marry her, someone who didn't make her skin crawl when he touched her. Until she found that man, she didn't know what to do next.

Josh looked up at her as they walked. He was growing tall. "I don't like that man — Boots doesn't, either."

"That's not nice," Emma said automatically.

"That man doesn't really like me," Josh said. "I can just tell. I thought Rider would be my daddy."

Her throat seemed to close up and she

reached to touch her swelling belly. "Rider's gone," she sighed, "and he won't be back. We'll have to do the best we can before we run completely out of food."

Josh took her hand. "You wouldn't marry that fat man, would you?"

She thought about sleeping with Herman and shuddered. Of course he would want his husbandly privileges. Later, he would expect her to produce children for him. Emma sighed. She felt she'd been slowly backed into a corner without any choices. What could she do?

She applied for jobs again, hoping things had changed. To Emma's puzzlement, no one wanted to even be seen talking to her. She tried to wait tables or cook at the cafe and begged for a chance at the town's dress shop since she knew how to sew and choose fabrics. She even tried to go to work at the small dairy, milking cows. Everyone avoiding looking at her as they told her they weren't hiring right now.

As far as finding a husband, men seemed to flee from her. Maybe it was because her swelling belly was becoming more noticeable, but she'd figured there was enough of a woman shortage that some man would be happy to marry her. She figured wrong.

Several weeks passed and she'd run out of groceries. Now she'd thrown away her pride and was back at Adams's general store. "Please, Mr. Adams, my child is hungry."

Herman smiled and shook his head. "My dear, you have my sympathy, but your prospects don't seem too good. Without a job or any husband, it doesn't look like you'll ever be able to pay me back."

"Give me a job," she asked with quiet dignity. "I'm strong, I can work —"

"My dear Mrs. Trent," he said softly. "I need a wife. You need a husband. I have plenty of money to look after you and your children. You'll be the richest woman in Oregon and I have a fine, big home. Why, it's almost a castle. Your son might freeze this winter in that old wagon. Now be sensible and marry me."

Beside her, Josh asked softly for a cookie. She looked down at her child and the dog. Boots's ribs were getting thin, too; she had no food for either of them. For her son and the child beneath her heart, she would sacrifice anything. "All right, Mr. Adams, you win. I'll marry you."

"Good!" He rubbed his fat hands together as he came from around the counter. "Now, you just take anything you want from the store and I'll get Mrs. Rivers over at the

516

dress shop to make you a wedding dress and a whole trunk full of beautiful clothes."

She pictured herself sleeping with this man and closed her eyes, trying to remember that he was a perfectly nice man who was going to take care of her little family. Maybe he wasn't the man she had dreamed of, but sometimes a toad, treated kindly, could be turned into a prince. "When shall we wed?"

Herman Adams thought a minute. "Well, this is going to be the biggest celebration this town has ever seen, so it'll take several weeks to get ready. We'll put on a dance and banquet at my big house and invite the whole town."

"Fine," she said without enthusiasm.

"Now," he said and began to pull delicacies off the shelf for her, "you just take anything you want, my dear, and I'll even get a juicy bone for the dog."

She was going to have to sleep with this man and let him put his hands on her. She tried not to shudder as she accepted the armful of supplies. "I'll let you make all the arrangements."

"Money will be no object." He reached up to kiss her cheek. "Good-bye, darling," he said. "I can hardly wait for our wedding day."

She nodded and left, knowing she had

sold herself to a man she did not like and could not love, but she would do her best to be fair to him and make him a good wife. Josh and her unborn child were depending on her.

Herman Adams stared after the girl as she left his store and smiled, licking his lips at the thought of bedding her. She was so trusting. Why, it had probably never occurred to her that Herman, with his money and power, could scare any would-be suitors away. Since he also owned the bank, he had threatened all the other little businesses with foreclosure if they dared offer Emma Trent a job. Herman Adams had planned well and had left the woman with no alternatives but to marry him. "All's fair in love and war," he said to himself as he watched her walk away, the child and the dog trailing after her.

That damned dog. Herman hated dogs. Once Emma was legally his and powerless, he would take that dog out and shoot it. As far as her two half-breed brats, he certainly didn't want to raise them. No, there was an orphanage he knew about that would take them, an orphanage that worked their children hard. Herman intended to breed Emma as fast as he possibly could. He wanted children, all right, but his own children. This marriage was going to be a fair exchange. The beautiful blonde would get fine clothes, a mansion, and money. Herman would get the pleasure of her nubile body and the many children she would give him. Once she was legally his wife, there wasn't much she could do about it if she weren't happy with the deal.

Well, Herman didn't give a damn whether she was happy or not as long as she ended up in his bed. Thinking about her made his groin ache. He glanced at the clock on the wall. Less than an hour 'til closing time and so many plans to make. He wanted this to be a wedding to show off his riches, the biggest wedding Oregon had ever seen.

He went to the window and watched the girl walking down the street. She shook her head and the sun caught her yellow hair and reflected off of it. Herman licked his lips, thinking of tangling his fat fingers in those golden locks. The ache in his groin became unbearable. He had to have a woman. Maybe now that they were engaged . . . no, Emma Trent wouldn't give in to him until after the ceremony. He wondered idly if she had liked sleeping with the half-breed gunfighter or just did it because the wagon train insisted?

In the silence, he heard the off-key piano from the Golden Nugget Saloon across the street. He owned that, too, in partners with that Francie Pettigrew. She said she had once been rich, but was now widowed. A likely story, Herman snorted. He didn't care to hear sad stories. Francie Pettigrew was a skilled whore and making plenty of money for him. She thought she was going to get rich, too, but he did the bookkeeping, so he'd already figured out a way to cheat her out of her share. In the meantime, he was enjoying the pleasures of her lush body. Now his need made him reach to hang out the "closed" sign in his store window early. He intended to marry Emma Trent, but that didn't mean he intended to give up Francie and the other whores at the Golden Nugget.

Rides the Thunder sat by the fire and looked at the snow falling outside the lodge.

Washakie sat cross-legged across from him and passed him the pipe. "We are most happy you decided to return to us."

Rides the Thunder sighed and accepted the pipe, then took a long draw of the fragrant tobacco. "I found no peace among the whites — my heart is here and here I will stay."

The other nodded, pleased. "You have

been bringing in much meat with your skilled hunting. What can we do to reward you?"

Rider stared out the lodge opening. Gamboling in the snow was a black-and-white spotted pony with a delicate muzzle and long, beautiful tail. "A very fine pony indeed."

Washakie turned to look and shrugged, puzzled. "It is much too small a mount for a man. Let me give you a bigger, finer horse."

Rides the Thunder shook his head. "I have no need of other horses besides Storm — I only thought of someone I knew who wanted a pony . . ." He did not finish, only smoked and stared into the fire. In the weeks since he had ridden out of the white settlement, his thoughts were constantly on Sky Eyes. That last night, he had been about to commit to her, planning to tell her he would become a farmer and sweat behind a plow if she would be his. Of course, now that he had had time to think, he realized, even as Emma Trent must know, that he could never be happy as a farmer. No, he was a Shoshoni warrior, free as the wind to hunt and ride at a gallop through the snow-capped mountains.

Washakie said, "I see that your heart is sad. You need a woman."

Rides the Thunder frowned. "I do not want to think of women right now."

"When it is cold and snowing as it is now," Washakie suggested, "it is good to have a woman, warm and loving in your blankets. You have surely noticed that some of our prettiest maidens are vying for your attention, hoping you will choose one of them."

"The truth is," Rides the Thunder sighed, "my heart already belongs to someone, but we were from two different worlds and it could not be."

The older man looked at him gravely. "Sometimes two worlds can become one if the love is strong enough."

He said nothing, remembering Sky Eyes in his arms. There would never be another love for him, never. "I think by now she has another man and has forgotten me."

"How do you know that?"

He shrugged. "I suppose I don't."

The old chief looked into the fire. "If she cared as much for you, she will wait for you."

Rides the Thunder shook his head. "You don't understand. I didn't ask her to wait or tell her that I loved her. I rode out before I could tell her this warrior's heart belonged to her now and forever."

"You should have told her," Washakie

said. "But most white women are not like our Shoshoni girls. They are weak and scolding and would never fit into our band. I suggest you choose one of our maidens."

Rides the Thunder stared out at the falling snow. It was a long way to that ragged little Oregon town and surely by now the white girl had married in desperation since he had abandoned her. What old Washakie said was true; there were many beautiful girls here in this camp who would happily warm his blankets. The trouble was, none of them were Sky Eyes.

The time had passed quickly, too quickly for Emma. The fabric shop had created a white dress for her of its finest lace and satin. Word had gone out that the whole town was invited to the wedding; all the shops and stores were busy with preparations. People who had snubbed her were now friendly and eager for her business.

Emma kept her mind on the preparations so she would not think about her wedding night. At least Josh and his dog were getting plenty to eat.

Now, finally, it was her wedding day. She had already dressed Josh and stood in her underclothes as she surveyed the satin wedding dress spread out over the old chest of her wagon. She'd hung blankets over each end of the wagon to keep out the cold.

"You going to marry old Adams?" Josh asked.

She looked at him. No longer a baby, he was tall and handsome. He was a son any man could be proud of. "Honey, we've been through this before. I'll marry him late this afternoon and we'll be moving into his fine home. Why, it's almost a castle. Remember — we always talked about a prince?"

"None of that matters," Josh complained. "I don't like him and Boots doesn't like him, either."

"Well, you must learn to like him," she answered as she brushed her hair and looked down at her swelling belly. "Herman Adams is going to give us a good home and plenty to eat. Now be quiet and let me get ready. Herman and the wedding party will be here in a few minutes."

"He's coming here?"

"Yes, he's driving a sleigh and the whole town will probably come along out of curiosity. After the ceremony at the church, there's going to be a big party with cake and everything."

"I don't care," Josh whined. "I want Rider."

Emma sighed and buried her face in her

hands for a long moment, remembering. "I like Rider, too, honey, but he's gone and after all, I came out here hoping to find a husband and a better future for you." She gritted her teeth and began to brush her hair again. She would think of how Adams's money would help her children and vowed to be a good wife to him, knowing that her heart would always belong to the half-breed gunfighter.

She stood up, dabbed a little fragrance behind her ears, and looked at the fine wedding dress with distaste. She had to go through with this. The fat storekeeper would see that she and her children were safe. She didn't feel very safe right now.

Josh stepped to the front of the wagon and peeked through the blanket. "Hey, they're coming."

"So soon?" She went to peer out. In the distance, across the snow, came a sleigh pulled by two white horses. The sleigh was all decked out in ribbons and bells, Herman Adams driving proudly along. Accompanying him was half the town, walking or riding horses, singing and talking. "At least the town is really looking forward to this."

Out back, Boots began to bark.

"What ails that stupid dog? Josh, go look."

Josh went to the back of the wagon and

looked out, giving a small cry of delight. Puzzled, Emma whirled as Rider stepped into her wagon. No, he was no longer the gunfighter; he was the warrior, Rides the Thunder, resplendent in buckskin and beadwork. Silver jewelry shone in his long black hair.

She could only stare in disbelief.

Josh ran to him with a glad cry and Rider hugged him. "I have gifts outside for you, Small Warrior."

"Presents for me?" Josh scampered out of the back of the wagon, leaving the two alone.

He looked at her a long moment. "You are as beautiful as I remember."

"Damn you, why have you come?" She couldn't hold back her fury. "I am to be married today to a very rich man. Look!" she gestured, "see the wedding party approaching?"

He peered out the front of the wagon. "I'm too late." He sounded crestfallen.

"Of course you're too late." She struggled to contain her sobs.

For the first time he seemed to notice her swelling belly and frowned. "His?"

"Of course not," she wept. "Yours!"

"Why didn't you tell me?" He reached for her.

She tried to pull away, but he was too strong and he held her tightly, pulling her into the shelter of his arms.

She laid her face against his wide chest and sobbed. "I tried to tell you. I didn't want to take your freedom, make you hate me."

"Sky Eyes, I could never hate you." Then he put one finger under her trembling chin, turned her face up to his, and kissed her tenderly.

She pulled out of his arms. "Why do you come back to taunt me?" She wiped at the tears on her face and reached for the wedding dress. "Go away, I'm going to marry Herman."

"But you love me?"

"Yes, damn you, I love you, you know that."

He jerked the dress from her hand, threw it on the floor. "That's all I need to know. I love you, too, more than I realized it was possible to love a woman. Will you come with me?"

She hesitated, almost unable to believe his words.

His shoulders slumped and he turned to go. "Very well, I have my answer. A life among the Shoshoni would be full of adventure and freedom, but there would be hardship, too. I suppose that doesn't measure up to being the wife of a very rich white man."

He was going. She stood frozen to the spot, staring after him as he started to leave her wagon. In the distance, she could hear the jingle of sleigh bells and the singing and laughter of the wedding party.

"Wait, Rider, don't leave me! I'll go anywhere with you — anywhere you want!" She threw herself into his arms and he held her so tightly she could scarcely breathe.

For a long moment, he held her, then climbed out onto the wagon tailgate and jumped down. Emma hesitated. It was cold outside and she wore only fancy lace underwear.

"I have a beautiful beaded dress and moccasins waiting for you back at Washakie's camp." He held up his hands.

She went into his arms, letting him carry her to his horse. He lifted her to his saddle where he wrapped a thick fox fur robe around her shivering form.

"Look, Mama!" Josh, clad in miniature furs, sat on a pretty little black-and-white pony. "Is it mine, Rider?"

He nodded and smiled. "From now on, call me Father, my son. Now let's get out of here. There's a long ride ahead."

She put her arms around his neck. He

held her close in the fur robe and she was safe now, forever safe.

Behind them, she heard shouts of dismay as Herman Adams and the crowd saw them and yelled in protest.

Rider looked down at her. "Are you ready, Emma?"

She smiled up at him. "I am now Sky Eyes and ready to be the wife of Rides the Thunder for now and forever more. Let's go, my dearest."

"Together forever, my only love." He kissed her face and with Josh on his pony by their side, they loped away through the snow, Boots running along behind, barking happily. Ahead of her lay the freedom and excitement of the Shoshoni world — she would not miss the life she was giving up. She was richer than any princess because she could count on Rider's love.

The two horses and the dog galloped away into the snowy wilderness, leaving the civilized world behind them forever.

Afterword

On a cold winter dawn, January 29, 1863, Colonel Patrick E. Connor and his troops attacked the hostile Shoshoni warrior Bear Hunter's camp on the Bear River in present-day Idaho. This resulted in the worst massacre of Indians in United States history. Bear Hunter and nearly three hundred Shoshoni men, women, and children perished. Colonel Connor went on to a long and glorious career, ending as a general.

Chief *Washakie* and his band, by staying at peace with the white invaders, managed to survive but were eventually sent to a reservation. Man Lost, the other hostile war leader, would continue to fight for a few more years before he and his followers were also exiled. We remember Man Lost best by his Shoshoni name, *Pocatello*. It is ironic or perhaps only just that Idaho's second-largest city is named for this hostile and valiant chief who fought in vain for his tribe's land and their freedom.

The employees of Thorndike Press hope you have enjoyed this Large Print book. All our Large Print titles are designed for easy reading, and all our books are made to last. Other Thorndike Press Large Print books are available at your library, through selected bookstores, or directly from us.

For information about titles, please call:

(800) 223-1244
(800) 223-6121

To share your comments, please write:

Publisher
Thorndike Press
295 Kennedy Memorial Drive
Waterville, ME   04901